A LESSON IN LOVE

In the next second she found herself pinned, helpless, to the ground, her legs trapped beneath his, her arms held above her head.

Furious and gasping, she glared up at him, ready to spit in his face until she saw the cold glitter in his azure eyes.

"I can do anything I want to you, and you won't be able to stop me," he said with maddening calm.

Slowly, so she was aware of every move, he took both her hands in one of his and lowered his free hand to her face. He touched her cheek, ignoring her flinch, and then stroked downward, over her throat, skimming the thin fabric of her shirtwaist.

The heat of his touch scorched her. . . .

HISTORICAL ROMANCES BY VICTORIA THOMPSON

Wild Texas Promise

Victoria Thompson

ZEBRA BOOKS
KENSINGTON PUBLISHING CORP.

Also by Victoria Thompson
Texas Treasure
Texas Vixen
Texas Triumph
Texas Blonde
Angel Heart
Bold Texas Embrace

ZEBRA BOOKS

are published by

Kensington Publishing Corp.
475 Park Avenue South
New York, NY 10016

First printing: August, 1990

Printed in the United States of America

To my Zebra editors, Carin Cohen, who saw promise where no one else did and literally taught me to write romance, and Wendy McCurdy, who makes even the hard times a pleasure.

Chapter One

Linc was dead. He knew he was. Nobody could feel this bad and still be alive.

Slowly, he opened his eyes. Sure enough, there was earth not six feet above his head, and God Almighty, he could hear flames crackling. His mother, rest her soul, had been right about his destiny.

He turned his head carefully toward the sound of the flames and was enormously relieved to see not the fires of hell at all but merely a small, smokeless campfire. To his surprise, a girl sat cross-legged beside it, slicing bacon into a frying pan. *His* frying pan.

Now he was sure he wasn't in hell because hell wouldn't have girls as pretty as this one. But who was she? Dead or alive, he would've by God remembered if he'd ever seen her before. And what was she doing beside his campfire? And where on earth were they, anyway?

They seemed to be in some sort of cave, but figuring it all out seemed entirely too difficult, at least for the moment. Instead he simply watched her, admiring the way the firelight picked up the gleaming red highlights in her auburn hair, which hung down her back, carelessly caught in a tattered ribbon that left loose strands wafting about her face. Every now and then she'd shake her head in a futile attempt to move the lock hanging over one eye.

She sat half-turned away from him, her delicate features squinched in concentration. He couldn't see the color of her eyes, but he liked the sweep of her lashes and the way her nose turned up on the end and the way her cheek curved softly. He judged her to be a few years younger than his own twenty-three, maybe no more than seventeen or eighteen. Her skin was lightly tanned, and her body slim but sturdy. The hands guiding the knife—*his* knife—through the bacon were strong and sure and capable. She wasn't one of those worthless hothouse flowers who called themselves ladies and never left the parlor. No, this was a real woman, he thought with a small smile, thoroughly intrigued.

When she was finished slicing, she set the pan over the fire, carefully wrapped the remaining bacon in its flour sacking, and tucked it into his saddlebag, which was lying nearby. Fascinated, he followed every movement of her graceful hands as she performed these homely tasks. When she finally reached up to push the strand of fiery hair out of her face, his gaze met hers at last. Eyes as green as spring grass widened in surprise.

"You're awake!" she said, scrambling over to him. Her voice was soft, like the sound of spring rain. "How do you feel?"

Lousy, he wanted to say, but the word came out as a croak.

She laid a hand across his forehead, then touched his cheek and neck, just the way his mother used to check for fever when he'd been a small child. Was he sick? Of course he was. Didn't he feel like he'd been stomped by a mean-tempered elephant? But how. . . ?

Before he could even think the question, she produced his canteen and lifted it to his lips, slipping her other hand beneath his head and raising it so he could drink.

The water was cold and fresh, not the stale, lukewarm brack he'd been expecting, and he gulped it thirstily.

"Easy," she said with a smile. "You'll choke." She took the canteen away, but he found her smile almost as refreshing as the water. It lit up her face, and her green eyes glittered like emeralds. "My goodness, you're soaking wet," she said, touching his shirt. "That's good, though, because it means your fever broke."

He tried his voice again. "Who . . . are . . . you?"

She sat back on her heels. "I'm Eden Campbell," she said, as if the name should mean something. It didn't.

"I'm—"

"—Lincoln Scott," she finished for him. "I know. I found the letter in your saddlebag, the one from Marcus Pauling asking you to come here."

"You know Marcus?"

Surprise flickered across her face, but then she smiled again. "Of course I know Marcus," she assured him, turning away for a moment to stir the

9

bacon with a stick. "That's why I decided to take care of you. Do you remember what happened?"

He tried to think, but his head ached too badly. "You must've been on your way to Marcus's ranch," she prompted.

Yes, he remembered, Marcus had sent for him, and it wasn't like all the other invitations he'd been sending for the past seven years. This time he needed help, the kind of help only Lincoln Scott's gun could provide. Linc recalled leaving the ranch where he'd been working in south Texas and heading north, traveling for days. He'd been close, almost there when . . .

"Somebody shot me."

"Did you see who it was?"

He strained to remember. "No, I . . . Some men. They started chasing me and . . . then everything goes blank," he said in frustration.

She nodded, her expression grim. "It was probably the Blaines, the ones Marcus wrote you about. They're brothers. They moved here about a year ago, settled on some land, and started putting up fences where they had no business putting them. Anybody who objected bought himself a whole peck of trouble."

"But why would they shoot at me?"

"That's easy. The reason I was on the road yesterday was to warn M—my father that we'd heard they were going to ambush him. He's on roundup, and he'd have been a sitting duck. The stallion you ride could be a twin to one he owns. They must've thought you were him."

"Caesar, where is he?" Linc asked in alarm,

searching the cave's shadows for the gray stallion.

"Back there," she said, indicating the depths of the cave. "There's another room behind this one. It's bigger, but it doesn't get much light."

"How'd you get him back there?" Linc asked in amazement. "Caesar doesn't let anybody touch him but me."

"It wasn't easy," she assured him. "Finally, I led my mare in, and he followed. In fact, that's how you got to the cave in the first place. You see, I was hiding in here from the men who shot you. I saw them on the road and didn't want them to see me. I discovered this place when I was a kid, and I never told anybody about it, so I thought I'd be safe here. Then all of a sudden, you came riding up. At first I thought you were one of them, but then I saw the blood and realized you were hurt. You were unconscious, and the only reason you didn't fall out of the saddle was you'd somehow managed to tie your hands to the horn before you passed out. You couldn't possibly have found the cave on your own, so I figure your stallion must've followed the scent of my mare."

She smiled again and shook her head. "Did you say his name was Caesar? He's something, all right. Wouldn't even let me unsaddle him until this morning."

"He let you unsaddle him?" Linc asked incredulously.

"Yes, he . . ." Color came to her cheeks. "I guess he smelled you on me. You never did say how you feel," she added hastily.

He glanced down at his prone body. She'd cov-

11

ered his six-foot length with a blanket so he couldn't see the damage. For a moment he tried to decide where he'd been shot, but the pain was too general. "How bad am I hit?"

"The bullet caught you about here," she said, pointing to her left side, just above the hip. "It went clean through. You bled a lot, and you had some fever last night, but from the looks of you this morning, I think you have a good chance."

He tried to make sense of it. He'd been shot, but somehow he'd managed to find a cave no one else knew about where a girl was waiting to save his life. Before he could figure it out, she said, "Oh, look, the bacon's done," and returned to the fire to fish out the greasy strips.

Linc suddenly noticed the smoky smell of the food, and his stomach cramped in response. He tried to remember when he'd last eaten, but he had no idea how long they'd been in the cave. The girl had said something about him having a fever last night. Had he been shot yesterday? And what time was it now?

Unfortunately, he didn't have the energy to ask any more questions. Of their own accord, his eyelids drooped and fell.

"Lincoln? Mr. Scott?"

It seemed only seconds had passed, but when he looked up, he saw she held the plate of bacon. Half of it was gone and the rest lay in a pool of congealed grease.

"I hated to wake you, but I want to get you fed and settled before I leave," she explained.

"Leave?" he echoed, feeling an irrational panic.

"Yes, you can't stay in this cave. It's cold and damp, and besides they might find you. I've got to get you back to the ranch as soon as possible, but you can't ride, so I'll have to fetch a wagon. It won't take more than a couple of hours. Here." She stuck a strip of bacon to his lips, and he obediently took a bite.

His stomach clenched again, reminding him of his hunger. Although he felt like a fool, he let the girl feed him, then help him get another drink.

"We'd better get you into some dry clothes, too. The stream runs right outside, so it's chilly when the fire's out. We don't want you catching pneumonia, do we?" she asked cheerfully as she began to unbutton his shirt.

"What are you doing?" he asked, experiencing a completely different kind of panic. Under certain circumstances, he didn't mind undressing in the presence of an attractive young woman, but not when he was as weak and helpless as a baby and certainly not when she was a decent woman. He'd never be able to look her in the face again, and Linc definitely wanted to look at this face a lot more.

"I'm taking your clothes off," she informed him, spreading the shirt open so she could ease it off his shoulder.

He grabbed her wrist. "Wait a minute!" Her eyes were even greener than he remembered, and for a moment he couldn't recall his objection. "You don't have to . . . I'll be fine," he managed.

"You most certainly will not be fine," she said, taking hold of the blanket with her free hand and jerking it off him.

Instantly he felt the chill of which she had warned him. "I mean, I can do it myself," he corrected, not wanting to seem a total fool. But when he tried to push himself up, he found out exactly where he'd been shot, as pain scorched out from his left side, convulsing him with agony and wrenching a cry from his throat. For a minute everything went red and hazy.

As from a distance, he heard her muttering something about fool men, and when she started easing the shirt from his shoulders again, he did not resist. In a few moments she had helped him into a dry shirt, and once the pain subsided, he had to admit he felt much more comfortable. He let out a long sigh of relief, but it strangled in his throat when she started tugging on his pants.

"No!" he yelped, grabbing for the waistband and hanging on tight. He didn't care if he did die of pneumonia. He didn't have a stitch on under those jeans, and he couldn't let her . . .

"Honestly," she snapped, sitting back on her heels in disgust. "If you're worried about your modesty, you're much too late."

It took a minute for his befuddled brain to completely comprehend the implications. He glanced down at his pants. The fly was unbuttoned, and through the opening he could see the white bandage she had wrapped around his middle. Then he noticed something even more alarming: these pants had no blood on them. They couldn't be the ones he'd been wearing yesterday.

"That's a really nasty scar you have on your . . .

14

uh, leg," she remarked with feigned nonchalance. "Knife wound, is it?"

The scar in question was indeed a knife wound, a souvenir from a little altercation with three Mexicans in a bar down in Laredo a few years back. But it wasn't on his leg, or at least most of it wasn't. If she'd seen the scar, she'd seen *everything*. He hoped his face wasn't as red as it felt.

"Are all the girls around here as bold as you?" he demanded, hiding his embarrassment behind anger.

Instantly, he regretted his defensiveness. Red splotches stained her cheeks, and those green eyes snapped. Planting her hands on her hips, she favored him with a glare that would've raised blisters on a rock. "Girls around here do what they have to when they need to save a man's life, and most men would be grateful. Maybe you'd rather I'd left your pants on and let you bleed to death?"

Linc briefly considered pretending to pass out again, but he figured she'd know he was faking. "I didn't mean . . . ," he tried, but she'd lost patience with him.

Without another word, she flipped the blanket back over him, reached beneath it, and with alarming ease, broke his grip on the pants and pulled them off his hips. He transferred his grip to the blanket and closed his eyes, pretending the pain was worse than it was so he wouldn't have to see the disgust on her pretty face.

"You only had two pairs of pants, so I have to put the bloody ones back on you," she was saying, talking while she worked. Linc winced, trying desperately to ignore the tantalizing feel of her hands against his bare flesh as she pulled his jeans into place under the blanket. "I washed them in the creek yesterday, so they aren't too bad, and with any luck, no one will see you anyway. There now, all done," she said when she was finished, smoothing the blanket and tucking it in around him. "And you'll be relieved to know I didn't see a thing . . . *that* time," she informed him acidly.

Linc winced again, but she ignored him. He was acting like a jackass, he knew. There was no reason for him to be so upset about her undressing him. He wasn't ashamed of his body or anything. In fact, he'd actually been complimented a time or two by girls who'd had enough experience with men to really know. Unfortunately, logic played no part in his feelings, and for some inexplicable reason, the thought of her stripping him down while he was unconscious disturbed him greatly.

"I'll leave the canteen right beside you," she continued in the same snappish tone. "Is there anything else you need before I go?"

Yes, he thought dismally, he needed to apologize for offending her. His upbringing hadn't included much training in etiquette, but any fool knew it wasn't right to insult a person who'd just saved your life. Besides, if he didn't make it up, she might be tempted to leave him in this cave to rot. "About what I said before, I'm sorry. You saved my life and . . ." He paused, hoping she'd stop him. Instead she waited, cocking her head to one side in silent challenge. This girl was something, all right. "And I'm grateful. Thanks."

Her lips twitched as if she were holding back a

smile. "Now see, that didn't hurt too much, did it?"

"You want the truth?" he replied ruefully. "I'd rather get shot again."

This time she didn't hold back. The smile lit up her face like a sparkler. "Then you'd better be careful how you talk to me from now on," she informed him and rose to her feet.

She brushed off her skirt and tucked in her shirttail. She was wearing some sort of riding outfit, dark green and cut shorter than a regular skirt, but her boots hid what he imagined were well-turned ankles. He admired the generous feminine curves beneath her shirt, and for the first time he noticed she looked mussed. She must have slept in those clothes if she'd spent the night in the cave with him. An unsettling thought occurred to him.

"Won't somebody be wondering where you've been all night?"

"Not likely. My father wasn't expecting me to come, and my mother probably heard about the shooting by now and figures I stayed the night at the roundup camp. I'm going to ride your stallion back to the ranch," she added, "and then—"

"He won't let you ride him," Linc warned. "Nobody rides him but me."

"Don't worry, we made friends this morning. Remember I told you?"

He did remember, and he remembered something else she'd said. "How could he smell me on you?"

She flashed him an impish grin. "Because I'm even bolder than you thought. I slept with you last night," she said just before she disappeared into the depths of the cave.

Linc stared open-mouthed after her, then glanced around the cave. The only set of blankets was his, and she wouldn't have been carrying any if she'd just been taking a message to her father, so she must have been telling the truth. He didn't know which was more disturbing: realizing she'd done it or not remembering it. Sharing a set of blankets with a girl like that would have been quite a highlight of his very eventful life, and he'd slept through the whole thing!

To make matters worse, he could hear her sweet-talking poor Caesar into letting her saddle him. The stallion had bitten hunks out of several grown men who'd tried it, but she didn't seem to be having any trouble at all.

Sure enough, in another minute she emerged from the depths of the cave leading a docile Caesar who whickered a greeting as they passed. For a moment, Linc was afraid she'd leave without saying good-bye, but once she had the stallion outside, she ducked back in.

"You never did say. Is there anything else you need before I go?"

"I dearly would love to have my gun to hand, Miss . . ." To his chagrin he realized he'd forgotten her name.

"Campbell," she supplied with amusement, hurrying to fetch the Colt from where she'd placed it in his saddlebag. "Eden Campbell, but after all we've been through together, you can call me Eden."

"Eden?" he repeated, not sure he'd heard her correctly.

"Yes, like in 'Garden of,' " she explained, laying

18

the pistol near his right hand. "Strange, isn't it?"

"No, it suits you," he said.

"Does it? How?"

Linc didn't want to say what he'd been thinking. "Uh, because of your eyes. They're green, like a garden," he explained lamely.

She frowned, and he wished he was better with words so he could've given her a more poetic answer.

"Well, I'd better get going," she said after a few seconds. "Marcus will skin me alive if I let anything happen to you."

Linc shook his head at the unlikely prospect of his old friend laying a finger on Miss Eden Campbell. "I'm the one most likely to get skinned when your father finds out we were together all night."

Eden flashed him her brilliant smile. "You're wrong there. You see, my father is Marcus Pauling."

Once again she'd shocked him into silence, and before he could gather his wits she was gone.

Marcus's daughter? Impossible! He'd known Marcus for seven years, and when they'd met on that cattle drive so long ago, Marcus didn't have kith nor kin anywhere in the world. Her last name wasn't even the same as his. How did she expect Linc to believe . . . ?

Slowly a memory drifted back to him, something from Marcus's letter. Yes, Marcus'd had more to tell him than just the news about his trouble with the Blaine brothers. At the ripe old age of thirty-six, Marcus Pauling had finally taken a bride, a woman named *Campbell*, a widow woman with a

19

little girl.

Little girl? Linc smiled to himself. If that's what the little girls around here looked like, he couldn't wait to see the full-grown women.

Eden did have a bit of trouble with the stallion. Scott had been right: Caesar didn't want her to ride him. He halfheartedly tried to buck her off, but she'd learned how to ride practically before she could walk, so Eden managed to keep her seat and show the animal who was boss. Soon they were trotting briskly toward the ranch.

As she rode, she recalled the scene back in the cave with Scott. She should probably still be angry with him in spite of his apology. After all, what right did he have to insult her when she'd saved his life?

Instead, she was amused. Who would have thought he'd be so upset to learn she'd undressed him? From what Marcus had told her about him, she never would've expected such a prudish reaction. Was this the same Lincoln Scott who'd wiped out a band of rustlers on the Rio Grande practically single-handed? Was this the same Lincoln Scott who'd faced down a Comanche war chief and saved not only his own scalp but every one of his men's? Was this the same Lincoln Scott who'd made a name for himself all across Texas by fighting for the underdog and winning?

Yet he blushed when a girl tried to take off his pants. Now wasn't that interesting?

In fact, everything about Lincoln Scott was interesting. She'd never expected a man who—at least to hear Marcus tell it—could walk through hell barefoot to also be so handsome. Marcus had certainly never mentioned it, but then Marcus hadn't actually seen Scott in seven long years, and Scott had only been a boy of sixteen then. He'd probably changed a lot in the intervening years.

He'd certainly turned out nicely, too. Even with his clothes on, he was an imposing fellow. She guessed he must stand at least six feet tall, and every inch of those six feet was solid muscle, as she well knew.

Once she'd managed to untie the rawhide thong holding his hands to the saddle, she'd been hard pressed to lower his bulk to the ground without breaking any bones—hers or his. When she'd gotten him on the ground, she'd had the unenviable task of dragging him inside the cave, where he would be hidden from the men who were no doubt seeking him.

She always carried a small pistol, and Scott carried one Colt strapped to his hip, another in his saddlebag, and a Winchester on his saddle. Still, she didn't think she wanted to try to stand off the Blaines and their gunnies, even with all that firepower. No, as her father had often said, sometimes it was better to pull your freight than to pull your gun, so she'd pulled Lincoln Scott's freight and her own into the cave and hid out until she was sure the danger had passed.

Just the same, she stayed off the road, riding cross country to miss anyone who might still be trying to find the wounded man, and watching over her shoulder all the way. Marcus had warned her often enough about what the Blaines would do to her if they caught her alone. He didn't seem to understand she could take care of herself, which meant not only that she wasn't afraid of the Blaines but that she also knew when to use common sense and avoid a showdown. Eden always listened to his warnings indulgently, though, recognizing his need to fulfill his duties as her stepfather. Then she did what she thought best.

In view of his protectiveness, she knew Marcus never would've allowed her to go riding off alone to warn him of the plot to murder him, but she'd certainly proved she could protect herself when necessary. Good thing, too, or Lincoln Scott would be lying dead somewhere right now.

The thought of him made her smile again. She liked the way his thick, dark hair curled slightly on his neck and the way his straight brows almost met over his nose. Several days growth of black stubble on his lean cheeks gave him a dangerous air belied by the gentle azure blue of his eyes.

Since he was so dark, she'd expected dark eyes, too. She could still feel the shock of looking into those crystal clear pools for the first time. It had been sort of like being lightly punched in the stomach, followed by a fluttery breathlessness. Luckily, he'd been in a fever at the time so he hadn't noticed what had no doubt been her stupefied expression and her odd inability to speak for several seconds.

Then he'd called her "Ma," and broken the spell. Imagine a tough hombre like Lincoln Scott calling for his mother. She'd been touched, however, and hadn't minded a bit. Later, when he'd been shaking with chills and fever and she'd had to crawl into his blankets with him to keep him warm, she'd actually been grateful for the misunderstanding.

How shocked he'd been to hear about it, too! Eden laughed aloud at the memory, earning a curious glance from the stallion, whom she patted absently. She'd better never let her stepmother hear about it. Poor Fiona would probably die of apoplexy. Of course, sleeping with him had seemed almost proper after the other things she'd done, things Fiona was also better off not hearing about. If Scott knew how much courage she had needed to strip that blood-soaked denim from his body, maybe he wouldn't have been quite so outraged. The memory still unsettled her.

Taking off his shirt hadn't been too bad. She'd seldom seen a man's naked chest, but she instinctively appreciated Scott's sculpted muscles and the thick pelt of raven hair that arrowed down his belly. At first she hadn't even thought too much about removing his pants. The logistics of doing so without hurting him had taken all her attention; then suddenly she was confronted with the reality of a completely naked man.

That had been the first time she'd jerked the blanket over him. Good heavens, who would've thought men looked like that? Most women would probably faint at such a sight. No wonder married people made love at night under the covers with the lights out. She knew they did because her bedroom was right next to the one Fiona had shared first with Eden's father and now with Marcus Pauling.

Eden knew far more about the nocturnal habits of married couples than was right for an unmarried girl to know, but she counted herself lucky. Her unusual knowledge blunted any curiosity that might have led her into temptation. Since seeing Lincoln Scott, her curiosity was deader than a doornail.

Or was it? she asked herself as she kicked the stallion into a gallop. Oh, she wouldn't ever have to wonder what men looked like beneath their clothes, but the memory of Lincoln Scott's lean hips and long, powerful legs stirred other, more disturbing emotions.

She also remembered the feel of his arms around her during the long night as he'd clung to her through his fever and pain. What would it be like to have those arms around her in passion? She shivered and told herself she was shaking off the ridiculous notion.

Still, the thought intrigued her. She never doubted for a moment she could have such an experience if she wanted it. She'd had enough male attention in her eighteen years to be certain of her attraction. If she set her cap for Lincoln Scott, he wouldn't stand a chance. The thought amused her, and she was still smiling when she reached the ranch.

Because of the creek and the steepness of the cutbank that formed the entrance to the cave, Eden and Pedro couldn't bring the wagon up close. All the way back from the ranch, Eden had tried unsuccessfully to figure out a way she and the fourteen-year-old Mexican boy could carry Scott out and up the hill. Eden was tall for a girl, almost five and a half feet, but Pedro stood several inches shorter than she and probably weighed even less than her one hundred and twenty pounds. Between the two of them, they might get him out of the cave, but they'd never get him up the bank. No, Scott would have to walk somehow. She only hoped he could.

Eden wished once again she'd been able to bring a full-grown man or two along to help. Unfortunately, all the hands were with Marcus, assisting with the spring roundup. Only Pedro had remained behind to help with what little work there was to do around the ranch. In most situations, Eden and Fiona could have managed perfectly well, but of course this wasn't a normal situation.

"Are you sure this is the place, señorita?" Pedro asked, looking around doubtfully when she told him to stop the wagon.

"Yes, the hill here is almost hollow. The opening is down in there," she said, pointing to a thick stand of weeds which blocked the entrance. As a child, she'd carried the seeds for those weeds from plants all along the creek bank in an effort to encourage abundant growth. Her labors had been rewarded. So far as she knew, not one other living soul had discovered the cave until Lincoln Scott had ridden up yesterday morning.

Pedro shook his head and muttered dubiously under his breath, but he jumped down from the wagon seat and reached up to help her alight. She hadn't taken the time to change her clothes, since she would have to ride her mare back separately from the wagon. Now that the day was heating up, she was beginning to regret her decision and hoped she didn't smell as rank as she was beginning to feel.

"Follow me, and be careful not to break any bushes," she cautioned as they scrambled down the bank. "If the Blaines are still trying to find Mr. Scott, we don't want to give them any more clues than necessary."

Pedro grunted impatiently, annoyed that a mere woman would instruct him in such a matter. Eden hid her grin. Gently pushing aside the stalks of undergrowth, she called, "Mr. Scott? It's Eden."

Hearing no response, she grew alarmed and hurried inside, blinking furiously in an attempt to see in the shadowed interior. "Mr. Scott?"

Behind her, Pedro grunted again, this time in surprise as he found the opening of the cave.

"Mr. Scott?" she tried again, hurrying to where she'd left him. He was no more than a darker shadow in the dimness, and he didn't move until she dropped to her knees beside him and touched his shoulder.

In an instant she was staring down the barrel of a Colt Peacemaker. She gasped in surprise.

Scott muttered a curse. "Miss Eden? God, I'm sorry," he said, hastily lowering the gun.

"Madre de Dios," Pedro muttered from the doorway.

"Who's that?" Scott demanded, lifting the gun again.

"It's Pedro. He's one of our men," she told him,

26

gently pushing his hand back down.

Scott squinted, trying to make Pedro out against the brightness of the cave opening. The boy stepped forward. "I am pleased to meet you, señor."

"She's a *little girl* and he's a *man*," Scott muttered.

"What did you say?" Eden asked, thinking he might be delirious again.

"Nothing," he replied, but she checked him for fever anyway. His whiskers pricked her hand as she touched his cheek.

"You need a shave," she remarked.

"Among other things," he said, making her smile.

"Pedro and I brought a wagon. We fixed a bed in the back for you and packed things around it so we could cover everything with a tarp and it would look like Pedro was coming back from town with supplies."

"You don't think they'll still be looking for me, do you?"

"If they are, they won't find you." She got up and began to gather his belongings. When she'd packed everything, she gave Pedro the saddlebags to carry out and proceeded to work on his bed.

He shivered slightly when she removed the top blanket. "I'm sorry. We'll get you out of here as quick as we can. I brought some bandages, but I don't want to unwrap your wound in here. I'm just going to reinforce the ones you already have on in case you start bleeding again."

This time he didn't protest when she eased the jeans down, probably because he knew she wasn't going to take them completely off. Pleased to see he hadn't bled much, she wrapped several lengths of sheeting around his middle and tied them tightly. He winced several times, but he didn't make a sound.

"How does that feel?" she asked when she was finished.

"Fine," he rasped, his expression telling her he wouldn't complain. Her admiration for him grew.

"I've been trying to figure out a way to carry you up to the wagon, but I don't think Pedro and I can manage it. Do you think you could walk? We'd help you, of course."

"I'll do what I have to," he replied.

When Pedro returned, they got Lincoln's boots on, and between the two of them, they somehow managed to get him on his feet and outside. They'd gone only a few steps when he asked to sit down on a rock.

Eden thought his weakness made it too difficult for him to go on. Indeed, his face was pale, but he said, "Miss Eden, do you suppose you could leave me and Pedro alone for a few minutes?"

She frowned, wondering why he'd want to get rid of her, but then she noticed he wouldn't meet her eye. "Oh, yes, of course," she murmured in embarrassment. "I'll make sure the wagon is ready." She hurried off before he could see her blush. If he had to relieve himself, she certainly didn't want to watch.

Busying herself with adjusting the blankets spread over a padding of hay in the back of the wagon, Eden kept a sharp lookout for signs of the Blaines. She and Pedro hadn't seen a soul this morning, but instinct told her the brothers hadn't given up. By now they must know the man they'd shot wasn't Marcus, and they didn't dare leave Scott alive in case he could identify them. Apprehension prickled the hair on her arms. She wouldn't rest easy until Scott was safely hidden at the ranch.

"Miss Eden!" Pedro called, and she hurried off to help with the maneuver up the hill.

The next few minutes were a nightmare as they tried to hurry without hurting Scott. Eden expected Blaine's men to ride up at any moment and catch them, but her fears proved groundless. They got Scott into the wagon without incident.

Eden sent Pedro back to the cave for the rest of the bedding and Scott's gun. Then she crawled into the wagon to check Scott's wound. Fresh blood was seeping through the bandage, but not much. He'd fared well. "You'll probably get hot under the tarp, so I won't cover you. Are you comfortable?"

He nodded, but his face was ashen, his eyes were clenched shut, and sweat stood out on his forehead. Feeling helpless, her heart aching, she patted his face with a corner of the blanket. "I've told Pedro to take it slow and easy, but we aren't far from the ranch. You'll be there before you know it," she promised rashly.

The ghost of a smile flickered across his lips. "Sure."

Her heart fluttered in her chest, and impulsively, she touched his cheek, stroking the roughness of his whiskers. "Just don't try to be a hero. If the Blaines do stop you, keep quiet. Pedro's a cool one. He can probably handle it."

"And if he can't?"

Eden withdrew her hand and swallowed a lump of apprehension. "Then I'll put your gun right here beside you."

When Pedro returned, she did just that after checking the loads for him.

It was time for her to leave, but she knew a strange reluctance, even though every second's delay placed them in danger. "Maybe I should ride along with you," she suggested.

"No, you'll just draw attention to the wagon," Scott replied, opening his eyes.

They were blue and clear and unyielding, and Eden felt the same shock she had the first time she'd looked into them. "I . . . I guess you're right. It would look suspicious."

He nodded, and she had the ridiculous impression that he was holding her there with the force of his gaze.

"I'd better get going," she said, making no move to.

He nodded again. "Be careful."

She couldn't resist a smile. "I should be saying that to you."

"I'm always careful."

"Not careful enough," she pointed out, touching his bandage lightly. "Just don't get any more holes pumped into you. Marcus will hold me responsible." Surrendering to another impulse, she squeezed his arm before scrambling out of the wagon.

Fighting an odd, burning sensation in her throat, she helped Pedro arrange some flour sacks across the back of the wagon to conceal their passenger.

When they'd finished tying down the tarp, she gave Pedro his instructions once again, ignoring his long-suffering expression. After seeing them safely on their way, she returned to the cave to fetch her mare.

Linc forced himself to relax and not to resist the jouncing of the wagon. He could already feel the warm ooze of blood soaking through the bandages Eden had wrapped around him, and the pain was extraordinary. It seemed to fill the entire space beneath the tarp, closing in around him like a throbbing, pulsing entity. At least he didn't have to worry about dozing off and not being ready if the Blaines approached the wagon, he thought with some irony.

Inside the warm cocoon Eden had prepared for him, Linc endured the torment for what seemed like hours until he heard Pedro say, "Looks like trouble, señor."

Instinctively, Linc's hand closed around the worn wooden grip of his Colt. Cursing his weakness, he lifted the gun, laying it across his chest so he would be ready to fire if someone raised the tarp. At least he would take one of them with him.

"Whoa!" Pedro called, and the wagon clattered to a precipitous halt. Linc gritted his teeth against a moan.

"Where you going, boy?" a man demanded.

"Home," Pedro replied with just the proper amount of deference.

"What you got in the wagon?"

"Supplies."

31

"Supplies? Seems like a funny time to be shopping. Don't the Pauling's usually go to town on Saturday?"

"Sí, señor Blaine," Pedro said, and Linc recognized the warning. This was one of the Blaine brothers himself. "I do not know why they sent me today. I do not ask questions when Señorita Campbell gives me an order."

Blaine chuckled lasciviously. "No, I don't reckon you do. Not many men would want to tangle with that little vixen." Blaine sounded as if he'd relish the opportunity, however, and Linc's finger tightened on the trigger. Taking care of Blaine might not be such an unpleasant chore after all. "You won't mind if we just take a look in your wagon, though, will you?"

Linc tensed.

"What are you looking for, señor?" Pedro asked, still sounding perfectly calm.

"A fellow who took a potshot at my brother yesterday. We figure he might be a hired killer."

"A hired killer?" Pedro repeated in awe. "Do you think I would hide a hired killer in my wagon?"

"You work for Pauling, don't you? Ace, pull back that tarp and let's see what the little greaser's got in there."

Linc eased back the hammer of his pistol. He was facing Blaine and this fellow Ace and maybe more. He listened carefully, trying to hear the creak of saddle leather that would tell him exactly how many and where they were.

"Boss, you don't really think he's in there, do you?"

"Just get down and look," Blaine snapped impatiently. The man called Ace swung out of his saddle. His footsteps came closer.

"Please hurry, señor," Pedro pleaded. "The señorita, she wanted me back by noon, and I am late already. I will help you."

Linc couldn't believe his ears. The wagon squeaked as Pedro leaned over the seat to untie the front corner of the tarp. Was he going to betray him?

"This man you are looking for, what kind of a horse does he ride?" Pedro asked as he fumbled with the tie.

"Why? Did you see any strangers around today?" Blaine asked sharply.

"Sí, I saw a man on a gray stallion this morning on my way to town," Pedro explained, pausing in his task. Linc could just picture his innocent expression as he described Linc's horse, and he smiled in spite of himself. "At first I thought it was Señor Pauling. The stallion was very much like his, you know?"

"Yeah, I know. Where was this fellow heading?" Blaine demanded.

"I do not . . . south, I think. Yes, south. I saw him near the Three Oaks Seep. You know the place?"

"Yeah, I know it. South you say?"

"Sí, he was riding fast, too. On a gray stallion like Señor Pauling's. Is that the man you are looking for?"

"Come on, Ace. Maybe you can track him *now,*" Blaine snapped, ignoring Pedro's question.

Ace muttered something, and his footsteps retreated. Saddle leather creaked again.

Linc heard horses galloping away and counted three sets of hooves. God, he wouldn't have stood a chance.

"They are gone, señor," the boy said through the tarp.

"You're a man to ride the river with, Pedro," Linc said in admiration. "I owe you one."

"If you help the señorita, we will be even. I will take you to her now. We are very close."

Pedro slapped the team into motion. Linc lowered the hammer on his pistol and let the gun slide back to his side, releasing his breath in a long sigh. The motion of the wagon jarred the pain to life again, the pain he'd forgotten momentarily, and he cursed once more. Damn, he'd hated lying helpless while a boy dealt with his enemy, but at least now Linc knew the kind of man he was up against. Blaine was mean and not overly bright and he'd been thinking about Eden in ways he had no business thinking about her. The memory of that suggestive laugh made Linc's hackles rise all over again.

Blaine wouldn't be very pleased when he found out Pedro had sent him on a wild goose chase, but by then they'd be safely at Marcus's ranch. The next time he and Blaine met, things would be very different.

After a surprisingly short ride, the wagon rumbled to a halt. "We are here, señor," Pedro announced, springing down from the seat.

He could hear Eden calling and her footsteps

running. "Did you have any trouble?" she asked. She was untying one corner of the tarp.

"Dirk Blaine and two of his men stopped us," Pedro reported casually.

Linc smiled at Eden's gasp of surprise. "They didn't find him?"

"No, I told them I saw a stranger riding a stallion like Señor Pauling's over at Three Oaks Seep this morning."

"Pedro, you're a genius," Eden exclaimed.

"Excellent job, Pedro," another woman said. Her mother, Linc supposed. "Mr. Pauling will be quite pleased."

In the next instant someone threw back the tarp. Sunlight blinded him for a moment.

"Mr. Scott, are you all right?" Eden asked.

The wagon shifted as two people climbed up and settled on either side of him.

Gradually, his vision returned, and he looked up into the two most beautiful faces he had ever seen. For a minute he recalled his earlier belief that he had died. If he had, he was most surely in heaven.

Eden smiled down at him. "Welcome to Paradise, Mr. Scott."

Chapter Two

"Paradise?" Linc echoed.

"Yes, this is the Paradise Ranch," the other woman said, her voice faintly musical. Her face was exquisite, as smooth and perfect as a porcelain doll's. "Didn't Marcus tell you?"

Linc couldn't remember, but she didn't wait for his answer.

"I believe the three of us should be able to carry him," she continued, addressing Eden and Pedro. There was something strange about the way she spoke, but Linc was much too tired to figure it out. "We'll use the blanket. Eden and I will each take one of the top corners, and Pedro you take the bottom two. We'll take him to Miss Eden's room."

Linc tried to protest being carried by two women and a boy, but before he could open his mouth, they'd dragged him out of the wagon bed and were hefting him up the porch steps. The beautiful girl had been right. They didn't seem to be having any trouble at all. Linc concentrated on not crying out when they accidently jarred him.

He caught a glimpse of the ranch house, a sturdy

adobe structure with a sprawling veranda. Then they were inside the cool, shadowed interior, but Linc was no longer very interested in his surroundings. Wincing with the pain and concentrating on biting back his moans, he saw nothing more for several minutes after they had finally deposited him on a bed.

As if from far away, he heard them instructing Pedro to go find Marcus and tell him what had happened. Vaguely aware that someone was moving his clothing to expose his wound, he forced his eyelids up. Eden had gone, and the china-doll girl was bent over him.

"I fear you've started in bleeding again," she said, her cornflower blue eyes full of apology and her cupid's-bow mouth turned down in a becoming frown. Her features were as fine as a princess's, and her hair looked like spun gold, every strand arranged with elaborate care into a bun on the back of her neck. She wore a simple calico dress, but the collar and cuffs were immaculate, her apron spotless and blindingly white. Although her face was that of an innocent child, her figure revealed her age. Full breasts swelled over a tightly cinched waist. Linc judged her to be at least as old as Eden — and he considered himself a good judge.

She rolled back her sleeves, picked up a pair of scissors from the nightstand, and began carefully snipping at his bandages. Her hands were small and delicate and lily white. This woman was the kind he most feared, a parlor-lady who turned up her little nose at gunfighters.

Or at least that had always been his experience until today. This lady didn't seem to care he was a gunfighter, but perhaps she just didn't know. In any case, she certainly didn't mind getting his blood on her pretty little hands.

Eden came in carrying a tray with a basin of water and a stack of fresh sheeting. She flashed him a quick smile before setting her tray down on the washstand. He glanced around the room, uncomfortably aware of its feminine decor. The headboard behind him was carved with rosebuds, and the canopy above was draped with pink ruffles. He remembered this was Eden's room, Eden's *bed*. The thought disturbed him.

"Eden, is this what I think it is?" the doll-lady demanded, holding up a bloody strip of bandage.

Eden widened her green eyes innocently. "What do you think it is?"

"Your brand new drawers! Eden, I sent all the way to Dallas for this lace," she said in dismay, "and you tear it up as if it were a rag!"

"I really didn't have much choice, did I?" Eden replied unrepentantly. "He was bleeding, and I didn't have anything else."

"But your underwear," the other began, then suddenly remembered Linc, who couldn't help but overhear this amazing conversation. "Oh, dear!" She blushed and quickly laid the scrap of material aside, then continued to remove his bandage.

Linc closed his eyes and distracted himself with visions of Eden pulling off her underdrawers. It was only fair for him to imagine it, he told himself, since she had actually done the same thing to him. The picture of Eden's slender white body came to him with surprising ease, and he wondered if he'd been at least partially conscious at the time. Thoroughly intrigued

38

by the thought, he almost forgot to feel the discomfort of his wound.

"I'm afraid I'll have to clean the wound," the other woman said a few moments later, again apologetically. Her warning instantly chased all the lascivious visions from his head. "It will hurt quite dreadfully, but I'm sure you'd rather suffer for a few moments than risk an infection."

Ever so gently, she bathed away the dried blood and the wet. Then, after warning him to brace himself, she poured a dollop of whiskey into the ragged hole. The agony clawed at his side, and Linc ground his teeth, determined not to scream. The pain closed over him like a tidal wave, blocking sight and sound and smothering him in its crimson embrace. For long minutes he knew nothing except the excruciating torment, then gradually it began to subside. When at length he could focus his eyes, he saw the two women staring down at him, their own eyes moist.

Eden gently patted the perspiration from his face with a soft cloth. Her emerald eyes swam with compassion.

The other woman was far more practical. She helped him swallow the remainder of the whiskey.

"I'm truly sorry, Mr. Scott," she said when the warmth had begun to spread through his body, "but it had to be done. Now I'll put a fresh bandage on you, and I promise not to cause you another moment's discomfort."

Suddenly he realized what it was about her voice. Unlike Eden, who spoke with the characteristic Texas drawl, this girl's accent was clipped and formal and . . . and *British!* Unfortunately, he had neither the energy nor the opportunity to pursue the matter.

With Eden's help, she quickly bound up his wound again. "Eden, please fetch one of Marcus's nightshirts, will you? We'll have you comfortable in no time, Mr. Scott," she added as the girl left.

She began to unbutton Linc's shirt, and he realized *she* was determined to strip him down! Twice in one day was simply too much.

"Wait! I mean . . ." He groped desperately for a reasonable argument, then recalled what it was he'd been trying to remember. "I thought Eden's *mother* was going to take care of me," he said, picturing Marcus's matronly bride. Surely he wouldn't feel quite so embarrassed being undressed by such a woman.

"I *am* Eden's mother," the doll-lady replied with a small smile. "Her stepmother, actually. I should have introduced myself. I'm Fiona Pauling."

Linc stared at this fairylike creature in disbelief. *"You're* Marcus's wife?" he asked, trying in vain to picture her with his old friend.

Her smile widened. "I'm really much older than I appear and not nearly so delicate. I've also been married three times, so you needn't worry. You don't have anything I haven't seen before."

Linc could only gape. When Eden returned with the nightshirt a minute later, Fiona chased her away again so she could undress Linc in privacy. To his great relief, she made short work of it, much as Eden had done. He hardly had time to get really red in the face before she was finished.

Clothed in Marcus's nightshirt and tucked up in Eden's bed with the pain in his side surrendering to Marcus's whiskey, Linc could no longer keep his eyes open.

"I'll make you some soup," Fiona said just before he fell asleep. "When you awaken, call, and I'll bring it right in."

As soon as Lincoln Scott was settled, Eden allowed Fiona to fix her a bath, and she luxuriated in the warm water for a while until at last she felt truly clean again. She smiled when she saw the dress Fiona had laid out for her to wear, a frilly little thing that left her neck and arms bare.

Exactly the one she herself would have chosen with Mr. Scott in mind.

"What is your opinion of our Mr. Scott?" Fiona asked later while Eden dried her hair.

"He's just the way Marcus described him, don't you think?" she replied coyly.

Fiona frowned. She may have been only twelve years older than Eden and she may have been no blood relation, but Eden had never been able to fool her. "I don't recall Marcus telling us anything about his appearance."

"I wasn't talking about his appearance," Eden replied innocently.

"Well, I am," Fiona informed her. "He's a handsome devil, don't you think?"

"Fiona!" Eden scolded, feigning shock. "You're a married woman."

"But *you* aren't, and the only reason is because you haven't found a man strong enough to match you. Someone like Lincoln Scott, for instance."

"You don't know if he's strong or not. We don't

"know anything about him," Eden reminded her.

"He's a friend of Marcus's. That's recommendation enough for me."

"Yes, but they haven't seen each other in seven years," Eden reminded her. "People can change a lot in seven years."

"They've corresponded, and we certainly know Mr. Scott by reputation. A man doesn't get that sort of reputation unless he's honest and courageous."

"Or ruthless and foolish," Eden said. "Maybe he just likes taking risks so he always chooses the losing side in a battle."

Fiona shrugged one small shoulder. "Mayhap you're right. Mr. Scott is probably a worthless scoundrel, and I should throw him out of my house immediately so he can bleed to death in the dust."

"Well, you don't have to do anything drastic," Eden said, no longer able to suppress a grin at Fiona's foolishness. "You're right, he is awfully handsome. Maybe we should at least give him a chance to show his true colors."

Fiona returned her grin. "You're very generous."

"I know," Eden replied.

Lincoln Scott slept for most of the afternoon. The two women were anxiously waiting for Pedro to return with Marcus when they heard horses in the yard.

"Hello, the house!" a strange voice called, giving the traditional western greeting. Fiona peeked out the front curtains.

"Oh, no, the Blaines!" she cried, hurrying to fetch a rifle from the rack. "What on earth are they doing

42

here? They should know better than to harass ladies."

"Unfortunately, the code of chivalry only applies if you happen to be a gentleman," Eden reminded her, taking up a shotgun and checking the loads. Looking outside, she saw Dirk Blaine astride the big bay gelding he favored. He had three of his men with him. She muttered a curse.

"Mind your tongue," Fiona chided. "Let's see what they want."

Eden opened the door and held it for Fiona, who maneuvered her rifle carefully through it. Eden followed her out.

"Good afternoon, Mr. Blaine," Fiona said, cradling the Winchester so the barrel was pointing politely at nothing.

The rifle looked so foreign in Fiona's frail arms, Eden felt an absurd urge to laugh out loud. If Lincoln Scott's life hadn't been at stake, she might have. Eden held her shotgun with the barrels pointed toward the ground. "What brings you out this afternoon?" she asked.

Blaine removed his Stetson, revealing his carefully oiled ash blond hair, and smiled. Eden supposed he must practice his smiles in front of a mirror. He wasn't bad looking, she'd give him that, but even if she'd liked his character, he was too much of a dandy for her taste. His vest and chaps glittered with silver ornaments, and some sort of feathers formed the hatband on his Stetson. And those eyes of his made her skin crawl. So pale blue they were almost colorless, they reminded her of the milky orbs of a rattlesnake just before it shed its skin. She stiffened in annoyance as he looked her over insolently, obviously appreciating the dress she was wearing for Scott and all the flesh it revealed. Her face went hot with fury.

"We were wondering if your boy Pedro ever made it home," Blaine said with oily charm.

"Yes, he brought us some supplies from town," Eden said.

"We'd like to have a little talk with him, then."

"He isn't here just now," Fiona informed him, her perfect face betraying nothing. Eden never ceased to be amazed at how cool her little stepmother could be. "I sent him on another errand."

"That's too bad." Blaine replaced his hat, settling it with elaborate care. "You see, we're looking for somebody, a fellow who took a shot at my brother. Tried to gun him down in cold blood from ambush. We think your boy might know something about it."

"He told us he saw you on the road this morning," Eden said, glad Pedro wasn't here. "Why didn't you ask him then?"

"We did, but he sent us on a wild goose chase. We think he lied to us on purpose because you all are hiding the man we're looking for."

"That's a pretty serious charge," Eden snapped, rage boiling inside her.

"It certainly is," Fiona said, her accent growing more pronounced with her annoyance. "I'm shocked at you, Mr. Blaine. You've as much as accused two ladies of harboring an assassin." She lifted her chin, affronted. "I'm afraid I'm going to have to ask you to leave."

Blaine grinned evilly. "We'd be only too happy to go, but first we'd like to take a look around."

"You've had a look around already," Eden said,

wishing she'd had Fiona's prim British background and all the training on how to be polite to people you detest. She knew her voice revealed her revulsion and possibly even her apprehension. Fiona had yet to even bat an eye.

"We'd like to look in the house, if you don't mind," Blaine explained with exaggerated patience.

Eden gasped aloud, but Fiona merely frowned. "We most certainly do mind. Surely you understand that two defenseless women cannot allow a group of men to enter their home. Eden and I must be careful of our reputations, and you must realize my husband would never approve."

This time Eden had to cough to cover a laugh. Not approve! Marcus would cut out Blaine's liver and feed it to the buzzards! But of course Marcus wasn't here.

"You're hardly defenseless, Mrs. Pauling," Blaine said, looking askance at their hardware. "We have no intention of harming either of you ladies or breaking up the furniture or doing anything the least bit objectionable. If you have nothing to hide . . ." He paused suggestively.

"It isn't a matter of hiding anything. It is a matter of propriety, Mr. Blaine," Fiona said, her sweet voice sharp with the anger she no longer bothered to suppress. "If you refuse to leave, we will have to use force."

Fiona lifted the Winchester to her shoulder. Since the rifle was almost as long as she was tall, the sight was ludicrous, and Dirk Blaine smiled.

"If you fire that thing, it'll knock you clear into next week, Mrs. Pauling."

"But it will knock you to kingdom come, Mr.

Blaine."

Blaine's smile disappeared.

"Boss, you won't win any friends if you mess with ladies," one of the other men said. "Let's get out of here."

"Shut up, Ace. No woman tells me what to do." Blaine rose in his saddle, preparing to dismount, and Eden's shotgun exploded.

The buckshot scattered at the horses' feet. The animals screamed in terror and danced away to safety, their riders shouting and cursing. Halfway out of his saddle, Blaine yelped in surprise, and his gelding reared, tossing him to the ground in an ignominious heap. Cursing, he jumped up again, reaching for his gun, but Ace yelled a warning above the squeals of the horses, and he froze.

Blaine found himself looking at two raised barrels, Fiona's rifle and the unfired second barrel of Eden's shotgun.

"My pa always told me a shotgun is a sure thing because you don't have to aim," Eden told Blaine. "Fiona might miss, but I'll cut you in half if you take one step toward this house."

Blaine stood in a gunfighter's crouch, glaring at her with murder in his snake's eyes, but he evidently believed she'd shoot because he damned her to hell and stomped off through the churning dust to catch his terrified horse while the other men brought their own mounts under control.

The man called Ace, a homely fellow with pockmarked skin and dark, beady eyes, touched his hat brim respectfully. "I'm sorry, ladies. Mr. Blaine, he's just upset what with somebody taking a shot at his brother and all."

Neither woman acknowledged the apology. Both continued to watch Blaine as he caught his horse, recovered his hat from the dirt, brushed off the worst of the dust, and remounted.

His face was scarlet, his pale eyes blazing with fury when he turned back to face them. "You'll be sorry you did that, Eden, and if I find out you're hiding the man I'm looking for, I'll burn this place to the ground."

Eden had no doubt he would try. She thought of Lincoln Scott lying helpless inside, and fear clogged her throat, blocking whatever smart reply she would have wished to make. She noticed the other men looked aghast at his threat, but that was small comfort.

Blaine jerked his reins and kicked his horse into a gallop. The others followed. Only when the dust in the yard began to settle did Eden lower the shotgun. Mildly surprised to find her hands were trembling, she glanced at Fiona. Her face had gone white, but her eyes sparked angrily.

"How dare he make a threat like that!" she demanded, lowering her own rifle. "Who does he bloody well think he is?"

"He thinks he's the strongest man in the county, that's who," Eden replied. "Obviously, he thinks he's strong enough to be a match for me, too." She shuddered at the thought.

"Which is all the more reason for you to find yourself a *good* man to protect you."

"I think I just proved I'm perfectly capable of protecting myself," she pointed out.

Fiona had just opened her mouth to reply when they heard a loud crash from inside the house.

"What on earth . . . ?" They both ran inside, straight into Eden's bedroom, where they found the washstand overturned, the pitcher and basin smashed, and Lincoln Scott sprawled on the floor beside it. In Marcus's nightshirt, with his long bare legs sticking out, he would have made a comic sight if Eden hadn't known how badly he was hurt.

"Don't move!" she cried, rushing to his side. Realizing she still held the shotgun, she handed it to Fiona, who quickly disposed of the two guns. "What in heaven's name are you doing out of bed?"

Although his face was ashen, his blue eyes twinkled with self-mockery when he looked up at her. "I had this crazy idea . . . you two ladies . . . might need some help," he explained hoarsely.

Eden stared at him for a moment before comprehension dawned. He held his Colt in one hand, and he'd encountered the washstand halfway between the bed and the window overlooking the front porch. Good heavens! He'd been covering them during their encounter with Dirk Blaine.

"Really, Mr. Scott, you had no business at all getting out of bed," Fiona said, kneeling beside him. "You've probably set your wound to bleeding again."

He nodded once, closing his eyes against the pain. "I'm sorry about the mess," he said after a few moments.

"Don't think of it," Fiona said, more gently this time.

"Certainly not," Eden agreed, feeling a warm glow in the general region of her heart. What did a little crockery matter when she had a genuine hero on her hands. "Fiona's right, though, we'd better get you right back in bed. Do you think you can walk?"

"I got myself here. I can get myself back," he replied, making as if to rise.

"Let us help you," Fiona said, taking his arm and placing it over her shoulder.

Eden did the same with his other arm, conscious of the weight of it and the tensile strength it held. They helped him get his legs under him, his long bare legs furred with the same dark hair she'd admired on his chest and arms. The last time she'd helped him walk, she'd been too concerned for his safety to notice much more. This time she savored the feel of his bare skin beneath her hand as she moved his leg, and the power of the shoulder leaning against her own.

His scent engulfed her, raw and alarmingly male. Her nerves tingled in response, and her stomach did a little flip, as if she were falling from a great height. No man had ever affected her this way before. Was Fiona right? Had she finally met her match? The thought made her stomach flip again.

They lowered him to the bed, and then Fiona shooed her out so she could check his wound. Alone in the parlor, Eden reflected on the events of the last few minutes. Oddly enough, she found the encounter with Lincoln Scott far more disturbing than the one with Dirk Blaine.

Fiona and Eden had long since finished supper when Marcus Pauling returned. The two women were sitting in the parlor working on their mending when they heard his and Pedro's horses approaching the house.

Fiona instantly put her work aside and rose from her chair. Lifting a hand to her hair, she murmured, "I must look a fright," and hurried to her bedroom which, like Eden's room, opened directly off the parlor. Eden knew she'd be checking her hair and pinching color into her cheeks in preparation for seeing her husband. Of course, Fiona didn't need any special preparation. Even when she was scrubbing floors, she looked better than most women did at their weddings.

Eden frowned. She had never known her stepmother to be so anxious about her appearance during her marriage to Eden's father. No, Fiona was worried about her relationship with her new husband and with good reason. Anyone could see there was something wrong between her and Marcus. Although they'd been married over six months, they didn't act like a married couple, or at least they didn't treat each other with the same ease of familiarity Eden had seen between Fiona and her own father. Something was definitely wrong. Eden only wished she knew how to help.

Usually, Marcus cared for his horse before coming inside, but he was apparently in too much of a hurry to see his old friend and had turned the task over to Pedro. Fiona had not yet returned when he came bounding up the porch steps and in the front door.

His tall, lanky frame filled the doorway as he paused and looked around. Eden figured he was searching for Fiona. He always looked for her first thing.

Eden stood up to welcome him home. "As usual,

you missed all the excitement."

He'd already pulled off his hat, and now he ran a hand through his thinning brown hair and smiled a greeting. No one would ever accuse Marcus Pauling of being handsome. His features were too irregular, his body too clumsily put together, but he had about him an aura of masculinity so strong it offset his lack of physical beauty. In any case, Fiona had proclaimed him "cute," and her opinion was the only one that really mattered.

"How's Linc?" he asked.

"He's fine. Fiona put him in my room."

Marcus sighed his relief, then scowled. "And thank God you're all right. What in the name of heaven were you thinking of to ride off alone looking for me in the first place?"

She suppressed her amusement. "It's a good thing I did, or your old friend would've bled to death."

Marcus's scowl deepened. She knew he was unwilling to let her have the last word but he was unable to think of a reply. "How's he doing?" he asked to change the subject, tossing his hat onto a peg beside the door and coming into the room.

"Pretty well, all things considered. He took a little fall this afternoon when Dirk Blaine was here, though."

"*Blaine?* He didn't . . . ?"

"No, he didn't find Mr. Scott." Briefly she told him what happened.

"I can't believe that son of a bitch had the nerve to try to get in the house!" he exclaimed in outrage. "Wait'll I get my hands on him. I'll . . ."

His attention wandered toward the door of his bedroom where Fiona had appeared. His light brown eyes took on a strange glow, the kind of glow a man has when he's in love. Indeed, Eden truly believed Marcus adored his bride, and when Fiona looked at him, her face held the same distinctive expression.

But Fiona didn't run to him, didn't throw her arms around him and kiss him the way a wife should have done when she hadn't seen her man for over a week. Instead she smiled tremulously, clasped her hands in front of her, and said, "Welcome home, Marcus."

He didn't go to her, either. Instead he shifted his feet awkwardly and cleared his throat. "I . . ." He swallowed and tried again, a flush rising on his neck. "Thanks for taking such good care of Linc. Pedro told me how you got him here, and Eden just told me about Blaine's visit this afternoon. I hope he didn't scare you too much."

She dismissed his concern with a graceful wave of her hand. "Dirk Blaine is a blowhard, and we were glad to take care of Mr. Scott. We know how much he means to you."

Marcus nodded and swallowed again. Eden had long since become accustomed to his reticence. He'd always been painfully shy with females, and as a child, Eden had spent months trying to break through the reserve of her father's new friend and neighbor. Her efforts had been rewarded with the friendship of a man who trusted only with difficulty. She could understand why he might once have found Fiona intimidating, but she simply couldn't understand why he still had such a hard time talking to her now that she was his wife.

"Do you want to eat or do you want to see Linc

first?" Eden asked to break the uncomfortable silence.

"I'll see Linc if he's awake."

"He asked me to send you in the moment you arrived," Fiona assured him with a smile.

He smiled back, or started to. His face froze midway into it, as if he'd caught himself doing something unseemly. "Thanks," he muttered, hurrying off to Eden's bedroom.

Linc woke up the instant he heard Marcus's voice in the other room. He couldn't make out the words, but he felt the warmth of excitement at the prospect of seeing his old friend again after so many years.

He'd often reflected on how strange their relationship had always been. They'd first met just after Linc had run away from home. His drunken father had beaten him one too many times, and with his mother dead, he no longer had any reason to stay.

Linc had decided to become a drover, one of the brave souls who dared to face the multitudinous dangers of driving herds of cattle north from Texas, across Indian Territory into Kansas to sell them. The job had seemed romantic to a boy barely sixteen who'd never been more than twenty miles from the place of his birth. He hadn't bargained for being the youngest member of the motley group of cowboys assembled for the job, and he certainly hadn't bargained for the hazing the others had proceeded to give him.

At first Mr. Pauling hadn't noticed. As foreman of the drive, he left camp early and returned late. By the time he got back, the men had settled down for the few hours of sleep they'd get before the backbreaking labor began again with the next dawn. He wasn't in camp when the other men put a rattlesnake next to Linc while he slept—it was dead, but Linc had still almost wet his pants—or when one of them "accidently" knocked his supper into the fire or when they made him ride the nastiest horse in the ramuda and he'd almost gotten killed. The first thing Mr. Pauling had noticed was that Linc only owned one motheaten blanket with which to make his bed at night.

Tradition said cowboys provided their own saddles and bedding, generally a heavy comforter called a sugan designed to withstand the bluest of blue northers. Of course Linc hadn't had the wherewithal to purchase or make a sugan, so he slept cold his first few nights on the trail until Mr. Pauling saw him shivering.

"Didn't any of these no good saddle bums offer to share their blankets with you?" he demanded angrily.

Terrified of the awesome foreman and even more terrified of offending the other men who had worn out a set of hobbles whipping the insolence out of him after supper, Linc had merely shaken his head.

"You'll catch consumption if you don't get some blankets, and I can't afford to lose a good man. From now on you sleep with me."

The suggestion wasn't so very outlandish. Most of the men shared blankets with a partner for warmth. Still, Linc couldn't quite bring himself to believe the exalted foreman of the entire crew really intended for the lowliest cowboy in the bunch to share with him.

But Mr. Pauling had hauled his bedroll out of the

chuck wagon and called Linc over to help him spread it out. When Linc made no move to join him, he looked up with some annoyance and said, "If you're gonna sleep with me, you'd better get those boots off, boy."

Needing no further invitation, Linc disposed of his boots in short order and joined Mr. Pauling for his first warm night since he'd left home.

For the first month, Marcus hadn't shown him any gentleness, perhaps guessing Linc's tough facade would crumble in the face of outright kindness. Without having to deal with the hazing, which stopped when the other men saw how the foreman trusted him, Linc could concentrate on learning his job. Gruffly but patiently, Marcus had taught him all the skills a drover needed: how to calm a herd in a thunderstorm, how to turn a stampede without getting killed, how to handle Indians who wanted fresh beef, how to deal with rustlers and herd cutters and bunch quitters and all the other varmints encountered along the trail north.

And most importantly, he'd taught him how to use a gun.

Linc had learned everything eagerly and thoroughly, desperate for the approval of the only man who'd ever treated him with respect. Finally, near the end of the drive, Marcus had said the words Linc had cherished ever since: "If I had a son, I'd want him to be just like you."

The only cross word they'd ever exchanged came over Linc's reluctance to stay with Marcus when the drive ended. Marcus finally had the means to get what he'd always wanted: a place of his own. At twenty-nine, he was more than ready to settle down, but the idea was too tame for Linc, who was just starting to sow his wild oats.

"I'll come back in a year or two," he'd promised with the ignorance of youth. In return Marcus had promised he'd always have a home waiting whenever he chose to claim it.

After seven long years, the time had finally come.

The door opened slowly. Linc grinned broadly and said, "Well, if it ain't the lord of the manor."

A smile split Marcus's weathered face, and the years fell away. "I'll be damned. Some men'll do anything to get into my daughter's bed!"

"Your *daughter?*" Linc hooted. "You never made anything that pretty on the longest day of your life!"

Marcus chuckled and took Linc's hand and shook it, grasping it with both of his. Linc's eyes stung, and Marcus blinked rapidly. For a moment neither of them could speak over the swell of emotion.

Marcus released Linc's hand reluctantly and said, "God, I'm sorry. If I'd known they'd ambush you, I never would've—"

"We think they were ambushing *you,* so this ain't hardly your fault."

Marcus's eyes grew bleak. "If I hadn't sent for you—"

"If you hadn't, I would've come anyway. It's past time, don't you think?"

Marcus nodded, a slow grin spreading across his face. "Past time and then some. I just hope to God you plan to stay."

Stay. The word was like a sword in Linc's heart. He'd never been welcome to *stay* anywhere in his whole life except with Marcus. He smiled wanly. "Who'd want to leave *Paradise?*" he quipped. "Especially after seeing the angels."

Marcus chuckled again, pulled up a chair, and sat down beside the bed. "They're something, ain't they?"

"How in the hell did you fall into a setup like this? And what on earth does a woman like that see in a bangtail like you?"

Linc's questions had been in jest, but Marcus's smile faded, and his brown eyes clouded. "You got it right, I fell into it. Dumb luck, just like how I got my spread in the first place."

"Let me have the whole story."

"Are you sure you're up to it?"

"If I start drifting off, just give me a poke," Linc said, adjusting the covers more comfortably.

Marcus leaned forward and ran a hand through his hair. It was thinner than Linc remembered, and he saw some strands of gray that hadn't been there seven years ago. The squint lines beside his friend's eyes were deeper, and his cheeks perhaps a little leaner, but otherwise he looked just the same.

"Well, you know how I got my place," Marcus began. "First person I met when I settled here was Jason Campbell, Eden's pa. He was a fine man, one of the best. His first wife had been dead a while, and he was raising Eden on his own. The three of us spent a lot of time together, but Eden was growing up, and we could see she needed a woman to help her. I guess Jason had been looking for a spell, but without much luck. Women are pretty scarce around these parts."

"They're scarce all over Texas," Linc testified, having seen most every corner of the state.

"Well, we got word that some rancher east of here had died, and his widow was selling out. Jason decides to look over her stock and takes Eden along with him. When he comes back, he's got the widow with him. They'd gotten married three days after they met."

"Fiona?" Linc guessed.

Marcus nodded.

"Is she English?"

"Exactly," Marcus said, doing a creditable imitation of Fiona's clipped accent. "Her first husband was the son of a duke or something. A remittance man," he explained.

Linc nodded. The West was full of British exiles who'd been sent to America by their families for one reason or another and who survived on the remittance checks their relatives sent them.

"His folks shipped him over here to make a man of him, but it killed him instead," Marcus said.

"Seems strange she didn't go back when he died."

"She likes it here, or so Eden says, although I can't figure it myself. Eden says she likes the freedom."

Linc could understand that, although he did wonder why Marcus had gotten the information from Eden instead of from Fiona herself. What he couldn't understand was how Marcus had ended up with her, but he'd already seen Marcus's reaction to the question. Before asking it again, he'd wait to see if Marcus told him on his own.

"Like I wrote you, the Blaine brothers moved in a couple years ago."

"A pretty mean bunch, I gather," Linc said wryly, touching his bandage.

"There's even more you don't know. At first they didn't seem too bad. Some of the cattle they brought had funny-looking brands, if you know what I mean, but plenty of perfectly respectable ranchers got their start the same way. Nobody minds so long as it's not their cattle that got stolen. Anyway, they homesteaded some land nobody else wanted. Then they started putting up fences, claiming the Land Act gave them the right. Trouble was, they fenced land didn't belong to them."

Linc knew all about the problems with fencing under the Land Act. Lately those were the problems he'd most often been called upon to settle with his gun. "They're entitled to fence land they rent from the state, even if they don't own it," Linc reminded him.

"They don't rent nothing from nobody, and they fenced land other folks owned free and clear. Didn't care if they fenced across roads and cut people off from town or even from their own land."

"Didn't anybody protest?"

"Sure, and whenever they did, nightriders burned their barns or fired shots into their houses or terrorized their womenfolk. Then, like I wrote you, our cattle started disappearing. Not many, but enough so we noticed. We don't have any law to speak of out here, so Jason Campbell made the mistake of trying to organize some vigilantes. We found him dead on the road one afternoon."

"Murdered?" Linc asked, outraged on Eden's behalf.

"We suspect he was, but we can't prove it. He'd been dragged by his horse. It could've been an accident, but you'll never convince Eden of it, or me either."

Linc nodded solemnly. "So you comforted the widow and . . ." he prompted, thinking he'd hit on the answer.

"Not exactly," Marcus hedged, and to Linc's surprise he turned beet red.

His friend didn't speak for several moments, and finally Linc said, "Then what, exactly?"

Marcus straightened in his chair and looked away, obviously embarrassed. "You know I never was much good with women."

Linc nodded, recalling what Marcus had told him of his motherless early life. Females were a mystery to Marcus Pauling and, like many men in the West, he feared only two things: a decent woman and being left afoot. He wasn't even too confident around *in*decent women. Linc remembered only too well the one time he'd known Marcus to patronize a lady of the evening and the disaster that had followed. "I figured you must've learned how to be charming in your old age," Linc tried.

Marcus didn't smile. "It was all Eden's doing. With Jason gone, the two of them were alone. Oh, they had their cowboys, but that's not the same as having a man to protect them. The Blaines started running cattle on their land, and we figured the next thing they'd do is start fencing. Jason's men wanted to fight, but with no one to lead them . . ."

He shrugged, and Linc nodded his understanding.

"I'm their nearest neighbor," Marcus explained. "Our spreads join at the creek, and we've always shared the water. It was only natural . . . I mean, Fiona needed a husband and . . ." He shrugged again.

"Are you saying you only married her because you wanted to protect her?" Linc asked incredulously, remembering the glorious creature who had tended his wound this afternoon. Not even Marcus could be that backward.

"Hell, no! I . . . Fiona's a fine woman . . ." he stammered, flushing again.

Linc smiled knowingly. "She ain't hard to look at, either."

"Eden came and asked me if I'd consider it," Marcus explained stiffly, ignoring Linc's remark. "They was afraid to be alone. Eden's always liked me, and I suppose Fiona must have, too."

"You *suppose?*" Linc scoffed.

"She respects me," Marcus corrected, not meeting Linc's eye. "She knew I wouldn't be afraid to stand up to the Blaines, not even after what had happened to Jason."

"And do you 'respect' her, too?" Linc teased.

"Fiona is a fine woman."

"You said that before."

Marcus's flush deepened. "You've had a rough life, Linc, just like me. We haven't had much truck with women like Fiona. She's different from the kind we're used to. She's special. She's . . ." He gestured vaguely with his hand as if groping for the proper word.

Linc had no trouble grasping his meaning, however. He'd seen Fiona for himself. She was everything Marcus had said and more, and so was her stepdaughter. "You must care for her," Linc suggested.

"Sure I do! What man wouldn't?" Marcus asked defensively.

"I'm awful relieved to hear that," Linc said with a grin. "The way you were talking, I was afraid you didn't even . . ."

Marcus straightened with a jerk, and his eyes blazed. For a second Linc thought he'd gone too far teasing his old friend, but then he realized Marcus was mortified, not furious. Maybe Marcus really *was* that backward.

"Hey, I'm sorry, partner," Linc tried. "It's none of my business."

"No, it ain't," Marcus said, but to Linc's relief his expression was self-mocking instead of angry. "But I don't want you to get the wrong idea. I mean, we're married, after all, and . . ." He grinned. "And I ain't entirely stupid. Besides, Eden said Fiona wants a family, and so do I."

Linc frowned. Eden said? Didn't Fiona ever tell him anything herself? But maybe Marcus was right. Maybe ladies like Fiona were different from ordinary people. She and Eden were certainly different from anyone Linc had ever met. Although they both had completely undressed him, he still couldn't imagine talking to either one of them about anything having to do with sex.

"So, enough about me," Marcus said in an obvious attempt to change the subject. "Are all those stories I've been hearing about you true?"

"Depends on which ones you've heard," Linc hedged, wishing Marcus had chosen a different topic. He hated talking about his reputation, built as it was on the bones of so many dead men.

"I heard you helped a lot of folks what needed it," Marcus said, his eyes telling him he understood. "I

62

never would've taught you how to shoot if I didn't think you were the kind of man who'd always use his gun for good."

"In a fight, sometimes neither side is good."

"I don't reckon you ever killed anybody who didn't need killing."

Linc had used that very argument to himself many times. He tried to remember the world was a better place without those men, but the justification didn't help him sleep any better. "I'd rather live in a world where men didn't need to go armed."

"We all would," Marcus said, suddenly looking older than his years. "But we can't so long as men like the Blaines are running around loose."

Yes, Linc thought, remembering the way Dirk Blaine had looked at Marcus's women. Someone would have to kill the Blaines before Eden and Fiona could be truly safe. The trouble was, what would a girl like Eden think of the man who did it once the gunsmoke cleared?

When Marcus came out of the bedroom after his visit with Linc, Fiona had a hot supper waiting for him. She sat with him while he ate, although he wasn't the sort of man who made conversation at meals.

Then she fixed a bath for him in their bedroom. After she left the room, he stripped off his filthy range clothes, lowered himself gratefully into the tub, and reflected on what a lucky man he was.

He'd told Linc the God's truth when he'd called his good fortune dumb luck. He'd have died an old and lonely man before he ever would have earned a bride like Fiona on his own. He knew she'd taken him out of desperation and need, but she'd certainly never thrown it up to him. Instead she made him feel as important as if he'd been the man of her dreams. Never having been married before, Marcus couldn't be perfectly sure, but he would've bet the entire Pauling-Campbell holdings that no man ever had a better wife.

He sat there for a while, letting the fatigue soak out of his muscles; then suddenly the door opened and Fiona came in. As always, she looked like something out of a picture book, her yellow hair brushed and bound, her tiny figure as neat as a pin, her face even more beautiful than he remembered. He'd worshiped the ground she walked on from the first moment Jason had introduced her as his new bride. Even after all this time, his mouth still went dry at the sight of her.

She must've thought he'd be finished, but she didn't look embarrassed at having caught him buck naked in the tub.

"I'm just about done," he said, feeling embarrassed for her. During their marriage he'd taken great pains not to expose his nudity to her, knowing how delicate her sensibilities must be. Fortunately, the cloudy bathwater covered the important parts, at least for the moment.

"Would you like me to wash your back?" she asked as calmly as if she'd performed this service for him every day of his life.

Marcus somehow managed to conceal his surprise and briefly entertained the idea of accepting her offer.

But as much as he wanted her to, he also knew how very dangerous such a thing would be. Marriage had done nothing to slake his desire for Fiona. In fact, having her had only made it worse. Concealing that desire was difficult at the best of times. Under the circumstances, he wouldn't be able to hide a thing. "Uh, you don't have to do that."

For an instant he saw the expression he recognized as impatience flicker across her face. No matter how hard he tried not to offend or irritate her, he always seemed to do it anyway. Her annoyance seemed to grow in direct proportion to how hard he tried to please her.

But her expression cleared instantly, becoming benign again. "I know I don't have to," she replied with what might have been determination. "I want to."

Before he could think of an appropriate reason to refuse, she had knelt beside the tub and taken up the washrag and soap. Mesmerized, he watched her tiny hands working up a lather, turning the bar over and over and over again until the white foam bubbled up and slid out between her fingers.

His breath rasped in his chest, and he fought to control it and the blood racing to his loins.

"Lean forward," she said, moving around behind him.

Seeing no other alternative, he obeyed, swallowing a groan when the hot, slippery rag touched his sensitized skin. She spread it slowly, sliding it across his shoulders and down and up again until she'd soaped his entire back. Then she clenched her fingers into a claw behind the rag and scraped it across his shoulder blade.

He couldn't hold back a strangled sound of pleasure.

"Does that feel good?"

Good hardly covered it. Marcus nodded, unable to get any words past his thickened throat.

She raked the rest of his back, stroking up and down and up and down, slowly, thoroughly, until every inch of his back tingled.

"Your friend seems like a nice man," she remarked, relaxing her hand to soothe the red furrows she had raised.

Marcus needed a minute to remember which friend she was talking about. "Linc's the salt of the earth," he said, hoping his voice didn't sound as strained to her as it did to him.

"We must think of a story to explain his presence here."

"A story?" Marcus repeated stupidly, wishing he had a little more control over his body so he could concentrate on something besides her hand moving rhythmically over his bare flesh.

"Yes, we certainly can't let anyone know he's the man the Blaines are looking for. So long as our cowboys are still on roundup, we can keep his presence a secret, but when they return, word will get out."

"Mmmmm," he murmured in agreement, aware only that her pause indicated some sort of response was required. The musical cadence of her voice was almost as hypnotic as her caress.

"We can't tell people he's a gunfighter, can we? At least not until he's recovered. If the Blaines learn his identity before he is able to defend himself, his life will be in certain danger. Therefore, we need a story."

"Yes, a story," Marcus muttered, hoping she didn't expect him to come up with one in his present condition.

"I thought perhaps we could say he was Eden's suitor."

She had said the one thing that could penetrate his sensual fog. "Suitor?" he asked, looking at her over his shoulder.

"Yes, we can say they met this winter in San Antonio when she and I were visiting there, and now he's come to court her in earnest. Since he's a guest, no one will expect him to ride the range and work cattle, which he won't be able to do until his wound heals."

"Have you talked this over with Eden?" Marcus asked as warning bells started to sound in his head. Eden might delight in arranging other people's lives, but she resented any interference in her own.

"I think it would be best if you suggested it," she replied, swirling the washrag in the bathwater to rinse off the suds. "She has great respect for your opinion, you know. If she thought this was your idea, I'm sure she'd be happy to support it." Pulling the rag out of the water again, she sloshed the drying soap from his back in a brand new sensual assault.

Marcus closed his eyes and gritted his teeth to hold back a moan of pleasure and tried to concentrate on what Fiona was saying. He didn't dare commit himself to anything until he had a chance to think over her idea when he was feeling completely sane again. "I'll talk to her," he said hoarsely.

When she'd finished rinsing his back, she rose to her feet beside the tub. "Oh, dear, I've soiled my gown."

She pointed to a wet spot on the skirt which Marcus thought would surely be dry in five minutes. Before he could say so, however, she'd started unbuttoning her bodice.

"I'd better change." She slid the dress from her shoulders, down over her hips, and stepped out of it. After shaking it out, she hung it carefully on a peg on the wall.

Marcus watched the whole procedure open-mouthed. He'd only seen her in her petticoat a time or two when he'd accidently walked in while she was changing. The sight of her bare arms and the ivory bosom swelling above the neckline of her chemise unnerved him. He knew exactly how she would feel and taste and smell if he were to bury his face in her softness. He swallowed against the thickness in his throat.

"You'd better get out of the tub before you turn into a prune," she told him with a smile, making no move to cover herself.

Was she crazy? he wondered frantically. Didn't she know what she'd done to him? Didn't she know that at this very moment his body was paying her its highest tribute, and if he stood up, she'd be shocked out of her mind?

And he certainly didn't dare get one inch closer to her. If she were within arm's length, he'd tear off what was left of her clothes and take her right there on the floor with water and soapsuds and everything.

But of course he wouldn't dare do such a thing. She'd think he was an animal and rightly so. By God, it wasn't even dark outside yet. He had at least another hour until bedtime. He drew a ragged breath. "I'll just sit here until you're gone," he managed.

Instantly her smile vanished and the roses in her cheeks turned scarlet. Without a word she snatched up the dress she'd just removed, threw it over her head, and marched toward the door, fastening the dress as she went. She threw the door open and slammed it shut behind her, making him wince.

He swore aloud, wondering what on earth he'd said to set her off this time.

Chapter Three

For the next few days Linc concentrated on getting well. Marcus stayed around, having sent word to his men back at the roundup that he was protecting Eden and Amanda from further harassment by the Blaines. Linc appreciated having a man to handle the more embarrassing aspects of his care, and as Linc's strength returned, the two of them used his increasing periods of wakefulness to fill in the gaps caused by their long separation.

After a few days, Linc began to venture out of the bedroom with Marcus's help. He'd grown somewhat accustomed to the feminine decor of Eden's room, so he wasn't surprised to discover the rest of the house bore an unmistakably woman's touch.

Aside from the whitewashed adobe construction and the fieldstone fireplace that covered most of one wall, the parlor could have been a fashionable room in a fancy Eastern mansion. Sofas and chairs upholstered in blue velvet mingled with finely carved tables and cabinets which Eden informed him had been imported from England. Linc figured they were a legacy from Fiona's first husband, the duke or whatever he had been.

Framed paintings of landscapes the likes of which Linc had never seen adorned the walls. He didn't need Eden to tell him they were pictures of a foreign country. Even Marcus was uncomfortable in such formal surroundings.

"Don't think I lived like this before I got married," Marcus explained one afternoon. "I had a one-room cabin over on the other side of the creek, but I couldn't ask Fiona to leave all this and move over there with me after we got married."

"Wouldn't make any sense," Linc agreed. "You've got a lot more room here, and privacy, too," he added with a wink.

Marcus glanced around glumly. "I just wish I wasn't always afraid of breaking something. I've got so I'm even scared to sneeze inside the house."

Linc nodded, in complete sympathy. "I reckon that's the price a man pays for getting himself civilized," he remarked, thinking the price wasn't very high at all. At least Marcus seemed to be adjusting pretty well. "And having a beautiful woman to share your bed must make things downright bearable."

Marcus flushed, but his grin affirmed Linc's theory.

By the fifth day, Linc felt well enough to join the family for supper in the dining room. They sat in ornate armchairs around a huge mahogany table held up by carved cherubs and draped with spotless

71

damask.

"We don't usually dine so formally," Fiona explained, indicating the glittering china and crystal and the multitude of silver utensils, "but we're honoring your recovery."

Linc would have preferred beef and beans on a tin plate to honor his recovery, but he smiled politely, and watched the others to see which of the several forks to pick up first.

Sitting across from him, Eden easily read his confusion. Catching his eye, she grinned mischievously and held up the correct implement. His smirk told her he appreciated her tip. Although he was plainly ill-at-ease, he made a valiant effort to behave correctly, and he even complimented Fiona on the meal.

"It's been a long time since I ate this good, Mrs. Pauling."

"Why, thank you, Mr. Scott, but I can't take all the credit," Fiona replied. "Eden really did most of the cooking."

Eden almost choked at the bold-faced lie. She'd have to have a talk with Fiona about her blatant matchmaking. Still, Eden couldn't help thinking that however wild Mr. Scott's past might have been, his behavior tonight showed he might possibly be housebroken to genteel living. That is, if a woman wanted to go to the effort.

The longer she watched him, the more Eden began to think the effort might be worthwhile. Marcus had given him a shave and a haircut earlier in the day, and Eden herself had ironed his shirt. The color was back in his face and his sky blue eyes glittered with health. She didn't need to imagine what the broad shoulders looked like beneath his shirt, or the rest of him either, for that matter, she thought, feeling suddenly very warm. No question about it, Lincoln Scott cleaned up very nicely, and he was every bit as brave as Fiona had suggested. Eden also liked the way he'd remained cheerful or at least tolerant during his recuperation. Yes, a man like that could definitely be housebroken.

Eden was glad she'd dressed so carefully tonight, selecting the same sprigged muslin Fiona had chosen for her the day Scott had arrived at their home. More than once she caught him admiring the way it hugged her breasts and bared a substantial amount of shoulder and bosom.

When they had finished off the apple and currant pie Fiona served up for dessert and the women had cleared the table, Marcus cleared his throat importantly.

"Could you girls leave the dishes for now? I'd like to have a little family discussion."

Linc rose from his seat. "I'll make myself scarce, then," he said with a smile.

"No, you're invited, too," Marcus assured him, looking more than a trifle nonplussed. "I mean, you're like a member of the family, and anyways, this concerns you, too."

Eden saw from Scott's puzzled frown that he was as mystified as she and Fiona. They adjourned to the front porch, where the evening breeze made the shade quite comfortable. Eden and Fiona sat in the swing while Marcus carried out two straight-backed chairs for the men. Eden wondered if Scott was growing tired, but he seemed fine. She kept her gaze on him anyway, pretending she was only concerned about his health.

Marcus rolled cigarettes for Scott and himself, and the two men smoked in silence for a minute or two. Eden had the uneasy feeling Marcus was working up his courage to tell them something.

"We've got a lot of things to settle between us," Marcus began finally. "But before we do, there's something I've got to tell you, something nobody knows but me. It started when I first got my ranch."

"We all know how you won it in a poker game," Eden reminded him.

"I never told you the whole story though, about Linc's part in it." The two men exchanged a glance, and Scott smiled slightly, as if at an old memory.

Intrigued, Eden turned to Marcus again. "What happened?"

"Well, you know how Linc and me met on the cattle drive."

"You've told us many times," Fiona said, even more intrigued than Eden.

"We got to be pretty good friends, and I taught him everything I knew, even how to play poker. Funniest thing, though, every time we played, I won."

"Nothing funny about it," Scott informed the ladies. "I'd never touched a card until I met Marcus."

Marcus frowned his disapproval at the interruption. "You know that ain't what I'm talking about. I'm talking about how the cards always fell my way, even when I played with the other men. I'm not much of a gambler, but anybody who's played very much knows when the luck is on him. It was on me that trip. I couldn't lose, not even when I tried. You remember?" he asked Scott.

His friend nodded. "I remember thinking you were a little touched the way you kept going on about it, too."

"I made up my mind I was going to find me a card game when we got to Dodge City," Marcus continued, ignoring Linc's barb. "I had all my summer wages coming plus a bonus for getting the herd in ahead of schedule. I'd always wanted my own place, and I knew I could win enough money for a stake."

"And you were even luckier than you'd thought," Eden finished for him, "because you actually won the deed to your ranch."

"It wasn't that simple," Marcus said. "You see, when I got to town, I had a little misfortune."

Scott grinned expansively. *"Miss Fortune?* Was that her name?"

Marcus flushed crimson, and Fiona stiffened to attention. "Marcus, were you involved with a woman?" she asked with great interest.

"I . . . It was a long time before I even met you," he hedged.

Fiona smiled. "Of course it was, but you must allow me to be jealous if I wish. Should I be jealous, Mr. Scott?"

Scott made a choking sound that might have been a suppressed laugh. "Not hardly, ma'am."

Marcus shot him an annoyed look, but Fiona

75

was undeterred. "You must tell us all about this woman, Marcus."

"Yes, tell them everything," Scott urged, making no effort to conceal his amusement.

Still red in the face, Marcus continued his story. "When we got to Dodge, I sold the cattle first thing and paid off the men. I sent a draft to my boss back in Texas, and then I went looking for a poker game. Along the way I ran into some trouble and got robbed of all my money. Then Linc—"

"Wait a minute," Scott protested. "I thought you were going to tell them *everything.*"

"Yes, when do we hear about Miss Fortune?" Eden asked, delighted by Marcus's discomfort and Fiona's avid interest.

This time Marcus glared at Scott, but he only grinned back beatifically. "I'll tell them if you're too embarrassed," Scott offered.

"The trouble I ran into was a . . . a lady," Marcus said, refusing to meet anyone's eye.

"Are you sure she was a *lady?*" Fiona asked archly.

"All right, she was a lady of the evening," Marcus explained grudgingly, giving Scott another black look.

"Marcus!" Eden exclaimed in feigned shock.

"I wasn't married then," Marcus insisted.

"And he sure didn't make a habit of going with women like that," Scott said gallantly. "Only a greener would've got caught with his pockets full."

Plainly Marcus disliked being called a greener, but to protest would have made him sound promiscuous. In any case, Eden and Fiona knew Marcus's character well enough to believe Scott's assertions.

Holding back a smile with difficulty, Eden said, "Marcus, I can't believe you let yourself get rolled."

"The woman had a partner," Marcus said defensively.

"They knocked him out cold and left him in an alley," Scott informed the ladies. "I found him with a swollen head and turned out pockets. He'd lost nigh unto a thousand dollars."

"Good heavens!" Fiona exclaimed.

"Then how did you get into the poker game?" Eden asked, equally shocked.

The two men exchanged another glance, and to Eden's surprise, this time Scott flushed.

"Linc bankrolled me," Marcus said. "He didn't have anywhere near what I'd lost, but he gave me his whole summer's wages."

"I figured if I didn't, I'd have to listen to him bellyache about how much money he could've won for the next fifty years," Scott defended himself, obviously as embarrassed as Marcus had been a moment ago.

"I hope he paid you back," Eden said slyly, earning a grin from Scott.

" 'Course I did," Marcus assured her. "Even gave him a bonus for serving as my lookout. You should've seen him. He sat right by my shoulder through the whole game watching to make sure nobody tried to cheat." Marcus smiled at the memory. "Gun strapped on his hip was as big as he was, but he'd started growing a beard and his hair was as long as an Indian's. Looked like the wrath of God, he did. Didn't nobody dare look crosswise."

"Under those circumstances, I'm surprised anyone would gamble with you," Fiona said, looking at Scott with admiration.

"They weren't about to admit they were scared of a kid," Linc explained. "Then when Marcus kept winning, some of them dropped out, but others joined the game, thinking they'd change his luck. We started drawing a crowd, and pretty soon we were the only game in town."

"We'd been at it all night when your old neighbor Perkins joined the game," Marcus continued. "I cleaned him out, but he wasn't about to let a used-up waddy and a snot-nosed kid beat him, so he put up the deed to his ranch. I liked to passed out when he offered it. For years I'd been dreaming of having my own place. I'd thought the money I won might buy me a little spot and a few cows, and then he lays down the whole ranch on top of everything else." Marcus shook his head, still unable to believe what had happened.

"Do you know how Marcus won?" Scott asked the women. They both shook their heads.

"He bluffed. Every single hand up 'til then he'd had the cards, but this time he got nothing, nothing at all."

"Perkins had a flush but he folded because he couldn't believe I didn't have better," Marcus explained.

Fiona's face was blank since she didn't understand the finer points of five-card draw, but Eden laughed out loud. "Oh, Marcus, what a wonderful story! Why didn't you ever tell us before?"

"Perhaps because he would have had to mention his lady friend," Fiona said, her lips pursed to hold back a smile.

Marcus frowned. "You still haven't heard everything. There's more that even Linc doesn't know."

"There is?" Scott asked curiously.

Marcus nodded. "It affects all of us, you two in particular," he added, gesturing to the women.

No one spoke for several seconds. Marcus drew a deep breath and turned to Scott. "Remember when I promised you'd always have a home with me?"

Linc nodded slowly.

"I didn't know if you'd come back like you'd promised, and life being an uncertain thing, I couldn't be sure I'd be here when you did. I wanted to be sure you were taken care of no matter what, so I put your name on the deed, too. You're half-owner of my ranch."

"What?" Scott exclaimed, coming half out of his chair. Eden started forward, automatically ready to stop him before he hurt himself, but he grabbed his side almost absently and sank back down again.

"You heard me," Marcus said solemnly. "The problem is that since I married Fiona and we combined the two ranches, all four of us own it together."

Eden saw her own surprise reflected on Scott's face, surprise and something more. Before she could identify the emotion, Fiona distracted her.

"That's not quite accurate, Marcus," she said. "Although Jason left the ranch equally to me and Eden, when you and I married, you became the legal owner of all my property. None of this affects me at all."

She was right, of course. However unfair it might be, the law was the law and a wife surrendered all her property rights to her husband. But Marcus was one step ahead of her.

"The last time I went to Dallas, I talked to a lawyer there and told him the situation. He drew up some papers for me. It makes both ranches legally one with all four of us equal partners. All we have to do is sign it."

"That's crazy, Marcus. I can't take part of your ranch," Scott objected.

"You aren't taking it. It's already yours," Marcus reminded him.

"Then I'll give it back. The three of you can work out whatever suits you, but I've got no claim on this place."

"Don't you, Mr. Scott?" Eden heard herself saying. "You've already been wounded just for thinking about protecting it."

"That don't mean I'm entitled to a quarter share," he said impatiently.

"Perhaps you will feel differently later on," Fiona said stiffly, and Eden noticed she was unusually pale, as if she'd sustained a shock. "Perhaps we all will. I think you must give us some time to think this over, Marcus."

"Sure, I never expected anybody to pick up a pen tonight," Marcus insisted, although Eden sensed he was dismayed by Scott's reaction and Fiona's strange lack of enthusiasm. Eden herself was mystified by Fiona's response. Any other woman would have been thrilled to discover her husband had taken legal steps to ensure she retained the rights to her own property.

"In any case, we have other, more immediate concerns," Fiona reminded him with forced brightness. "Our men will return from the roundup soon, and they will be wondering who Mr. Scott is. What shall we tell them?"

"You're making a problem where there isn't one," Eden scoffed. "We'll simply tell them the truth."

"Shall we tell them he's the man the Blaines shot?"

"Of course not!"

"Wait a minute," Scott tried, but the women ignored him.

"It might be a week or more before Mr. Scott is able to ride," Fiona continued. "How will we explain why he lazes around the house, not earning his keep?"

"Oh, dear," Eden said, glancing at Scott, who seemed as perplexed as she at the problem.

"Maybe I should go off somewheres and lay low for a while," Scott suggested, but Fiona ignored him again.

"Marcus, you had an idea, didn't you?" she prompted.

Amazingly, Marcus flushed again. "I . . . uh, yeah, I was going to talk to you . . . to both of you," he corrected, gesturing to Scott and Eden, "but . . . I guess this is as good a time as any. Fiona thought . . . I mean, we both thought Linc ought to have a reason for being here, something that would explain why he didn't do any work and . . . well, if he was a guest, he wouldn't be working cattle, now would he?"

"But an ordinary guest wouldn't be resting on the porch swing all day, either," Fiona prodded.

"So we thought . . . that is, it would make sense if . . . ," Marcus stammered.

"If what?" Eden asked in exasperation.

"If people thought Linc was here to court you."

Eden felt her face grow hot, and Scott's eyes had widened in disbelief.

"It's perfectly logical," Fiona insisted. "We'll tell everyone the two of you met when Eden and I went to San Antonio this winter. Mr. Scott was smitten and has come to court you. That will explain why he is staying in the house and why he never leaves your side."

"What an interesting plan, *Marcus,*" Eden said sarcastically, recognizing Fiona's fine hand. She had to admit it was a good one, though. She only wished someone had consulted her about it privately first. Finding out in front of Lincoln Scott was humiliating. She glanced at him. Their eyes met for one excruciating moment before they both looked guiltily away. Obviously he felt the same way. Eden could have groaned aloud.

"I can see this is something else that requires some thought," Fiona said, rising from the swing. "Perhaps we should leave Eden and Mr. Scott alone to discuss the matter. I have some dishes to wash. Marcus?"

"What?"

"Don't you have something to do?" Fiona prompted sharply.

"Oh, yeah, I guess I do." He rose from his chair.

"It's really for the best, and you won't have to do it very long. Linc'll be his old self in a few days and—"

"Marcus!" Fiona snapped. "Let's go."

Frowning, he followed her into the house, leaving Linc and Eden alone on the porch. Frantically Eden tried to think of something to say to break the uncomfortable silence, but what did a woman say to a man who had just been instructed to pretend to be in love with her? Nothing appropriate came immediately to mind.

"Is your side bothering you?" she asked at last, noticing he was rubbing it.

"Oh, no, it's just starting to itch."

"That's a good sign," she replied inanely.

He nodded and looked away again.

"Look, you—"

"You don't have—"

They spoke at once and stopped in an agony of embarrassment.

"Ladies first," he suggested.

"No, what were you going to say?" she urged.

He drew a ragged breath and shifted in his chair. "I was going to say you don't have to do this. I'm well enough I can go off somewheres and hide for a week or two until I'm completely healed."

"That's ridiculous. You might get sick sleeping on the ground, or somebody might find you and figure out who you are."

"They'll find out sooner or later anyway. The minute Blaine sees Caesar, he'll know."

"Then we'll keep Caesar hidden. Listen, you're probably right about them finding out sooner or

83

later, but don't you think it would be better if they found out a lot later? Meanwhile, we'll keep you close to home until you're well again."

"But you don't have to pretend . . . I mean, there's no need. . . ." She thought he flushed, but the light was growing dim.

"I don't mind," she said, amazed to realize it was true. "I mean, Fiona is right. It's the safest thing for you. That is . . . unless *you* mind."

"No!" he assured her, as if the very thought were insane. "It might be embarrassing for you, though."

"Why? Are you such a boorish lout that you'll shame me?"

His lips twitched into a grin. "I'll try not to be."

He had an utterly charming grin. "Well, then, I don't see any problem. We'll just have to learn to act as if we're . . . well, you know."

He nodded, and his grin disappeared.

Eden gave a little push with her foot, setting the swing in motion. They stared at each other across the porch for a long moment, and Eden admired the lean, masculine lines of his body. When she considered the novel situation, she felt a tingling anticipation. "Maybe we ought to practice a little before the men get back from the roundup though."

"Practice what?" he asked warily.

"Practice looking like a courting couple," she explained, amazed at how appealing she found the prospect.

"I reckon we'd better since I don't have much experience."

Eden could have rubbed her hands with glee, but she managed to control herself. "So I see," she said solemnly. "If we were really courting, you'd be sitting next to me on the swing."

For a moment she thought he wouldn't take the hint, but then he carefully unfolded himself from his chair and strode over to her. She watched, looking for signs his side was bothering him, but he gave none. She held her skirt aside, but she didn't scoot over to make more room. If they were really courting, she'd want to sit close to him, wouldn't she?

He eased himself down onto the seat, taking great pains not to touch her, and she experienced a mild disappointment. For a second he seemed at a loss as to what to do with his arms. Laying one across the back of the seat would be entirely too forward, of course, and if he put his hands in his lap, his elbow would brush hers. He crossed his arms over his chest, staring straight ahead.

Biting back a smile, Eden studied his profile. She liked the strong line of his nose and the way his long lashes curled up on the ends. "You seemed awfully surprised to find out you were half-owner of Marcus's ranch," she observed.

He turned to face her, his cerulean eyes startling in their intensity. Eden's breath snagged somewhere in her chest.

"I'm *not* half-owner of his ranch," he insisted. "I know Marcus meant well, but in my whole life I never took anything I didn't earn. I ain't gonna start now."

"Maybe he thinks you did earn it, by being his

friend," she suggested. "He cares for you very much, you know."

"I know, and I'm grateful. Marcus is the best friend I ever had, but that doesn't mean he owes me anything."

Eden knew an urge to smooth the furrows from his broad forehead, and she curled her hands into fists to strengthen her resistance. "Suppose you're able to help us get rid of the Blaines. Would you feel you'd earned a part of the ranch then?"

"How come you're so worried about me? Seems like you'd be glad I don't want to claim a share. A third of two ranches is a whole lot better than half of one."

"What if I said I never took anything I didn't earn either? The only thing I have a right to is half of Paradise, my father's original ranch. Your share comes out of Marcus's ranch, and I don't have any claim on his property at all."

He frowned, obviously impressed by her reasoning. She wished he seemed a little more impressed by her nearness. "Oh, dear," she said with a laugh she hoped didn't sound forced. "I'm afraid we're off to a bad start."

"What do you mean?" he asked suspiciously.

"I mean this isn't at all the sort of thing courting couples talk about."

"You know a lot about it, I guess," he said. Perhaps she only imagined he sounded disgruntled, but she didn't think so. She certainly didn't mind if he were a tad jealous of her other suitors.

"A lot of men have called on me, if that's what you mean. All cowboys like to talk foolishness to

86

girls, Mr. Scott."

"Not all of them," he said acerbically. "And if we're supposed to be courting, you shouldn't call me 'Mr. Scott.' "

"All right, *Lincoln,* which reminds me, how on earth did you get that awful Yankee name?"

As she had hoped, he grinned. He had the most interesting teeth, large and white and just slightly crooked. "My mother was a Lincoln, but I think she really did it just to rile my pa. He was off fighting in the war when I was born, for the Confederacy, of course."

"Of course," Eden said like any loyal Texan.

"Anyway, I got a lot of black eyes when I was a kid because of it."

"I'm sure you gave as many as you got."

His grin widened mischievously.

Eden sighed with exaggerated relief. "There now, we're doing much better. This is just the sort of thing courting couples talk about. Unfortunately, we already talked about *my* strange name, so now we'll have to think of something new."

She tilted her head coquettishly and pretended to consider the problem. He stared back cautiously and folded his arms more tightly across his chest.

"Lincoln, I'm afraid that won't do," she said, indicating his folded arms.

"What?" he asked, looking down at his chest.

"If we were courting, you wouldn't be sitting so . . . so primly."

"Primly?" he asked, straightening immediately.

"Yes," she deadpanned. "Gentlemen who are courting are much . . . bolder."

"What do you mean by 'bolder'?"

Eden bit her lip to keep from smiling. "Oh, my!" she said, touching her cheeks as if she were blushing. "I never should have brought this up."

"I told you we don't have to go through with this—"

"We most certainly do!" she objected. "Remember, we're trying to protect your life." She drew a deep breath as if overcoming her maidenly modesty. "I just meant that a man would be more . . . If he really liked the lady, he would . . ."

"Try to put his arm around her?" he supplied.

At last! she thought, but she said, "Well, yes. Of course, you don't have to if you don't want to—"

"I don't mind if you don't," he said.

Gratified to hear a hint of eagerness in his voice, she managed a modest smile and said, "Certainly not. We want this to look real, don't we?"

She thought something flickered in his eyes, but she couldn't be perfectly sure in the dim light. Ever so slowly, he unfolded his arms and curled his right one around behind her until it rested on the back of the swing. She nodded her approval and leaned back until she was just touching his sleeve.

His long legs rocked the swing back and forth several times. She glanced at Lincoln, but he was staring off into space as if oblivious to her presence, as if having his arm around her meant nothing at all. She was trying to think of something shocking to say to regain his attention when he glanced at her. His blue eyes glinted suggestively, and he said, "What else do courting couples do?"

Linc couldn't quite believe he'd asked such a provocative question, not when he knew perfectly well he had absolutely no right to be sitting here on a swing in the twilight with a girl like Eden Campbell. Still, she'd started it. Linc wasn't such a greener that he didn't recognize flirting when he saw it. Although he didn't have much experience with nice girls, he figured it was all pretty much the same except you couldn't take her upstairs afterward. Or anyplace else either. On the Paradise Ranch, Eden Campbell was forbidden fruit.

She drew a deep breath, lifting her bosom until her nipples strained against the thin fabric. He wondered if she knew what that did to him or even what simply being in her presence did to him. He hoped not.

"Sometimes the man will compliment the girl," she suggested, her green eyes glittering even in the shadows. She was enjoying this, so Linc decided he would, too.

He let his gaze drift over her as if searching out something worthy of flattery. She'd worn her auburn hair up tonight, baring the long, graceful curve of her neck, and her dress didn't have sleeves or a top, leaving her half-naked from the waist up. All evening he'd been feasting his eyes on the sight of creamy white flesh softly rounded in all the right places and imagining what it would feel like under his hands or his mouth.

Such thoughts were crazy, of course, and certainly wouldn't form the basis for any decent compliment. His gaze moved lower, touching the swell of her breasts and her tiny, corseted waist. Briefly, he envisioned releasing her from her corset, her full breasts spilling free to fill his hands, and then . . .

He caught himself just in time. "Uh, nice dress," he managed after clearing his throat.

She pouted her disapproval. "Not very ardent, I'm afraid."

"What should I have said?" he asked in amusement.

"Oh, something about my beautiful eyes or my lovely hair," she said immodestly. "But I already know my eyes remind you of trees, so don't bother mentioning it again."

"Trees?"

"You said they were green like a garden so my name suited me."

He held back a smile at the memory. She was just lucky he hadn't said what was really on his mind, then or now. "Oh, well, then, nice hair."

She rolled her eyes, then pretended to take him seriously. "Do you really think so? I've always hated the color."

"Why?" he asked in amazement. In the dark, the red highlights were invisible, making her hair look merely brown, but Linc could still imagine its lustrous length draped across his chest or trailing over her naked breasts. His breath caught at the thought.

"I guess because nobody else I knew had hair this color. I always wanted yellow hair like Sue Ellen Cartwright's until she got scarlet fever and it all fell out. It grew back in brown, even duller than mine."

"Your hair's not dull."

"It isn't? Why not?"

"Well, because . . ." He ransacked his brain for the proper words. "It shines like . . . like it's got fire trapped inside."

Her eyes widened in surprise. "Goodness gracious, Mr. Scott, I had no idea you were a poet."

Linc didn't think he'd said anything poetic. In fact, he thought he'd probably made a fool of himself. "Well, it does," he insisted.

She smiled like a cat with a mouthful of feathers. "I'm starting to think you've had more experience with courting than you let on."

She was right, of course, Linc thought with a pang, remembering a girl back in Uvalde who'd let him come calling until she found out who and what he was. He pushed the memory away. "No, I'm just a fast learner. What's next? Are you supposed to say something nice about me now?"

"Oh, yes, I have to simper and marvel at what a big, strong man you are."

"Simper?"

"Yes, like this." She demonstrated, startling a laugh from him.

The laugh jarred his wound unexpectedly and quickly turned into a groan. Clutching his side, he grinned ruefully. "Some big, strong man."

"I didn't say the compliments had to be accurate," she replied impishly. "Flattery seldom is, you know."

Linc experienced an almost overwhelming urge to kiss the impudence right off her sweet little mouth, but he managed to resist it. When the pain in his side eased, he straightened in his seat, conscious that his arm still lay across the back of the swing, only a fraction of an inch from her bare shoulders. The heat from her body radiated in a golden glow and her flowery female scent teased his senses. He sounded a little hoarse when he asked, "Is that all there is to this courting business? We just sit together a lot and tell each other lies?"

Hearing the strain in his voice, she wondered if it had anything at all to do with how close they were sitting. She looked up at him through her lashes and tried to decide just how far she wanted to take the little game she'd started. "That depends on whether or not we're engaged."

"Engaged!" he croaked, as shocked as she had intended.

"Yes," she replied coolly, aware she was playing with fire and enjoying the heady sense of power. "If we aren't engaged, you may try to kiss me, but of course I won't let you."

His eyes narrowed speculatively. "And if we *are* engaged?"

Something in his expression stopped her breath. "Then . . . I'd have to let you, wouldn't I?" she said, her voice as strained as his.

"Are we?"

For some reason Eden no longer felt in control of the situation. "Are we what?"

He leaned fractionally closer. "Engaged."

"I . . ."

He came closer.

". . . don't . . ."

Instinctively, she raised her face to his.

". . . know."

His mouth touched hers tentatively, his breath

warm and scented with tobacco. She gasped in surprise, amazed at how soft his lips were. Instinctively leaning into the kiss, she lifted her hand to his chest. His heart clamored beneath her palm, and her own began to race, sending blood roaring to her ears.

The arm behind her encircled her shoulders while the other found her waist. Her own arms slid around his neck, seeking a closeness she'd never known before. He crushed her to him, overwhelming her with the strength she'd sensed, and she surrendered willingly, clinging tightly.

Her breasts flattened against the solid wall of his chest, and her breath rasped in her throat. The world seemed to spin out of control for just a second before he wrenched his mouth from hers.

He muttered something savage that might have been a curse and bolted up from the swing. Instantly he groaned and doubled over, clutching his side.

"I'm sorry!" she cried, jumping up, wanting to comfort him but not knowing how. "I forgot about your wound. I didn't mean—"

"You didn't do anything," he told her through gritted teeth. "I just got up too fast."

He straightened slowly, one hand pressed to his side. Eden stared at him in confusion. If she hadn't hurt him, why had he ended the kiss so abruptly? Striving to renew their light flirtation, she managed a smile. "I guess we'll have to be engaged, won't we?"

"No, we won't," he said grimly. "We won't be anything at all."

"What do you mean?"

"I mean you don't have to pretend we're courting. After what just happened, you must realize this isn't a good idea."

"Nobody said you had to kiss me," she said, stung. "If you find it so unpleasant—"

"It wasn't *unpleasant*," he said angrily. "I told you before, I don't take anything I haven't earned."

She stared at him for a long moment while the meaning of his words sunk in. "You didn't 'take' that kiss. I gave it."

"Then you shouldn't have," he snapped. "You don't know anything about me, and if you did, you wouldn't be spooning with me on your front porch."

She wanted to protest. She wanted to say she knew everything she needed to know about him and she wouldn't mind if he kissed her again, but of course she didn't. Instead she said, "You're taking this whole thing too seriously."

"One of us better, and I don't think you have any idea how serious it might get if we don't put an end to it right now."

"We're just pretending, Mr. Scott, and we're doing it to save your life."

"I don't need to hide behind a woman's skirts."

"You didn't mind my help a few days ago when I found you bleeding to death in that cave!" she reminded him furiously.

To his credit, he winced. "No, I was grateful then, and I still am, but I already owe you too much. You don't need to put yourself out for me anymore. Good night, Miss Campbell."

He moved amazingly fast for a man still recovering from a gunshot wound. He was already at the door by the time Eden got her mouth open. "Lincoln!" she called, but he ignored her.

Impulse told her to go after him, but pride forbade it. She certainly wasn't going to beg him to pretend they were engaged! Of all the rude, boorish, pigheaded ingrates! How could Marcus be friends with such a man?

Outraged, she waited until she heard her bedroom door close before storming off to the kitchen in search of Fiona. Her stepmother was leaning over the dishpan when Eden burst into the kitchen.

"You won't believe what that man said to me," she began before she noticed Fiona was crying. "What's wrong?" she asked in alarm.

"Nothing," Fiona said, scrubbing ineffectually at her tears with her sleeve.

"Oh, sure, you're dripping into the dishwater because you think it needs more salt. Fee, I haven't seen you cry since we buried Papa. What is it? What's happened?"

Fiona drew an unsteady breath. "Marcus is going to divorce me."

"What? He told you that?" Eden asked incredulously.

"Not in so many words, but it's obvious," she said, sniffing. "Why else would he be signing over part of the ranch to me?"

Eden stared at her in amazement. "Because he loves you and respects you, and he wants you to be financially independent."

Fiona snorted contemptuously. "As long as I'm

Marcus's wife, I don't *need* to be financially independent! The only reason I'd need my own money is if I no longer had a husband. We both know Marcus is too honorable to turn me out with nothing, so he went to this solicitor and—"

"Fee, you're being ridiculous," Eden insisted, although Fiona's theory made more sense than she wanted to admit. A man's wife benefited from what he owned, even if she didn't have any legal right to it herself, so why would he have to give her that right? And hadn't she sensed a problem with their marriage? But divorce was simply unheard of. "Why would Marcus want to divorce you?"

Fiona stiffened and turned her attention back to the plate she had been washing when Eden came in. "Our marriage is a sham," she said bitterly. "Marcus can hardly stand the sight of me."

Eden knew that wasn't true. "Are you crazy? He adores you!"

Fiona placed the plate into the rinse water with elaborate care. When she looked up, her blue eyes were bleak, her perfect mouth pressed into a thin, bloodless line. "I'm not an innocent young girl, Eden. I've been married twice before, and I know how a man in love should act."

"But the way he looks at you," Eden protested, even as Fiona shook her head.

"We both know he only married me because we needed help so desperately and because he's such an honorable man."

"That wasn't the only reason. He cares for you, too, I know he does!"

Fiona's smile was heartrending. "I wish you were right. I'd give anything if you were, but you aren't."

"I'll ask him," Eden announced. "He'll tell you you're wrong!"

"Don't you dare!" Fiona snapped, her cheeks blazing. "I'll never forgive you. Don't meddle, Eden. Things are bad enough as they are."

"Then you ask him. Fee, you can't go on suspecting without knowing for sure."

"Yes, I can, and I have every intention of doing so. If he's trying to work up his courage to tell me, I'm not going to ease his way."

Eden didn't know whether to laugh or to cry. She was beginning to think the whole world had gone mad and she was the only sane person left. Her stepmother had always been the one person she could confide in, but now it seemed cruel to burden her with the tale of Lincoln Scott's boorish behavior on top of all this. Eden would just have to work out her own problems and, in spite of Fiona's warning, figure out a way to help her and Marcus, too.

At first Linc thought he had a hangover. He awoke groggy and disoriented, his head throbbing. Then he remembered his argument with Eden the night before and the nearly sleepless night he'd spent tossing and turning and trying to blame the hole in his side for his restlessness.

What could he have been thinking of to kiss Eden Campbell? A man like him didn't even have the right to speak her name aloud. Lying in her bed until the wee hours of the morning, he had alternately cursed himself for a fool and relived the glorious moment when he had held her in his arms.

You'd better enjoy the memory, he'd told himself, because it damn well won't ever happen again.

On top of that, he'd been haunted by Marcus's offer to make him a partner in the Paradise. Seven years ago he had refused Marcus's offer of a home, and in those seven years Linc had learned just how precious was the gift he had rejected.

But no matter how desperately he might want to, he couldn't possibly accept it now, either. What he'd told Eden was absolutely true, he could never take something he hadn't earned. Still, he also couldn't forget Eden's question: "Suppose you're able to help us get rid of the Blaines. Would you feel you'd earned a part of the ranch then?" He hadn't answered her last night, and he found he still had no answer.

The only thing he knew for sure was that he couldn't allow Eden to pretend they were engaged. He couldn't even be trusted to spend five minutes with her in the porch swing without forcing himself on her. Pretending to court would be tempting fate entirely too much.

When he finally sat up, he realized the hour was later than he had thought. Someone had already brought his breakfast tray, which was sitting on the bedside table. The food was cold, but even cold, Fiona Pauling's grub was the best he'd ever eaten. Not wanting to wait a moment longer to tell Marcus he and Eden had decided not to go along with his plan, Linc made short work of the meal and hurried to get cleaned up and dressed.

He'd just finished shaving with the lukewarm water he'd found in the pitcher when the door opened and Marcus came in.

" 'Morning, or should I say afternoon?" he asked cheerfully.

"Is it that late?" Linc replied, returning Marcus's smile as he slipped on his shirt and buttoned it.

"Not quite, but I was getting ready to put a mirror to your mouth to see if you could still fog it. Our men got back late last night, and I want you to meet them. If you don't feel up to it, I'll just bring in our foreman. He's a good man, and we can trust him not to—"

"Marcus, has Eden talked to you about . . . about your plan?"

"She hasn't talked to me about anything. I had breakfast with the men this morning, so I haven't seen her since I left her with you last night."

"Well," Linc began, wondering how to explain without revealing his breach of conduct, "we talked it over, and we decided it wouldn't be necessary to pretend we're . . . you know."

Marcus frowned. "Damn, I already let the cat out of the bag."

"Who'd you tell?" Linc said, fighting a ridiculous sense of panic.

"Everybody, all the men. I told them some poor fool come all the way from San Antonio traipsing after Eden and the real reason I hadn't gone back to the roundup was so's I could chaperone you two."

Linc sighed wearily and sank down on the bed. "I don't suppose you could tell them you made a mistake, could you?" he asked wryly.

"Not hardly. Do you think Eden'll be mad? We can always say you two had a fight and broke it off, but then they'd wonder why you didn't leave."

From outside, they heard several men yelling.

"There she is!"

"Hey, Miss Eden, where's your fella?"

"Yeah, bring him on out so we can horsewhip the rascal."

"Couldn't you find nobody around here, Miss Eden?"

" 'Course she couldn't. Everybody around here knows she's got a temper to match that red hair. They prob'ly had to send to Louisiana to find her a man."

"Who told you I had a fella?" Eden demanded from the porch. Linc exchanged a grim look with Marcus. Linc could just imagine her outrage.

"The boss. He told us we was all out of luck."

"That'll teach me," another man wailed in mock despair. "I'll never go on another roundup again."

"Where is he, Miss Eden? He ain't afraid to face us, is he?"

"Why would he be afraid of a bunch of shiftless no-accounts like you?" Eden scoffed. Linc frowned. Why wasn't she denying it? "I'll go see if I can hunt him up. It may take awhile, though. I have to keep him locked up so he doesn't run away."

Their howls of laughter followed her.

Linc could hear her coming into the house and crossing to the bedroom door. Marcus hurried to open it for her, and Linc rose, prepared to endure her wrath.

"Oh, Marcus," she said in surprise. "Is he up? The men are calling for him and—"

"I'm up," Linc said. She peered around Marcus at him.

"Then I guess you heard. They want to meet you."

Linc waited for her to say something more, but she turned back to Marcus. "Maybe you ought to do the honors."

Before Marcus could agree, she turned and walked off.

Linc and Marcus exchanged another look, this time one of confusion. "She didn't seem mad," Marcus said. "You sure she didn't want to go through with it?"

As a matter of fact, Linc distinctly recalled she hadn't minded at all. He was the one who'd resisted, but he couldn't go back on it now without embarrassing Eden. "I guess she's just a good sport," Linc said. "Let's get this over with."

He followed Marcus outside, onto the porch and into the blinding morning sunlight. Half a dozen men loitered in the yard, talking in small groups until Linc appeared. All conversation stopped, and the men stared openly for several seconds. Then one of them came forward, a stocky fellow of average height. Orange hair straggled down from beneath his hat, and about a million freckles spotted his face and the backs of his hands. He grinned expansively.

"You must be Lincoln Scott," the fellow said, offering his beefy hand. "I'm Jed Titus."

Linc strode down the porch steps and took his hand. "Pleased to meet you."

"Jed is my foreman," Marcus said, "but then, I already told you all about him, didn't I?"

"All good, I hope," Titus said.

Linc feigned seriousness. "Yeah, and I believed most of it, too, except the part where you walked on water."

Titus chuckled in delight and clapped Linc on the shoulder. Linc flinched slightly, gritting his teeth against the stabbing pain and somehow managing to smile. He'd have to be careful not to be too clever in the future. If somebody slapped him on the back, he'd probably go over like a pole-axed steer.

"I reckon all these other fellas want to meet you, too, only they're too shy to say so," Titus said. "See, all of 'em are in love with Miss Eden theirownselves, so they ain't real happy to see you."

Linc felt certain this was true, although the others denied it vehemently as they marched forward to shake Linc's hand and welcome him to Paradise. Most of them made a comment on Linc's bravery and/or foolishness in courting Eden Campbell.

The last man to come forward was a tall, good-looking fellow about Linc's age and height. He wore a long, drooping mustache that made him look as if he were frowning, and his large brown eyes put Linc in mind of an old hound dog. "Mel-

102

ancholy Jones," he said, shaking Linc's hand with challenging firmness. Linc hoped his answering grip was strong enough. "I got my name because Miss Eden turned me down so many times," he announced plaintively.

"Horsefeathers," Eden scoffed, having somehow materialized at Linc's elbow. "If I ever said yes, you'd make dust walking away, and if Melancholy ever told the truth, he'd say he was thankful to see any man who was going to marry me, Lincoln," she added, slipping her arm through Linc's and smiling sweetly up at him.

Linc blinked in surprise but dredged up an answering smile until Jed Titus said, "Hey, when's the wedding?"

"As soon as you boys find out who's rustling our cattle," Eden replied ingenuously before Linc could think of an appropriate lie. "Lincoln and I certainly hope you find them soon, don't we, darling?" She batted her eyes and simpered.

Linc felt the heat rising in his neck at the men's suggestive laughter, and the regret he'd felt for the embarrassment she might suffer evaporated. She enjoyed taunting him, and she seemed intent on raking him over the coals, probably as a punishment for kissing her last night.

"If he's in such an all-fired hurry, maybe Lincoln would like to give us a hand finding them rustlers," Melancholy suggested morosely.

"Oh, no, you don't," Eden chided. "Lincoln's not leaving my sight. Heaven only knows what you boys might tell him if you get him off alone somewhere."

"Oh, nobody's gonna try to talk him out of anything," Jed Titus assured her cheerfully. "Life around here sure would be a lot more peaceful if you was brought to heel, and from the looks of him, Scott here seems like the one man who can tame you."

Linc almost laughed out loud at Eden's chagrin. Somewhat mollified, he said, "Now, Jed, no man in his right mind would take on a task like that."

"Are you going to tell us you like her just the way she is?" Jed challenged.

Linc could have bitten his tongue. He glanced around at the men's knowing grins and then down at Eden's pout. No matter how tempted he was to get back a little of his own, instinct told him he'd better make it up with Eden. Whether he'd wanted her to or not, she'd swallowed her pride in order to protect him, and he owed her. Lincoln Scott always paid his debts. "Yeah, I like her just the way she is," he said with more truth than anyone would have guessed.

Eden's emerald eyes widened in surprise, and for a moment he didn't even hear the whoops of laughter from the men.

"She's got the Indian sign on him for sure," someone said, and Linc figured it might well be true. He only hoped Eden didn't suspect.

He could almost feel the animosity drain out of her. She squeezed his arm and smiled, her green eyes twinkling. "I'm afraid you'll have to excuse us now, gents," she said to the others. "Lincoln and I have a wedding to plan."

"I'll see you later," Lincoln told them, but they

104

expressed their doubts amid general hilarity as Eden drew him back into the house.

As soon as the door closed behind them, Eden released his arm and stepped away, her expression guarded once again. "Did Jed hurt you?"

For a second Linc couldn't think what she meant, then he recalled the friendly slap the foreman had given him. She must've been watching from the house. "No, I'm fine."

"You'll have to be more careful."

"I know. I was afraid somebody might get real friendly and knock me on my face." He stared down at her, admiring the way her auburn hair fell in gentle waves around her cheeks. She had it down, pulled back with a ribbon the way it had been the first time he'd seen her. "I . . . Thanks for going along out there."

She shrugged one shoulder. "I told you before I didn't mind. I was just surprised. After what you said last night, I thought . . ." She shrugged again.

"Marcus told the men before I had a chance to talk to him about it."

"Oh."

"I'm sorry for all the teasing. That was one reason I didn't think this would be a good idea."

"Jed has been teasing me since I could walk. I'm used to it."

"Oh."

They stared at each other for a long minute.

"Well, I guess you need to rest," she said at last. "Fiona is making soap today, and I promised to help."

"Won't the men be suspicious if they see you

outside?"

"They'll be riding out soon. I'll wait until they're gone."

Linc felt a perverse urge to ask her to stay with him for a while, but he resisted it. "I'll go lay down. Call me for dinner."

"All right," she said. He watched until she disappeared down the hallway to the kitchen, admiring the way her hips swayed gently beneath her simple brown skirt as she walked, and imagining the long, shapely legs it concealed.

He drew a deep breath, and muttered a prayer for strength.

Chapter Four

Eden studied Lincoln Scott surreptitiously across the dining room table. She still felt the sting of his rejection after the kiss they'd shared last night, and she didn't like the feeling one bit, but she now saw a way to get a little of her own back. The idea had come to her this morning when the men had started teasing her about her new beau. At first she'd been stunned to realize Lincoln hadn't informed Marcus of the change in plan, but then she'd also realized the possibilities.

Not that she wanted revenge, exactly, just a little satisfaction to soothe her wounded pride. Plainly the idea of pretending to be her fiancé disturbed him, so she would simply be the most devoted sweetheart imaginable. Such devotion wouldn't do any harm, but it certainly seemed likely to drive Mr. Scott to distraction.

"You're going to have to help keep Linc occupied for the next few days," Marcus said, as if on cue. "He's liable to get cabin fever not being able to ride and all."

"We can't have that, now can we?" Eden replied with a guileless smile. "What would you like to do this afternoon?" she asked Lincoln.

He frowned, obviously uncomfortable with Marcus's suggestion. Perfect, she decided.

"You've probably got more important things to do," he demurred.

"Not at all," she replied agreeably. "I'm always glad for an excuse not to make soap, aren't I, Fiona?"

"What?" Fiona asked absently. Eden felt a pang of guilt. She'd momentarily forgotten how upset her stepmother was over her problems with Marcus. All morning she had refused even to discuss the subject while they stirred the rancid vat of melting fat and turned it into soap.

"Marcus thinks I should entertain Mr. Scott this afternoon instead of helping you," Eden explained.

"Oh, yes, by all means. We were almost finished anyway."

"Fiona, are you all right?" Marcus asked with some concern. "You look a little peaked. You haven't been working outside without a hat on, have you?"

"Certainly not," she snapped. Angry color came to her pale cheeks, and Marcus's expression grew perplexed. He looked as if he wanted to say something else, but thought better of it and resumed his eating without another word. Eden had to bite her tongue to keep from interfering.

"Do you like checkers, Mr. Scott?" Eden asked to fill the silence.

"I can play," he replied without much enthusiasm.

"If you prefer, we can play cards. My father taught me poker, although Marcus insists a woman can never master the game because she can't control her expression. I always smile when I get a good hand."

"Linc never was much good at poker either, as I recall," Marcus said, "although he might've had some practice since I last saw him."

"I've had some practice, but I'm not much better than I was. I do know how to keep a straight face, though." Lincoln's blue eyes issued a silent challenge that Eden readily accepted.

"Poker it is, then," she replied, eagerly anticipating the afternoon to come.

But the promised game never occurred. Before they'd finished their meal, a rider interrupted them to report that a neighbor woman had gone into labor and needed help from the ladies of the Paradise Ranch. Fiona and Eden hurried to pack for an overnight stay.

Eden was in her room, stuffing things into a carpetbag when she felt a presence behind her. She turned and found Lincoln Scott watching her from the doorway.

"Sorry," he said. "I didn't realize you'd be in here."

"That's all right," she said, returning to her packing. "I'll only be a second."

She thought he might leave, but instead he stayed where he was, watching her. "I guess I never even thought to wonder where you've been sleeping," he said after a minute.

"There's a room off the kitchen with a cot. When we have a cook, he sleeps there, but Fiona prefers to cook for us herself."

"There's no reason I couldn't stay there and let you have your room back."

Eden put the last garment in the bag and turned to face him again. "You wouldn't get much rest. It's noisy during the day with me and Fee working in the kitchen. You're better off here."

"I don't like putting you out. Maybe I should move to the bunkhouse."

"Don't be silly. You couldn't rest there, either, and what if one of the men noticed your bandages?"

He shrugged. "I just don't think you should have to give up your room."

"When you can ride again, I'll let you sleep in the kitchen," she said, closing up her carpetbag and fastening the buckle.

She started to lift it, but he hurried forward. "I'll take that for you."

His hand closed over hers for an instant as he reached for the grip, but he quickly pulled away. She felt the rough abrasion of his callused palm for several seconds after it was gone, and she smiled at the tingle of awareness rippling over her. Did he feel it, too? Was that why he'd let go so swiftly?

He reached out, silently offering to take the bag, but she shook her head. "You can't carry this. You might break open your wound," she reminded him, hefting the bag herself.

He frowned. "How long do you think you'll be gone?"

Was he going to miss her? The idea was delicious. "Probably only until tomorrow." She almost added that Mrs. Cartwright already had five children and usually gave birth quickly, but a lady simply didn't discuss such things with a gentleman.

"Will the men think it's funny that I'm not going with you?"

"No, men only get in the way at times like this. Even Marcus won't be staying after he delivers us."

"What if the Blaines show up?"

"They wouldn't dare, not with so many people around. Other neighbor women will come, too, and Mr. Cartwright will be there."

He nodded, but he looked far from pleased.

She tilted her head as if trying to get a different perspective on him. "My goodness, Lincoln, anybody'd think you were concerned for my safety."

His blue eyes flickered, but she couldn't tell what emotion they reflected. "Of course I am. Dirk Blaine rode right up to your front door the other day and demanded to come inside. What's to stop him from finding you on the road?"

"Nothing, I suppose, but it's not very likely, and Marcus will be with us. You wouldn't be much help right now no matter what happened," she reminded him gently. "The best thing you can do is concentrate on getting well so your bride-to-be will be perfectly safe under your protection."

Playfully, she lifted one hand as if to straighten his collar, but he grabbed her wrist and held it fast. Startled, she looked up at him, and for several pounding heartbeats, he held her gaze. His blue eyes blazed into hers, and she noticed irrelevantly that they had darkened a shade. She felt as if someone had squeezed all the air from her lungs.

"You aren't going to try to kiss me again, are you?" she asked breathlessly.

"No," he said hoarsely, but his face came closer. She knew she should resist, but all the strength seemed to have drained from her body. Helpless, she lifted her mouth to his. His lips touched hers as tenderly as before, but only for a second. In the next instant, his arms were around her, crushing her to him, his mouth devouring hers.

She opened to his sensual assault, and his tongue swept the interior of her mouth, stirring emotions she couldn't even name. Her body yearned toward his, drawn by forces beyond her control. She clung to him with the hand he had grasped moments before, burying her fingers in the lush thickness of his raven hair. He molded her to him, and she yielded eagerly to his strength.

"Eden? Are you ready?" Fiona called from the parlor.

They wrenched guiltily apart, and Eden saw her own astonishment reflected in his eyes. Well, well, well, it seemed Lincoln Scott wasn't nearly as determined to resist her as he pretended to be. She lifted her free hand to her throbbing lips, but before either of them could speak, Fiona came into the room.

"Eden, are you —? Oh, excuse me." She frowned, as if sensing the tension between them. "Is something wrong?"

"No," Eden said too quickly, her voice high and strained. She and Lincoln each took a hasty step back, widening the space between them.

Fiona's speculative gaze darted back and forth between them again, and her frown deepened. "Are you ready to go?"

Eden glanced down, surprised to find she still held the carpet bag. "Yes."

"Well, then," Fiona said briskly, "perhaps Mr. Scott would like to see us off."

"Sure," he agreed, also too quickly.

Eden tried to catch his eye, but he refused to look at her. When she started for the door, he followed, making no move to take the bag from her again. Eden's mind was racing. Now she was sure: Lincoln Scott did find her attractive. But if that were true, why had he rejected her last night? she wondered in frustration.

Unfortunately, she didn't have time to pursue the matter further at the moment.

Outside, Marcus waited with the wagon. He loaded Eden's bag and helped Fiona up onto the seat. "I'll be back in a few hours," he told Lincoln. "If you need anything, Pedro is in the barn." Then he reached for Eden, but she hesitated, turning back to Lincoln.

He seemed even taller than usual, but his face was carefully expressionless as he looked down at her. She wondered if Marcus and Fiona could tell they had been kissing passionately just seconds ago. Eden's stomach quivered from the memory.

"Take care now," she said, unable to think of anything more profound.

He nodded. "You, too."

Reluctantly, she surrendered to Marcus, who assisted her into the wagon. Then he climbed up beside Fiona and slapped the team into motion. Eden couldn't resist looking back. She waved, and Lincoln lifted his hand in a silent salute, looking slightly forlorn.

She smiled. This was much sweeter than revenge.

When they arrived at the Cartwrights' house, the yard was full of wagons. Mr. Cartwright came out to greet them.

"You're too late, I'm afraid," he told the ladies with a broad smile. "The missus had a little boy not more'n an hour ago."

."Congratulations," Marcus said, grinning broadly.

"Is Mrs. Cartwright doing well?" Fiona asked in some concern.

"Right as rain. I'm just sorry you folks came all this way for nothing. As you can see, we've got more help than you can shake a stick at, so you might as well head on home."

"Not until we've had a look at that boy of yours," Eden said, already climbing down.

"And we've brought some food, too," Fiona added.

After Eden and Fiona had finished admiring the new arrival, they found Marcus enjoying a cigar with the new father and several other men who had accompanied their wives to the birthing.

"Linc'll sure be surprised to see us back so soon," Marcus remarked when they were on their way again.

"Since we're already out, why don't we stop in

town?" Fiona suggested. "Mr. Scott needs some clothes to replace the ones that were ruined," she explained, "and Eden and I can make a few visits while we're there."

"Good idea," Marcus said enthusiastically. "I've been wanting to catch up on the news anyway. Being stuck in the house with Linc, I've kind of lost track of what folks are saying."

Neither Eden nor Fiona asked what news he hoped to hear. They both knew he wanted to find out if any of his neighbors had fallen victim to the rustlers recently.

He dropped the women off at Deal's General Store, left the wagon there, and walked across the dusty street to the Gay Paree Saloon. The town itself was nothing more than a small collection of weathered buildings, each of which housed an enterprise essential to the cattle business. Besides the mercantile, there was a livery where the blacksmith carried on his trade, a schoolhouse that doubled as a church, a few houses where the townspeople lived, and the saloon.

To a man who had seen the fine drinking establishments along Dodge City's infamous Front Street, the Gay Paree was a sorry spectacle. The dirt floors were covered with sawdust to soak up tobacco juice and any other liquids that might befall it. A ramshackle bar stood at one end of the room. Behind it, a crude shelf made of discarded wooden egg crates held an assortment of bottles and glasses. Someone had decorated the rough walls with lewd pictures torn from the *Police Gazette*. Several scarred tables filled the open space in the room, and a couple cowboys Marcus knew by sight sat at one of them, nursing beers. He nodded to them and made his way to the bar.

" 'Afternoon, Marcus," the bartender greeted him.

"Howdy, Sam. Draw me a beer, will you?"

Sam Ferguson took a glass from the shelf behind him and limped toward the keg sitting at the end of the bar. He was a short, wiry man who had once worked as a cowboy. A mean-tempered bronco had ended his riding days, so now he made his living by listening to the complaints of those who still rode.

He limped back and set the glass in front of Marcus. "What do you hear?" Marcus asked, blowing the foam off his drink and taking a sip.

"Same old thing. Guess you know what happened at the roundup."

Marcus nodded. "My calf crop was down almost half of what it should've been. Some was hurt even worse."

"Most folks are suspicious because the Blaines didn't lose as much as everybody else."

"Yeah, if somebody's running off our calves, everybody ought to suffer equal, but it seems like the rustlers have took a dislike to anything with the Blaine's daisy brand on it."

"It is a hard brand to cover," one of the cowboys at the table offered, referring to the practice of "covering" the brand of a stolen cow with a new one. "In fact, was I thinking of running stolen cattle, I'd pick one just like it."

Marcus grinned at the implication. It was one

he'd heard many times before. The daisy brand would easily cover just about any brand in the county, including the Paradise P and Marcus's own Flying Circle.

"I heard the Blaines paid your womenfolk a visit the other day," Sam said.

Marcus scowled into his glass. "Only Dirk. That bastard tried to go into the house."

"I'm surprised Miss Eden didn't shoot him down."

"She would've if he hadn't've backed off," Marcus said proudly. "Maybe next time he won't be so polite, and we'll be rid of him once an' for all."

Sam snorted his agreement. "I reckon the cows around here'll be a lot more fertile once that happens."

At the general store, Eden and Fiona browsed leisurely, taking advantage of the unscheduled visit to town to pick up a few small items. Although they usually made their fashion purchases in Dallas, the store here in Centreville carried just about everything else they needed on its well-stocked shelves.

"Why don't you pick out a few shirts for Mr. Scott?" Fiona suggested. "He'll need some trousers, too."

"Should I get him a nightshirt?" Eden asked, knowing Fiona would frown her disapproval.

She didn't disappoint her stepdaughter. "Really, Eden, you are such a forward girl. It comes of never having had a governess, I expect."

"And growing up wild, raised by a bunch of men," Eden added wryly. "What about under-drawers?"

"Eden," Fiona cried in exasperation. "Just find some shirts and a pair of trousers. I'll take care of the rest."

Grinning, Eden strolled over to where the ready-made shirts were stacked. Since Lincoln had been wearing Marcus's clothes, she didn't have to wonder about the size. She found the correct pile and began to sort through it, looking for appropriate colors.

Yes, blue would be perfect, she thought, pulling one out to examine it. She could just picture the yoke-fronted shirt stretched across Lincoln Scott's broad chest.

"Well, now, imagine seeing you again so soon," Dirk Blaine crooned from behind her.

Eden cringed, and the hair on her neck prickled in warning. She turned slowly, gathering her composure as she did so. "I wish I could say it was a pleasant surprise."

He smiled insolently, and his pale eyes took her in from head to toe, making her feel unclean. She wanted to shudder in disgust, but she refused to let him see her reaction.

"What've I ever done to make you dislike me, Eden?" he wondered with an evil grin.

"You started breathing for one thing," she replied.

His grin vanished. "That ain't no way for a lady to talk, but then, maybe you ain't really a lady. Is that it, Eden? Do you like it rough?"

118

Before she could think, he grabbed her arm.

"Let me go!" she cried furiously, struggling against his grip.

"What's going on?" the storekeeper demanded, hurrying from behind the counter. Fiona was already coming at them from the other direction.

Blaine dropped her arm immediately and smiled his feral smile. "Excuse me, Miss Eden," he said with exaggerated politeness. "Sometimes I forget myself with pretty girls."

"Blaine, you'd better mind your manners when you're in my store," the proprietor said. Ben Deal was a scrawny, middle-aged man, but his bald head and wire-rimmed spectacles gave a false impression. Like most Texans of his time, he'd fought Yankees and Indians and outlaws to make himself a place on the frontier, and he wasn't about to tolerate abuse of ladies in his establishment, not from Dirk Blaine or anyone else.

"I told her I was sorry," Blaine said mildly. "I sure never meant no offense. Maybe you'll let me buy you and Mrs. Pauling a sarsaparilla."

"Certainly not," Fiona said before Eden could tell him exactly what she'd like him to do with his sarsaparilla. "Mr. Blaine, I told you my husband wouldn't approve of your coming into my home, and I certainly don't think he would approve of you accosting Eden. It seems your upbringing was deficient in certain social skills."

To Eden's surprise, Blaine's face went scarlet and his eyes blazed with outrage. "You leave my upbringing out of this. If you wasn't a woman, so help me God—"

119

"Dirk!" a man called from the doorway. "What's going on?"

Blaine recovered himself instantly. "I'll see you *ladies* later," he warned savagely, then turned on his heel and strode toward the figure in the doorway.

Eden recognized his brother, Alvin. She never would have expected to be glad to see the other Blaine brother, but now she fairly trembled with relief. The two men left the store instantly.

"I'm awful sorry, Miss Campbell. I hope he didn't say anything too offensive," Mr. Deal said.

"Oh, no," she lied, not wanting to start any gossip. She managed a small smile. "It's just that after what happened the other day, I'm a little frightened of Mr. Blaine."

"Can't blame you for that. Imagine trying to bust in on a couple of ladies when their men was away." Neither woman expressed surprise that Mr. Deal knew of the incident. Gossip spread as quickly as if it were carried on the wind. "If they'd done you any harm, you can bet every man in the county would've turned out to lynch them."

"A very unusual custom," Fiona remarked, her British accent pronounced. "One I'd never seen the need for until lately. Thank you for coming to Eden's rescue, Mr. Deal."

"Glad to do it, Mrs. Pauling."

"Have you made your selection?" Fiona asked, indicating the shirt Eden still held.

"Not yet," Eden said, shaking off the last vestiges of her fright. Her arm still ached where Blaine had grabbed her, and she supposed she would have bruises to remind her of the encounter.

If only she were a man . . .

"We have a little more shopping to do, thank you, Mr. Deal," Fiona said, dismissing him. He moved away, watching them over his shoulder to make sure Eden was all right.

As soon as he was out of earshot, Fiona said, "What did that scoundrel say to you?"

"Nothing important. He was just trying to scare me, I think."

"He must have succeeded. Your face went quite pale."

"Did it?" Eden said, not caring much. "If I was a man, I'd shoot him down like the dog he is."

"Eden, what a horrid thing to say! I'm afraid living in this wild country is turning you into a barbarian."

"We both know he killed Papa. Wouldn't you like to shoot him, too?"

"If he really did kill Jason, then yes, I would, but we have no proof," Fiona reminded her. "Your father's death could well have been an accident."

Eden started to deny it, but caught herself just in time. Although Eden had endured her grief by indulging in rage against her father's killers, Fiona had been unable to bear the thought he had been murdered. There was no use in stirring up painful memories now. "I'm sorry, Fee. I guess Blaine upset me more than I realized."

"That's all right, dear. Now let's select some clothes for Mr. Scott and get Marcus to take us home. Suddenly, I don't feel like making any visits."

"Oh, dear! I just realized Marcus is over at the

saloon alone. What if the Blaines find him there?"

This time Fiona's face paled. She whirled in a swish of skirts and made for the door just as her husband came through it.

"Marcus!" she cried. "Thank heaven!"

"Was that the Blaines I saw coming out a minute ago?" he demanded, taking Fiona's arm as she went weak with relief.

Eden realized with some surprise this was the first time she'd seen Marcus touch her in months. She thought of Fiona's concerns and wondered if her stepmother didn't have some justification for them.

"Yes," Fiona replied. "Dirk Blaine accosted Eden. He said something unspeakably rude, although she won't tell me what it was."

"The hell you say," Marcus exclaimed, and Eden judged the extent of his outrage by the fact that he'd never sworn in front of Fiona before.

He turned as if to go after Blaine, but Fiona grabbed his arm. "No, Marcus! You can't!"

He looked down at her as if she'd lost her senses. "Fiona, if he insulted Eden —"

"He didn't insult me," Eden insisted. "He was just trying to be friendly. If anyone else had said the same thing, I would've been flattered." She hoped they couldn't tell she was lying through her teeth. "We were just going to find you so we could warn you they were in town. We didn't want them to catch you alone."

Marcus scowled, obviously affronted. "I can take care of myself."

"Two against one is pretty poor odds in anyone's

game," Eden pointed out.

"She's right," Mr. Deal said. "You've got a bone to pick with Dirk Blaine, all right, but only a fool would go after him alone when his brother's backing him."

"Please, Marcus," Fiona begged, and something in her face convinced him.

"Well, all right," he agreed reluctantly.

"Thank heaven," Fiona breathed.

"Yes, thank heaven," Eden echoed. "Let's finish up here and get home."

"I thought you wanted to do some visiting," Marcus said.

"Not any longer," Fiona said, straightening and releasing her hold on him. "Unless . . . Are the Blaines still outside?"

"No, they rode out," Marcus said. Now he was looking at her as if he'd never seen her before. Eden suspected he was marveling over how frightened she had been for his safety. He shouldn't have been surprised. It was only a wife's normal reaction, but she knew Marcus and Fiona didn't have a normal relationship. They stared at each other for a long minute before Marcus cleared his throat and said, "Have you got everything you need?"

"No," Eden replied. "We still have to pick out some clothes for Lincoln. Maybe you can help."

Marcus made short work of the selection, insisting one shirt was as good as another and Linc wouldn't care a fig which one they chose. Mr. Deal wrapped their purchases, and Marcus carried them out to the wagon and helped the women up onto the seat. The whole time he kept watching Fiona, though, as if waiting for her to do or say something.

Eden tried to figure out what he was waiting for, but without success.

Dirk and Alvin Blaine rode straight out of town without looking back. Dirk cursed savagely for the entire first mile, furious at his brother for not letting him find Marcus Pauling for a showdown. Alvin simply rode.

No one would have picked them for brothers. While Dirk was tall and handsome, his older brother stood barely five feet, seven inches and had a face that could only be described as homely. Nurture had further ruined what nature had begun. Alvin's beaklike nose leaned to one side, as if someone had once tried to knock it off his face with only partial success. A knife scar divided one thick eyebrow; and his colorless eyes, the only feature he shared with his brother, didn't always point in the same direction.

What he lacked in looks, he made up for in cunning, however. "You don't have the sense God gave a ripe gourd," he informed his brother.

"You don't know what that bitch said to me. She said my upbringing was . . . was . . . *deficient*."

"It was. We grew up in a whorehouse, in case you've forgot."

"I haven't forgot anything," Dirk snarled, "but I also don't want some limey bitch throwing it up in my face."

124

"That limey bitch is the wife of a highly re-spected rancher, and you'd better remember folks in Texas don't take kindly to having their womenfolk insulted."

"And that's another thing," Dirk said, aggrieved. "How many of her husbands are we going to have to kill before we get the Paradise?"

"We ain't gonna kill nobody else at all, not after what happened the other day. We're gonna wait until the man I hired gets here and let him take care of Marcus Pauling."

"I could've done it myself," Dirk insisted.

"You shot the wrong man," Alvin reminded him brutally. "You'd better pray he's lying dead some-wheres, too. If he ever comes back—"

"He hasn't, has he?" Dirk snapped. "Anybody could've made that mistake, even your hired killer. I just don't like bringing in a stranger. What if he wants part of the Paradise?"

"Are you worried about the Paradise or are you worried he might want part of that red-haired girl?"

"You leave Eden out of this."

"I'd sure like to, but you won't let me. Dammit, Dirk, when're you going to start thinking with your head instead of with your pecker?"

Dirk grinned at his brother. "I ain't done too bad so far."

"You might've done all right when we was kids, but you're not trying to shine up to a bunch of whores anymore. Them women made you think the world stops to look every time you take a leak, and it just ain't true. That Eden girl hates your guts, and if you don't want some outraged citizens stretching your neck, you'd better stay away from her."

"I can handle Eden," Dirk said stiffly.

"Oh yeah? Like you handled her the other day at her ranch?"

Dirk reddened. "She won't get another chance like that."

"Damn right she won't, because you ain't going within sniffing distance of her again. You understand?"

"Dammit, Alvin, you ain't my mother."

"No, our mother's dead and burning in hell where she belongs. She never gave a damn whether either of us lived or died, and all we've ever had is each other. I been taking care of you for a long time, and I ain't gonna let you get yourself killed now over some fool woman."

"Sometimes I think you're jealous, Alvin."

Alvin made a rude noise, but Dirk grinned again.

"Yeah, that's it, you're jealous, but don't worry. When we get the Paradise and I get little Eden all to myself, I'll let you have the other one, the limey bitch. Maybe having a woman of your own will sweeten you up some, big brother."

Alvin shot his brother a disgusted look and kicked his horse into a gallop.

At first Linc thought he was dreaming when he heard Eden's voice in the other room. He'd lain down for a nap, but he was pretty sure he hadn't slept the clock around.

The bedroom door opened slowly, and Marcus crept in carrying Eden's bag and a package.

"I'm awake," Linc said, pushing himself into a sitting position. "Did Eden come back with you?"

"Yeah," Marcus said, setting the bag down and coming over to the bed. "Fiona did, too. The baby had already come by the time we got there, and they didn't need no more help, so we came home. We stopped in town and got you some things." He handed Linc the package.

"Things?"

"Clothes, to replace the ones you bled all over."

"Oh, thanks," Linc said, setting the package aside. He looked up at his friend again. Marcus's eyes were troubled. "What's wrong?"

Marcus sighed and reached for the chair sitting beside Linc's bed. He straddled it and ran a hand through his thinning hair. "We saw Dirk Blaine, or at least Eden did."

Linc swore, instantly overcome by an impotent rage. "What happened?"

"Nothing much, according to her. She and Fiona was in the store getting that stuff," he explained, gesturing toward the package. "I didn't even know the Blaines was in town, or I never would've taken the women in. Dirk somehow ran into them in the store. He said something to Eden and grabbed her arm."

"That son of a bitch!"

"Didn't come to no more than that," Marcus assured him. "Deal, the storekeeper, stepped in, and then Alvin Blaine showed up. He's Dirk's brother, and he keeps him in line as much as anybody can. Dirk apologized to Eden and left town with his brother."

"I was afraid this would happen if she left the ranch," Linc fumed, furious at Blaine and his own helplessness.

"The thing that scares me most is how Eden don't take it serious," Marcus mused. "She's a feisty girl and can hold her own in an argument, but I don't think she's got any idea the kind of danger she's in."

"You mean she don't know about . . . ? Hasn't Fiona told her?" Linc asked, thinking he might have taken advantage of a totally innocent girl.

"Oh, she knows what can happen. She just don't think it can happen to her. She thinks she's too smart for Dirk Blaine. I've tried to tell her smart don't matter when a man twice your size throws you down on the ground, but she don't believe me. She always pats my hand and tells me she can take care of herself."

"Damn fool!"

"The worst part is, I don't think he just wants to rape her. I figure after he has his way, he'll force her to marry him so he can have a legal excuse for moving in on the Paradise."

Linc swore again.

"That's one of the reasons I sent for you," Marcus continued. "I can't watch her all the time. What with running the ranch and all, I've got my hands full just keeping up with Fiona, and she don't go riding off to God-knows-where every time the mood takes her."

"Eden rides off alone?" Linc asked incredulously.

Marcus nodded, his expression grim. "I was hoping you could keep an eye on her for me. When Fiona suggested pretending you two was courting, I thought it was a perfect idea, and Eden don't seem to mind much. Taking care of you has kept her close to home, but she won't stay put much longer, if I know Eden. When she takes off again, I sure wish you'd be with her."

Linc tried to tell himself he was crazy to agree to such a plan. He'd be tempting fate and courting disaster and all sorts of other horrible things. "Of course," he promised, knowing he had no other choice. "I won't let her out of my sight."

"That shirt looks good on you," Eden told Linc that evening after they had seated themselves in the porch swing. Eden had noticed how Fiona and Marcus made themselves scarce after supper, but she didn't mind a bit.

"Thanks," Lincoln said self-consciously. "I reckon these jeans'll be fine once they're washed, too."

Eden smiled, having noticed him walking stiff-legged in the unyielding denim. She waited in vain for a return of her compliment. She'd worn a barred muslin, light green to match her eyes and cut tightly to accent her figure, but he'd hardly looked at her all through supper, just like he was not looking at her now. He pushed the swing back and forth, staring straight ahead and very carefully not putting his arm around her.

The silence stretched until she realized he wasn't uncomfortable with it. Probably he actually preferred it to talking with her. Heaven knew, their conversations usually ended in dramatic ways, so she couldn't blame him, not if he was still dead set on denying their attraction for each other. But she wasn't going to let him ignore her any longer.

She cleared her throat, and he glanced at her suspiciously. "If you didn't want to pretend to be engaged to me, you should have told me to tell Marcus," she said.

"It's not that I didn't want—" He caught himself, probably realizing how dangerous that explanation might be. He settled for, "No harm done."

"So now we'll have to do some serious courting," she informed him solemnly.

His eyes twitched slightly, almost as if he were wincing. "What do you mean by 'serious'?"

She smiled coyly, wondering if he appreciated how infrequently she bothered to actually flirt with a man. "We'll have to be inseparable. People who are in love never want to be apart, you know."

"No, I didn't know," he replied grimly.

She resisted the urge to punch him and somehow held her smile. He hardly seemed to notice, though. He looked out at the ranch yard again, still pushing the swing back and forth with dogged determination, as if the persistent effort would get them somewhere.

Of course, she didn't have to hit him to get his undivided attention. "How many men have you killed?" she asked sweetly.

As she had expected, his head jerked back

around and his blue eyes darkened like a stormy sky. "I never talk about that," he snapped.

"Aren't you proud? Most men would be—"

"I'm not most men, and anyway, you're wrong. Only a jackass like Dirk Blaine would brag about how many men he's killed. There's nothing honorable about it."

"Not even when the other man needs killing?"

"Nobody has the right to decide who lives or dies."

"I'd kill the man who murdered my father if I knew who he was."

"If you knew who he was, why not go to the law?"

"What law?" she replied.

She had him there, and she knew it. His lips tightened, and he didn't respond.

"If that's the way you feel, how come you're a gunfighter?" she demanded.

"I'm not a . . . ," he started, but stopped when he realized the denial was absurd. His eyes grew bleak. "I never set out to be one."

Eden stared at him in surprise. She'd somehow never expected to see pain when he spoke of his reputation. She'd always assumed men who fought for right were immune to regret. Impulsively, she laid a hand on his arm. "I'm sorry," she whispered. "I . . . How did it happen?"

For a moment she thought he'd refuse to answer, then she felt the tension drain out of him as he surrendered to an impulse of his own. "It just happened. I was working at this ranch down near the border. We'd been having trouble with Mexicans taking our cattle across the river. The rangers and the army couldn't follow, so we did. I wasn't even the leader, but I was the best one with a gun. The greasers ambushed us, and we had to shoot our way out. When the smoke cleared, they were all dead. We brought back the cattle and got branded as heroes."

He sounded strangely bitter. "But you *were* heroes. Do you know how many thousands of head of cattle the Mexicans have stolen through the years?"

His scowl told her he knew far better than she. "If we'd been a little smarter, we might not've gotten ambushed and maybe we could've gotten the cattle back without any shooting."

"Now you're being ridiculous," she chided, withdrawing her hand. "You know as well as I do the Mexicans never give anything back without a fight."

His frown deepened. "Seems like nobody gives up without a fight."

She couldn't resist prodding him a little. "I suppose you're in a position to know since you've been in most of those fights." Once again pain flickered in his startlingly blue eyes, and she regretted baiting him. "I'm sorry. I—"

"No, you're right, I have been in more fights than I care to remember. Marcus seems to think I was always on the right side, too, but sometimes there just ain't a right or a wrong, just a winner and a loser."

"And you always win, don't you?"

He shrugged, as if the answer were of no importance. Eden began to wish she had never opened this sensitive subject.

"My goodness," she said with forced brightness, hoping for a lighter note. "You're awfully cross tonight. What's put you in such a bad mood?"

"Marcus told me you saw Blaine in town today."

His outrage surprised and pleased her. She tried a simper. "Are you jealous?"

"Jealous?" he croaked as if the word were strangling him. For a long minute he glared at her, his fierce expression driving every thought from her mind. "I'm starting to wonder about you, Miss Campbell. Maybe Dirk Blaine ain't completely to blame for all this. Maybe you've been leading him on—"

"Leading him on!" she cried. "How dare you suggest such a thing to me!"

"Yeah, maybe that's it," he mused as if she hadn't spoken. "He's a good-looking fellow, and you've been flirting with him—"

"I have not!"

"—so naturally he thinks he can put his hands on you whenever he wants."

"I've never flirted with Dirk Blaine or anyone else," she insisted, "and a lady never lets anyone take advantage of her!"

"You let me."

She stared at him, speechless, as the heat rose in her face. "That . . . that was different," she muttered, mortified by his contempt.

"How was it different?" he demanded, and suddenly she realized he wasn't contemptuous at all. He was *angry*. Why on earth should he be mad

133

because she'd kissed him?

"Because . . . because we're pretending . . . So people will think . . ."

"Nobody saw us. You didn't have to pretend that much."

She thought she might choke on her rage. "Do you think I kiss every man who comes by here?"

"I don't know. That's why I'm asking."

"You . . . Of all the insolent . . ." she sputtered. Rage overwhelmed her, and she threw back her hand to slap him, but he caught her wrist in a bone-crushing grip.

"Do you?" he demanded.

"Do I what?" she snapped, struggling in his grasp.

"Do you kiss every man who comes along?"

"No!" She clawed at his wrist, but he caught her free hand and pulled it away.

"Then why did you kiss me?"

Startled, she met his gaze, and her anger died a quick and silent death. So that's what he wanted to know! Her heart stopped for a long second as she debated telling him the truth. "Because I wanted to," she said at last.

He went perfectly still, and his grip on her wrists gentled as she ceased to struggle. Mesmerized, she watched his expression soften as his own anger drained away, and for several pounding heartbeats, neither of them moved or even breathed.

After what seemed an eternity, he whispered, "Eden."

Her name had never sounded so sweet, almost as sweet as his lips when they covered hers. Sweet and

134

soft and warm, his breath tasting of tobacco and Lincoln Scott. She leaned into the kiss and found her hands suddenly free to caress him.

"Eee-haaa!"

The rebel yell split the evening air, and they instantly jolted apart.

"What the . . . ?" Lincoln muttered, looking around in alarm.

"Hey, much obliged, Scott," Melancholy Jones called from the bunkhouse porch. "You just won me ten dollars!" Two other men stood with him, grinning from ear to ear.

"Melancholy Jones!" Eden cried, jumping to her feet. "You weren't *betting* on . . . on . . ."

"On whether he'd kiss you or not," Jones supplied helpfully. "Yes, ma'am, we were."

"Of all the low-down, dirty, rotten things to do! You were *spying* on us!"

"If you're bashful, you oughta do your spooning in private," Jones advised, looking as morose as usual but sounding annoyingly cheerful.

Lincoln rose beside her and when she looked up at him, she saw he was frowning. "Did you know they were watching?" he asked softly.

"Of course not!" she cried in exasperation. This time she wanted to kick him. Did he honestly believe she fell into his arms just to promote the lie that they were engaged?

"I'll have a little talk with them," he said and before she could reply, he was down the steps and halfway across the yard.

Since she couldn't very well call him back in front of the others, she stormed into the house.

135

Conscious of her fury, Linc walked slowly across the yard to where the other men waited, cursing himself with every step. Why on God's earth couldn't he keep his hands off Eden Campbell? And what was wrong with *her?* Didn't she know she was asking for trouble, tempting him the way she did time after time?

Unfortunately, he knew exactly what was wrong with her, because Marcus himself had told him just this afternoon. She labored under the delusion that she could take care of herself, that she could handle him and Dirk Blaine and any other man who couldn't resist her charms.

Ever since Marcus had told him about her encounter with Blaine this afternoon, Linc had tortured himself with suspicions that she might have led Blaine on the same way she'd been teasing Linc. He didn't want to believe it, had driven himself half-crazy picturing it in his mind, and he'd been unable to stop himself from accusing her of it just now.

Her reaction to his accusation had convinced him he'd been wrong to even consider the possibility, but that still didn't ease his mind any when it came to explaining why she'd been so eager to fall into *his* arms every time he'd come within reaching distance. She'd said she kissed him because she wanted to, but why would she be letting a no-account drifter with an unsavory reputation, a man she barely knew, take such liberties?

Before he could decide, he'd reached the bunkhouse porch where Jones and his two companions waited. He managed a fierce scowl. "You fellows make things awful tough on a man."

Melancholy Jones shook his head solemnly, his doelike eyes remorseless. "You can't blame us, Scott. We've all been trying to get Miss Eden to fall in love with us for years, and then you come along without so much as a by-your-leave and steal her out from under our noses."

The other two men nodded assent, obviously feigning their outrage. If only they knew how far off the mark they were. "You don't expect me to apologize, do you?" Linc asked, unable to hold back a grin.

"A pat on the back don't cure saddle galls," Melancholy said morosely. "However, if you was to leave the state, we might consent to forgive you."

"You boys shouldn't be so eager to run him off," Jed Titus said from the doorway, his red face split in a wide grin. "We could sure use an extra gun around here."

Linc managed not to wince, knowing he should be flattered by the foreman's confidence in his abilities.

"I reckon you're right," Jones agreed with a long-suffering sigh, "but he'd better be even better'n we've heard if he expects us all to step aside and let him have Miss Eden."

Titus hooted with laughter at Jones's presumption, and the others coughed suspiciously, covering their smiles. Linc kept a straight face, but only with difficulty. "I'll do my best to earn the right to her," he said, only half in jest.

Could he ever hope to earn the right to Eden Campbell? He wasn't sure, and until he was, he knew he'd have to be mighty careful not to be alone with her again.

Eden found Fiona sitting alone in the parlor, working on some needlepoint.

"Where's Marcus?" Eden asked without thinking.

"Out somewhere," Fiona replied stiffly, her accent more pronounced than usual. A sure sign she was upset. Eden recalled her remark to Lincoln that people in love liked to be together as much as possible, and her heart ached for her stepmother.

Eden sank down on the sofa beside her. "Men are the most infuriating creatures alive."

Fiona didn't reply for several seconds. Then she said, "What has Mr. Scott done now?"

Eden opened her mouth to explain, but caught herself just in time. Fiona would never approve of all the kissing that had been going on between her and Scott, so she was hardly likely to offer sympathy. Choosing her words carefully, Eden said, "I think you were right about Lincoln being a good man."

Fiona laid her needlework down and turned her speculative gaze on Eden. "Then why are you upset with him?"

"It's not him exactly. See, every time we start talking and I think we're really starting to get to know each other, something happens, like just now. Melancholy and some of the other boys were spying on us, and they started to tease, and . . ." She shrugged.

"Yes, it is difficult to get acquainted with someone when you don't have any privacy," Fiona mused, and Eden got the impression she was talking about more than just Eden and Lincoln Scott. Surely she didn't mean her and Marcus, though. They had privacy by the bushel whenever they closed their bedroom door.

Or did they?

Eden began to wonder if they knew she could eavesdrop on them whenever she wished and sometimes when she didn't wish at all. Was her presence part of the problem between the two of them?

"Perhaps you should try to get him away from the ranch," Fiona suggested, distracting her from her other concerns.

"But he can't ride yet."

"You could take the buggy, and you wouldn't have to go far. Perhaps you could plan a picnic at the place where your father and I used to go."

Eden nodded, recalling the secluded spot only a short ride from the ranch. It was incredibly romantic, with the small creek running among the sweeping willow trees. She wondered briefly if Fiona had ever taken Marcus there for a picnic and decided she probably hadn't. Something would simply have to be done about the two of them, but first Eden had her own problems to worry about. "Do you think he'd be willing to go on a picnic with me?" she asked, recalling his studied reluctance to be alone with her.

"Of course. He promised Marcus he'd watch over you."

"What!" Eden asked in outrage.

"Marcus is deeply concerned about your safety,

particularly after your encounter with Dirk Blaine this afternoon. He told me he asked Mr. Scott to look after you."

"And Lincoln agreed?"

"You don't honestly think he would refuse, do you?"

"Well, no," she admitted, realizing even the most churlish of men wouldn't turn down a request from his best friend in all the world. Eden just wished she knew whether Scott had agreed reluctantly or willingly.

"So you see, you have no problem. If he refuses to accompany you, simply threaten to go alone. I believe Marcus said he has promised not to let you out of his sight."

"Well, now, fancy that," Eden said, imagining all the delightful possibilities once she had Lincoln Scott alone. "What do you suppose we should pack for our picnic?"

Chapter Five

"It's a beautiful day for a picnic, isn't it?" Eden asked as she guided the buggy out of the ranch yard.

Linc grunted a reply, wishing he could appreciate the gorgeous weather. The spring sun shone brightly in the crystal blue sky, making the whole world appear to be in sharper focus. The purple bluebonnets and the scarlet Indian paintbrush stood out in bold relief against the emerald green of the new grass.

Sitting alone with Eden Campbell in the confines of the buggy, Linc could only appreciate the emerald green of her laughing eyes. They were definitely laughing, too, as if she were rejoicing in her cleverness. Had she suspected he'd decided never to be alone with her again? If so, she also knew of his promise to Marcus, since she'd played on it so well. Imagine threatening to go off on a picnic all alone if he didn't agree to come with her. She was undoubtedly trying to drive him crazy, and succeeding admirably.

"You're not mad at me are you?" she asked.

"Why should I be mad?" he replied warily, wishing her hair didn't smell quite so much like wildflowers.

"I haven't the slightest idea. You should be extremely grateful to me for getting you out of the house, but instead you're pouting."

"I'm not pouting," Linc informed her with a scowl.

"Looks like it to me. Are you mad because I wouldn't let you drive the wagon?"

"No, I'm mad because I *can't* drive the wagon," he said, grasping at this straw. "I figured I'd be able to ride by now."

"No one likes being laid up. I can still remember how much I hated having the measles when I was six." She gave an exaggerated sigh. "I was just worried you didn't like picnics."

"I don't know if I like them or not. I've never been on one before."

"What!" she cried in surprise. "You're not serious."

"Well," he allowed, "I've eaten outside plenty of times, but I don't think you'd call it a picnic."

At least her green eyes weren't laughing anymore, but Linc wasn't sure whether he was really glad about it. Now she was looking at him as if she'd never seen him before.

"My goodness, Mr. Scott," she said at last, "as Fiona would say, your upbringing has been sorely lacking. I know that's what she'd say because she says it to me quite frequently. In any case, I can teach you everything you need to know about picnics in short order, and I expect you'll be getting lots of practice in the future. Courting couples go on lots of picnics."

"Probably so they can be alone," he guessed grimly.

Eden batted her eyes innocently. "You needn't look so worried, Mr. Scott. Your virtue is safe with me."

Linc wished he could make her the same promise.

They rode for a few more minutes in silence until she said, "There it is, down there."

The buggy rattled down a slight incline to the bank of a tiny ribbon of water snaking through a tangle of willows. Probably a branch of the creek running by the cave where Eden had found him, he supposed. Nobody could have found a more secluded or romantic spot for two lovers to be alone unless it was the cave itself. Eden pulled the horse to a halt. "What do you think?"

Linc thought he was in big trouble. "It's nice," he hedged, wondering how she'd found this place and who else she might have brought here. The thought of her sitting under the willows with someone else burned in him like a hot coal.

"Fiona used to bring Papa here for picnics," she explained, setting the brake and tying off the reins.

Linc swallowed down hard on the hot coal and managed a grin. "Doesn't she come here with Marcus?"

Eden frowned. "I don't think so. She and Marcus aren't . . ."

"Aren't what?" he asked when she hesitated.

She shrugged. "I don't know. I'll get the basket.

143

Can you bring the blanket?"

Before he could reply, she was out of the buggy, reaching behind the seat. When she had lifted the basket out, he found the blanket and climbed out himself.

Watching her slender figure disappear into the tangle of willows, he muttered, "God help me." Drawing a deep breath, he plunged in after her, brushing aside the veil of leaves to find her critically surveying the shaded bower inside for a likely spot.

"How about right here?" she asked, indicating a fairly level place. She stooped down to remove a few rocks and sticks, and Linc's breath caught as he watched the dappled sunlight reflecting off the fiery highlights of her hair and the way her full breasts strained against the fabric of her shirtwaist. For an instant he imagined those breasts filling his hands, soft and warm and . . .

"All right," she said, looking up, her green eyes glittering.

"All right what?" he asked hoarsely.

"We can spread the blanket now." She stood up and reached out. "Give me an end."

He quickly unfolded the blanket and handed her two corners. In a few seconds they had it spread.

"Sit down," she said, dropping to her knees on one corner and pulling the basket closer. "How are you feeling? Did the ride hurt your side any?"

"No, I'm fine," he said, cautiously lowering himself onto the exact opposite corner, as far from her as he could get. This was going to be torture, he thought, glancing around at the leafy enclosure.

They might as well be the only two people on earth. His one hope was to keep the conversation going. Considering how little practice he'd had at such things, he didn't think he had much hope at all.

"Take off your hat and stay awhile," Eden said, indicating his Stetson. He lifted it off and carefully set it aside. "You probably won't need that gun, either, and it must be a weight to carry around."

Reluctantly, Linc unbuckled his gunbelt and laid it aside, too, although he kept it within easy reach, unable to forget Dirk Blaine was still running around loose somewhere.

He watched while Eden emptied the basket. She set the food out and unwrapped each container. The tantalizing aromas drifted around him, but Eden was still the most inviting dish on the blanket.

"Would you like a breast or a thigh?" she asked.

"What?"

"A breast or a thigh? The chicken." She pointed, giving him a quizzical look.

"Oh, uh, white meat," he said, too quickly.

Still quizzical, she filled his plate with chicken and pickles and cold biscuits and a hard-boiled egg and a thick slice of pound cake. She set it next to him and proceeded to fill her own plate.

Linc had never been a finicky eater, but his normally reliable appetite seemed to have fled, so he had no trouble at all waiting until Eden had poured them each a glass of cider and settled herself on the blanket to eat.

To Linc's chagrin, she moved closer to him, easily within reach, he noted in dismay. Tucking her legs beneath her, she spread her skirt modestly and took the plate into her lap.

Used to eating around a campfire, Linc usually squatted, holding his plate in one hand and his knife in the other, and shoveled the food into his mouth. Such an approach hardly seemed appropriate under the circumstances, so he settled for crossing his legs and accepted the fork she handed him.

"This is good," he remarked when he'd devoured a good bit of his meal.

"Fiona made most everything. You've probably figured out by now I'm not a very good cook. Fiona says I'll have a hard time catching a husband if I don't learn. Is that true?"

"Why're you asking me?" Linc asked in alarm.

"To get your opinion. Would you marry a girl who couldn't cook?"

Linc swallowed a mouthful of cake while he studied her, noting her silken skin and her tempting mouth and the enticing curves beneath her shirt. He couldn't help thinking he wouldn't miss food at all if he had Eden Campbell to nibble on, but of course, he couldn't say a thing like that. "I don't reckon cooking's so important."

For some reason, his answer pleased her, and Linc had the impression he'd made a tactical error in doing so. She looked entirely too smug for his peace of mind. He'd have to be more careful.

All too soon he'd cleaned his plate and finished the seconds she pressed on him. When she'd packed up the foodstuffs, he started to rise, thinking the picnic was over and they'd be heading back, but instead of getting up, Eden sat back down and reclined on one elbow as if she were prepared to settle in for quite a spell.

Out of necessity, Linc stretched out to ease the ache in his side, but he was careful to leave a respectable distance between them. Suddenly he was once again aware of how isolated they were and how easy it would be to reach over and take her in his arms. With a renewed sense of foreboding, he realized this was exactly what he *would* do if they were really courting. He cast about frantically for something to say to fill the silence.

"Marcus said you were the one who got him and Fiona together," he tried.

"Oh, yes, I arrange all of Fiona's marriages," she explained with an impish grin. "Well, I didn't arrange the first one, of course. Fiona eloped with Bruce in England. His family didn't approve because she was poor and so was he."

"I thought he was a duke or something."

"Oh, no, just the youngest son of a viscount. Over there the oldest boy inherits everything and the others have to marry heiresses. Bruce didn't, so they sent him to Texas to run a ranch they'd bought as an investment. He didn't know anything about ranching, and the place went broke. Their babies got sick and died—Fiona had two children—and then Bruce got gored by a bull."

Linc whistled softly in sympathy.

Eden nodded her agreement. "By the time we met up with her, she was in a bad way. Papa had gone to buy some of her cattle, and he'd taken me along. Everybody thought she'd be going back to

England, but she'd decided she would stay here if she could find a good man to take care of her. As you can imagine, she'd had plenty of offers, women being so scarce out here and all, but she'd turned them all down. I guess she didn't trust her own judgment, what with being so sad about Bruce dying and everything.

"Anyway, when Papa and me showed up, she made friends with me right away. Papa liked her a lot, and when I found out what a pickle she was in, I convinced her he was just the man she needed. They only knew each other a few days before they got married, but it worked out real fine. They would've had a good life together if . . ."

Her voice trailed off, and Linc regretted stirring up unpleasant memories. "So how did you convince her to marry Marcus?" he asked to distract her.

"Oh, I didn't have to convince her at all. In fact, Marcus was her choice. She'd known him almost as long as she'd known Papa and me, and he's such a dear. Once we realized we'd need a man on the place if we wanted to hold onto it, Marcus was the one she picked. The only problem was getting him to agree."

"I can't believe you had any trouble talking him into it," Linc scoffed.

"Marcus is awfully shy," she reminded him. "In all the years he'd known her, he'd never even called Fee by her first name. I had to practically hog-tie him to get him over here to ask her. Just between us, I don't think he ever did ask. I think Fiona had to propose to him." She frowned thoughtfully. "I'm not sure I did them a favor by getting them together, though."

"Why not?"

"Because they don't seem very happy together. Haven't you noticed?"

He certainly hadn't. "Marcus is happy as a weevil in high cotton."

"He is?"

"Well, sure. What man wouldn't be?"

"He doesn't act happy. He practically ignores Fiona most of the time."

"He's been pretty busy," Linc reminded her. "He's got the ranch to run, and the rustlers to deal with, and the Blaines."

While she mulled over his theory, he remembered another thing Marcus was concerned about.

"And he's worried about you."

"Me? Whatever for?"

"Because of the way Dirk Blaine is chasing after you," he said, feeling the burning in his chest again. The mere thought of Blaine touching Eden filled him with unspeakable rage.

She dismissed the threat of Dirk Blaine with a wave of her hand. "He's just a lot of hot air. If he ever really tried anything with me, I'd put him in his place."

"What would you do, slap his face?" Linc asked contemptuously, reminding her of when she'd tried to do just that to Linc.

Obviously, she remembered her failure. Red spots burned on her cheeks, and she lifted her chin defiantly. "I can handle the likes of Dirk Blaine."

Linc knew an impotent fury at her complacency.

Didn't she have any idea of the danger she was in? "Can you now?" he challenged. "And what would you do if he grabbed you like this?"

Linc grabbed her arms. Her eyes widened in surprise, but she instantly accepted his challenge.

"I'd fight him like this," she announced smugly, glad for a chance to prove herself once and for all.

She wrenched out of his grasp, or tried to, while at the same time she started thrashing, kicking her feet and pushing at his chest. Instead of freeing her, he pushed her down flat on the blanket. Furious now, she beat on his chest and tried to scratch his face, but he dodged her claws and captured her hands. Struggling in his grasp, she landed a telling blow near his wound with her elbow. His grunt of pain gave her one second of remorse, but only one second, since it didn't seem to affect him at all.

Her feet were still free, so she aimed for his shin, but her slippers were no match for his boots, and she cried out in her own pain when she jammed her toe against the unyielding leather.

Enraged, she resorted to the only weapon left in her arsenal and jerked her knee up straight for his crotch.

But his own knee deflected hers with a bruising blow that overpowered her. In the next second she found herself pinned, helpless, to the ground, her legs trapped beneath his, her arms held above her head. Frantically, she continued to struggle, arching her back against him until he pressed his chest to hers, using his superior weight to still the last vestiges of her resistance.

Furious and gasping, she glared up at him, ready

150

to spit in his face until she saw the cold glitter in his azure eyes. "Have you put me in my place yet?" he taunted.

"You bastard!" she cried in frustration, renewing her fruitless struggle for a few more seconds until forced to surrender to exhaustion. Panting, she sputtered out more invectives until he lowered his full weight onto her, stopping her breath completely.

Suddenly she realized she didn't know this man at all. Might he actually harm her? "I . . . can't . . . breathe . . ." she gasped, panic welling within her.

"No, you can't," he said with maddening calm, "but I can do anything I want to you, and you won't be able to stop me."

Slowly, so she was aware of every move, he took both her hands in one of his and lowered his free hand to her face. His touched her cheek, ignoring her flinch, and then stroked downward, over her throat, skimming the thin fabric of her shirtwaist, until his palm covered her breast.

The heat of his touch scorched her, and she cried out, horrified at the violation and terrified to realize she was powerless to resist it. Tears stung her eyes, tears of rage and frustration and fear. Pride forbade her to beg him to stop, but the plea had already formed in her throat when, in one swift motion, he released her.

One second he held her completely motionless, and in the next she was free. He rolled away, pushing up to a sitting position, knees updrawn, arms draped over them, head hanging. For a minute,

Eden couldn't move, unable to quite believe it was over. She lay there gasping for the breath of which he'd robbed her, trembling in the aftermath of terror.

Instinctively, she crossed her arms over her chest, as if to deny her own vulnerability. When she was sure she wouldn't cry, she struggled upright and looked over at Lincoln. He hadn't moved a muscle. Conscious of her gaze, he lifted his head, and when she saw the anger still blazing in his eyes, her breath lodged in her throat again.

"Now do you understand?" he demanded.

"I . . . I . . ." She shook her head in confusion.

"Did you see how easy that was for me?" he asked almost desperately. "I wasn't even trying to hurt you. I didn't even get out of breath, for God's sake. Now do you understand what Dirk Blaine could do to you?"

Eden gaped at him in outrage. "Were you trying to teach me some kind of *lesson?*"

"Somebody had to," he replied defensively.

"And who appointed you for the job?" she raged, jumping to her feet. "Or do you just enjoy terrorizing women?"

"Marcus asked me," he informed her.

"Did Marcus ask you to paw me like a lecher?" she cried, glad to see him wince. "I wonder if he'd still think you were such a good friend if I told him how you threw me down and put your hands all over me?"

She could see her words had stung him, hitting him where he was most vulnerable, threatening his friendship with Marcus. She wanted to hurt him

152

even more as vengeance for scaring her so badly, but something held her back. Perhaps it was her common sense which warned against angering a man whose power she had just seen so clearly demonstrated. She settled for glaring at him, arms akimbo, until he looked guiltily away.

"Marcus said you wouldn't believe him when he told you how dangerous Blaine could be," he explained, his voice expressionless. "I figured the best way was to just show you."

Eden didn't know what made her more furious, what he had done or the fact that he seemed so totally unaffected by it. She was still shaking from head to toe, and she could still feel the impression of his body against hers and the imprint of his hand upon her breast. How dare he cause her such distress and be unmoved?

Because her legs refused to support her any longer, she sank down on her knees beside him, drawing his attention again. To her surprise, he no longer seemed angry. In fact, his clear eyes were full of concern. "Are you all right?"

"Certainly," she snapped, straightening her shirtwaist with a jerk.

"Look, I didn't . . . enjoy that, no matter what you think."

"Hmmph." Nothing could have infuriated her more. Hadn't he even liked being so close to her? A lot of men would've given a year's pay to hold Eden Campbell in their arms. She reached up and began to angrily repair the damage to her hair.

"I know you probably think I'm a . . . a . . ."

"A cad? A bounder?" she offered acidly.

A muscle twitched in his jaw, but he held on to his temper. "If it's any comfort to you, I know I . . . or rather *we* shouldn't have . . . Well, I'd already decided I'd never lay a hand on you again."

Was that supposed to be good news? she wondered incredulously. How dare he kiss her and make her feel things she'd never felt before and then calmly tell her it was all some kind of mistake in judgment?

He watched her closely, as if expecting some sort of response. The longer he watched, the more angry she became. Did he want a response? Well, she'd give him one he wouldn't soon forget.

When she was satisfied with her hair, she lowered her arms and said, "I think we'd better go now."

He rose instantly and even offered her a hand up, which she ignored. She stood up so they were facing each other, brushed her skirt, drew a deep breath, and looked him directly in the eye.

"You probably should have apologized," she informed him just before she stuck out her foot, caught his calf, and yanked, backheeling him as she had seen cowboys do in fights from the time she could walk.

He went down on his rump with a roar of surprise that ended in a howl of pain as he clutched at his side.

"Oh, no." she cried, covering her mouth in horror. "Oh, Linc, I'm sorry. I forgot! Oh, Linc."

She dropped beside him and eased him back onto the blanket, unable to look at his face contorted in agony. He clutched at his side, but she gently removed his hands and began to unbutton

154

his pants.

"What are . . . you doing?" he gasped, feebly attempting to stop her.

"I have to see if you tore it open. Oh, Linc, I'm so sorry. You made me so mad, I just didn't think." Pulling his shirttail loose, she saw with some surprise he wore no bandage. To her great relief, the wound appeared undamaged. "Everything looks fine," she assured him unsteadily. "Just lay still, and I'm sure it'll stop hurting in a minute or two."

He shuddered, and she laid a comforting hand over the angry red scar. Tears of remorse blinded her for a moment, and she closed her eyes over them.

His skin felt hot beneath her palm, and she stroked it tenderly, willing away the pain. His stomach rose and fell unsteadily with the jerky rhythm of his breathing.

After a few moments, he said, "Eden?"

Alarmed by the rasp in his voice, she opened her eyes and looked at him.

"Eden, you'd better stop that."

"Why?" she asked, stilling her hand instantly.

"Because if you don't, I'm going to pull you down here and kiss the daylights out of you."

Her heart came to a lurching halt as she saw the same heat she felt beneath her palm flickering brightly in his eyes. She knew she should jump up and run. She was furious at him, wasn't she? She hated him, didn't she?

Except she'd only hated him because she thought he didn't feel anything for her. At this particular moment, he seemed to be feeling a lot of things. Defying his warning, she slid her hand farther up inside his shirt until she found a flat male nipple which puckered instantly at her touch.

Linc groaned, and this time she knew it wasn't from the pain in his side. Before she could even blink, he reached up, grabbed the back of her head and pulled her face down to his.

This kiss was nothing like the others. This time he was fierce and demanding, his mouth hot and open. His arms closed around her, dragging her across his body and rolling her over until she lay flat on the blanket and he loomed above her.

The kiss went on and on, until she gasped for breath, and the instant she opened her mouth, his tongue plunged inside. Startled by the invasion, she tried to force it out with her own. His moan of pleasure filled her mouth as the strange duel stirred sensations she'd never known before.

Every one of her nerve endings prickled to attention, clamoring for his touch. His hands moved over her, molding her to him, but it wasn't enough, not nearly enough. Her own hands were both inside his shirt now, exploring the sinewy expanse of his back. His skin felt like warm satin, and her own skin heated from the fever burning within.

Her breasts seemed to swell and strain against the confines of her clothing, and she tried to hold him close to ease the pressure. As if he understood her need, he once again caressed her breast, but this time she welcomed his touch, needing it in some elemental way she couldn't begin to understand.

She arched her back, offering herself to him, until he'd claimed both gifts. He kneaded her gently, sending pleasure spasming through her. She'd never dreamed a man's touch could affect her so, and she wondered if her touch had the same effect on him.

Experimentally, she slid her hands around from his back to his chest, pushing his shirt up and delving into the thick pelt of hair she found there. Linc gasped in response and quickly unbuttoned his shirt to grant her better access.

Staring up at the perfection of his body, she hardly noticed when he began to release the buttons on her shirtwaist. Indeed, she instinctively helped him, knowing somehow that she would die if she couldn't feel his flesh against hers. He spread the garment open slowly, almost reverently, and she wondered vaguely if he could actually see her heart slamming against her chest.

Surely he could see practically everything else. Only her chemise covered the breasts her corset lifted so invitingly, and she felt as if she might burst through the thin fabric. Hardly able to breathe, she lay perfectly still, silently willing him to continue. Something flickered in the depths of his sky blue eyes and his head came down, carefully, deliberately, until his lips touched the tiny, shadowed valley just above the lacy edge of her chemise.

She gasped in joyful surprise, burying her fingers in his raven hair to hold him to her. But he had no intention of leaving her. He kissed her again and again, touching and tasting her eager flesh until he had dewed every inch exposed to him and she longed to tear away the restraining fabric so he could have *everything.*

She didn't have to. He breathed her name and slipped his fingers tentatively beneath the edge of her chemise until he found the nipple pouting for his touch.

Desire clenched in her belly and twisted into an aching knot as his fingers teased each nipple in turn, pushing aside their covering to expose them to the heat of first his gaze and then his avid mouth. Nipping, tugging, he suckled like a starving man seeking sustenance.

The knot in her belly tightened until her body wept its need of him. When she thought she might go mad, he pulled away, gathering her and lifting her. At first she had no idea what was happening, but she soon understood and followed as he rolled over on his back and lifted her onto his body.

Her hair had come loose, and it spilled over her shoulders, surrounding them in a silken curtain that narrowed their private bower into an even more intimate space.

"You're so beautiful," he whispered raggedly, weaving his hands into her hair and drawing her down to him.

She splayed her hands across his bare chest, brushing aside his shirt so she would encounter no barrier. Slowly, resisting his insistent hands tugging on her hair, she lowered her breasts until just the sensitized tips touched the furred wall of his chest.

His breath caught, strangling in his throat, and she watched his eyes darken. "God, Eden," he gasped and then enveloped her in his embrace, crushing her softness against him. His heart pounded like a sledge so they both trembled from the force of it. He found her mouth and once again claimed it as his own.

She clung to him, reveling in the intoxicating sensations of her flesh meeting his as they melded together in the radiance of desire. When his lips left hers to nibble on her throat, she sighed with bliss and said, "I thought you weren't going to lay a hand on me again."

"You were the one who laid a hand on me first," he reminded her hoarsely. He clutched at her hips, pressing her against the hard evidence of his arousal. Response tingled up the backs of her legs.

So this was what love felt like, she thought wildly. She'd never imagined it could be so glorious. She couldn't get enough of touching him and tasting him. How could she have ever thought he didn't want her? He *adored* her! Giddy with her knowledge and her power, she felt compelled to test it to its limits.

When he rolled her over again, she did not resist. This time she took his weight gladly, holding him to her while she explored his body more boldly than before. She let her hands wander lower, down to his waist, and found his pants were still loose from when she'd unbuttoned them.

Feeling deliciously wicked, she slipped her fingers inside the waistband. Delighting in his hair-roughened flesh, so different from her own, she stroked his bare flanks, coaxing a moan from deep in his chest. The sound rumbled through her, stirring instincts she hadn't known she possessed. As if of their own accord, her hips moved beneath his, seeking solace for the burning emptiness.

Almost frantically, he clutched at her hips, stilling them while one hand wrestled to find her beneath the layers of petticoats. She gasped when he touched her hip through only a thin layer of cotton. He shouldn't really be touching her down there, and she wasn't too far gone to know it, but she certainly wasn't afraid. She was still in control.

His knee parted hers while his hand caressed her hip, her thigh. Need pooled in her loins as her bones turned to jelly, and someone moaned Linc's name.

He rose up over her, pressing his mouth to hers as his hips sought the cradle of her thighs.

"Oh, God!" he cried as bare flesh touched bare flesh. Some part of him had met her secret spot through the opening in her pantalettes, a part of him that was hot and hard and strong.

Her gasp echoed his surprise. Apparently, he hadn't known women's drawers were open down there, and she certainly hadn't remembered his jeans were unbuttoned. She should have pushed him away, and she would have except it felt too good, too wonderful, too right.

Her hips moved again, responding to primitive urges she could not deny, and heat scorched through her. It burned away all vestiges of sanity and left her a creature of sensation only. Linc touched her, just *there,* and she shuddered in response. She wanted something, something more. Wordlessly, she pleaded for it, clutching at him with hands and lips.

Linc muttered what sounded like a protest, but she kissed him to silence. Down below his hips moved as feverishly as hers until, at last, his strength stilled her, opened her, and filled her.

"Yes," she breathed when she first felt the hot, hard length of him prodding. This was what she wanted so desperately. She grasped his flanks to urge him on, and with a strangled groan, he plunged into her.

Unexpected pain shot through her and wrenched a cry from her throat. She arched her back in protest as sanity suddenly returned. Good God, what had she done?

But Lincoln left her no time for regrets. His lips caressed her face and his hands soothed her hurt, finding the sensitive spots to coax the flames of desire to life again. He whispered her name over and over, calling her back to the realm of mindless delights.

Her body responded before she realized what was happening, and when he moved inside of her, sanity fled again. The scorching heat streaked through her, warming her blood and melting her bones. She clung to him mindlessly as he stoked the flames higher and higher until she couldn't think, couldn't see, couldn't even breathe. Nothing existed except she and Linc and their passionate quest to become one.

The end came with an incendiary roar as she convulsed into white-hot oblivion. Above her, he cried out her name and shuddered his own release while she clutched at him desperately.

For several minutes they rode the aftershocks, gasping and clinging, kissing and cuddling, unwilling to let the closeness end. But at last it did end, and too soon Eden emerged from the fog of passion into the scathing light of reality.

What had she done?

What had happened to her control, her power? What had happened to *her?* She looked to Linc for the answer, but if anything, he seemed more confused than she.

He levered himself up on his elbows, relieving her of his weight, then muttered something and rolled off of her. As he made hasty adjustments to his clothes, Eden became aware of her own state of undress. Quickly, she wrapped her shirtwaist over her bare breasts and flipped her skirt down. She felt moisture between her thighs, blood or something else, but she couldn't think about it now.

She struggled upright and, turning her back to Linc, awkwardly rearranged her chemise to its proper position and rebuttoned her shirtwaist.

Behind her, Linc sat up, too, having finished his task. "Are you all right?"

He'd asked her the same questions just a few minutes—or was it a lifetime?—ago. This time she was not so certain of the answer.

"I'm . . . fine," she replied after a few seconds, wondering if it were true. When she was once again decently covered, she turned to face him. Hoping to see the adoration she had imagined he felt, she saw only a wary uncertainty. Her heart constricted.

"I didn't mean for that to happen," he said.

She hadn't meant for it to happen either, but she couldn't blame him, she realized with a stab of guilt. If she hadn't been so intoxicated with her power over him . . .

When she didn't respond, he said, "I don't usually . . . I mean, I never . . . Like I said before, I don't enjoy terrorizing women."

"You didn't exactly terrorize me," she reminded him, willing him to smile. Dear God, why did he look so grim?

He stared at her for a long minute, and she wondered what he saw, what changes had been wrought by their intimacy. Self-consciously, she brushed the hair out of her face and wished she'd brought a comb.

Linc watched the gesture and knew a brand new wave of longing. God, how he wanted to take her in his arms and hold her close and tell her how she'd made him feel. But if there were words to say such things, he didn't know them, nor did he think she would welcome his embrace right now, not after what he'd just done. At least she didn't look angry, only frightened. Her fear tore at his heart. When he spoke, he kept his voice soft.

"We haven't known each other very long," he began, feeling his way through dangerous territory. "There are a lot of things you don't know about me." And a lot of things he didn't know about her, he added mentally, thinking the more he learned about her, the less he understood.

Still, he knew the most important thing of all: he wanted her. He wanted her for today and tomorrow and for the rest of their lives. He would have her, too, because now they would have to get married. The idea of marriage had never really appealed to him before, but after knowing Eden, he understood perfectly what drove men to it. Losing his freedom was a small price to pay for a lifetime with the woman he loved.

The thought swelled in his chest and settled like a lump in his throat. He had to clear it to speak again. "Eden, I guess you know we ought to get married now," he said, carefully keeping the elation from his voice.

"We *ought* to?" she echoed suspiciously.

"Well, yeah," he said, proceeding cautiously. He didn't want her to think he was forcing her into it or, worse, that he'd seduced her just so he could have her. "I mean, if folks found out . . ."

"How would they find out?" she asked in alarm.

"Not from me," he assured her, wondering if she knew what they'd just done might result in a pregnancy that would announce their act to the world. If she didn't, he certainly wasn't about to explain it to her. "Look, Eden, I'm not such a prize. Ordinarily, Marcus wouldn't let a man like me within a mile of you. You deserve a fellow with something to offer you, a home and a—"

"I certainly do."

"What?"

She lifted her chin defiantly. "I deserve a much better man than you."

He blinked in surprise, uncertain how to respond.

Before he could, she said, "And you needn't worry, I have no intention of trying to force you to marry me."

"You don't have to force me—"

"Perhaps you got the wrong impression," she said stiffly, ignoring his interruption. "I was only teasing you with all that talk about us being engaged. I saw it made you uncomfortable, but I certainly never . . . I have no intention of marrying you, Mr. Scott, so you don't have to try to convince me I shouldn't."

Eden could hear the faint British accent she had unconsciously adopted along with Fiona's British reserve. She only hoped it disguised her utter mortification and the tears of humiliation that even now burned behind her eyes. She fairly trembled with the effort of holding them back, but she'd die before she'd cry in front of Lincoln Scott.

"I wasn't trying to convince you you shouldn't," he said, apparently surprised by her attitude. Who was he trying to fool?

"Well, you did," she informed him, feeling stronger by the minute. If only she could get back to the ranch and out of his sight before she broke down. "And you're right. Two strangers have no business getting married for any reason. It's not like we're in love or anything."

The words almost choked her. She'd thought he loved her, and she was very much afraid she had fallen in love with him. What else could explain her obsession with winning his regard? Or her eager surrender just now? Nothing, she admitted with a wrenching agony, but she fought the pain. She couldn't succumb to it just yet.

"Wait a minute, Eden," he was saying. "We're

getting off the track here. Maybe you think I'm just after a part of the ranch—"

"You already own part of the ranch," she reminded him bitterly. Did he think he had to make excuses for seducing her?

"I told you before, I never take anything I haven't earned . . ."

His voice trailed off as they both realized the absurdity of his claim in light of what had just happened. He had the grace to flush.

"I think we'd better get back to the ranch," she said briskly, stuffing her shirttail into her skirt with almost frantic haste. Her control was beginning to slip, and she didn't know how much longer she could hold onto it.

"Eden, you're upset now, and maybe you're not thinking straight—"

"I'm thinking perfectly straight," she assured him, hating him for being so damned polite. Why couldn't he act like the cad he was? Fighting a welling panic, she started to rise, only to realize her hair still hung loose. What on earth could she do with it? If only she could find her pins.

With a haste born of desperation, she ran her hands over the blanket in search of them. When Linc realized what she was doing, he helped, finding far more than she in her distracted state.

Without looking at him, she allowed him to drop the pins into her outstretched palm, then turned away to make what repairs she could. Finger-combing the long, auburn strands, she managed to work out the worst of the tangles and twist her hair up into a semblance of her former style. She jabbed the pins in helter-skelter, praying they would hold until she got home.

Home. The word conjured thoughts of refuge and comfort and blessed privacy, away from Lincoln Scott's prying eyes. The instant the last pin was in place, she jumped to her feet. "Can you bring the blanket?" she asked as she scooped up the basket and fairly ran for the buggy.

"Eden, wait!" he called, but she ignored him. If he had more to say to her, he'd have plenty of opportunity on the drive back to the ranch. Meanwhile, she needed a few seconds in which to restore her tenuous composure.

By the time he'd strapped on his gunbelt, retrieved his hat, and folded the blanket, Eden felt in control again. She sat in the buggy, ramrod straight and acutely aware of the ache between her thighs. She did not deign to glance at him as he stowed the blanket and climbed up beside her. She could actually feel his searching gaze upon her.

"Eden, before we go back, we have to talk."

"Talk!" she cried, alarmed to hear the shrillness in her voice. "I think we've talked enough already," she said, consciously softening her tone.

His expression was cautious, as if he were handling a wild creature whose actions he could not predict. "What are Marcus and Fiona going to say about this?"

"You don't think I'm going to tell them, do you?" she asked incredulously. "I'm not interested in arranging a shotgun wedding, if that's what you're worried about."

She reached for the reins, but her shaking hands

167

could not untie them from the brake handle. With an exasperated sigh, he leaned over and released them with one jerk.

Eden gasped at his nearness, so he withdrew instantly, a strange expression in his eyes that she might have mistaken for hurt if she hadn't known better.

"You . . . you can't drive," she stammered as he slapped the horse into motion.

"Neither can you. You're shaking like a leaf."

It was true. She clasped her hands tightly in her lap, but she couldn't stop the trembling that had started in her heart and now radiated outward.

"You don't have to be afraid," he said with surprising gentleness.

"I'm not afraid," she lied, terrified of things she couldn't even name.

"I'm willing to do right by you."

"Do right?" she scoffed. "You should have 'done right' a few minutes ago!"

"I can't change what happened, but I'll marry you and—"

"I don't want an unwilling husband!"

"I'm not unwilling," he protested.

"Then why did you try to talk me out of it before you even asked?" she demanded, near tears.

"Dammit, I didn't try to talk you out of it—"

"Stop it!" she cried, horrified to feel the moisture flooding her eyes. She covered her mouth with both hands, blinking furiously.

Linc reined to a stop. "Oh, God, Eden, don't cry," he begged, turning to her, reaching out.

"Don't touch me!" she screamed as hysteria

welled within her. She fought it desperately, but if he so much as laid a hand on her . . .

"All right," he said, holding up his palms in surrender. "Just don't . . . We won't talk anymore. I'll take you home. Everything'll be fine. You'll see."

She recognized the meaningless assurances as an attempt to calm her and accepted them as such. Wrapping her arms around her middle protectively, she withdrew as far as possible into the corner of the seat. He slapped the horse into motion again, glancing nervously at her every few seconds.

Staring straight ahead, she concentrated on breathing in and out at regular intervals and blinking hard to keep her eyes clear. Whatever would she say to Fiona, who was bound to notice her condition? However would she face her stepmother or anyone else again?

They reached the ranch before she came to any conclusions, and the instant Linc stopped the buggy, Eden jumped out. He called after her, or she thought he did, but she didn't look back, didn't stop, didn't even breathe until she'd entered the house, run through the parlor and down the hall to the kitchen into the tiny room where she'd been sleeping since Lincoln Scott had come into her life.

Slamming the door behind her, she collapsed on the bed, surrendering at last to her tears. She buried her face in her pillow to muffle the sobs and wept out her grief and her pain and her humiliation.

* * *

Linc put the buggy away and turned the horse loose in the corral. Carrying the picnic basket and blanket, he trudged slowly to the house, where he fully expected to be met by an irate stepmother intent on nailing his hide to the barn door.

But the front room was empty, and he heard no sounds from any other part of the house. Setting the basket and blanket down just inside the front door, he waited a minute or two, trying to decide what to do. His only two choices were to go after Eden or to wait for Fiona to come to him. Since he knew Eden didn't want to see him just yet, he went to his room—Eden's room—to await the inevitable.

Closing the door behind him, he glanced longingly at the bed. As much as he hated to admit it, Eden had been right about him driving. His side was burning like hellfire. Of necessity, he sat down, pulled off his boots, and stretched out on the inviting length of Eden Campbell's feather tick.

Drawing a deep breath, he let it out in a shuddering sigh. What in the hell was he going to do now? When Marcus found out—and Linc didn't doubt for a minute that he would—their friendship would be over. After promising to protect Eden from Dirk Blaine's lust, Linc had seduced her himself. He'd betrayed Marcus's trust, something no man could forgive.

Of course, if Eden would just agree to marry him, everything would be fine, but that didn't seem at all likely. He could certainly understand why a woman would be hesitant to hitch up with a gunfighter. Hadn't he been the one who pointed out all the reasons why she shouldn't? But how had she gotten the idea he didn't *want* to marry her? And how could he convince her otherwise? And could he do it before Marcus blew his head off?

By the time Eden heard Fiona moving about in the kitchen, she had managed to stop crying. It would never do for Fiona to guess the truth, but how could she explain why she was so upset and the fact that she never intended to speak to Lincoln Scott again?

As Fiona's footsteps came closer to the door, Eden cast about frantically for an explanation. It came to her just as Fiona knocked.

"Eden, are you in there?"

"Yes," Eden said, scrambling upright and scrubbing the last of the moisture from her face.

Fiona opened the door. "Why are you . . . ? Good heavens, what happened?" she demanded, coming inside and closing the door behind her.

"Linc and I had a fight," she said, glad to hear her voice sounded steady.

"A fight? What on earth do you have to fight about?" She sat down on the bed beside Eden. "He didn't . . . make any improper advances, did he?"

"You could say that," she said, not bothering to hide the break in her voice.

Fiona cried out in distress. "I'll speak to Marcus at once. He'll—"

"He won't mind a bit," Eden said, striving for a martyred expression. "Scott was only doing what Marcus told him to."

"What are you talking about?"

"Marcus told him to protect me from Dirk Blaine, so after we'd finished our picnic, Scott started to lecture me on how I needed to be careful. Of course I told him I wasn't afraid of Dirk Blaine—"

"But you should be, darling," Fiona assured her, laying a hand on hers.

"Well, I certainly am now! Scott scared the living daylights out of me."

"What did he do?" Fiona demanded, outraged.

Eden drew a steadying breath, grateful she'd discovered a logical reason for her distress. "First he tried to scare me by telling me what Blaine might do. When that didn't work, he grabbed me and threw me down on the blanket and asked me what I'd do if Blaine did the same thing. Of course I fought him. I thought he was only teasing and . . ." Her voice broke, and she blinked at tears, angry to discover she wasn't as calm as she'd thought.

"Go on," Fiona said gently.

"Oh, Fiona, it was awful! I fought like crazy, but he's so strong. I felt helpless. I had no idea . . ." A tear slid down her cheek, and she swiped at it angrily.

Fiona slipped an arm around her and pulled her close. "I know. It's frightening to discover just how helpless we are. But Mr. Scott actually did you a favor."

"A favor!" Eden cried in outrage. "I haven't told you everything. He wasn't satisfied with just frightening me or showing me how weak I am. Oh, no,

172

once he had me pinned on the ground so I couldn't move a muscle, he . . . he *touched* me . . . here."

Eden touched her left breast, striving to remember her revulsion at the time and not the burning ecstasy that had come later.

Fiona stiffened, even more outraged than Eden had been. "That scalawag! That varlet! That . . . that *gutterpup!*"

In spite of herself, Eden smiled at Fiona's proper British version of profanity. "Gutterpup?"

"How dare he violate you in such a shocking manner?" Fiona continued, oblivious to Eden's amusement. "Marcus will horsewhip him."

"Oh, no!" Eden protested automatically, then caught herself. Why on earth was she defending Lincoln Scott? After what he'd done to her, didn't he deserve to be horsewhipped?

But of course, she knew he didn't. He hadn't done anything she hadn't invited him to do. As much as she detested him, she couldn't allow him to take all the blame. "Marcus wouldn't really . . . I mean, we don't have to tell him, do we?" Eden asked guiltily.

"Don't you want him to at least reprimand the scoundrel?"

"Marcus might not think what he did was so bad," Eden ventured. "After all, he was the one who asked Linc to watch out for me."

"I'd hardly call what he did 'watching out' for you," Fiona sniffed angrily.

Fiona was right, of course, and she didn't even know the half of it. Why couldn't Eden bring herself to agree? Why did she feel so strangely protect-

173

ive of a man who had just seduced and abandoned her? Maybe she really was in love with the "gutter-pup." The thought terrified her.

"There now, don't cry," Fiona urged, patting Eden's shoulder. "I can understand why you're upset, but why all the tears? You're making far too much of the whole thing."

Once again Fiona was right. Eden's feeble explanation couldn't possibly explain the depth of her despair. She would have to cheer up quickly if she didn't want to arouse her stepmother's suspicions. "I guess I am acting like a baby," she admitted, "but he frightened me."

"I'm quite certain he only did it for your own good."

Eden didn't have to feign her skepticism.

"Of course, he didn't have to take liberties with you," Fiona amended tactfully.

"I don't think I can face him. Could I have supper in my room tonight?" Eden asked.

Fiona frowned. "I'm surprised at you, Eden. You aren't acting like yourself at all. Are you certain you've told me everything that happened?"

Eden knew a moment of panic before she recalled the best way of handling Fiona. "No, I guess I'm not acting like myself," she said defensively, "but then I've never been manhandled before, either. I'm sorry if you're disappointed in me, but I can't—"

"Oh, Eden, *I'm* the one who's sorry!" Fiona said, instantly contrite. "It's just that you're always so brave, and you never react like a gently bred lady should. I'm simply surprised, and *pleased,* I might add, to see you're finally developing a properly delicate nature."

Eden almost gagged at the thought. The last thing she wanted to develop was a delicate nature, but it was certainly in her best interest to let Fiona believe she was. Somehow she managed to hide her revulsion. "So you'll let me have supper in my room?"

"Of course, if you feel you must, but you can't hide in here forever."

At the moment, nothing sounded more appealing, but Eden wouldn't give Lincoln Scott the satisfaction of thinking she was hiding away in shame. No, by tomorrow she would certainly feel braver and stronger. By then surely she would have the courage to face him.

And then what would happen?

Chapter Six

Linc awoke with a start. He hadn't meant to fall asleep, but for the second time that day, his body had slipped out of his control. With a curse he pushed himself up, trying to judge how long he'd slept by the position of sun outside. He guessed it must be close to suppertime.

The thought of sitting down opposite Eden at the table just now was not appealing, and he figured she probably felt a lot more apprehensive about it than he did. Of course, by now she might have told Fiona how he'd attacked her, and maybe they'd be kicking him out of here the minute Marcus and the other men got back to the ranch.

The possibility filled him with a nameless sorrow, and not just because he didn't want his best friend to know he'd betrayed his trust. Of course, he also didn't want to leave Eden, but it was even more than that. For the first time in his life, Linc had found a place he might be able to call home. Marcus had already told him part of it belonged to him, and although he couldn't accept it as an outright gift, Linc thought there was a chance he might eventually earn a place here. The vision of a home here with Eden by his side was the closest thing to heaven Lincoln Scott could imagine. He wasn't going to give it up without a fight.

But in the meantime, he knew he couldn't keep living in her house so long as Eden felt the way she did about him. The best thing right now would be to put a little distance between them. Not a lot, because he still had every intention of winning her, but enough so they weren't tripping over each other all the time.

Ignoring the twinge in his side, Linc rose from the bed and began to gather his belongings. He'd just finished stuffing them into his saddlebags when someone knocked on the bedroom door. Instantly wary, he called, "Yeah?"

"It's me," Marcus called back, coming in without waiting for an invitation. He glanced at the saddlebags in surprise. "What're you doing?"

"Packing up."

"Why?"

Linc didn't know how to reply. Did Marcus know what had happened? "Have you talked to Eden yet?" he asked reluctantly.

Understanding lighted Marcus's eyes. "I know she's pretty upset, but that don't mean you have to leave. The fact is, I'm grateful for what you did."

"Grateful?" Linc stared at him in surprise.

"Yeah, you proved once and for all that she don't stand a chance of fighting off Dirk Blaine. I reckon that's the main reason she's mad and not because you got yourself a little feel while you had

177

her pinned. Fiona don't think you should've been so rough with her, but I reckon it's for the best."

" 'A little feel'? Is that what Eden said?" Linc asked, still confused.

"I don't know what Eden said 'cause I haven't talked to her. Fiona said you put your hand on her bosom. Now that ain't exactly proper, and as her stepfather, I gotta warn you to keep your hands to yourself in the future," Marcus said with mock sternness, "but under the circumstances, I think you did the right thing. Linc, you all right?"

Linc sank down on the bed and ran a hand over his face. "Yeah, I'm . . . just a little tired," he muttered. Good Lord, she'd carried it off. She'd said she wouldn't tell Marcus and Fiona, but he'd thought she wouldn't have any choice when they saw how upset she was. He'd known they'd guess something terrible had happened and what possible explanation could she give? Personally, he'd completely forgotten about their little set-to over Dirk Blaine, but Eden hadn't. His considerable admiration for her grew even greater.

"How come you're packing your things?" Marcus asked after a minute. "Hey, you didn't think I'd run you off, did you?"

Linc managed a self-mocking grin. "I wasn't sure, but I figured it was time I gave Eden back her room, anyway. I doubt she's going to want to see my face around here for a while."

Marcus frowned. "She did say something to Fiona about having supper in her room."

"Then that settles it. I'll move down to the

bunkhouse and eat with the men from now on."

"Are you well enough for that?"

"I drove the buggy back from the picnic today, and I'll take old Caesar out for a run tomorrow. If everything goes well, you can put me to work in a day or two."

Marcus still wasn't convinced. "Won't the fellows wonder why you moved out of the house?"

"I'll tell them me and Eden had a fight. They'll be real tickled to hear it."

Marcus chuckled. "I reckon they will. It won't be far from the truth, either."

Linc only wished his problems with Eden were as simple as Marcus thought. Apparently, his expression betrayed the bleakness of his thoughts, because Marcus clapped him on the shoulder reassuringly.

"Don't worry. Eden's got a mean temper, but she don't stay mad very long. In a day or two she'll forget this ever happened."

Linc doubted this, but he managed a half-hearted grin. "I sure hope so."

"Say, you're not sweet on her, are you?" Marcus asked in amusement.

"Don't bother to act surprised. You knew I would be before you ever sent for me, didn't you?"

Marcus widened his eyes. "How could I know a thing like that?" he asked, not very convincingly. " 'Course, I wouldn't have no objections if the two of you was to hook up."

"Unfortunately, it ain't your decision," Linc replied bleakly.

179

"Now, don't fret yourself. Like I said, Eden ain't one for holding a grudge. Give her a little time to cool down, and she'll come around. She'll probably even realize what you did was for her own good."

Linc somehow managed not to groan.

"Well, look what blew in with the tumbleweeds, boys," Melancholy Jones said as Linc approached the bunkhouse, his bedroll under his arm, his saddlebags slung over one shoulder.

Jones and the other men were gathered on the porch awaiting the cook's call to supper. Linc ignored the others and spoke directly to the foreman, Jed Titus. "You got room for one more down here?"

Jed grinned broadly. "What'd you do to get tossed out of the big house?"

Linc grinned back. "They're pretty strict on manners up there. I reckon they didn't like the way I slurped my soup."

"Are you saying Miss Eden threw you out?" Melancholy asked dourly.

"I ain't saying nothing to you," Linc reminded him good-naturedly.

Jones's prodigious mustache drooped ominously. "You didn't try anything funny with her, did you?"

Linc felt the accusation to his soul, but he didn't even blink. "You don't expect me to talk about her, do you?" And of course, a gentleman never did. They all knew it and grudgingly acknowledged his civility.

Jed Titus chuckled aloud. "If you've had a falling out with Miss Eden, how come you ain't leaving the ranch altogether?"

"Marcus asked me to stay because he can always use an extra gun, but mainly I'm staying because I'm hoping the falling out with Miss Eden ain't permanent."

Melancholy sniffed derisively. "You prob'ly think if she sees you moping around, she'll feel sorry for you and take you back."

Linc shook his head solemnly. "Oh, no, Jones, that ain't my plan at all. If Miss Eden could be won with pity, you'd've caught her a long time ago."

The others hooted their approval, and while Jones sputtered in outrage, Linc could see it was mostly bluster. When Jones finally found his tongue, he glared at Linc. "Well, I hope she does take you back. It'd serve you right to get hitched up to that sharp-tongued little vixen."

Linc could appreciate the humor of the remark and smiled his approval. "Meanwhile, where can I stow my outfit?"

"There's an empty bunk down on the end you can have . . . *temporary*," Jed Titus told him slyly, pointing to the door.

Nodding his thanks, Linc strolled inside, ignoring the other men's knowing grins. He found the unoccupied bunk just where Jed had indicated. Above the bed was a row of pegs for hanging clothes and equipment. A straw-stuffed mattress had been rolled up on the bed. Linc set his burden down and unrolled it before spreading out his bedding.

Within five minutes he had emptied his saddlebags and hung up his few belongings. Although he'd lived in bunkhouses his entire adult life and made a point of owning nothing more than could be carried on the back of a horse, Linc now looked at his meager possessions in a new light. He'd been perfectly right to tell Eden he didn't have anything to offer her. Of course, his reputation would always be worth money to anyone who needed an extra gun hand, but Eden seemed unlikely to be impressed by such a thing. He drew in his breath and let it out on a weary sigh.

"Hey, Scott, you deaf or something?"

Linc turned to see Melancholy Jones scowling at him from the doorway. "The cook's been ringing his bell for half an hour."

Linc grinned at the exaggeration. "I was just waiting to see if somebody'd come to escort me in to supper."

"Well, somebody better," Jones informed him acerbically. "Might be you couldn't find your way to the cookhouse without help."

"And I reckon finding the cookhouse is the thing you do best," Linc countered. "Let's get going. I'm hungrier than a woodpecker with the headache."

Melancholy's mustache twitched suspiciously, but he humphed in disgust and stomped out, making sure Linc was right behind him.

Linc bit back a grin. At least one good thing had come of his disaster with Eden. He'd made a friend.

As usual, Fiona was already in bed when Marcus came in. He always allowed her time to undress so she could preserve her modesty. She had the covers pulled up to her breasts, and her hair hung across one shoulder in a flaxen braid. He looked quickly away, not wanting her to think he was lusting after her.

Sitting down on his side of the bed, he pulled off his boots, then carried them over to the other side of the room, where his clothes hung in an elegant mahogany wardrobe. He set the boots inside and stripped down to his long johns, carefully hanging his clothes on the pegs inside the wardrobe. With a grimace, he reached for the nightshirt he'd begun wearing after his marriage to Fiona.

He felt like a damn fool in the thing, but a man couldn't very well climb into bed buck naked as he'd been wont to do when he'd been a bachelor, certainly not when he had a wife as modest as Fiona. Making sure he was hidden by the wardrobe door, he skinned out of his long johns and pulled the nightshirt over his head. Buttoning it, he padded over to the bed, bent down, and blew out the lamp.

Fiona had thoughtfully turned down his covers, so he slid beneath them, relishing the cool, clean sheets and the soft, feather tick. Inhaling deeply, he could smell the lavender scent Fiona dabbed on herself before bed each night. His body quickened automatically, and he cursed silently. Didn't she know what she did to him with her softness and her pretty smells? His whole body ached for her, but of course he couldn't take her tonight, not when he'd just had her last night. What would she think?

She'd think he'd married her just to get her luscious body, which of course had been one of the most attractive features of their arrangement, but he certainly didn't want Fiona to know it. She'd be appalled. No, he'd made a little rule for himself not to make love to her more often than every three days. Even that seemed like it might be too frequent, but he could hardly stand to wait even that long, and since she hadn't complained, he supposed she didn't mind too much.

Sleep came hard on the off nights, though, lying so near her, smelling her and remembering what she felt like beneath him. A man could go crazy. Marcus closed his eyes in the darkness and prayed for strength.

Several minutes passed, and Marcus thought he might actually survive when Fiona broke the silence.

"I'm concerned about Eden."

"Why? She seemed fine at supper."

"Didn't you notice how quiet she was?" Fiona turned to face him in the dark.

"Texans don't talk much when they eat," he reminded her. He thought she should understand that by now, as long as she'd lived here herself.

"But she hardly said a word all evening, either."

"She's probably still stewing about her fuss with Linc."

"Eden is never quiet when she's angry, though. If she were 'stewing', she would have also been reminding us of what a blackguard he is. She never conceals her feelings, but she was concealing them tonight."

"What do you think is wrong?" Marcus asked, beginning to share her concern.

"I don't believe Eden told us everything that happened between her and Mr. Scott."

"What else could've . . . ?" His voice trailed off as he thought of a very unpleasant possibility. "You don't think they . . . ? Linc wouldn't . . . *Eden* wouldn't."

"I certainly hope not, but Eden was much more upset than her explanation justified. When I found her, she was shut up in her room, and she'd been crying for quite a while. I can't imagine anything else that would disturb her so."

"That son of a bitch. I thought he was my friend, and here he—"

"Marcus, we don't know anything for certain," she reminded him, laying a hand on his arm. She touched him so rarely, he felt it to his toes and was momentarily distracted from his fury. "We must believe that if Mr. Scott had forced Eden, she would have told us. She would have told *you* particularly so you could deal with the situation

185

appropriately."

"Yeah, like cutting off his pecker and sticking it down his throat—"

"Marcus!" Fiona chided, and he was instantly contrite. For a minute, he'd forgotten to whom he was talking. "Perhaps he didn't force her at all."

"What are you talking about?"

"Well, sometimes, if the woman loves the man or finds him particularly attractive, she . . . she might welcome it."

Marcus was glad for the darkness and figured Fiona was, too. Good God, what a thing for her to say to him! "You think Eden might've *let* him?"

"It's possible. She's always been a reckless girl, and I'm sure you've noticed how attracted they are to each other."

"But if she let him, why would she be mad about it later?"

"Perhaps she found the experience . . . unpleasant."

As much as Marcus hated to admit it, Fiona's theory made perfect sense. "That son of a—" This time he caught himself. "I'll stomp all over him till there ain't nothing left but a greasy spot. I'll—"

"I don't think it would be wise of you to take any action whatsoever at this time."

"What? You tell me some no-account drifter took advantage of my girl and—"

"That 'no-account drifter' is your best friend, and your 'girl' hasn't uttered one word of complaint. Remember, this is all speculation on our part. The only thing we can do now is wait and see what happens. Perhaps Eden and Mr. Scott will work things out for themselves."

"Well, I'm gonna have me a little palaver with Mr. Scott and—"

"Don't you dare! What if we're wrong? What if nothing happened? You'll look like a fool and offend a good friend into the bargain."

She was right, of course, but doing nothing wasn't Marcus's style. If he had something stuck in his craw, he liked to spit it out. "Why don't you try to get Eden to tell you then."

"I will. Meantime, we must behave as if nothing were amiss."

Fiona's hand was still on his arm. She laid her head on his shoulder. "Eden is very fortunate to have such a loving stepfather." She slid her hand around his bicep and snuggled closer until her breasts pressed against him. His breath caught as his body quickened once again. "Remember what I told you," she whispered. "If a woman loves the man and is attracted to him, she welcomes his advances."

Marcus hardened instantly and his heart slammed against his ribs as if it would burst from his chest. God in heaven, didn't she know what she was doing to him? All this talk about sex had gotten him stirred up and now this. It was almost as if she were trying to tempt him, but of course she would never do a thing like that consciously, not Fiona. She'd probably faint if she knew what he was thinking right now.

"I . . ." He had to clear his throat. "Thanks for

telling me this about Eden. If you want me to do anything, talk to her or Linc, just say the word." Relieved to hear his voice sounded almost normal, he eased out of Fiona's grasp and rolled over on his side, giving her his back. His body throbbed like one giant toothache. Only forty-eight more hours to wait, he told himself grimly.

"There she is," Melancholy reported. He and Linc were sitting on the bunkhouse porch, their chairs tipped back against the wall, enjoying the Sunday afternoon sunshine. Jones was whittling while Linc worked on braiding himself a new reata.

Linc glanced up to see Eden coming out of the ranch house. The sight of her hit him with the force of a blow and for a moment he couldn't seem to get his breath. She wore the same riding outfit she'd been wearing the first time he'd ever seen her, the time she'd saved his life. A flat, black, Spanish-style hat sat pertly on her head, hiding most of her hair and shading her eyes so he couldn't see her expression, couldn't even tell where she was looking.

"Uh-oh, she's heading this way," Melancholy informed him unnecessarily. Linc could see perfectly well where she was heading. From the purposeful way she strode across the yard, her full breasts jiggling provocatively beneath her bodice, she meant business, too.

Linc swallowed to moisten a dry throat and

steeled himself for a confrontation. He'd had forty-eight hours to think things over—forty-eight hours during which Eden had studiously avoided him—and he'd decided he wasn't going to leave, no matter what kind of a fuss she put up. She was his woman, and he was going to stay right where he was until he could claim her.

Linc let his front chair legs drop with a thunk, and he prepared to rise as she approached, but at the last second she veered away without so much as a glance in their direction.

Melancholy whistled softly. "She's got a bee in her bonnet, all right. What do you reckon she's up to?"

They found out soon enough. Eden stopped right in front of where Jed Titus lounged with several of the other cowboys farther down the porch.

" 'Afternoon, Jed," she said brightly.

" 'Afternoon, Miss Eden," he replied, obviously aware she was up to something and delighted to be included in her plans.

"Jed, I'd like to go for a ride this afternoon, but you know how Marcus worries about me. He won't let me go alone, so I was wondering if you'd go with me."

"Well, now, Miss Eden," Jed said, lifting his hat to scratch his thatch of carrot-colored hair, "I'd be purely honored to accompany you, but don't you think you'd have more fun if you took a younger man instead? I'm sure any one of the boys would be tickled to go."

The men sitting with Jed all murmured their

189

willingness. Melancholy Jones let his own chair drop and cleared his throat importantly. "Linc'd be right proud to escort you, wouldn't you, Linc?"

Linc could have cheerfully strangled him, but Eden pretended she hadn't even heard the offer. Instead she turned her brilliant smile full force on Jed Titus. "If I wanted somebody else to take me, I would've asked him," she purred. "I want you, Jed. Pretty please?"

Now Linc knew an urge to strangle Eden. She was giving Jed the same look she'd given Linc when she'd been teaching him the finer points of courting. He knew it, and she knew he knew it.

"Well, now, how could any man turn down an offer like that?" Jed asked of the group at large, and without waiting for a reply, he rose from his seat and walked off with Eden toward the barn.

As they passed, Jed shot Linc a sly grin and gave him a broad wink while Eden simply ignored him. Linc cursed himself, knowing perfectly well he had no reason to be jealous of Jed Titus, who clearly thought of Eden as a daughter. All the same, he couldn't deny the bitter gall burning in his throat.

In a few minutes they emerged from the barn, Eden mounted on her pretty little mare and Jed riding beside her on a piebald gelding. As the two of them rode off, Melancholy stopped his whittling for a moment and stared after them.

"If she was my girl," he remarked, "I sure as hell wouldn't let her go riding off with another man."

* * *

Jed and Eden rode for a while in silence while Eden savored her victory. She'd certainly shown Lincoln Scott. Walking across that ranch yard had taken just about every ounce of courage she possessed, but now he knew she wasn't afraid of him and she certainly wasn't going to hide in her room for the rest of her life, overcome with shame.

No, she'd proved she could hold her head up and successfully pretend Lincoln Scott didn't even exist. Unfortunately, the problem with ignoring him so thoroughly was that she didn't get to see his reaction to being ignored. She wished she could ask Jed if he'd happened to notice, but of course she couldn't.

Instead she determined to enjoy herself. Today the broad Texas sky was filled with billowing clouds, and over to the east a pair of hawks swooped and soared in a freewheeling game of tag. The rolling grassland sparkled like a giant emerald, and in the distance, Eden could see a clump of cattle grazing lazily. She felt a fierce pride in all she surveyed, knowing it was here because of her father's courage. It would remain because of hers.

Jed chuckled, startling her out of her reverie. "You sure are a piece of work, Miss Eden."

"What are you talking about, Jed?" she asked warily.

"I'm talking about how you snubbed poor ol' Linc back there. It worked, too. I don't think I've ever seen a man with his nose more out of joint."

"I'm sure I don't know what you're talking about," she tried, hoping she might dredge a few more details out of him.

"Come on, girl, this is Jed you're talking to. I used to wipe your nose for you when you was a young'un. You can't fool me for a minute. You made one mistake, though."

"What?" she asked before she could stop herself. She pretended not to see Jed's knowing smirk.

"If you wanted to make him jealous, you should've invited Melancholy or one of the other men. He ain't likely to worry too much about an old bangtail like me."

"You're not an old bangtail," Eden protested, managing to conceal her uneasiness. She certainly couldn't explain that she'd chosen Jed *because* he posed no threat. After her encounter with Scott, the thought of flirting with another man and possibly even fending off his advances appalled her. She hadn't examined her feelings too closely—they were still much too tender—but she simply wasn't ready to deal with men just yet. She gave Jed what she hoped was a guileless smile. "Really, Jed, you're quite a prize if you want to know the truth. I don't know why some woman hasn't snatched you up years ago."

"You ain't gonna get me off the track with a bunch of flattery," he chided. "I want to know what happened between you and young Scott and when you're gonna put him out of his misery."

"What do you mean?" she asked apprehensively.

"I mean he's been moping around the bunkhouse like he's trying to put Melancholy out of a job. Anybody'd think the two of them was having a contest to see who could look the most miserable, and so far, Linc's winning."

Well, now, this was fascinating news, and Eden was duly fascinated. "I can't imagine why he'd be so sad," she ventured.

Jed snorted his disgust. "Try to remember who you're talking to, girl. We both know you kicked Linc out. He won't say a word about it, but knowing you, I figure you got into a tizzy about something silly that don't amount to a hill of beans, and—"

"You don't know anything about it," Eden snapped, mortification burning her cheeks.

"I know everything about it. Us redheads understand each other, don't we?" he asked slyly.

"It's not something silly," she allowed, unable to hold his probing gaze. "It's . . . I have reason to believe Lincoln really doesn't care for me."

"Are you loco?" Jed demanded. "The boy's half-crazy about you. You should see his face when somebody mentions your name."

"Perhaps he's got a guilty conscience for treating me so badly," she suggested.

Jed stared at her in amazement. "You can't really believe that. Look, Eden, I don't know what you two fought about, but I can tell you for sure that if you sent him packing because you thought he didn't love you, you're dead wrong."

Their horses had slowed to a walk, and Eden reined her mare to a complete stop. Jed did the same and waited expectantly while she digested what he'd said. Could he be right? Was it possible Linc really did love her?

She tried to remember exactly what Linc had said to her two days ago. At the time she'd been sure he was trying to get out of marrying her, but on the other hand, she'd been awfully upset and not thinking straight about anything. Could she possibly have misunderstood him? Certainly he'd denied her accusation that he was unwilling.

"He told me he's only staying around because he hopes you'll take him back," Jed offered.

"He did?" Eden could hardly allow herself to believe it.

"He sure did. Honey, maybe if the two of you just had yourselves a little talk, you could settle the whole thing, and we could have us a wedding at the Paradise after all."

"I . . . Maybe you're right, Jed," Eden said thoughtfully. It would be awkward, and she had no idea how she would open such a conversation, but if Jed was right . . .

"Hey, do you smell smoke?" Jed asked suddenly, lifting his nose to scent the air.

Eden sniffed and thought she caught the faint scent of burning. "What could it be?" she asked, briefly considering the terrifying prospect of a grassfire and then discarding it. The conditions simply weren't right.

"Your eyes are better than mine," Jed said. "Do you see anything?"

She squinted into the distance, scanning the horizon for a telltale plume, and then she saw it. "There," she said, pointing at the barely visible trail.

"Let's go take a little look-see," Jed said, kicking his horse into motion.

"What could it be?" Eden asked again above the pounding of their horses' hooves.

"Looks like a branding fire to me, but honest men rest on the Sabbath," he called back.

Eden felt a frisson of excitement. They might catch some rustlers in the act.

The smoke came from behind a hill which all but hid it from those at the ranch. If she and Jed hadn't gone for a ride, no one from the Paradise would have noticed it. Jed led them around so they approached from the blind side. He reined in and motioned for Eden to stop, too.

"I'm going to get a closer look, and I want you to wait here for me," he told her. "If there's any trouble, you hightail it back to the ranch."

"What do you mean by 'trouble'?"

"I mean if they see me, which they shouldn't. I'm only planning to find out who's there, then we'll go for help. You understand?"

Eden nodded, apprehension twisting in her stomach. "Be careful, Jed."

He smiled grimly and kneed his horse around. Eden watched until he was out of sight. Her heart was pounding so hard she wondered if the rustlers could hear it, and she held her breath every few seconds, listening for Jed's progress. Only then did she recall the derringer she had tucked in her pocket. What a ninny she was to have forgotten it! If Jed needed help, she at least had her gun.

The breeze died, and the blazing sun beat down. Sweat formed on her upper lip and trickled between her breasts. She shifted in the saddle, vainly seeking a more comfortable position. What was taking so long? Eden fought an urge to go after Jed, knowing she might only succeed in betraying him to the rustlers, if rustlers they were.

Finding a handkerchief, she dabbed at her face, wishing she had thought to bring along a canteen. Then she heard it, men's voices raised in anger. She couldn't make out the words, but she knew they must've spotted Jed.

She'd already turned her mare when she heard the shots. They came almost at once, so close together she couldn't even tell how many had been fired, and then an ominous silence. Dear Lord, if Jed were still alive, he'd keep firing, wouldn't he? She hesitated. Should she go to help him? What if he were wounded? But he'd told her to go to the ranch, and what could she do with just a two-shot pistol?

She was still debating when she heard the clatter of horse's hooves. For one wild moment, she thought it was Jed, returning to catch her before she could ride away; then she realized the sound was of a horse galloping off in the other direction. Rising in her stirrups, she could just make out the dusty cloud the rider was churning up in his effort to escape.

"Jed!" she cried, her decision made. His assailant had fled, and if Jed was wounded, she couldn't leave him here. Spurring her mare, she leaned low in the saddle as the little horse bolted off, following Jed's trail.

Coming around the hillside, she first saw the fire and the cows with their calves, a half-dozen of them milling about in terror, the calves bleeding from the mouth. Someone had cut their tongues so they couldn't nurse anymore. That way no one would see them sucking on a cow with a different brand. Then she saw Jed's horse, dancing skittishly beside Jed's prone figure.

"Jed!" she screamed, terrified when he didn't move. Sawing on the reins, she brought her mare to a sliding halt and vaulted from the saddle. "Jed!" Catching up her skirts, she raced to his side.

He still didn't move, and when she dropped to her knees beside him, she saw the neat, round hole in his forehead. "No, Jed!" she screamed in protest, but his eyes stared sightlessly up at her. Tears blinded her, and she choked on a sob. Why had she let him go? Why hadn't she insisted they both return to the ranch for help. Why . . . ?

"Where in hell did you come from?"

Eden jumped and looked up to find Alvin Blaine glaring down at her. Her anguish turned instantly to fury. "You killed him!" she shrieked, reaching for the gun she'd hidden in her pocket.

She jerked it free and tried to aim, but Blaine's boot struck her arm and the pistol went flying. Eden cried out in pain, clutching her arm as she cast about frantically for another weapon. Where was Jed's gun?

Before she could find it, Blaine grabbed her by the scruff of her neck and jerked her to her feet.

"You bastard!" she cried, whirling on him in a flurry of arms and legs. She lashed out, heedless of the pain in her arm, but she landed only one blow before Blaine smacked her. Stars burst before her eyes, and she plummeted to the ground.

Her ears rang, and the whole side of her face went numb. She fought a wave of nausea, but she struggled upright, managing to reach a sitting position before Blaine's voice stopped her.

"Stay right where you are, girlie."

Half-blinded by pain, she fought to bring him into focus. "You're a murderer!" she gasped. "And a rustler, too! I saw you. You're finished around here, now. They'll hang you —"

"Not if you don't tell anybody," he replied smugly. His feral grin made Eden's flesh crawl.

"You can't stop me!"

"Oh, maybe I can."

"You wouldn't kill a woman," Eden informed him with more confidence than she felt at the moment. Not many men would harm a woman, but at the moment Alvin Blaine looked like he might well be one of them.

"No, I reckon I wouldn't," he said, to her immense relief. "Brother Dirk would have my hide if I did. Seems he's got some plans for you."

"No!" Eden said in a hoarse whisper, instinctively sidling away from him.

"Yeah, he's been telling me for a long time what a sweet little piece you are and how much fun he's going to have breaking you to saddle. I been trying to talk him out of it, but now things've changed. Now I reckon we're gonna need you on our side."

"I'll never be on your side!"

"Oh, a few days with Dirk'll change your mind." Blaine's pale eyes glittered, and for the first time Eden knew real terror. "First he'll slap you around a little to take the fight out of you. Then he'll strip you down and tie you to the bed so's you can't give him no trouble. Then he'll—".

"No!" she cried, covering her ears. She scrambled to her feet, knowing she had to get away, but Blaine was too fast for her. Catching her around the waist, he pulled her against him. The sickening stench of sour sweat again brought the gorge to her throat, and she actually gagged as he breathed out with his fetid breath every obscene detail of what his brother intended to do to her.

She tried not to listen, struggling against his grip, but he wrapped his other arm around her throat, cutting off her wind until she slumped, helpless, against him. Tears ran unheeded down her face as he poured out his filth, desecrating the act she had shared with Linc in love.

"And if you still won't see things our way when Dirk's done with you, we'll start sending in the rest of our boys. I reckon they'd all like a little turn with Eden Campbell."

Eden shuddered in horror. "Don't . . . do . . .

this . . ." she gasped. "They'll . . . hang . . . you . . ."

"Not if you're Dirk's wife," he replied with maddening calm. "We'll marry you up with Dirk and won't nobody be able to do a thing about the way he treats you."

"I'll never . . . marry him!"

"You'll be glad to when we're finished," he grunted, releasing her at last. "Get on your horse, and let's get out of here." He gave her a shove in the right direction.

"Hold it right there!"

Lincoln! Eden staggered, trying not to fall, and turned toward his voice. He sat his stallion, pistol raised and pointing at Alvin Blaine's heart.

Behind her, Blaine muttered a curse, but instead of obeying Linc's command, he lunged for her. Linc's gun exploded, but he must have missed. Once again Blaine's arms closed around her, and once again she fought until she felt the barrel of Blaine's Colt pressed against her temple.

"Let me go, or I'll kill her," Blaine shouted. Eden thought she heard a note of panic in his voice, but her blood roared so loudly in her ears, she couldn't be sure.

"That'd be a stupid thing to do, because then you wouldn't have anybody to hide behind," Linc replied.

The coldness in his voice sent chills up Eden's spine, and she felt the jolt of Blaine's reaction, too.

"I'm taking her with me," Blaine tried, now unmistakably panicked.

"How far do you think you'll get? Every man in the county'll come after you when they find out you've got her. Your only chance is to give it up—"

Bang! Blaine's gun blasted, and for an instant Eden thought she must be dead. Then she realized the gray fog was powder smoke. Blaine had fired at Linc and was dragging her toward his horse. Was Linc hit? Tears blurred her vision, but when she found his stallion through the smoky haze, she saw he was no longer in the saddle.

"Lincoln!" she cried in terror, clawing at Blaine's arm and digging in her heels.

Blaine swore and lifted her off her feet with a strength born of desperation. She kicked furiously, aiming for his shins, trying at least to trip him up as he lurched clumsily for his horse.

A gun exploded, not Blaine's gun. *Linc!* Blaine's horse danced skittishly away, and Blaine swore again. In the next second she was on the ground, and Blaine's gun barked over her head, once, twice, and Linc returned fire.

Instinctively, Eden curled into a ball, covering her head. Linc's gun spit flame again, and Blaine cried out.

"You bastard!" he screeched.

Eden looked up to see a crimson stain spreading on his shirt front, but her relief was short lived. His wild eyes found her crouching at his feet, and with a maniacal laugh, he took aim at her.

She screamed, or tried to, as the gun exploded,

but no flame belched from it and she felt no impact. Instead Blaine's head jerked back, and he sat down abruptly, a startled expression on his face. Part of her realized the dark hole in his forehead was the cause of his strange behavior, but the rest of her knew a hysterical urge to laugh.

She watched, mesmerized, as the gun slipped from his hand and he slumped over sideways, still looking completely astonished.

"Eden? Are you all right?"

Linc had a habit of asking her that question at the most inconvenient times, she thought wildly.

"Eden?" Now *he* sounded panicky, she noted with an odd detachment.

She tried to call to him, to reassure him, but her body wouldn't respond. In fact, she couldn't seem to move at all. She heard the sound of running feet, then Linc was beside her.

"Are you hurt? Did he hit you?"

With gentle hands he turned her over, seeking wounds that weren't there. Or perhaps she really had been shot. That would certainly explain why she felt so weak, why she couldn't speak, and why everything seemed to be happening at a great distance.

She stared up at him, marveling at how upset he seemed. She wanted to reassure him, but her voice still wouldn't work right. All she could manage was, "Linc?"

"Yes, sweetheart, it's me. It's all right. He can't hurt you anymore."

Hot tears welled in her eyes. "He said . . . he

was going to take me . . ."

"He can't take you now." Linc's arms closed around her, gathering her to him. He felt so blessedly real and strong and familiar.

"Oh, Linc," she sobbed, clinging to him. He held her fast, cradling her while she wept against his chest. "He killed . . . Jed . . ."

"Yes, I know," he crooned, running his hands over her back.

"I . . . I wanted to help . . . but Jed made me wait. . . . He said I should go back to the ranch but . . . They shot at him, Linc, and he didn't shoot back!"

"I know, I know." He patted her soothingly, but she couldn't be soothed.

"I knew he'd been hit. I was going to go for help, but then I saw somebody ride away. Linc, he rode away, I know he did!"

"I saw somebody, too. There must've been two of them."

Two of them! She'd never thought of that. "I . . . I went to help Jed, but he was . . . was . . ."

"Shhh, don't think about it." Linc's arms tightened, as if he could protect her from the horror.

"Then Blaine grabbed me and—"

"Blaine? Was that Dirk Blaine's brother?"

Eden knew a moment of surprise until she realized Linc had never seen Alvin before. "Yes, he . . . he said he was going to take me back to Dirk to . . . to . . ."

"Don't say it," Linc commanded. "Don't even think about it. He can't hurt you or anyone else

203

again, and the only place you're going is home to the Paradise. Come on."

He began to rise, taking her with him. She wanted nothing more than to go home, but her legs couldn't seem to hold her. When she stumbled, he murmured a curse and lifted her like a child, high against his chest.

She wrapped her arms around his neck, inhaling his blessedly familiar scent. "Oh, Linc, I'm so glad you came."

"So am I," he whispered hoarsely. "Do you think you can ride?"

"I . . ." She had no idea.

Reading her uncertainty, he whistled shrilly, and Caesar came running. He set Eden in the saddle and mounted behind her, settling her across his lap. When she realized his intention of riding away, she cried out in protest.

"What about Jed?"

"We'll have to bring a wagon back for him. Meanwhile, I want to get you back to the ranch in case that other fellow went for help."

Feeling a renewed terror, Eden nodded and buried her face against Linc's shoulder so she wouldn't have to see Jed's poor body lying so forlornly on the prairie.

As they rode, her mind raced. There would be war now. Blood had been shed on both sides, and Dirk Blaine wouldn't take the killing of his brother lightly. He'd also deny that Alvin had been branding Paradise calves and claim Jed had attacked without provocation. None of the people who knew Jed would believe such a story, but outsiders might, and Dirk could drum up some sympathy and perhaps even some supporters.

And they would all be after Lincoln Scott.

She and Linc were almost home when her mind cleared enough to settle on the one unsolved mystery of the whole afternoon. She studied Linc's face for a moment, somewhat surprised to find him so calm, but perhaps he was only hiding his feelings as he so often did. "Linc, how did you find me?"

She thought he stiffened slightly. "I was following you," he admitted reluctantly.

"You were following me and Jed?" she asked in amazement. "Why?"

He didn't answer immediately. "Marcus asked me to."

"He asked you to follow us?" she demanded skeptically.

"He asked me to keep an eye on you."

"So following us was your idea?" she prodded.

He nodded reluctantly.

She wanted to ask him why, to demand an explanation, but this wasn't exactly the time for such a discussion. Besides, she already knew the answer. Poor Jed had told her just before he died. Right up to the last, he'd been thinking of her happiness. Tears stung her eyes, but she blinked them away. If she started crying now, she wouldn't be able to stop. Somehow she'd wait until they got back to the ranch.

Somehow she did.

* * *

Dirk Blaine hadn't been home long when the rider came racing into the yard with news that brother Alvin had shot the Paradise foreman. Dirk had spent the night at the area's excuse for a brothel, a hog ranch located several miles out of town and known for its rotgut whiskey and aging whores. This morning Dirk had awakened with a pounding head and a woman he couldn't remember ever having seen before. God knew, he never wanted to see her again. She'd probably given him the French pox into the bargain.

Dirk took the news of the shooting with equanimity and even amusement. "Well, if that ain't a shot in the eye. Here Alvin's been giving me hell for stirring up trouble, and he goes and shoots their foreman. What happened?" he asked, momentarily forgetting his headache.

"Mr. Blaine was showing me how to cover the Paradise brand when this fellow comes riding up," the cowboy reported. He was new, and Dirk couldn't quite recall his name. He looked scared shitless, too, which probably meant they'd have to get rid of him. Alvin would be furious at him for running off anyway.

"You mean he just came out shooting?" Dirk asked in amazement.

"Well, no, he was sneaking around. We figured he was spying, trying to see what we was doing, but Mr. Blaine spotted him and yelled at him. He yelled something back, something about how now he had the proof he'd been needing, so Mr. Blaine pulls out his gun and plugs the fellow right between the eyes."

Dirk whistled in admiration. "Didn't Titus even get off a shot?"

"Well, yeah, I reckon so. It happened awful fast," the boy allowed, wiping his brow with his forearm. He looked oddly pale, as if he might pass out. "Look, Mr. Blaine, I didn't sign on for no killing. I want to draw my wages."

Dirk snorted his disgust. "I reckon you might as well be gone when Alvin gets back. He won't take kindly to you leaving him like that."

"He . . . he sent me back to bring you word," the boy tried, but he wasn't very convincing.

"Pack your gear and come up to the house when you're ready to go," Dirk told him in disgust, rubbing his bristling chin. His mouth tasted like the bottom of an outhouse and the sunlight made his eyes feel like they were going to pop out. He spat contemptuously as the cowboy scurried off to the bunkhouse to gather his gear. "We'll be better off without that son of a bitch," he muttered as he went back into the house. At least Alvin would be pleased to find him gone.

"I can't believe it," Marcus said grimly when Linc had told him and the other men the story. The instant he and Eden had arrived at the ranch, Fiona had taken Eden into the house and put her to bed. Marcus and the other men stood in the yard while Linc explained what had happened.

Linc had barely known Jed Titus, but in their brief acquaintance, he had come to like and respect the man. He could see from the other men's reactions that they felt they had lost a good friend.

"We owe you, partner," Melancholy said. "If you hadn't've been there, Blaine would've got away with killing Jed and carried off Miss Eden, too."

The reminder brought the red tide of fury roiling up in Linc again, but he resisted the urge to surrender to his anger. He had important things to do now. "I owe you, too. You were the one who suggested I follow them this afternoon." He refused to consider what might've happened if he'd been too proud to go traipsing after Eden. If Melancholy hadn't shamed him into it . . . "We'd better get a wagon hitched up. I figure that fellow'll bring Dirk Blaine and his crew, and I don't want them carrying Alvin's body away and driving off those cattle before somebody else gets to see them."

"You're right. Melancholy, I want you to ride around to the neighboring ranches and tell them what's happened. We'll leave everything just the way it is until they get there so they can see for themselves. Linc'll take the rest of us out there to stand guard."

Linc followed Marcus to the corral for a fresh horse. On the way, Marcus clapped Linc on the back. "I can't tell you how grateful I am for what you did for Eden." He managed a sad smile. "At least your troubles with her are over now. You'll be her hero."

"Hero?" Linc echoed incredulously. "Are you crazy? Marcus, I killed a man right in front of her. She'll never want to see me again."

Chapter Seven

Dirk Blaine stood on his front porch and squinted into the distance, trying to make out the approaching rider. He knew a moment of irritation when he realized the man wasn't Alvin. Where in the hell was his brother? Hours had passed since the cowboy had brought word of the trouble with the Paradise foreman. Dirk had expected his brother to ride in even before the cowboy had left after collecting his gear and his pay, but of course he hadn't. Now Dirk was cursing himself for not having inquired more closely as to where the shooting had taken place. Without that information, he couldn't even go looking for his brother.

Not that Alvin needed anybody to go looking for him, Dirk reminded himself. Alvin had taken care of that bastard Jed Titus, and he could handle anything else that came along, too. Probably his horse had gone lame or something. Yes, that would explain his delay in getting back. Nothing could happen to Alvin.

Meanwhile, Dirk had to deal with whoever was riding up to his front door. Dirk's hangover still lingered, and he felt little patience for the task. Scowling, arms crossed belligerently over his chest, he waited for the rider to rein up in front of the house.

" 'Afternoon," the fellow said. He was young, probably not even twenty, but he had a hard look about him Dirk recognized. The twin Colts strapped to his thighs told Dirk all he needed to know. "The name's Garth Hamilton. You Mr. Blaine?"

Dirk nodded.

"You sent for me."

The boy was entirely too cocky for Dirk's taste. "I never sent for nobody."

Hamilton frowned in confusion. "I got the telegram right here. It's signed 'Alvin Blaine.' "

Suddenly, Dirk remembered. This was the gunfighter Alvin had hired to kill Marcus Pauling because Dirk had failed to do so. His irritation swelled into anger. "Alvin ain't here."

"You his son or something?"

"Brother," Dirk snapped.

"Then you must've known I was coming," he insisted. "He said he has a job for me."

"I knew," Dirk said, looking the boy over contemptuously, "but he said he'd sent for a man, not a snot-nosed kid."

Hamilton's downy cheeks went scarlet, and his baby blue eyes narrowed with fury. "Well, even if you ain't heard of me, your brother has, and he knows I ain't no kid."

"Maybe he does and maybe he don't. We'll let him speak for himself when he gets back."

The two men stared at each other for a long moment. The rules of hospitality demanded Dirk invite Hamilton to get down from his horse and find himself a place in the bunkhouse, but he waited long enough before making the offer to let the kid sweat a little.

"Ace!" Dirk called to his foreman, who had been watching the exchange from the other side of the yard. "Show this fellow where to stow his gear."

"Thanks," Hamilton grunted sarcastically, kneeing his horse around and heading for the corral.

Fuming, Dirk went back into the one-room cabin that served as a combination home and office for him and his brother. The place sure could use a woman's touch, Dirk thought grimly, glancing around at the unmade bunks and the clothes and gear scattered on the floor. A cobweb hung in one corner and dust had congregated in the corners. Yeah, once he got little Miss Eden Campbell broken to his bed, he'd set her to work scrubbing his floors. The thought made him grin.

A little while later, he was lying on his bunk trying to sleep off the remnants of his hangover when he heard Ace shouting from outside. "Riders coming, boss!"

"What the hell is it this time?" he muttered, dragging himself out of his bunk and over to the door, not even bothering to straighten his clothes or his hair. Who would be coming to see him at suppertime on a Sunday evening? And why in the hell wasn't Alvin back yet? If he hadn't shown up by the time they'd eaten, he'd send Ace out to see what he could turn up.

Squinting against the fading sunlight, Dirk recognized one of the riders as his neighbor, Gus Olsen. The burly German sat his horse like a sack of potatoes, Dirk noted in derision. Olsen had three other men with him. One was a fellow rancher, and the other two were ordinary cowboys. They rode purposefully into the yard, their expressions solemn, and for the first time Dirk knew a twinge of concern about his brother. Had he been caught?

Dirk lifted his hand in greeting. "Funny time for a social call," he remarked as the men brought their horses to a halt.

"Ain't a social call," Olsen said, crossing his beefy hands on the saddle horn. "I'm afraid we've got some bad news for you."

"Bad news?" Dirk echoed, breaking out into a sweat. Somehow he managed a small, unconcerned smile.

"Yeah, about your brother. Seems he and Jed Titus got into an argument because Alvin and another fellow was trying to put your brand on some Paradise calves."

"The hell you say. Whoever told you a story like that is a damned liar! My brother never—"

"We saw the calves," Olsen said doggedly. "And we saw the bodies."

"Bodies?" Dirk's sweat turned cold. There should only have been one body, unless that damn cowboy lied!

"Yeah. Alvin killed Jed Titus, and when Eden Campbell went to help—"

"Eden? What in the hell was she doing there?"

213

Dirk demanded in confusion.

"She and Jed were out riding together when they saw the smoke from Alvin's branding fire. She went to help Jed, and Alvin threatened to kidnap her so she couldn't tell what had happened. Luckily, another one of the Paradise's men came along before he could. The two of them shot it out. I'm sorry to tell you, but your brother's dead."

Dirk felt as if the ground had opened beneath him. Alvin dead? He couldn't be, not Alvin! "This is all a damn lie!" he blustered. "If Alvin's dead, where's his body?"

"Marcus Pauling took both bodies back to his place. He said to tell you you can come and get it any time."

Dirk swore viciously. "You're damn right I'll go get it, and I'll take my men with me! I don't know who told you a story like this, but my brother ain't no rustler. If they killed him, it was an ambush."

"Dirk," Olsen said patiently, "we saw the proof. Marcus sent for every rancher around so we could see for ourselves."

"I notice he didn't send for me!" Dirk shouted. "He set it up to look bad so his man wouldn't get blamed for killing Alvin."

"You can believe what you want," Olsen said. "The rest of us believe Marcus. Like I said, you can go get your brother any time."

Olsen kicked his horse into motion, and the others followed suit, riding away at a slow trot. Dirk watched them go as if through a haze. Alvin, dead? It couldn't be true! What would he do now?

Ace came loping over, having overheard the conversation from his position in front of the bunk-house. "Do you reckon it happened the way they said?" he asked, his homely face twisted into a frown.

Dirk barely heard him. "That damn cowboy. If he hadn't've left Alvin, this wouldn't've happened. And that Campbell bitch! What'd she have to do with it, anyways?" For a moment grief and rage overwhelmed him, shutting out everything else as he pondered his great loss.

"Boss? *Boss?*"

At last Ace's urgent appeal registered and brought Dirk out of his fog. He shook himself. "Tell the boys to get their guns. We're riding to the Paradise."

Dirk turned abruptly and strode into the house. Ace followed on his heels. "We can't just ride in there shooting."

"They killed Alvin!" Dirk shouted, jerking a Winchester from the gun rack.

"And they'll kill the rest of us if we give them a chance! We've got to think of a plan."

A plan. Of course they'd need a plan. Alvin would've thought of one, but Alvin wasn't here. Rage boiled up inside of Dirk until he couldn't see straight. All they'd ever had was each other, and now Dirk was alone. What would Alvin do in his place?

He certainly wouldn't let his killer get away. Dirk broke open the rifle and checked the loads. "Tell the boys to saddle up. We won't ride in shooting, but we're going for my brother, and if nothing else we'll find out who killed him."

"What about the new man?"

Dirk hesitated. As much as he wanted to send the little shitkicker packing, they might well need his gun. He must have a reputation, or Alvin wouldn't have sent for him. "We'll take him along."

"What are you going to say?"

"Say about what?" Dirk snapped, closing the rifle with a jerk.

"About what happened. They're calling your brother a rustler."

Dirk swore again. Alvin would know exactly what to say. He was always so clever. "I'll . . . I'll think of something."

Linc toyed with his food, unable to swallow more than a few mouthfuls of the delicious supper Fiona had set before him. How had he ever let Marcus talk him into taking his meal with the family? But Marcus had insisted, saying Eden wanted him there. She didn't seem like she did. She'd hardly glanced at him, keeping her red-rimmed eyes lowered to the plate she'd barely touched.

It was just as well, because he knew what he'd see in her green eyes if she did look up at him. He'd seen it before, in another girl's eyes, the time he'd been working down near Uvalde. Her name was Susie, and her father owned the store in the tiny town near the ranch where Linc had been helping to patrol for rustlers. A pretty girl, she'd enjoyed the attentions of the cowboys who were all smitten with her, but she encouraged none of them until Linc. Why she chose him above the others, he never knew, but she had, and her parents had welcomed him into their parlor when he came calling.

He and Susie had courted chastely, furtively holding hands in the evening shadows of the porch, and they'd talked of a future in which he would have a place of his own with a small house for Susie to keep for him. All of it had seemed possible, a dream that might really come true, until the trouble.

One day Linc and the other men caught some rustlers. They disposed of the men in typical frontier fashion, hanging them from the nearest cottonwood. No one faulted them for dispensing justice so cavalierly, no one except the brother of one of the hanged men. He rode into town a few weeks later seeking revenge, and he found Linc.

When Linc closed his eyes, he could still recall the scene vividly: the blazing sun, the gunman standing alone in the dusty street; the shouted challenge, the burst of flame, and his own gun bucking in his hand. Then the other man falling, and a crimson stain in the dirt.

Linc could still taste the metallic bite of fear and feel the cold sweat beading on his skin. He'd never killed a man face-to-face before, and the act sickened him. What a tragic waste. He hadn't even known the man's name.

That night he went to Susie's house, seeking a haven and someone in whom he could confide his feelings. Instead her father met him at the door and ordered him away. Susie stood behind her father, staring at Linc as if she'd never seen him before, a look of abject horror in her eyes.

"My daughter doesn't want any truck with a killer," her father had said. "No decent girl would."

Even now the words still stung, but Linc knew they were more true today then they had been then. No decent girl *should* have anything to do with a man like him, a man who made his living with a gun and whose hands were bloodied from killing.

"Mr. Pauling, Dirk Blaine's coming," Melancholy Jones called from outside.

The four people sitting at the table were up in an instant. Marcus and Linc sprinted for the front door while Fiona and Eden hurried along behind.

"He's brought his army with him," Marcus noted when he and Linc reached the porch. Jones and the rest of the men had congregated on the bunkhouse porch, ready to offer assistance, Linc saw with approval. He wondered how good they'd be in a fight, if a fight was what Blaine wanted. Then he thought of Eden and her stepmother and knew they must avoid a fight at all costs.

"Stay inside," Marcus told the women when they would have joined them. Eden murmured a protest, but Fiona pulled her back into the house.

Instinctively, Linc reached for his Colt and loosened it in the holster so it would be ready if he needed it. Marcus and the other men still wore their side arms from this afternoon, also. If Blaine was looking for trouble, he'd find it.

They waited for what seemed a long time until Blaine and his crew rode into the yard. From the expression on Blaine's face, Gus Olsen had delivered the message he'd volunteered to carry.

"Where's my brother?" Blaine demanded the instant his horse stopped in front of the house.

Marcus gestured toward a wagon parked near the barn.

Jerking his horse's reins, Blaine trotted over, his foreman right behind him. The two men dismounted and strode to where the blanket-wrapped figure lay in the wagon bed. Blaine flipped back the blanket and examined his brother's body.

"You can see he wasn't shot in the back," Marcus called.

Linc watched the rest of Blaine's men carefully, lest any of them make a move. Jones and the other Paradise hands slowly fanned out behind the riders until they were surrounded. Linc's tension eased somewhat at seeing this evidence of Marcus's crew's fighting ability, but he still couldn't forget Eden was in the house behind him. The thick adobe walls would provide some protection, but if a bullet went in through a window or Eden decided to come out to help . . .

On the other side of the yard, Blaine and his foreman mounted their horses and rode back to the house. Blaine's face was mottled with rage. "I want to know which son of a bitch killed my brother."

"I did," Linc replied before anyone else could.

Blaine started, then looked Linc over contemptuously. "Who the hell are you?"

"That's Lincoln Scott," Melancholy informed him morosely.

Blaine's head jerked to the right where Melancholy flanked him. His eyes narrowed as he glanced left and realized he'd let his men be surrounded.

"Maybe you've heard of him," Melancholy continued, sounding almost cheerful.

"Can't say I have," Blaine said derisively.

"I have," one of Blaine's men offered.

Linc looked directly at the man for the first time. The young fellow seemed vaguely familiar, but perhaps only because he held himself with the arrogant swagger of a professional gunman. No name came immediately to mind.

"Lincoln Scott is a low-down, dirty, back-shooting sidewinder," the fellow informed them all.

Linc felt his hackles rise, but he knew better than to surrender to his anger. Before he could respond, Marcus chuckled tolerantly. "Sounds like you lost out to Linc once or twice."

The fellow went red in the face. "He tried to run my brother off his land, and when he couldn't, he killed him. Maybe you remember Wilson Hamilton, Scott, or maybe you've murdered so many men, you can't keep track."

Wilson Hamilton. Of course Linc remembered. The man hadn't been worth the powder it took to blow his brains out. Unfortunately, that wouldn't matter to a brother bent on revenge, as Linc knew from bitter experience. "I remember. You couldn't have been more than a kid when it happened."

"I'm not a kid anymore. Maybe you've heard of me, Garth Hamilton."

"Garth's working for me, now," Dirk said, obviously irritated at being left out of the proceedings. "And I won't stand for you telling people my brother was a rustler, Pauling."

"Then you should've stopped him from stealing other people's calves," Marcus replied calmly.

220

Blaine's face went crimson. "He wasn't stealing anything. It was one of our men, a new fellow I hired. We started suspecting him, and Alvin followed him today to try to catch him in the act. I guess he did, but your man shot him before he could explain what was going on."

"Let's see this cowboy, then," Marcus said. "I'd like to hear his side of the story."

"So would I, but I don't know where he is. He must've took off when the shooting started."

"Nice try, Blaine," Linc said, his voice tight with fury, "but I was there. I heard what your brother said to Miss Campbell, and all he was interested in was keeping her from telling what she'd seen."

"Maybe *Miss Campbell* would like to speak for herself," Blaine snarled angrily.

"I'd be happy to," Eden said, stepping out onto the porch.

"Eden, get back inside," Marcus snapped, but Eden shook her head.

"I think Mr. Blaine deserves to hear the truth, and besides, I don't think any of these men would start shooting with a woman around, would you, boys?" she asked Blaine's men. None of them would meet her eye except Blaine, who glared murderously. "No, only a fool would start shooting when he's surrounded. Are you a fool, Dirk?"

Linc wanted to shake her. Was she crazy to taunt the man like this? From the expression on Blaine's face, he could have done a lot more than shake her.

"Some man needs to take you in hand, Eden Campbell," Blaine said through gritted teeth.

221

"Oh, Linc plans to," Melancholy informed him. "Did we forget to mention it? Linc and Miss Eden are getting married."

Now Linc's wrath turned to Jones, but the damage was done. Blaine's face was almost purple when he growled, "Is that true, Eden?"

She'd deny it, of course, Linc thought with a measure of relief, but instead, she stepped over to his side and lifted her chin defiantly. "It most certainly is, but you'll forgive me if I don't invite you to the wedding."

They'd pushed Blaine too far. One more insult, and he'd blow, regardless of the fact that his men would be caught in a crossfire and a lot of innocent people would get hurt. "Eden, go back in the house," Linc said, his voice hard.

For a second he thought she might refuse him as she had refused Marcus, but to his surprise she said, "Yes, Linc," with more meekness than he ever would have dreamed her capable of and hurried inside.

Slightly relieved, he turned his attention back to Blaine. "You came for your brother, but I see you didn't bring a wagon. I'm sure Marcus will lend you one under the circumstances."

"I don't want anything from you," Blaine snarled, turning his horse. His men followed him to where the body lay.

The Paradise crew kept their vigil, watching every move the others made. It wasn't a pleasant task. In spite of Blaine's bravado, they found they couldn't get the stiffened body onto a horse, and Blaine was forced to send his foreman to thank Marcus for the loan of his wagon. When it had been hitched, one of Blaine's men drove it away with the others following.

Blaine was the last to leave, lingering for one long look at Linc. "I'll see you again, Scott," he promised.

Watching from the window, Eden shuddered. "I shouldn't have gone out there and rubbed his nose in it," she told Fiona.

"No, you shouldn't have, but I doubt it made much difference. Dirk Blaine would have hated Mr. Scott quite thoroughly even without your interference."

"Oh, Fee, when I think how close I came to being that man's prisoner—"

"Shhh, don't fret yourself," Fiona urged, slipping her arm around Eden's shoulders.

"If Linc hadn't come along—"

"Stop it! I won't hear another word about what might have been."

"But poor Jed is dead, and it's all my fault!"

"All your fault?" Fiona echoed in amazement. "How have you reached such an absurd conclusion?"

"If I hadn't made him take me for a ride, we never would have found the rustlers." Eden swiped at a tear.

"Nonsense. It isn't as if you purposely led Mr. Titus to his doom, and he was the one who decided to spy on them. If I were inclined to speak ill of the dead, I should point out he used very poor judgment indeed by putting you in such danger when he should have brought you straight home

223

and procured some assistance from the other men."

Eden wished she could agree with her stepmother and assuage some of her guilt, but she knew she would carry at least part of the burden of Jed's death until the day she died herself. "And now I've put Linc in danger, too. Did you see the way Dirk looked at him?"

"I expect Mr. Scott has been in danger the most of his life," Fiona said acerbically. "Honestly, Eden, you simply cannot assume responsibility for the behavior of grown men. As you know, men usually do what they wish and the devil take it. Seldom if ever do they consult women or pay any heed to their advice when they do. You must stop blaming yourself for this situation."

Eden swiped at her eyes again and sniffed loudly as she tried to take Fiona's advice to heart.

"I'm curious about one thing," Fiona said after a moment. "I thought you loathed Mr. Scott. If you have no intention of marrying him, why did you make such a spectacle of yourself just now?"

Eden felt the heat rising in her cheeks and tried to turn away, but Fiona's delicate arm held her fast. "I . . . I've changed my mind about him."

"Have you now? And why is that?"

"Because he . . ." How could she explain? She wasn't even certain of the reasons herself. "Because I thought he didn't love me, but now I know he does," she tried.

"Has he told you so?"

"No, of course not. There's hardly been time since . . ." Her voice broke, and she had to clear the tears out of it. "You see, I asked poor Jed to

take me for a ride to make Linc . . ." She hesitated, uncertain exactly how to explain her motives.

"To make him jealous?" Fiona guessed.

"Not exactly. Even Jed said he wasn't likely to be jealous of a man old enough to be my father. I suppose I just wanted Linc to know I was ignoring him. I was so sure he didn't care about me, and I wanted him to think I didn't care right back, but Jed set me straight." Tears flooded her eyes, and for a long moment she couldn't speak. "He told me . . . he told me Linc was crazy about me, and that he was hanging around because he hoped he could win me back."

"How would Mr. Titus know such a thing?"

"Linc told him. Jed had just asked me if I'd try and settle things with Linc when we saw the smoke from the rustlers' fire."

Fiona patted Eden's shoulder comfortingly. "Are you certain Mr. Scott is the kind of man you want to be involved with, my dear? You heard what that scoundrel said about him a few moments ago. He's killed men. He killed a man right before your very eyes."

"He saved my life!" Eden protested. "The man he killed had just murdered Jed and was going to turn me over to Dirk Blaine so he could rape me!"

"There now, don't upset yourself," Fiona said, leading Eden over to the sofa. Eden sank onto it gratefully. "I'm not trying to change your mind. I simply want to be certain you know exactly the sort of man you'll be getting," she said, sitting down beside her.

"I do know, and that's why I want him. Fee, he's

exactly the kind of man you said I needed, strong and good and . . . and . . ."

"And he can make you obey him," Fiona added with a small smile.

The memory rankled slightly. "I only came back inside because I realized I'd put Linc in danger."

"I'm sure Marcus will have a few words to say on the matter after the way you defied him."

Eden sighed. "I wish somebody *would* yell at me instead of treating me like I'm made of glass."

"I'll mention it to Mr. Scott," Fiona said with twinkle. "Perhaps he'll take you over his knee."

"He won't have to go that far," Eden replied, smiling in spite of herself. "I'm sure a few harsh words will make me well and truly repentant."

"Harsh words it shall be, then. Shall I inform Mr. Scott you wish to see him?"

See him? She wanted to do much more than see him, but Fiona needn't know the extent of her desires. "Please," she replied primly.

"You wanted to see me?" Linc asked.

Eden looked up in surprise. She hadn't heard him come into the parlor. To her relief, she saw he was alone. Fiona must have told Marcus to make himself scarce. "Yes, please come in," she said a little breathlessly.

He took off his Stetson, hung it on a peg by the door, and ran a hand through his hair. Tentatively, as if not quite certain of his welcome, he came closer.

"Sit down," she said, patting the sofa beside her.

He walked over and lowered himself slowly, almost reluctantly, onto the seat. The gun he still wore drew her eye, reminding her of the way he had used it to protect her this afternoon. Her stomach did a nasty little flip at the memory, and her heart clenched with pain. As if sensing her reaction, he hastily unbuckled the gunbelt and removed it, laying it on the floor beside the sofa, out of sight. When her gaze met his again, his expression was guarded.

Eden swallowed nervously, resisting the urge to throw herself into his arms. They had too many things to settle first. "I never thanked you for what you did this afternoon."

"No need. Anybody else would've done the same thing."

"I don't think so. Alvin Blaine was a very dangerous man. It took a lot of courage to face him."

"Or a lot of stupidity. I wasn't trying to be a hero. I just wanted to get you away from him."

"I know. I . . ." Eden shivered at the memory. "Did you hear what he was saying to me?"

"A little," he said curtly, telling her he'd heard more than a little.

"I don't think I've ever been so frightened in my life. I tried to fight him, but of course I couldn't, and after what you showed me, I knew it was hopeless to even try."

He looked quickly away, as if he were embarrassed, and Eden sighed in frustration. This wasn't going at all the way she'd planned. She wanted him to put his arms around her and tell her everything was going to be all right. Instead he seemed to be growing more distant every minute, and everything she said made things worse.

"Linc?" Warily, he turned back to face her. "You may be right that most men would have tried to rescue me, but not many men would've been able to do it the way you did."

"Oh, you're right there," he exclaimed bitterly. "Not many men can kill the way I can."

Eden stared at him in astonishment. "If you hadn't killed him first, he would've killed us both. You didn't have a choice!"

"No, I didn't," he replied, jumping up and jamming his hands into his pockets. "So now I've got *two* men after me for killing their brothers."

He paced restlessly while Eden gaped, unable to comprehend his mood. "Are you afraid?" she asked at last.

He gave a bark of derisive laughter. "Hell, yes, I'm afraid! I'm afraid I'll have to kill two more men just because I already killed their brothers. Where will it all stop, Eden?"

At last she understood. She rose and hurried to him. "Oh, Linc, I'm so sorry!" But when she would have put her arms around him, he grabbed her and held her away.

"Don't touch me! Don't you understand? I'm not fit to be in the same room with you."

"Where did you get a crazy idea like that?" she demanded.

His face twisted with what she recognized now as bitterness. "It's not a crazy idea. It's the way things are, no matter how much I might want to change them."

"Do you want to change them?"

Pain flickered in his eyes and was gone. "It doesn't matter whether I do or not. I can't." He dropped his hands from her arms and turned away.

"Don't I have any say at all in this?" Eden asked in frustration.

"You can't say anything that would make a difference. I'm a hired killer, Eden, and that's all I'll ever be. When I first came here, I thought maybe . . ."

She grasped at this straw. "You wanted to change, and you still want to!" She tried to take his arm, but he shook her off.

"But I can't! Don't you see? No matter what I might want, there'll always be a Garth Hamilton or a Dirk Blaine out there hunting for me."

Since she had no argument for that, she tried another tack. "So that means you have an excuse not to behave like an honorable man," she said, crossing her arms righteously.

"What do you mean?"

"Have you forgotten what you did to me?"

He flinched as if she'd struck him, and a guilty flush rose on his neck. "No, I haven't forgotten," he said tightly, "but you said you didn't want me to . . ." He paused, obviously at a loss for words.

"I was upset. Maybe I've changed my mind since then. After all, you ruined me."

He scowled, but he wouldn't be moved. "That's not a good enough reason to ruin the rest of your life by tying yourself up with a killer."

"You aren't a killer! You aren't like the Blaines and the rest of them."

229

"How do know? You don't know anything about me."

"You're Marcus's friend!"

"He hasn't seen me for seven years. A lot can happen to a man in seven years."

"I know, and obviously, a lot has happened to you. It made you angry and bitter, but you can't let it ruin the rest of your life. You can't let it keep you from finding happiness and . . . and love!"

He went perfectly still, and for a moment his startlingly blue eyes searched her face. "Are you saying you love me, Eden?"

Of course she was, but pride forbade her from declaring herself, especially when he had just rejected her again. "I . . . What if I did?" she asked defensively.

"Then I'd tell you you're a fool. Don't throw yourself away on a man like me."

"Because you can't love me back?" she demanded, stung.

"Because I won't be around to try."

Fear clutched at her heart. "Do you think they'll kill you?"

"If they don't, I'll kill them, and then I'll be riding out again."

"But why? This is your home now. Marcus said—"

"It doesn't matter what Marcus said or did. I can't take something I haven't earned."

"Oh, yes, I forgot. You don't take anything you haven't earned," she said sarcastically.

She saw she'd struck a nerve, reminding him again of how he'd taken her virtue, and the color came back to his face. "Look, Eden, that was a mistake, one I'll regret as long as I live, but I'm not going to make it worse by messing up the rest of your life, too."

"But it's *my* life! Don't you think *I* should be making that decision?"

"Not if you're going to make the wrong decision."

She stared up at him in disbelief, fighting the urge to shake some sense into him. He was the most stubborn, exasperating man she had ever met! If he loved her . . . But perhaps he didn't love her after all, she thought with a stab of pain. What if Jed had been wrong? What if Linc had simply been pretending, using her as an excuse to explain why he didn't leave? Fear dried her mouth. "Are you trying to tell me you don't care about me?"

His eyes were terrible, bleak and full of despair. "I'm trying to tell you I *can't* care about you or anyone else. I gave up that right when I killed the first time, and now there's no going back."

"You don't have to go back!" she tried, desperate now. "You said you changed in seven years, but if you don't like what you've become, you can change again."

"Only if the Blaines and the Hamiltons of this world will let me, and that doesn't seem very likely."

"Are you going to let men like that control you?" she challenged. "If you are, you're not the man I took you for."

His face went scarlet, but whether from anger or some other emotion, she couldn't tell. For a long moment he didn't speak, and she thought she might have gone too far. Literally holding her breath, she waited.

At last he released a ragged sigh. "There's nothing in this world I want more than . . . than a life like the one you're talking about. But I can't just walk in and take it."

"Then fight for it!" she cried.

"A man doesn't get those things by spilling another man's blood, and that's the only way I know to fight."

Now she wanted to pound some sense into him. She wanted to cry and scream and stamp her foot, but she knew none of those things would move Lincoln Scott. Instead she drew herself up to her full height and looked him straight in the eye. "Well, then if you want those things, you'll just have to find a new way to fight, won't you?"

Dirk could never remember feeling so desperate, not when his mother had gotten drunk and thrown him and Alvin out into the pouring rain, not when he and Alvin had gone for days without food, not even when they'd left St. Louis without a dime between them. Of course, all those other times, Dirk had had Alvin to take care of things.

Now Alvin was a stiffened corpse wrapped in a bloody blanket and lying in the back of a borrowed wagon. And it was all Eden Campbell's fault.

"Boss?"

Ace's voice brought him back to the present.

They had just arrived back at the ranch.

"Should I get a couple of the boys to build a coffin?"

Dirk nodded. "Better get a hole dug, too." Dirk swung down and mechanically began to unsaddle his horse.

"Boss?"

Dirk turned back to his foreman in irritation.

"You came up with a good story. We'll just tell everybody it was Shorty who was rustling, and Mr. Blaine had been trying to catch him at it."

"Yeah," Dirk said, gratified by the praise. He really had come up with a good story. Suddenly, he felt better. It was his word against Eden Campbell's and that gunnie's. Who the hell *was* that bastard, anyway? Dirk looked around for the new man. "Hamilton?" The boy looked up. "Come over to the house when you're finished. I want to talk to you."

A few minutes later, Dirk met him on the front porch. Hamilton's cocky air no longer irritated Dirk. Instead he found it reassuring. "How do you know this Lincoln Scott?" he asked, sitting down on the step.

Hamilton took a seat beside him. "I ran into him a couple years back, right after they passed the Land Act. He was working for the big ranchers, trying to drive all the smaller ranchers off their land." His eyes kindled with fury. "My brother got in their way, so Scott killed him."

Dirk nodded in sympathy at the boy's outrage. "What else do you know about him?"

Hamilton pursed his lips thoughtfully. "They say

233

he's killed thirty men, though you can figure that's mostly bullshit. He's fought in some of the range wars and even a few feuds. He's supposed to be a fast-draw artist, though not many men've been brave enough to face him down."

"And what about you? How many men have you killed?"

"I've killed my share," Hamilton snapped defensively. "Only a jackass cuts notches on his gun."

Dirk nodded again. He didn't really care what the kid's past was, any more than he cared whether he was an even match for Scott. If Scott killed him, Dirk would simply be saved the expense of paying Hamilton off. On the other hand, Hamilton might accidentally kill Scott and save Dirk the trouble.

"I don't reckon you'd mind then if I gave you the extra special job of seeing that Lincoln Scott don't live to get much older," Dirk said.

"Hell, I'd've come here on my own if I'd known he was here. I'll be more than happy to take care of him for you," Hamilton replied with the cockiness Dirk was beginning to admire.

"There's a hundred-dollar bonus in it for you if you get him, and I don't particularly care how you do it."

Hamilton stiffened. "I ain't no backshooter. It'll be a fair fight."

"Figure to make your reputation, do you?" Dirk taunted.

"My reputation's already made," Hamilton insisted. "I just want Scott to know who's finally giving him what he's had coming for a long time."

"Well, whatever," Dirk said, dismissing the subject with a wave of his hand. "So long as Scott ends up dead, I don't care how it happens."

The folks at the Paradise laid Jed Titus to rest the next morning. Representatives from every ranch in the area save one came to pay their respects to a man who'd been one of the earliest arrivals here.

Eden and Fiona had been cooking all morning, and the other women brought food, too, so the funeral spread was generous.

"Jed would've enjoyed this," Eden remarked at one point, surveying the crowd gathered through misty eyes. "He loved a party."

When the minister finished, Marcus said a few words in eulogy, as did several other ranchers who had known Jed for many years. Then they lowered his rough wooden casket into the earth. Fiona sobbed softly into her handkerchief, and Eden wept silently, letting the tears flow unchecked down her face as she watched the men shovel dirt into the grave.

If only she hadn't been so proud, Jed would still be alive, Eden kept thinking. She tortured herself by imagining all the things she could have done or not done to prevent Jed's death, and nothing anyone said could comfort her. The only person whose solace she wanted wouldn't even meet her eye, and Eden supposed Linc must also be suffering the tortures of the damned as he recalled arriving too late to save Jed.

When the men had finished filling the grave,

Linc followed them back to the ranch yard where the other mourners had gathered. Still feeling that the stench of death surrounded him, he avoided the food table where Eden stood, and wandered over to the group of ranchers gathered around Marcus. He had met the men when they had come to inspect the scene of Jed's killing, and they greeted him warmly.

Linc knew they respected him for the way he had taken care of Alvin Blaine, but he also knew Jed Titus might well be alive if he hadn't botched things so royally with Eden. He didn't allow himself to dwell on the irony of the situation, however. Better men than he had gone crazy by trying to make sense of such things.

"Marcus here is trying to convince us we should go after Dirk Blaine and his bunch," Gus Olsen told him. "But the rest of us ain't so sure that's a good idea."

"How much more proof do you need?" Marcus asked, his face red with exasperation. "You saw the calves with your own eyes."

"And don't forget what Miss Eden said," Linc reminded him. "He was going to kidnap her so she couldn't tell what she'd seen."

The other men glanced away, and Gus Olsen shook his head. "She was pretty upset, seeing Jed killed like that and all. You know how women get. Maybe she just misunderstood."

"I didn't misunderstand when I saw him put a gun to her head," Linc replied coldly.

"I ain't saying he was innocent," Olsen hastened to assure him. "We all figure Alvin got what he

236

deserved, but so far as we know, Dirk and the rest of his men haven't done anything."

"What about the rustling?" Marcus insisted.

"Maybe Dirk was telling the truth," Olsen said. "Maybe it really was the fellow who lit out."

"And maybe it was all of them," Linc suggested, holding his temper with difficulty.

"But we've got no proof of that," Olsen said doggedly, and the others murmured their consent.

"How many more good men have to die before you're convinced?" Marcus snapped.

"We just don't want to hang somebody, then find out later we'd made a mistake," Olsen said, equally annoyed.

As furious as he was, Linc realized Olsen was right. There had already been enough senseless killing.

"If it's proof you want, we'll find it," Linc said, effectively ending the discussion. "And when we do, you'd better be ready to ride."

The crowd lingered until late in the day, and by the time everyone was gone, Eden wanted nothing more than the privacy of her bedroom. Having slept little the night before, she collapsed exhausted into her bed and knew nothing until morning.

When Marcus came in later, he discovered Fiona had already retired. Or at least she'd gone to their bedroom. He found her lying fully clothed on their bed, weeping softly into a soggy handkerchief. A lamp burned low on the bedside table.

He couldn't even imagine how horrible all this violence must seem to a gentle creature like Fiona. Feeling totally helpless in the face of her grief, he ransacked his brain for something comforting to say. He sat down on the edge of the bed and cleared his throat.

"I'm awful sorry about Jed," he tried. "You must've got to know him pretty well."

Fiona dabbed at her tears and pushed herself up slightly. "He was a fine man. Eden was quite fond of him, too, and I'm afraid she's suffering dreadfully. It seems she feels somewhat responsible, although I've tried to convince her otherwise."

"Responsible? She's no more responsible than I am. Jed was a grown man, and he did a damn fool thing. He should've gone for help."

"I tried to explain that to Eden, but she remains unconvinced. Perhaps you could speak with her tomorrow."

"Sure," Marcus muttered, looking askance at the tears still flowing down Fiona's pale cheeks. "Look, you shouldn't take it so hard. Nobody's to blame except Alvin Blaine, and he's paid his dues."

"It's not just poor Mr. Titus." Fiona's voice broke, and she covered her face with her handkerchief as she surrendered to a new spate of weeping. Her slender shoulders shook with sobs while Marcus looked on in anguish. He'd never seen a woman cry like that. What on earth should he do?

Awkwardly, he laid a hand on her shoulder, but she jerked away as if he'd burned her.

"Don't touch me!" she cried. "How dare you!"

"I . . . I'm sorry," he stammered, not certain what he'd done wrong.

"No you aren't! You aren't one bit sorry. Sometimes I think you must actually *enjoy* humiliating

238

me!"

"Humiliating?" Marcus echoed incredulously. "What are you talking about?"

"You know perfectly well what I'm talking about." She angrily dashed the moisture from her cheeks, threw her legs over the edge of the bed, and got up. "I'm going to retire."

While Marcus gaped, she began to unfasten the bodice of her black bombazine gown with quick, furious motions. She had it halfway off when she looked up and caught him watching. "Be careful, Marcus, I'm going to undress now," she said in warning. "It's time to hide your eyes so you won't have to look at me."

Won't have to look at her? What was she talking about? None of this made a lick of sense. "You're pretty upset," he tried. "Maybe I oughta ask Eden to come in and—"

"Oh, yes, let's wake up that poor, exhausted girl to deal with your grief-stricken wife so you can go down to the bunkhouse and talk to your precious friends."

"I don't want to go to the bunkhouse," Marcus protested, starting to feel a little frightened. He'd never seen Fiona like this. She was always so calm and reserved, but now . . .

Fiona pulled off her skirt and stuffed it into the wardrobe. She started trying to untie her petticoats, but she was too upset to see straight.

"Fiona, maybe if you tell me what's wrong," he offered, rising from the bed and taking a few tentative steps toward her.

"*What's wrong?*" she repeated shrilly. "I'll be

239

only too glad to tell you what's wrong. I'm distraught from wondering whether or not you will manage to get yourself murdered before you have the opportunity to divorce me!"

"Divorce you?" Marcus couldn't possibly have heard her right. "Where did you get a crazy idea like that?"

"You didn't think I knew, did you?" she asked with a toss of her head. "I'm really much more intelligent than you give me credit for being. The instant you explained you were giving me a portion of the ranch, I knew!"

"You knew *what?* Fiona, none of this makes any sense at all," Marcus complained in exasperation.

"Oh, it makes perfect sense," she insisted, planting her hands firmly on her hips. "You wanted to turn me out, but your conscience wouldn't allow you to leave me penniless, so you provided me a portion of the ranch."

Marcus shook his head, completely bewildered. "Why would I want to turn you out?"

"Because you detest me! And don't bother to deny it," she continued when he would have protested. "You never kiss me, you never touch me, you never even *look* at me!"

Stunned, Marcus couldn't speak for a moment. "I . . . I do . . ." he said lamely, but she ignored him.

"Well, you needn't worry about turning me out. I'll leave of my own accord." She swiped angrily at a tear. "I can always go back to England . . ." She swiped at another. ". . . where people are civilized and . . ." Her voice broke on a sob. ". . . and they don't . . . shoot at . . . each other. . . ."

She covered her face with her hands, and Marcus was beside her in an instant. He'd never dealt with a hysterical woman before, but he responded instinctively, out of love, and took her in his arms. She struggled, fighting his touch, but he held on. God dammit, how could she say he never touched her? Pulling her close, he ran his hands over her precious body, dismayed at how fragile she seemed. Cushioning her wrenching sobs, he silently offered the comfort he could not speak while she wetted his shirtfront with her tears.

When at last she slumped weakly against him, he bent down, scooped her up, and carried her to the bed, where he laid her carefully down. Her sobbing had dwindled to an occasional hiccup, and he pulled a bandana from his pocket and gently wiped her face.

"Don't cry anymore, please," he begged, his heart aching.

"What do you care?" she asked dejectedly.

"I care a lot!" he insisted.

"Ha!" she said. It was meant to sound haughty, but came out as a pathetic croak.

"Fiona, I don't know what's got into you. You're my wife. Of course I care about you."

"It's too late for lies, Marcus."

"Dammit, I'm not lying! You're my wife and I love you!"

"Oh, yes," she cried, fury bringing the color back to her cheeks. "Of course you love me. You love me so much you can barely stand the sight of me."

"Whatever gave you an idea like that?" he asked in total confusion.

"Perhaps the way you never look at me!"

"I look at you all the time!" he insisted.

"Not the way a man looks at a woman. Not the way a man looks at his *wife!* And you never . . ."

But she didn't finished her sentence. Closing her mouth with a snap, she turned away in a huff.

"I never what?" he demanded, as angry as she now. "What don't I ever do?" When she refused to respond, he took her arms and forced her to face him. "Tell me, Fiona."

"You never make love to me!"

That was a bold-faced lie! "Now I know you're crazy," he informed her. "I make love to you every week! Sometimes twice a week!"

"Yes, *every week,*" she shrieked, "as if it were some onerous chore to be dealt with as swiftly as possible!"

Too stunned to reply, he could only stammer a few syllables, but she wasn't listening anyway.

"You forget, I've been married before," she continued relentlessly, shaking loose of his grip. "I know how a man treats a woman he loves."

"And how's that?" he demanded, as angry as she now.

"With *passion!*"

Passion? Hellfire, Marcus had as much passion as any other man! If she wanted passion, he could damn well give it to her. He started pulling off his boots.

"What are you doing?" she asked when the second one hit the floor.

With the same angry motions she had used a few minutes ago, he began to unbutton his shirt. "I'm getting undressed," he informed her, fairly ripping his shirt from his body. He couldn't remember ever being so furious. "Take your clothes off." He stood and began unbuttoning his pants. "Take them off or I'll tear them off!"

Her eyes widened, and suddenly Marcus realized he'd gone too far. He hadn't meant to frighten her, but . . .

And then she smiled, a slow, provocative, *passionate* smile. Marcus could hardly believe it until he saw she was untying her petticoats with far more success than she'd had a few minutes ago. The realization spurred him to action, and by the time he got his pants off, she had skinned out of her petticoats and flung aside her corset.

Desire roared through him. He had one knee on the bed before she stopped him, holding up both hands to ward him off. "Take off *all* your clothes, Marcus," she said, her voice husky. "I want to see you."

Clumsy in his haste, he could barely manage the myriad buttons on his long johns, and as he worked, Fiona slowly, lazily pulled loose the ties of her camisole. By the time he got his arms free, he could hardly breathe.

He paused then, still hesitant to expose himself to her lest she be frightened by the swollen evidence of his desire, but she smiled again, as if reading his thoughts. Sitting up, she pulled her camisole open and let it slide down her arms.

He'd never seen her naked before, and the sight

of her staggered him. Her small, round breasts rose and fell unsteadily with her breath, and the rosy tips puckered, begging to be touched. No longer hesitant, he pushed his drawers down over his hips and let them drop. She didn't look at all shocked. In fact, she looked pleased, and this time she didn't stop him when he came toward her.

"Maybe you'd like to undo these buttons yourself," she suggested, lying back against the pillows. She guided his trembling hand to the opening of her pantalettes and helped him when he fumbled. When the last button slid free, she helped him again, lifting so he could ease the garment from her hips.

At last she lay as God had made her, and Marcus felt helpless again, awed in the face of such beauty.

"You may touch me," she whispered, but he didn't know how, so she showed him, lifting his hand to her breast. When flesh touched flesh, instinct took over. His mouth found hers as his hands continued to explore the heated satin of her body. Responding to her moans of pleasure, he grew more bold, stroking down and down until he found the mound of golden curls and the moist core of her.

"Now, Marcus, please," she urged, and her eager fingers closed around him. He gasped at the sensations, fighting for control until, at last, he sank into her sweet depths.

He groaned her name, or thought he did, but then she wrapped her legs around him and every rational thought fled. He took her in a frenzy of need, so crazed he no longer knew where his body ended and hers began. The end came like a thunderbolt, striking him senseless with ecstasy and jarring his very soul. Beneath him, Fiona cried out and raked his back with her nails as she shuddered out her own release.

After what seemed a long time, Marcus came to himself, aware he was crushing Fiona with his weight. Wearily, he pushed up on his elbows and looked down at her.

She was crying.

"Oh, God, did I hurt you?" he asked, horrified, and tried to pull away, but she clung to him with arms and legs and wouldn't let him go.

She shook her head frantically. "No, you didn't hurt me. Please, don't move!"

He stayed where he was, still resting on his elbows and holding most of his weight off her. "Why are you crying, then?"

To his astonishment, she smiled up at him, her eyes still glistening with tears. "Because I'm so happy. Oh, Marcus, I love you so very much, but I thought you didn't love me in return."

"You *love* me?" he echoed in disbelief.

"Of course, you silly man. Why did you suppose I married you?"

"Because you needed my protection," he reminded her. "At least that's what Eden said."

Fiona laughed aloud at this, and Marcus, who still rested inside her, gasped at the odd sensation. He knew in all decency he should withdraw, but Fiona still held him tightly. He felt the heat in his face, and Fiona laughed again.

"Are you embarrassed?" she asked.

"Are you?" he countered.

"Not in the least," she assured him cheerfully, running her hands lovingly over his back. "Marcus," she asked after a few moments, "did you honestly not know that I care for you?"

Marcus was having a hard time thinking coherently at all. "I . . . I never really thought about it, I guess. I mean, that was too much to ask for. Just having you for my wife was more than I ever imagined."

"Oh, Marcus, I do love you," she cried, pulling his face to hers for a long, lingering kiss.

When they paused for breath, he eased the upper part of his body off to one side so he could collapse against the pillow. She turned her face so their noses were almost touching. Marcus inhaled her sweet scent and released his breath in a wondrous sigh.

Suddenly Fiona frowned. "Marcus, you do love me, don't you?"

"Of course!"

Her smile returned, impish now. "You haven't said so."

"I . . ." He started to say that he had, just a few minutes ago, but the words had been uttered in the heat of anger and if she didn't remember, he didn't mind saying it again. "I love you, Fiona."

When he saw her happiness, he wondered why he had never told her before.

"But if you love me, why did you treat me so badly?" she asked.

"I didn't," he insisted, but she shook her head.

"You most certainly did. I used to think you were simply shy, but you behaved exactly the same way after we married, as if we were virtual strangers. Why, I don't think you ever even looked at me unless I was speaking directly to you."

"I looked at you plenty," he insisted.

"Not that I could tell, and certainly not when I was undressing. I thought you found me repulsive!"

"What?" he asked unbelievingly. "I was only trying to . . . to be a gentleman. I didn't want you to think . . ."

"To think what?" she prompted when he hesitated.

"To think I married you just to get you in bed."

"Oh, Marcus," she purred, stroking his cheek. "Is that why you never took me to bed, too?"

"I wish you'd stop saying 'never,' " he said crossly, making her grin.

"Well, then, how about 'seldom'?"

"Yes," he admitted grudgingly. "God knows, I wanted you all the time, but I was trying to be a gentleman. I didn't think you liked it."

"Well, I didn't like it when you performed as if it were your duty and you couldn't get it over with quickly enough. But tonight was quite enjoyable," she added provocatively before he could take offense. "And from now on you must forget all that nonsense about being a gentleman."

Marcus thought he would gladly do so, except for one thing. "But you're a lady," he reminded her.

"In the parlor, I'm a lady," she corrected him. "In the bedroom, I'm your woman." She ran her fingers over his bare hip, and he quickened inside her. "Do you understand?"

"Yes," he croaked, wondering if she knew what she was doing to him.

"A lady would probably faint at the very thought, but as your woman, I shall be quite annoyed unless you make love to me again, immediately," she informed him, removing the last of his doubts.

He was only too happy to comply.

Chapter Eight

The next morning, Linc took his breakfast with the men in the cookhouse. They were almost finished when Marcus finally strolled in looking amazingly relaxed for a man with more problems than he could shake a stick at.

He nodded a greeting, poured himself a cup of coffee, and sat down with the rest of them. "I reckon we need to make some decisions, boys," he told them gravely. "I've been thinking about who the new foreman should be." He looked meaningfully at Melancholy.

"Before you say anything, boss," Melancholy replied, "the boys and me've been talking things over, and we was wondering if you'd consider Linc here for the job."

Linc started in surprise. "Me? Why?"

Melancholy looked even more somber than usual. "We like the way you handle yourself, the way you took care of Alvin Blaine and stood up to his brother. 'Course, it ain't our decision to make, but we kinda figured after what happened, the boss'd approve."

"I sure do approve," Marcus said. "I just didn't want you boys to think I'd pick an outsider over any of you. What do you say, Linc?"

Linc glanced around at the other men, easily reading their support. "Before we decide, I reckon there's a few things you need to know about me. First off, I didn't come here to court Miss Eden." He silenced their murmurs of surprise with a gesture. "The truth is, me and Marcus is partners from way back. When the trouble started here, he sent for me. I was on my way to the ranch when somebody ambushed me."

"What do you mean, ambushed?" Melancholy started to ask, but caught himself. "Wait a minute. Was you the one the Blaines shot?"

Linc nodded. "We figure they thought I was Marcus because our horses look so much alike. I was hit pretty bad, but I managed to get away. Eden found me when she went out to warn Marcus and brought me back here."

"Why didn't you tell us all this before?" Melancholy asked with a scowl.

"Because we didn't want to chance the Blaines finding out," Marcus explained. "I know you boys wouldn't ever purposely tell anybody Linc was the one they was looking for, but if you didn't know, you couldn't accidentally say anything either. We wanted to keep it a secret until Linc was back on his feet."

"Seems like he is now," Melancholy observed dryly. "But why'd you tell us all that business about him courting Miss Eden?"

"So you wouldn't wonder why he was hanging around here. If I'd hired him, you'd expect him to be working, so we let you think he was a guest."

Melancholy nodded sagely, then suddenly perked up. "That means he and Miss Eden ain't engaged after all," he informed the others.

"No, we ain't," Linc confirmed, ignoring the spasm of pain the admission cost him.

Melancholy stroked his long mustache thoughtfully. "You don't look real happy about it, neither."

Linc certainly didn't want to discuss his personal feelings at this particular time. He straightened in his seat. "Now you know I came here to fight, so I've got no objections to doing it. I'm still a little peaked, but I'll pull my weight around here or die trying. If you still want me as your foreman, I'll be proud to do it."

He glanced at Marcus, who grinned over his coffee cup. The others murmured their approval. "I reckon it's settled, then," Marcus said. He reached across the table and shook Linc's hand, then the others followed suit.

"What are our orders?" Melancholy asked when everyone had congratulated Linc.

"Linc and me'll have us a little palaver, first, so just sit tight for a while," Marcus said, rising from the table. Linc rose, too, and followed him out into the yard.

When they were out of earshot of the other men, they paused and leaned up against the corral fence. Linc pulled out the makings and rolled himself a smoke. When it was lit, he drew deeply on

251

it and studied his friend's face for a long moment. "What do you want me to do about Dirk Blaine?"

Marcus sighed in disgust. "Not much we can do until we can prove he's involved with the rustling. You heard what the other ranchers were saying yesterday at the funeral. They figure there might be some truth to the story that Alvin had only caught one of his men at it. I don't reckon we can expect folks to string Dirk Blaine up for what you say his brother said."

Linc took another drag on his cigarette. "So all we can do is keep our eyes open."

"At least we know who we're looking for now. The way I figure, Alvin was the brains of the outfit. With Dirk running things, they'll screw up, sure as shooting. We've just got to be ready to catch them when they do."

Linc shook his head. "I'm already tired of waiting."

"Well, there's plenty of work to keep you out of trouble, Mr. Foreman."

Linc smiled grimly. "I guess you're right. You going to tell me what you want done?"

"Just the usual stuff. Melancholy can give you a rundown on the way we work. I'll . . ." Marcus looked away self-consciously. "I'll be up at the house."

Linc frowned in concern. "Is something wrong?"

Marcus flushed. "Oh, no, I . . . I just thought I'd spend a little time with Fiona before I left for the day. She's been pretty upset, what with Jed getting killed and all."

"Yeah, sure," Linc said, wondering what had

suddenly come over his old friend. Hadn't Eden said something about how Marcus never paid any attention to Fiona? Things had certainly changed in the past few days, or else Fiona was a lot more upset than she'd appeared to be yesterday. "I'll give you a holler when we're ready to go."

"Thanks," Marcus called over his shoulder, already on his way.

Linc watched him go, shaking his head in wonder.

Marcus found his wife in the kitchen rolling out pastry dough. He grinned when he heard her humming. She looked up as he entered, and a brilliant smile lighted her face. Out of habit, he hesitated for a moment before going to her and planting a kiss on her upturned mouth.

"What are you making?"

"Currant pies," she told him happily. "Your favorite." She wiped her hands on her apron and slipped them around his waist.

"*You're* my favorite," he replied, pulling her hips snugly against his.

"Then perhaps I shouldn't waste my time in the kitchen today. If you'd rather I worked in the bedroom . . ."

Marcus frowned his disappointment. "I'd like to take you up on that, but I've got work to do. I've made Linc the new foreman, and somebody's got to show him around."

"Melancholy could do it," Fiona said, nuzzling his neck, but he steeled himself against the temptation.

"I'm the boss," he pointed out hoarsely.

"Which gives you the privilege of ordering someone else to do the work," she countered, nipping his ear and sending chills up his spine. "In any case, Eden and I should be afraid to stay here alone. You simply must leave someone here to protect us."

Marcus groaned in surrender, crushing her to him and claiming her lips with his.

That was how Eden found them a few minutes later when she came in looking for some breakfast.

"Oh, my!" she exclaimed before she could stop herself.

They broke apart guiltily, all flushes and silly grins.

"Excuse me," she murmured in bemusement. What on earth was going on?

Fiona laughed self-consciously and smoothed her hair back into place. "What did you want, dear?"

"My breakfast," Eden said. Marcus refused to meet her eye, and no wonder. If she wasn't mistaken, he'd had his hand on Fiona's breast when she walked in. Now wasn't that interesting?

"I . . . I've got a few things to take care of before I leave," Marcus muttered. "I'll be in my office when Linc comes."

"Marcus!" Fiona wailed.

"I'll stay home tomorrow, I promise." He hurried out.

Eden watched him go in amazement, then turned back to Fiona. "Well, well, well," she said, crossing her arms, "am I to assume Marcus is *not* planning to divorce you?"

254

Fiona's fair cheeks pinkened. "I think not. It was all a terrible misunderstanding. What would you like for breakfast?"

"Just some biscuits and jelly," Eden replied, moving to get the leftover biscuits from a tin on the table. "And just who misunderstood who?"

Fiona handed her the jelly jar and a knife. "It was all my fault, really. I was judging dear Marcus by my other husbands. I forgot he had no experience at marriage and had no idea how he was supposed to behave."

"I see he's got the idea now," Eden said, not bothering to hide her amusement, "but you'd better warn him about saving all that affection for more private moments."

"I most certainly will not," Fiona replied. Eden noted with delight that her normally angelic stepmother looked devilishly smug. She was glad *someone's* love life was starting to work out. Sitting down at the table, Eden couldn't suppress a sigh.

"Is something wrong?" Fiona inquired. "You aren't still blaming yourself for poor Mr. Titus's death are you?"

"Yes, but that's not why I'm sighing," she hastened to explain when Fiona would have argued. "I had another fight with Linc."

"Last night? I didn't think the two of you so much as spoke to each other yesterday."

"We didn't. It happened the night before, when you sent him in to talk to me." Eden absently rubbed her forehead and sighed again.

Fiona filled two cups with coffee from the pot

on the stove, sat down across from her, and shoved one of the cups under Eden's nose. "My mother always gave me tea at times like this, but I believe coffee will serve the same purpose."

Eden gratefully swallowed a mouthful of the bitter brew, and idly began to spread jelly on a biscuit she had no appetite for.

"What did you argue about?" Fiona asked when Eden did not offer to begin the conversation.

"The silliest thing."

"It usually is."

"He doesn't think he deserves me."

"He said this, in so many words?"

"Not exactly. He gave me all this hog wallow about how he's a gunfighter and he's killed all these men and he can't settle down."

"Perhaps he's simply making excuses because he doesn't *want* to settle down," Fiona suggested gently.

"I wish I could believe that. Then I could forget about him, but I have this awful feeling that he really wants to settle down more than anything in the world and he truly believes he doesn't deserve to have a real home."

"If you will forgive me for saying so, you've taken an unusual interest in Mr. Scott's well-being."

Eden smiled sadly. "If that's your proper British way of asking me if I've fallen in love with him, I'm afraid I have. But even that doesn't make any difference to him."

"You told him you loved him?" Fiona asked in amazement.

"Of course not! I mean, a woman shouldn't commit herself until the man does. Isn't that what you always told me?"

Fiona frowned and looked away, staring at the wall thoughtfully for a few minutes. "Perhaps my advice was not entirely correct."

"What do you mean, not entirely?"

"Well, I . . . You see, men are so much more easily discouraged than women, particularly in matters of the heart. Sometimes . . . and mind you I'm not saying this is true in every case or even quite often, but *sometimes* a man needs to know a woman cares for him first so he will have the courage to admit his own feelings."

Eden wondered if Fiona's advice sprang from some recent personal experience, but decided not to inquire into such a delicate subject. She would concentrate on her own problems. "Then you think I should tell Linc how I feel?" she asked eagerly.

"I'm not certain. I mean, I have no idea if he returns your feelings or not, but perhaps you do. If you believe your coyness has hindered matters between you, you might try being a little more frank with him."

Eden sipped her coffee thoughtfully. "The problem is I'm still not absolutely sure, and I don't know how I ever will be now that he's avoiding me."

"One does need time to make such a determination," Fiona agreed, "and the situation couldn't be worse. Marcus just informed me he has made Mr. Scott the foreman, so he'll be occupied from dawn to dusk every day from now on."

"Oh, no!" Eden cried. "How could Marcus do this to me?"

"I doubt he had any inkling he was ruining your life when he made the decision," Fiona told her with a small smile. "It would seem your only hope of spending time with Mr. Scott is to become one of his cowboys."

Eden started to laugh at the suggestion until another thought occurred to her. "And why shouldn't I?"

"Why shouldn't you what?"

"Become one of his cowboys. I can ride and rope just as good as any of them, and Marcus said the other day they're short-handed. They should be glad for my help."

"You can't be serious!" Fiona scolded.

"I'm perfectly serious. If I could team up with Linc, we'd be together almost every waking hour. What better way to find out how he really feels about me?"

"Or drive him to murder you," Fiona said acerbically. "This simply will not do. Marcus will never allow it."

"We'll see about that. Oh, thank you, Fiona!"

Eden jumped up and ran out of the room.

"Eden, you didn't eat!" Fiona called after her, but Eden couldn't stop for anything as mundane as food. In her bedroom, she threw open the trunk where she stored the clothes she seldom wore. After some frantic digging she found exactly what she was looking for. Knowing she didn't have much time, she hastily stripped off her calico dress.

When Melancholy had finished giving Linc the lay of the land and Linc had divided the men into pairs and assigned them each a section of the ranch to patrol, he headed back to the house to get Marcus.

As he climbed the porch steps, the front door opened and Eden appeared. As always, the sight of her stunned him for a moment. Before he could recover, he saw how she was dressed and sustained a second shock.

"What in the hell are you got up for?"

She smiled beatifically. "I'm your new man," she said, gesturing to her outfit. She was dressed exactly the way he was, man's shirt, leather vest and *pants!*

But she most certainly didn't look like anybody's *man.* Linc had never seen a woman in pants before, and he'd never imagined they would look so different on a female form. The sight of Eden's long, shapely figure lovingly encased in denim made his mouth go dry.

Forcing his gaze back to her face, he gave her what he hoped was a fierce scowl. "What are you talking about?"

"I'm going to ride with you fellows today, and don't look so skeptical. I've been riding since I could walk, and I can rope as well as any man on the place. Marcus will tell you."

"Does Marcus know about this?" Linc demanded.

"Does Marcus know about what?" Marcus

asked, coming out of the house behind Eden. He stopped dead when he saw her. "What in the hell . . . ?"

"I was just telling Linc I'm going to be riding with them today," Eden informed him cheerfully.

"You most certainly are not," Marcus replied. "Are you crazy? Get back in the house right now before the other men see you in that getup."

"Eden." Fiona cried as she came out, too, and saw her stepdaughter.

"Fee, you were the one who said I should help out since we're short-handed," Eden insisted. "And if I go, then Marcus can stay here with you."

For some reason Linc couldn't understand, this last piece of information instantly swayed Fiona to Eden's side.

"Well, of course, I can't approve of you riding around the country dressed like a hoyden, but Marcus, dear, you didn't intend to go off and leave me here alone, did you?"

Marcus seemed a bit flustered. "Well, Pedro'll be here."

"But he's only a boy. What if Dirk Blaine and his men come back? Have you forgotten he threatened to burn the house?" She pulled a handkerchief from her pocket and dabbed at her eyes. "And his brother was going to kidnap Eden. I simply can't bear the thought of being here unprotected."

"Now don't cry, honey," Marcus said, putting a comforting arm around her shoulders.

Linc could hardly believe the change in Fiona. She'd always seemed like such a sensible person, not at all likely to become hysterical. But then he recalled what Marcus had said about her being upset over Jed's death. She must've really taken it hard.

"We could leave one of the men here," Linc offered, earning a warning glare from Eden.

"There's no reason why Marcus can't stay himself if it would make Fiona feel better," she pointed out.

"Oh, please, Marcus," Fiona sniffed, lifting her cornflower eyes to him in a look Linc knew any man would've been hardpressed to resist.

"But somebody's got to show Linc around," Marcus protested weakly.

"I can do that," Eden said. "Come on, Linc." Before he could resist, she took his arm and led him down the porch steps.

"Wait a minute," he managed before they'd gotten too far, but she silenced him with another glare.

"Stop being such a dolt!" she whispered fiercely, hurrying him along toward the corrals. "Can't you see they want to be alone?"

"What?" Linc glanced back at the couple on the porch. Marcus now had both arms around Fiona as she wept against his chest.

"They want some time alone together. That's why I decided to go out with you today. You don't think I *want* to do this, do you?" she asked in disgust.

"Uh, no," he said, thinking he really had no earthly idea what she might want.

"Then stop arguing."

As they approached the corrals where the others were selecting their horses for the day, the men noticed Eden for the first time.

"Glory be," one of them murmured, alerting the others, who responded in varying degrees of surprise.

Melancholy looked her over sourly. "What's going on?"

"I'm going to work with you boys today," Eden informed him with a dazzling smile. Her good humor was beginning to get on Linc's nerves. "Can you recommend a horse for me, Melancholy?"

Ignoring the request, Melancholy looked to Linc for confirmation of this astonishing plan.

Linc nodded reluctantly. "We thought maybe Marcus should stay here. Mrs. Pauling is kind of scared to be here without a man, what with all Blaine's threats to burn the place down."

Melancholy nodded. "But why does Miss Eden have to go with us?"

"Because you're short-handed," Eden replied before Linc could get his tongue unhinged. "And someone has to show Linc around."

"Who're you gonna ride with?" one of the other men asked hopefully.

"I don't know yet," she replied, still smiling like a cat with a mouthful of feathers.

"I'll be glad for you to go with me," another man offered.

"Me too!" a third said.

Melancholy's mustache twitched. "I'd be right proud if you'd go with me, ma'am. You're about the best hand we've got on the place."

Linc told himself he had no right to feel it, but he knew the bitter taste of jealousy. He called himself a fool, but still he said, "Thanks, boys, but I reckon she'll go with me. She can show me around, and Marcus asked me to keep an eye on her." He pretended not to see Eden's amazed response to his lie. "Pedro, can you cut out a gentle horse for Miss Eden?"

The boy was in the corral, roping the horses each man selected. "Sí señor," Pedro replied with a grin.

"Pedro, you know I don't need a gentle horse," Eden called. "How about Old Gray?"

The boy nodded, still grinning, and roped a big gray gelding for her.

Linc frowned his disapproval, and Eden laughed. "Pedro, maybe you ought to give that gentle horse to Mr. Scott," she said, slapping a halter on her mount and leading him off to be saddled.

Good God, Linc thought, watching her go, she looked even better walking away in those pants than she did coming forward. Mesmerized, he studied the provocative sway of her hips for a long moment until Melancholy laid a sympathetic hand on his shoulder. "The worst part is, you don't never get used to it, neither," he informed Linc sadly. "If women ever take to wearing pants all the time, this world'll sure go to hell in a hurry."

"You're right there."

A few minutes later, Linc had saddled his own horse, and he found Eden mounted and waiting for him. She was still smiling and looking like butter wouldn't melt in her mouth.

"Where are we going?" she asked when Linc had mounted and allowed his horse to buck out its morning energy.

"I figured we'd cover the area from the seep to the old cottonwood."

She nodded approvingly. "You talk like you know the place pretty well."

"Melancholy gave me the landmarks." One cowboy could give another directions from one side of the country to the other simply by naming a few important natural formations. "Trouble is," he admitted reluctantly, "I ain't too sure which direction to head."

"South," she said, turning her horse and kicking him into motion. Linc followed her into the clear, cool morning.

Automatically, Linc made a mental note of the terrain, glancing back over his shoulder periodically to get his bearings, since things always looked different going the other way.

Still, he found himself watching his companion far too often. As if drawn by a magnet, his gaze kept returning to her slender figure atop the big gray horse. She rode well, he'd give her that, her body moving naturally in rhythm with the animal.

Too naturally, if the truth were told. He kept thinking about her long legs spread wide over the saddle, her full, round bottom bouncing gently, and all that white velvet flesh beneath her denim trousers . . .

Up ahead she yelled something and pointed, jarring him out of his fantasies. Then he saw them, too, a small herd of cattle clustered nearby. Setting his mind resolutely on business, he followed her toward the group of animals.

By unspoken consent, they rode around the herd in opposite directions, checking the animals with practiced eye for new calves and signs of weakness or sickness or injury. He saw all the calves had already been branded, but when he met Eden at the other side of the herd she said, "That old mossy horn's got a big gash on his side."

Linc picked the animal out easily. The wound would have to be treated immediately before the blowflies had a chance to go to work.

"Your horse is a good cutter," she told him. "You cut him out and rope his head. I'll get his feet."

"No, *you* rope his head, and *I'll* get his feet," he corrected, assigning himself the more difficult task.

Eden was right about his mount, at least. Linc had no more than indicated which cow he wanted than the horse moved into the herd and separated it from the rest. Linc merely went along for the ride. When Linc lifted his reata from the saddle horn, he saw Eden was already swinging hers for an overhand catch. To his surprise she caught the animal's horns on the first pass and swiftly looped the rope around her saddle horn.

Before the steer could charge her, Linc threw a heeling catch and captured the animal's rear legs. As he tied off his own rope, his horse backed up, pulling the steer's legs out from under him and rendering him momentarily helpless, held as he was between the two horses.

Linc reached into his pack for the screwworm remedy and jumped down from his horse. He was glad to see the gash was superficial. Although it was already swarming with worms, the medicine would kill them, and the steer would be fine in a few days.

He worked quickly, dodging the steer's murderous front feet, and when he was finished, he leaped into his saddle again. The moment he was seated, Eden moved her mount forward, releasing the tension on her rope, and deftly flicked it free of the steer's horns. Linc likewise released his own rope, and the two of them rode swiftly away for about a hundred feet while the steer lumbered up, bellowing ferociously.

They waited, watching while the steer tossed his head, searching frantically for his attackers, then snorted and pawed the ground menacingly.

"He's all talk and no action," Linc said when the beast finally gave up and trotted off to join the herd again.

He looked over to find her studying him. "You're pretty good for somebody just out of a sickbed," she said, her green eyes smiling at him.

He couldn't stop his answering smile. "And you're pretty good for a *girl*," he replied recklessly. "Where'd you learn to rope like that?"

"Oh, my father taught me . . . and Jed," she added, looking away for a moment, but when her gaze came back he could see she'd shrugged off the painful memories, at least for the moment. "When I got really good, my father decided he'd

266

better get me a mother before I was ruined completely."

"So that's when he found Fiona."

"No, that's when he started looking. It took a couple of years, and by then I was completely wild. I'd taken to wearing pants all the time, but when Fiona came, she put a stop to it. This is the last pair I had left. I was afraid they wouldn't fit me anymore."

"They are a little tight," he said without thinking. Mortified, he tried go make amends. "I mean . . . they can be uncomfortable if they don't fit . . ." He gave up in an agony of embarrassment.

Her eyes sparkled with suppressed laughter. "If you're trying to convince me to take them off, you'll have to do better than that," she tossed out as she reined her horse around and headed away.

His face burning, Linc followed, forcing himself to study the terrain and look for cattle instead of watching Eden's cute little bottom bouncing on the saddle.

When they got to the seep, they found a cow mired in the mud, bawling piteously. Linc rode in as far as was safe, threw a loop around her horns and dragged her out. The instant he released her, however, she started back in again. Swearing, he caught her once more and dragged her forcibly away, although she struggled violently, bellowing her rage.

From the corner of his eye, he saw Eden riding into the mud hole. He was yelling for her to stop when she tossed her rope around what appeared to be a stick protruding from the mud, but as her horse began to back out, the stick proved to be the leg of a drowned calf whose muddied body Eden dragged to dry land.

As soon as Eden released the calf, Linc let the cow go, knowing now why she had wanted so desperately to return to the mud and why she no longer needed to.

"Poor little thing," Eden said when she joined him. For a moment they watched as the cow futilely tried to nudge the calf to its feet. Then, unwilling to linger over the animal's grief, they silently turned their horses and rode away.

For several hours they rode, inspecting each small herd of cattle they encountered, doing whatever was necessary with each group. Eden watched Linc closely for signs his wound was bothering him, and finally she noticed him slumping in the saddle and rubbing his side.

"There's a tree up ahead with some shade," she called over to him. "Do you mind if we stop and rest a few minutes? I'm afraid I'm not used to all this riding."

"Sure," he said, straightening instantly, although she could see the weariness in his eyes.

The tree was a scrubby live oak that gave no more than a patch of shade, but they sought it eagerly. The cool morning had given way to a warm afternoon. After pulling the saddles from the horses, they collapsed on the ground. Eden offered Linc a pull from the canteen she'd brought, and Linc offered her a strip of jerky. Working so far from the ranch, cowboys would ordinarily skip

268

the noon meal. Eden chewed the dried beef grate-fully.

"I'm starting to regret my generosity," Eden said when she had finished it, shifting her sore bottom on the hard ground. Linc was stretched out, lying on his side.

"What generosity?" he asked. He looked excit-ingly virile, even in repose, with his long, muscular legs filling the denim of his pants and his broad shoulders straining the fabric of his shirt. Remem-bering how it felt to be pressed against that body, Eden felt warm all over.

"The generosity that inspired me to give Marcus and Fiona some time alone. This cowboy business is a lot harder than I remembered."

"Everything's more fun when you're a kid." He frowned thoughtfully. "Fiona must've been real up-set about losing Jed. I never would've expected her to carry on like she did this morning."

"We were all real sad about Jed, but I think there's more to it than his death. Have you noticed anything peculiar about Marcus since yesterday?"

Linc tried to think of something. "He was real worried about her is all. He even wanted to go back to the house to spend some time with her before we left this morning."

Eden considered this. "I caught them kissing in the kitchen."

"What?" Plainly Linc considered this odd behav-ior, too. She smiled at the memory. "Yeah, and they don't usually carry on like that at all. In fact, I don't recall ever seeing them kiss, not even at their wedding. And then . . ."

"Then what?" he prompted.

Eden didn't quite know how to explain without revealing the subject of her conversation with Fiona. "Do you remember I told you I thought something was wrong between them?" He nodded. "Fiona said some things to make me think she and Marcus had made it up. She said they had a misunderstanding, something about Marcus didn't know how a husband was supposed to act, but he seems to be doing real fine now."

"So you arranged for them to be alone."

She shrugged. "It's hard to spoon when people are watching."

He made a face. "Yeah, I remember."

"What do you remember?" Eden asked, feeling a pang of jealousy over the unknown girl with whom he'd tried to spoon.

"I remember when Melancholy made a bet on whether I'd kiss you," he explained.

"Oh, yeah," she said, absurdly relieved. "I thought maybe . . . maybe you had more experience at it than you'd let on."

"More experience at what?"

"Courting."

"Oh."

"Do you?"

"A little."

She waited, but he volunteered nothing. "With lots of girls?" she asked, hating herself for inflicting such torture but unable to resist.

"No, just one."

"Did you love her?"

Linc sighed, and Eden imagined it was with regret. "She was a nice girl and real pretty. No other girl had ever paid me any mind before."

"You must've cared for her," she insisted, wishing she didn't have to know.

"I liked her a lot. Any man would've."

Eden frowned, dissatisfied with his reply. Of course, she hardly wanted to hear of his undying devotion to another woman, either, she reminded herself sternly. "Did you ask her to marry you?"

"Never got the chance," he said, his beautiful blue eyes suddenly going hard. "I killed a man in a gunfight, and her father ran me off."

"How awful! Didn't she have any say in it at all?"

"She didn't seem to mind. I reckon she didn't want to be mixed up with a killer either."

Suddenly everything fell into place and all Linc's protests began to make sense. "What a ninny she must have been!" she exclaimed in outrage.

Linc idly picked up a twig. "Most folks would say she showed good sense," he remarked with seeming nonchalance, but the twig snapped in his fingers and he tossed it away.

Eden let a few moments of silence tick by. "Well, now I feel silly."

"Why?" he asked, wary again.

"For trying to teach you how to court. I guess you're a lot more experienced than you let on."

"I never—" He stopped himself from completing the sentence.

"You never what?" she prodded, intrigued.

"I never courted like you showed me."

"Oh," was all she could think to say. What did

he mean? Was he talking about their lovemaking or something else? Before she could decide, he stirred restlessly and made a move as if to get up. Knowing she had to stop him from ending their conversation, she said the first thing she could think of. "Was the man you killed the brother of that man who works for Dirk Blaine?"

Instantly she regretted her question. Linc's azure eyes clouded. "No, he was somebody else's brother," he said bitterly. "Wilson Hamilton came along years later."

"But why would that Hamilton fellow want revenge? I can't believe you shot his brother down for no reason."

Linc's mouth stretched into the parody of a grin. "Funny thing is, I didn't shoot him at all, at least not that I know of."

"What do you mean?"

"He was killed in a shootout with our whole crew. Nobody really knows who got him, but I was the leader, so . . ." He shrugged eloquently.

"Why were you in a shootout with him?"

"You heard his brother," he said stubbornly. "I was trying to steal his land."

Eden made a disgusted noise. "You can't expect me to believe you'd do a thing like that."

"What if it's true?" he countered.

She studied his face for a long moment, not a bit surprised to see how closely he was guarding his true emotions. She smiled. "Because I know you, Lincoln Scott, and you're not the kind of man who'd steal somebody's land. Now tell me the truth."

Surprise flickered in his eyes, and pleasure, too, if Eden hadn't imagined it in the second before he masked his emotions again. "Wilson Hamilton did have some land, but he was squatting on it. He'd never filed a legal claim, and he never made much effort to really work. He ran a 'three-cow outfit' and lived off the beef he stole from his neighbors. They got tired of it and tried to fence him out, but he cut the fences. They warned him, and he started taking potshots at everybody who rode by his place. Finally, there wasn't nothing else left to do."

"You should tell his brother all this!" Eden exclaimed righteously.

"He probably knows, but even if he don't, it won't matter. The kid wants revenge, and he probably wants a reputation, too."

"What kind of a reputation?"

"As the man who killed Lincoln Scott," he told her baldly.

Stunned, she stared at him for a long moment, and before she could think of a reply, he was on his feet. "Let's get going," he said gruffly. "We don't get paid to sit around."

"I don't get paid at all," she reminded him in an attempt at lightness, but he was already picking up his saddle.

She still wasn't ready to end this conversation, but he no longer seemed disposed to linger here with her. Resigned, she hoisted her own saddle, and in a few minutes they were riding again. Several more times that day Eden tried to get him to talk, but apparently he'd decided he'd already said too much, and she couldn't get more than two or three words out of him at any one time.

It was still early when she noticed he was rather pale and favoring his left side. "Do you suppose Marcus would fire us if we headed in a little early?" she asked. "I'm about to drop clean out of this saddle, and Marcus did ask you to look after me, didn't he?" she added slyly.

He frowned at the reminder of his lie. "I had to think of a reason not to let you go off with one of the other boys."

"Why?" she asked eagerly.

"Because . . ." Plainly he regretted the admission. "Because if something happened, Marcus would hold me responsible anyways."

"What do you think could've happened with one of the other men?" she asked in delight.

He gave her a murderous scowl, but she didn't even blink. "Anything," he finally said. "Let's get back to the ranch."

This time he rode ahead of her, but not so fast that Eden couldn't keep up. The whole way she kept wondering how successful her day had been. She and Linc had talked a bit, and he had seemed uncomfortable whenever the subject worked its way around to her or to her and him. And he'd passed up a marvelous opportunity to take advantage of her, so she was now sure he wasn't just after whatever physical pleasures she could offer. But she still wasn't certain how he felt about her. This was going to take more time than she'd originally anticipated.

Marcus met them in the yard when they arrived

back at the ranch. The other men were still out, and Marcus greeted them with a worried frown. "Is something wrong?"

"Oh, no, I asked Linc to knock off early. I'm not used to this cowboy business," Eden explained before Linc could.

"How'd she do?" Marcus asked Linc as he swung down from his saddle.

"She's pretty good with a rope."

"Don't sound so surprised," Eden chided.

"For a girl," he added, but she saw the glint in his eye and merely grinned her reply.

"How's Fiona?" Eden asked Marcus.

"Fiona? Why, she's fine," he said, nonplussed. "Why shouldn't she be?"

"Because the last time I saw her, she was crying on your shoulder," Eden reminded him.

"Oh, yeah, well, she's fine now," he stammered.

"Is there something you're not telling me?" Eden asked, becoming alarmed by his unease.

" 'Course not. If you don't believe me, go see for yourself. I'll take care of your horse."

Only too glad to be relieved of the duty, Eden hurried across the yard and into the house. "Fiona?" she called the instant she crossed the threshold, but Fiona was sitting in the front room, calmly embroidering a pillowcase.

"What is it, dear?" she asked, her voice serene.

It took a minute for Eden's eyes to become accustomed to the interior light. When she could finally focus, Fiona stood in front of her, her expression as serene as her voice.

"I was a little worried about you. Marcus

said . . ." Her voice trailed off as she noticed more than just Fiona's expression was serene. Suddenly, Eden realized just how strained Fiona had been these past weeks, because now all the strain was gone. Her eyes, her face, even the way she held her body, spoke of peace and happiness. "What on earth happened to you today?"

"Whatever do you mean?" Fiona asked as color stained her delicate cheeks.

"I mean, you look . . . I don't know what."

"Well loved?" Fiona suggested, her lips quirking into a smile.

Eden nodded, returning her smile. "And extremely happy. I'm beginning not to mind my saddle sores too much if spending the day alone with Marcus had this effect on you."

"Oh, dear, are you really very sore? Here sit down," Fiona urged. "That is, if you can."

"Just barely," Eden said, lowering herself gingerly onto the sofa. "What went on here while I was gone, anyway?" she asked suspiciously.

"Things about which an unmarried girl should know nothing," Fiona countered slyly. Eden winced, thinking how shocked Fiona would be to know she understood far more than she should. "Now tell me how your day with Mr. Scott went."

"Well, he seemed to like my britches," she replied.

"Eden!" Fiona scolded. "Of all the shocking . . . You really are beyond the pale. I'm afraid I've failed you miserably."

"Well, he did. Couldn't keep his eyes off me all day, although he certainly tried to pretend he wasn't looking. I found out he had a girl once, but she broke it off when she found out he was a gunfighter."

"My goodness, you seem to have made good use of your time together."

"Not good enough. I'm going out with him again tomorrow."

"You most certainly are not! You will be the scandal of the state riding around dressed like a common ranch hand."

"Well, you were the one who said I'd never get any time with him unless I did, and you were right. Besides, if I'm gone, you and Marcus will be alone again."

She could see Fiona was tempted, but her proper British upbringing was too deeply ingrained to permit her to be swayed. "Nonsense, Marcus and I don't need to be alone. Besides, Marcus will probably want to go out himself tomorrow."

"Not if he had as much fun today as you did," Eden guessed. "Tell me, does he make love to you in the parlor when there's no one to see?"

"Eden, what a shocking thing to ask!"

"Well, I've seen some shocking things lately, like Marcus kissing you in the kitchen. Come to think of it, maybe I will stay here tomorrow. Maybe by watching you two I'll find out those things an unmarried girl isn't supposed to know."

Fiona was scarlet now, so Eden decided to show a little mercy. "Do you suppose I could have a hot bath to soak in for a while before supper?"

"Of course," Fiona said, amusingly eager to change the subject. "I'll have it ready for you in a few moments."

Eden didn't raise the subject of her plans for the next day again that evening, but neither Marcus nor Fiona seemed to notice. They were too busy exchanging long, lingering looks with each other, looks that reminded Eden painfully of the kind of relationship she wanted with Lincoln Scott. Since Linc had taken his supper with the men, she was only too glad to retire early and leave the two of them to moon over each other in privacy.

The next morning she was stiff and sore and extremely sorry she had ever conceived of the idea of being a cowboy, even for one day. Her aches still weren't enough to alter her purpose, however, so she once again donned her britches and sauntered down to the cookhouse just in time to join the men for breakfast.

Melancholy ostentatiously cleared a place for her next to him at the table, and one of the other men jumped up to get her a plate. Linc pulled his hat brim down low so she couldn't see his eyes, but his mouth wasn't smiling. A good sign, she thought.

"Who're you gonna ride with today, Miss Eden?" Melancholy asked, giving Linc a sidelong glance.

"I don't know. That's up to the foreman, isn't it?" she asked innocently, thinking that if he assigned her to ride with one of the other men, she would suddenly remember a previous engagement.

"How about it, Linc?" Melancholy asked. "You gonna have pity on one of us?"

"Not on your life," Linc replied lightly. "I wouldn't trust any one of you waddies alone with Miss Eden for a minute."

"And what makes you so trustworthy?" Melancholy wanted to know.

Eden cheerfully helped Linc out. "Linc doesn't have to worry about compromising me since we're already engaged. He can only marry me once, you know."

She expected the others to laugh, but instead they looked at her strangely. Before she could ask what was wrong, Linc cleared his throat.

"Let's decide where everybody goes today."

Melancholy once again described the various sections into which the ranch had been divided for patrol, and when he came to the western section, Eden impulsively said, "Linc, let's take that one."

His expression was curious, but he said, "All right." Plainly he had no idea why she'd selected the area. She'd let it be a surprise.

The morning passed quickly as they chased wandering cows back in the right direction and treated injuries and earmarked a few newborn calves for future branding. There was one bad moment when they spotted two other cowboys off in the distance and Eden identified them as Dirk Blaine's men.

"What're they doing here?" Linc asked, his hand going automatically for his gun.

"That's Blaine's land over there. They're riding the line, same as us."

Linc swore eloquently as the two men turned tail and rode off in a cloud of dust. "I'm going to take you right back to the ranch."

"You most certainly are not. We've got work to do."

He argued some more, shouting when she simply ignored him, and finally she said, "If you want me to go back to the ranch, you'll have to carry me there, bodily."

He was silenced by the image that called up, and the argument ended instantly. She noticed he was much more wary from then on, watching their back trail and constantly scanning the horizon.

At least she knew a place where such vigilance would not be necessary, and she felt a rising sense of excitement as they neared the destination she had in mind. Never doubting her ability to convince Linc to go there, she only hoped something momentous would happen once she did.

They were near when they spotted a small herd of cattle and discovered one of the young steers had been badly mauled.

"Panther, maybe," Linc said. "Looks like it might've happened last night."

The animal would die if they didn't treat the wound, but the steer was understandably skittish. Linc cut him from the herd, but he circled back twice before Linc could get him completely away and in a position for Eden to rope him.

His horns were cockeyed, and she needed two passes to finally get the rope over them. By then the steer was furious, and he fought the rope, bellowing with rage and threatening to charge Eden's horse.

Linc forced himself not to hurry, knowing he needed to catch the animal on the first pass and so couldn't afford a mistake, but the steer was going crazy now. At last Linc saw a chance and threw his rope, but he caught only one leg.

"Give him some slack!" Linc shouted as he fought to free his rope so he could try again, but the steer went wild when he felt his hoof captured. He danced in a circle, jerking the rope from Linc's hands, and when he came around again, he charged right for Eden.

"Eden!" he cried in warning, but she'd seen the danger, and her range-bred horse was already reacting, bolting out of the path of the deadly horns. Seeing the maneuver, the steer changed course but not quickly enough, and Eden's horse sidestepped as the steer hurtled past.

For an instant Linc thought Eden was safe until he heard her cry of pain. She grabbed her thigh, but not before Linc saw the jagged edge of torn cloth. The steer's horn had caught her. How badly, he couldn't tell, but he knew he had to make sure the son of a bitch didn't get a second chance.

Spurring his own horse, he pulled out his pistol and galloped after the running steer, who was circling back on its quarry. He cut the animal off and fired a warning blast right in the steer's face. Screaming in terror now, the animal promptly swerved, with Linc pounding right on his heels. A few more shots sent him on his way, and when Linc was sure he wouldn't be back, he used the spurs again as he raced back to Eden.

He brought his horse to a sliding halt near where she still sat her own horse. She had just finished tying her bandana around the wound.

"How bad is it?"

She looked up at him, her face pale, but she managed a smile. "Not too bad," she assured him. "I think he just grazed me."

Briefly he debated the wisdom of examining the wound then and there and decided not to. If it was as bad as Linc feared, Eden was better off not knowing until she was safe. "I'll take you right back to the ranch," he said, reaching for her reins.

"No!" she cried, stopping him. "It's not bad, really. If we can just clean it out, I'll be fine."

"Clean it out with what?" he demanded, glancing around the empty prairie.

"There's a creek near here. You know, the one beside the cave? Just over that rise," she said, pointing.

He considered for a moment, then finally decided it would be better to clean the wound at once and bind it up. Then he could take her back to the ranch. "Can you ride?"

"I think so. It's not bleeding much."

Deep puncture wounds usually didn't, Linc thought with growing apprehension. God, if she was badly hurt, how would he bear it? "Hold on, I'll lead your horse," he told her, not surprised to see his hand tremble as he reached for her reins again. "Holler if you feel like you're going to faint or anything."

She nodded, gripping the saddle horn with both hands.

The ride seemed to take forever. Linc alternately watched for the creek and watched Eden's face. She was doing well, but she still looked pale. The wound wasn't bleeding, either. A clean gash would have soaked her pant leg by now.

Fear clogged his throat by the time the creek came into view.

"The cave is right there," she said, indicating the clump of undergrowth he recognized. "We could get in out of the sun."

And out of sight of any of Blaine's men who might be around, Linc thought. He climbed down and found the opening, then led Eden's horse and his own to it. She started to climb down, but cried out in pain. Linc was beside her in a minute, lifting her gently and carrying her inside. He laid her down carefully on the cool ground.

"Don't move," he commanded, then led the horses inside and into the inner room. He was back in an instant. By then she had untied the bandana, and when Linc saw how little blood was on it, a brand new terror claimed him.

Kneeling beside her, he tried to see the wound, but the tear in her pants was too small and the light too dim. He reached into his boot and pulled out the knife he kept concealed there.

"What are you going to do with that?" she demanded, obviously terrified.

"I'm going to cut your pant leg open."

"No, you'll ruin them! Let me take them off."

Linc glanced down at the form-fitting garment with a sense of foreboding. "I don't suppose you've got anything on under those things, do you?" he asked gruffly, fighting the stirring of desire.

She glanced down at them and then back up at

him. "Uh, no," she admitted sheepishly.

Muttering a curse, he swiftly unbuttoned his vest and stripped it off.

"What are you doing?" she asked, still sounding frightened.

"I'm going to give you my shirt to cover up with." The cool air of the cave raised gooseflesh on his bare skin as he peeled the shirt off his shoulders. He reminded himself Eden was hurt. He had no business thinking the things he was thinking. Handing her the shirt, he found he had to clear the hoarseness out of his voice to speak. "Do you need some help?"

"I . . . uh, yes, my boots."

Without further instruction, he carefully pulled her boots off and set them aside. She was already unbuttoning the fly of her jeans. Linc averted his eyes until she made an odd noise, almost like a laugh, which brought his gaze immediately to her face.

"I was just thinking how I took *your* pants off in here," she said with a strained smile. "Do you remember?"

How could he ever forget? He managed to smile back. "Sure. If I've got it right, this is how it goes." He picked up his shirt and spread it over her lap.

Beneath the covering, she eased the pants over her hips, and Linc assisted by pulling on the legs. Her pants fit much more snugly than his, so it took a little maneuvering, but at last he pulled them free.

And there she was, the luscious Eden Campbell,

284

stretched out on the cave floor with her long, beautiful legs looking impossibly white against the rock, and her glorious green eyes staring up at him in complete trust.

Gently, carefully, he lifted the edge of his shirt to reveal the angry red gash on her thigh. "Oh, my God."

Chapter Nine

Eden glanced down her thigh where the trickle of blood from the long scrape had already dried. "I told you it wasn't bad," she said, shaking her head. "You were going to ruin a perfectly good pair of pants for nothing!"

Linc ran a hand over his face and released a ragged breath. "You acted like it hurt," he reminded her indignantly.

Naked from the waist up, he looked so overwhelmingly appealing, Eden felt slightly breathless. "It *does* hurt," she insisted. "It'll probably be black and blue for a month."

He glared at her for a long moment. She tried a placating smile, but that only seemed to irritate him more. "I reckon we'd better clean it up anyways," he muttered finally, pulling a bandana from his pocket as he rose to his feet.

"Where are you going?" she asked.

"For water," he replied, not bothering to look back.

"Well," Eden huffed, adjusting his shirt more

modestly across her hips. Suddenly she wondered how she looked after a morning in the saddle. Pulling off her hat, she ran her fingers hastily over her hair, smoothing it as best she could until she saw his figure filling the doorway again. Leaning back on both elbows, she looked up at him and smiled.

He didn't so much as glance at her. Kneeling down, he pulled off his Stetson, set it carefully aside, and held out the dripping bandana.

"Uh, would you do it?" she asked coyly.

"No," he snapped, thrusting the bandana toward her.

Stung, she struggled to a sitting position so she could accept the cloth, but as she took it from him, she noticed he still refused to meet her eye. What on earth was wrong with him, anyway? she wondered in annoyance, but the answer came to her almost at once: if she was disturbed by his state of undress, wouldn't he be equally disturbed by hers?

Smiling with renewed confidence, she laid the bandana on her injured leg, sighing at the cooling relief. Beside her, he sat back on his heels.

"Are you going to be all right?" he asked after a minute.

"I'd like to rest a little while, if you don't mind. It feels good to be out of the sun."

"Maybe you're cold," he ventured. His gaze met hers for a moment before darting away again.

"Maybe you are," she countered, admiring the dark hair blanketing his bare chest. "If you want your shirt back . . ." She made as if to give it to him.

"No!" he assured her almost frantically. "I mean, I'm not cold." He looked away again, up at the cave opening and all around, anywhere except at her. Her guess had been right: he was disturbed, but not the way she wanted him to be. Remembering how Fiona and Marcus had stared at each other the night before, Eden stifled another sigh.

"Linc?"

"What?" He looked her right in the eye, holding his gaze steady as if to shift it might mean disaster.

"Do you think I'm attractive?"

"What . . . What difference does it make?" he hedged.

She shrugged. "I guess it doesn't, but I can't help thinking . . ." She let her voice trail off provocatively.

"Thinking what?" he asked as if the words were being dragged from him by force.

"Well, seeing you like that," she indicated his bare chest, "reminds me of the time I undressed you." He folded his arms self-consciously across his chest, but she pretended not to notice. "I thought you were very attractive, and I was just wondering . . . well, if you thought I was, too."

"You already know the answer to that," he said gruffly.

"I do? How?"

"From what happened . . . at the picnic." His eyes were bleak again, just as they had been yesterday when he spoke of his past.

Determined to solve the mystery of the picnic once and for all, Eden frowned. "But when you refused to marry me, I thought — "

"I never refused to marry you!" he insisted, genuinely shocked.

"Well, maybe not," she conceded, "but you did your best to convince me I shouldn't *want* to marry you."

"I wasn't trying to talk you out of it," he protested.

"Oh, and I suppose you haven't been trying to talk me out of it since then either," she reminded him, not having to feign her outrage.

"That's different. I . . . I came to my senses and — "

" — and decided you didn't want me for a wife," she supplied bitterly. "Don't worry, if you don't think I'm pretty — "

"Dammit, Eden!" he swore, but she ignored him.

" — or you just don't like me, all you have to do is say so!"

"You know it isn't that! I've told you!"

"You haven't told me anything that makes any sense!"

"I've told you no woman in her right mind would want anything to do with me!"

"Maybe I'm not in my right mind! Maybe I'm crazy in love with you!"

The words hung between them for several heartbeats, the air so thick Eden could hardly breathe it. Had she gone too far? Suddenly, she remembered she was lying here half-naked and completely vulnerable. If he wanted to take advantage of her . . .

But he didn't move, didn't breathe, didn't even blink for what seemed a long time. At last he said, "You'd *have* to be crazy to be in love with me."

She swallowed the lump in her throat and managed a rueful smile. "Then I guess somebody ought to lock me up, because I do love you, Linc. I just wish you loved me back."

Anger kindled in his eyes. "Don't tease me, Eden. You know how I feel about you."

"That's just it, Linc, I don't have any idea how you feel! Do you care for me at all?"

"God, yes!" he cried, already reaching for her when he caught himself.

"Do you love me?" she demanded, her heart pounding, her hopes soaring.

"Eden, don't do this," he begged desperately.

"Please, Linc, I have to know!"

He hesitated, his eyes full of despair, and for a moment she thought he would deny it.

"Yes, I love you," he said at last, his words no more than a hoarse whisper.

"Oh, Linc!" she cried and, heedless of her injury, launched herself into his arms.

He caught her and held her fast, crushing her to him with the same desperation with which he'd tried to hold her off a few seconds ago. Eden wanted to laugh and cry at the same time, but instead she kissed him, pressing her mouth to his joyfully.

His lips opened over hers, as if he would devour

her, and she responded, granting him access to the sensitive inner recesses which he explored with loving thoroughness. The invasion stirred memories, and her body warmed in response. She ran her hands greedily over the heated satin of his back, and desire clenched in her belly.

His hands were moving, too, caressing her shoulders and down and down, until they encountered the end of her shirttail and the naked skin beneath. He gasped, dragging his mouth from hers.

"Eden, where . . . where's my shirt?"

"I don't know," she murmured, pressing a string of kisses along his jaw.

With what must have taken superhuman will, he grasped her waist and pushed her gently away. "Eden, stop!"

She stopped, looking up at him quizzically.

"If we keep this up . . ." He cleared his throat and tried again. "You'd better get your clothes on."

She smiled wickedly. "Isn't it easier with my clothes off?"

"Eden," he said in warning, but she was having none of it.

"You might as well take advantage of me because I'm going to say you did anyway."

"What?"

"I'm going to tell Marcus that you lured me into this cave and tore off my clothes and had your way with me. Then I'm going to beg him to force you to marry me."

"You won't tell Marcus anything," he scoffed. "You said you didn't want a shotgun wedding."

291

"I didn't when I thought you didn't love me. Now, of course, everything is different," she informed him, running her hands down his chest and raking her fingers through the dark swirls of hair she found there.

His breath caught on a gasp. "You'd really do that?"

"If I have to," she replied sweetly. "Will I have to?"

He stared at her for what seemed ages; then finally, slowly, he shook his head. For the first time, she saw actual joy glittering in his eyes. His hands came up to cup her face tenderly. "Eden, will you marry me?"

"Oh, yes, Linc! Yes, yes, yes!" Punctuating her reply with kisses, she toppled him over until they lay side by side on the cold floor of the cave.

But Eden felt nothing except the solid strength of Linc's body pressed against the length of hers. They kissed until they were breathless, and when they pulled apart, Linc gasped, "I'm not made of stone, honey. You'd better get those pants back on or else."

"Or else what?" Eden asked, widening her eyes in feigned innocence.

"You know what," he replied with a grin, and once again Eden felt the tantalizing flutter of desire.

"Yes, I do," she said, untangling herself and pushing up to a sitting position.

Linc rolled to his back, arms flung wide, breath coming in ragged gasps. She studied him a moment, thinking how wanton he looked and how very much she wanted him.

So instead of reaching for her pants, she began to unbutton her vest. She had it off before Linc realized what she was doing. His shock had hardly registered before she started unbuttoning her shirt.

"Eden?" The word held a wealth of questions.

"Better get those boots off, cowboy."

He scrambled upright. "Are you sure?"

"Darn right I'm sure," she said, purposely misunderstanding him. "You can't get your pants off until you get rid of those boots."

Grinning at her nonsense, he swiftly pulled off his boots and tossed them away. Just as swiftly, he unbuckled his gunbelt and laid it carefully aside. But instead of removing the rest of his clothes, he reached for his shirt, which Eden had lost a few moments ago.

She opened her mouth to protest, then saw he was spreading it behind him on the floor of the cave. Suddenly the logistics of the matter began to occur to her, and as she considered lying beneath Linc's weight on the stony ground, her passion cooled considerably.

But Linc was peeling out of his jeans, and Eden knew it was too late to change her mind even if she'd wanted to. Once again the body that had haunted her dreams lay naked before her, boldly aroused and blatantly masculine. She shivered, all thoughts of logistics forgotten.

She'd unbuttoned her shirt, but it still covered her from neck to thigh. Linc reached for her. Half-expecting him to remove the garment himself, she was surprised when he simply cupped the back of her head and drew her mouth down to his. His kiss was infinitely sweet, and the sweetness spread through her like warm honey.

Feeling weak, she could not resist when he pulled the rest of her down until her body covered his with only her shirt between them. While his mouth continued its loving exploration of hers, his hands stroked her back and buttocks, finding the end of her shirt and groping beneath for the chilled flesh.

His hot, callused palms seemed to scorch her as he kneaded her soft curves, and she reveled in the delicious abrasion of his hair-roughed legs against her smoother ones. Beneath her belly, she felt the hard evidence of his desire, and her own body ached with emptiness.

Gooseflesh rose on her legs, sweeping up and up, into her very core, and she shuddered with need. Her heart hammered, or perhaps it was his heart. They were so close, she couldn't tell. But they weren't close enough.

She breathed his name against his heated skin, and he parted her legs, gently stroking the sensitized flesh of her inner thighs. Instinctively, she moved her hips against his, seeking the union she craved.

When would he turn them over? she wondered wildly, half-crazed with want, but he didn't turn her over at all. Instead he lifted her, spreading her legs, gently so as not to hurt her wound, until she straddled him. At first she didn't understand, but then she felt the hot hardness of him prodding.

"Oh!" she cried, surprised and delighted. With patient hands he tutored her, guiding her until their bodies joined and his shaft penetrated and filled her. Sighing her ecstasy, she arched her back and responded to his unspoken commands until she sat astride him, filled with the promise of his love.

But he wasn't finished yet. Slowly, so she could resist if she wished, he opened her shirt and spread it, revealing the breasts that ached for his touch. She yearned toward him, offering herself, and the hands that had given her so much pleasure closed over the white orbs.

With another sigh, she let the shirt slide off her shoulders and tossed it aside, then lowered her own hands to his chest where she let her fingers tunnel into the dark hair to find the flat, masculine nipples.

"Oh, God, Eden," he groaned. "I've been dreaming about this for two days."

"This? Exactly this?" she marveled breathlessly.

"Yes, the whole time . . . I was watching you . . . bouncing in that damn saddle . . ."

She could feel the strain in him. It slickened his skin and darkened his eyes. "Bouncing?" she echoed mischievously. "Like this?"

He groaned and grabbed her hips, stilling them. "Not so fast!" he cautioned, his voice ragged. "Slowly."

She followed his lead until his fingers slid down her belly into the auburn curls. Sensation streaked through her, numbing her to everything except the pleasure his touch gave her.

His free hand caressed her, teasing her nipples to pebbled hardness and cupping her bottom for restraint when she grew too urgent. Passion coiled in her, pulling tighter and tighter until she could bear it no longer. She collapsed onto his chest, clutching at him, her mouth seeking his desperately.

He held her to him, as desperate as she, and together they rode out the storm, gasping, panting, clinging. He called her name, arching and thrusting one last, shuddering time, flooding her with life and shattering the last remnants of her control. The end came in a glorious, wrenching spasm that curled her fingers and toes and tore an anguished cry of release from her lips.

For a long time they lay together as more spasms echoed through them. Linc held her to his heart, whispering words of love in the disjointed phrases of delirium. But Eden understood, being half-delirious herself. Was this the kind of loving Marcus and Fiona had engaged in yesterday, the kind of loving that had put such a glow on her stepmother's face? Eden imagined her own must be absolutely shining.

Still sprawled across Linc's beloved body, she stroked the moist velvet of his skin, pressing kisses to his collarbone and inhaling the intoxicating scent of him. Entranced, she closed her eyes and dozed.

She awoke some time later when the chill of the cave had cooled her passion-heated skin. Only warm where she touched Linc, who still slept soundly, she decided she would be wise to take his advice, however belatedly, and put some clothes on. Easing out of his embrace, she snatched up the shirt she had previously discarded and slipped it on, grateful for its warmth.

Only then did she dare look at Linc. He was, as she had often thought, magnificent, even when the urgency of his passion had been tamed and lay limp and still. His broad chest rose and fell with the rhythm of his breathing, his powerful arms relaxed in repose. She admired the length of his legs, like two sturdy trees, symbolizing his unyielding strength.

Lincoln Scott would never bend for any man, but he had bent for her, surrendering to the power of her love. He was hers now, and nothing would ever change that. Smiling with satisfaction at the thought, she started to get up and felt a stab of pain in her thigh.

Oh, dear! She'd completely forgotten her encounter with the steer this afternoon. Odd how she hadn't felt so much as a twinge while she'd been busy with Linc, but now she could see her prediction had been correct. The wound was already changing color. Maybe she ought to put another cold rag on it, she thought. And maybe she ought to wash up a bit before struggling back into her jeans, she added with a smile.

Retrieving Linc's bandana from where it had fallen, she crept out of the cave, trying not to waken Linc. Having him see her naked when they were making love was one thing. Letting him see her wash up afterwards was quite another.

Slipping through the undergrowth, she found the creek running clear and cool over its rocky bed. No more than a few inches deep and icy cold, it wouldn't provide much of a bathing spot, but Eden knelt by its edge and, opening her shirt, splashed handfuls of frigid water over the parts of her most in need of freshening.

The initial shock brought an involuntary cry to her lips, but she bit back the rest of them, shivering silently so as not to disturb Linc. When she was done, she dipped the bandana into the water and laid it on her aching leg. With a sigh, she closed her eyes and savored the relief.

"Well, now, what a nice surprise."

Eden jumped, and when her eyes flew open, she found Dirk Blaine standing on the bank above, leering down at her. With a cry of horror, she realized her shirt still hung open, completely exposing her. Snatching it shut, she lurched clumsily to her feet. "What are you doing here?" she demanded, wondering whether or not she should try to alert Linc. Would he bring his gun or would he be too groggy to think of it? Before she would risk it, she would try to get rid of Blaine herself.

"I've been looking for you all day, Miss Eden," he said with mock civility. "Ever since some of my men told me you was out riding."

"I'm not alone," she tried, hoping to scare him away.

He glanced around contemptuously. "I can see you're not. You don't expect me to believe you've been rolling around in the bushes buck naked with some cowboy, now do you?"

Eden felt the heat scalding her face, but before she could think of a reply, he laughed evilly. " 'Course, that's exactly what you're gonna be doing in just a minute."

He started down the bank, skidding and slipping.

"No!" she cried, backing toward the cave, but she caught herself. She couldn't lead Blaine in there where he could catch Linc by surprise. "Get out of here, Dirk Blaine!" she shouted.

"Are you scared?" he taunted, still grinning lasciviously. "I like it that way." He rubbed his crotch obscenely and jumped across the thin ribbon of water.

"Linc!" she screamed, and Blaine grabbed her arms. She fought as she had fought his brother, kicking and clawing, but her bare feet thudded ineffectually against his boots and he easily held her arms away from his face.

"Let's see what we've got here," he said, holding her away from him. Her shirt had fallen open in the struggle and once again she was completely exposed.

"You bastard, let me go!" she shouted, writhing in humiliation and praying Linc could hear her. *"Linc!"*

"He's not gonna save you this time," Blaine sneered. "Now let's get this thing off you and get down to business."

Eden screamed as he fought to tear the shirt from her back. Raking his hands with her nails, she thrashed frantically.

"Turn her loose!"

Linc's command startled them both. For a second, Blaine relaxed his grip on her, and she wrenched free. Unfortunately, she wasted a precious second to cover herself, and in that second Blaine recovered. Before she could run, his arm closed around her neck. He hauled her against him, oblivious to her struggles, and jerked out his pistol, ready to shoot his rival, but he had no target.

Gasping for breath, Eden searched wildly for Linc, but he was nowhere to be seen.

"You whore!" Blaine hissed, tightening his grip until she couldn't breathe at all. "You *were* out here with him! I should've known you were no better than the rest of them. Well, just you wait until I get you home."

He was muttering something, something about his plans for her, but the roaring in her ears drowned it out. Dark spots danced before her eyes, her body no longer obeyed her commands to fight him, and she felt consciousness slipping away.

Then something exploded, and Blaine jumped in surprise, whirling around and dragging her with him. The hasty movement loosened his grip, and she gasped, desperately drawing air into her beleaguered lungs. "Linc!" she managed to croak, but still she saw no sign of him.

"Come out and fight like a man!" Blaine shouted, brandishing his pistol.

"Stop hiding behind a woman, and I will!" Linc

replied.

His voice came from behind them, and Blaine whirled again, firing blindly into the undergrowth. One, two, three shots. Eden screamed her protest, expecting at any moment to hear Linc's cry of pain as one of the bullets pierced his flesh, but when Blaine's gun ceased, all she heard was the pounding of her own heart and Blaine's string of curses.

"Come out or I'll kill her!" Blaine tried, still scanning the entire area with an air of desperation.

"A dead woman's no fun!" Linc called from off to Blaine's left. Blaine fired again, once, twice!

Five shots! Most men only carried five loads in their six shooters so the hammer rested on an empty chamber and couldn't go off accidentally. She tried to remember if his gun had clicked on an empty chamber the first time but couldn't. Don't come out yet! she cried silently, willing Linc's safety.

She could actually smell Blaine's fear, a stink that made her gag. His breath came in furious gasps as he scanned the creekbed.

Linc must be part Indian, Eden thought wildly, to move so silently. Where was he now? Had one of Blaine's bullets struck him?

Suddenly, Blaine started moving, scrambling backward into the creek. Eden tried to resist, digging in her heels, but Blaine was too strong, and her bare feet offered little resistance. The icy water closed around her ankles and the slippery rocks gave her no purchase.

"Going somewheres?" Linc taunted, this time

from a different spot, but this time Blaine didn't fire. He must have been counting his bullets, too.

"I'm going to my horse!" Blaine called back. "I'll let her go as soon as I'm away from here, but if you follow me, I swear to God, I'll kill her."

They were at the cutbank. Blaine started backing up it, but his feet slipped in the mud, sending them both sprawling. He swore as Eden broke free of his grasp and rolled away, splashing into the creek and scrambling across it.

Seeing his advantage lost, Blaine turned and ran, clawing his way up the bank as Linc's bullets slammed into the dirt around him. Still swearing, he hauled himself over the top and sprinted away.

Behind her, Eden heard the pounding of Linc's feet as he emerged from his hiding place, jumping over her, splashing through the water and darting up the bank after Blaine.

"Be careful!" she cried, but just as he disappeared over the top, she heard the sound of a horse running.

Blaine was fleeing. With a cry of relief, Eden sat up in time to see Linc bounding down the bank again.

"Are you all right?" he demanded, sloshing barefoot through the stream again and dropping down beside her, his pistol still in his hand. He was clad only in his jeans.

He looked so dear, she wanted to cry, and she blinked at the hot sting of tears. "Oh, Linc, I'm sorry!"

"Sorry? What for?"

"I shouldn't have gone outside without looking around! I knew you were worried about Blaine all morning, but I never thought . . . How on earth did he find us?"

"Probably tracked us. It wasn't your fault. Hey, don't cry!"

But Eden had no control over the tears flooding her eyes and spilling over onto her cheeks. Linc's arms came around her, and he pulled her to him. Conscious of the gun he still held, Eden cried even harder as she thought of how many times Blaine had fired. If one of those bullets had hit Linc . . .

"Eden!" Linc said sharply after a moment.

Eden lifted tear-filled eyes to him.

"We don't have time for this. We've got to get out of here. Blaine might come back, and he might bring some of his men with him. I want to get you home first."

She nodded, scrubbing the moisture from her cheeks with both hands. Her tears could wait until later.

"Splash some water on your face, then go inside and get dressed. I'll keep watch."

She nodded again, still unable to speak. He helped her over to the water with gentle hands. After washing her face, she lurched to her feet and on trembling legs hurried back inside the cave. From the inner room, one of the horses whickered questioningly, and she managed to make a few soothing sounds as she collected her scattered clothing.

Eden could still feel Blaine's touch and the mem-

303

ory defiled the beauty of her and Linc's lovemaking. Ashamed and humiliated, she struggled into her jeans, buttoned her damp shirt, and slipped on her vest. Retrieving her hat, she stepped into her boots and stomped them on. Determined to show Linc a brave face, she dried what was left of her tears on her shirt sleeve and marched back outside the cave.

Linc stood with his back to her, watching and listening, his long legs spread, bare shoulders tensed, his gun ready. Once again she remembered how she had thought him unyielding. He would never let anything happen to her.

If only nothing happened to *him!* How would she bear life without him now that she knew his love?

Clearing the roughness out of her voice, she said, "I'm ready."

He turned and looked her over from head to foot as if doubting her word. "Here," he said softly after a moment, carefully pressing his pistol into her hand. "If you see anybody, call me."

He disappeared inside the cave, and she blinked rapidly to keep the moisture from blurring her vision. Entrusted to guard him, she had no intention of letting him down.

In a few minutes he returned, fully clothed. Only his eyes gave evidence of what they had just endured. She wondered if she looked equally unscathed, and doubted it.

Taking the gun from her, he looked at her closely and asked, "Are you all right?"

Fighting a hysterical urge to laugh at the question he always asked at the most terrible times, she nodded.

"Can you get the horses?"

She drew a deep breath and nodded again. Action would help keep her from remembering what had just happened.

He touched her cheek tenderly with his fingertips. "Go inside and bring the horses out then. I'll climb up onto the bank and take a look-see. Don't bring them up until I call you."

But he didn't see anything or anyone. Plainly, Dirk Blaine had hightailed it for safety. Linc had to help her mount because her leg was still sore, but soon they were on their way back to the ranch.

Although she tried, Eden couldn't stop remembering the scene with Dirk Blaine, how he had leered at her nakedness and made her feel filthy and defiled. He'd also degraded her love for Linc, making her feel cheap and immoral.

And how did Linc feel? Eden watched him surreptitiously. His face was expressionless, the way he was when he was trying to hide something from her, and he hadn't so much as looked at her during the entire trip back to the ranch. Did he, too, think Blaine had defiled her? Could he no longer stand the sight of her?

She had to know, and although she wasn't sure her emotions were stable enough to discuss it just yet, she also knew she couldn't wait until they got back to the ranch. The minute Marcus learned what had happened, all chance for her and Linc to speak privately would be gone. When the ranch buildings came into view, Eden sucked up her courage and said, "Linc?"

He turned to her instantly. "Are you all right?"

She fervently wished he would stop asking her that. "I . . . Yes, I'm fine. Uh . . . Could we talk? For a minute, before we get to the ranch?"

He reined in, and she followed suit, stopping her horse beside his. "If you're worried about what I'm going to tell Marcus, don't be," he assured her with a smile that warmed her heart. "I don't want a shotgun wedding any more than you do."

The warmth instantly evaporated. "I . . . I guess you don't want any kind of wedding at all now."

He blinked in surprise. "What? What are you talking about?"

Tears burned her eyes, but she refused to weep. "I can't blame you. I mean, after what Blaine did, I can hardly stand to touch myself. You must—"

"Eden, you're talking crazy!" He reached for her, but her horse shied, dancing away a step.

With a curse, he bolted from his saddle and hurried around to pluck her from hers. Fury burned like blue fire in his eyes, and Eden flinched as he set her on her feet. "Linc, don't," she pleaded, knowing she couldn't bear his scorn.

"Don't what? Eden, listen to me! Nothing's changed between us."

"Everything's changed!" she wailed. "He . . . he called me a whore." Eden covered her face with both hands as she recalled her boldness in the cave. Did Linc think her a wanton, too?

His arms came around her, fiercely possessive. "Dirk Blaine is a stupid son of a bitch!" he raged. "When I think of what he did to you, I want to cut his eyes out and—"

Eden convulsed on a strangled sob.

"Don't cry," he begged her, but she couldn't help it.

"I . . . I feel so dirty," she choked, and his arms tightened protectively. "You can't even look at me anymore!"

"What?" he demanded, pushing her slightly away so he could see her face. When she wouldn't uncover it, he pulled her hands away. "What are you talking about?"

"You haven't looked at me once since we left the cave," she accused.

He gaped at her. "I've been watching for Blaine and his men."

But she was past listening to logic. Teetering on the ragged edge of hysteria, she couldn't stop herself. "You . . . you think I'm cheap!"

"Don't tell me what I think!" he cried, grabbing her by the shoulders and shaking her sharply.

Her head snapped, shocking her to attention. She stared up at him, frightened once again by the fury in his eyes.

"Listen to me!" he commanded. "Dirk Blaine is going to pay for what he did to you, but he didn't make me think you're a whore or cheap or anything else. And I swear to God, as long as I'm alive, neither Dirk Blaine nor any other man is going to lay a finger on you again. Do you understand?"

"Do you . . . do you still want to marry me?" she asked timidly.

"God, yes! Why wouldn't I?"

She had no intention of answering such a question. "It doesn't matter to you? What happened, I mean?"

"Oh, it matters plenty," he assured her grimly. "And maybe it'll mean *you* won't want to marry *me*."

"What do you mean?"

"You told me before that if I wanted you, I'd have to find another way to fight, but Eden, I don't know any other way. I'm going after Blaine, and when I find him . . ."

His voice trailed off ominously, and Eden felt the high tide of raw terror swelling within her. "No, Linc! You can't. He'll kill you!"

Linc's eyes grew bleak. "You don't have much faith in me, do you?"

"Oh, I know you could beat him in a fair fight, but he's too much of a coward to face you! He'll shoot you in the back."

"Then I'll *make* him face me. Don't worry about me, Eden. I know how to take care of myself."

But she *was* worried and would always be because she loved him so much. Slipping her arms around his waist, she held him close, comforting herself with the reassuring thumping of his heart beneath her ear.

He held her gently, stroking down her back and tugging on her auburn braid. At last he said,

"Eden, will it make any difference between us? If I kill him, I mean?"

She shook her head against his chest, dislodging her hat, which fell to the ground unnoticed.

"Then you'll still want to marry me?"

She almost laughed aloud. How could he even ask such a question? Managing a small smile, she drew back and looked up at him. "If I don't, you can always complain to Marcus that I've ruined you. I'm sure he'll force me to marry you."

His lips twitched into a reluctant grin. "Don't think I won't try it."

"You won't have to," she promised. "Oh, dear!" she remembered suddenly. "We can't even announce our engagement since everybody thinks we're already engaged."

"No, they don't," he corrected her. "I already told the boys the whole story the other day. They were all pretty relieved to hear you were still free, too. Maybe we shouldn't tell them any different for a while. One of them might shoot me in the back before Blaine gets a chance to."

Shooting Linc in the back wasn't a subject about which Eden felt like joking, but she smiled bravely. "Of course we'll tell them, and you'll just have to take your chances. I want the whole world to know."

He touched her face, grazing her cheeks tenderly with his fingertips. His eyes were full of wonder. "I never thought . . ."

"You never thought what?" she prodded when he hesitated.

"I never thought a girl like you would ever want anything to do with a man like me."

She shrugged, feigning nonchalance. "I probably wouldn't have if I hadn't had to take your clothes off first thing. Of course, after that . . ." She laid a hand over her heart and fluttered her eyelashes.

He hauled her back into his arms, grinning wickedly. "Any time you want to do it again, just say the word."

"Oh, Linc, I love you so much!" she cried, flinging her arms around his neck.

He kissed her then, a long lingering kiss that wiped away all the ugly memories. She would have gone on kissing him, but he set her firmly away from him. "Did you forget they can probably see us from the house?"

She didn't care if Marcus and Fiona saw them or not, but she knew they'd be worried, wondering why they didn't just come on into the ranch.

"We need to tell them we had a good reason for coming back early today, too," Linc said.

"Oh dear. I'll have to tell them about the cave, but what will we tell them about what were we doing in there?" she asked, assaulted by a new wave of guilt.

"Let me do the talking and just go along with whatever I say," he told her, leading her over to her horse.

After another long kiss, he helped her back into her saddle and mounted his own horse. When they rode into the ranch yard, Marcus and Fiona were both waiting on the porch, their expressions worried. Fiona took one look at Eden and said, "Oh, my!" Eden supposed her appearance betrayed her ordeal.

"I'm all right, Fee," she assured her stepmother, sliding off her horse and hurrying up the porch steps.

"What happened?" Marcus addressed his question to Linc, who dismounted more slowly.

"Dirk Blaine. We saw a couple of his men this morning, and I reckon they saw us, too. They must've told Blaine Eden was out, so he came looking for her. We figure he tracked us. Eden was alone by the creek, doctoring a scrape she got from a steer who didn't like being roped."

"You were injured?" Fiona asked in concern, looking down at the tear in her jeans.

"It's only a scratch," Eden assured her. "It hardly broke the skin." Linc scowled at her, but she ignored him.

"He must not have known I was nearby," Linc continued, "and tried to attack her, but she screamed for me. I ran him off and brought her straight back here."

"Did he hurt you?" Fiona asked, holding Eden's arms and looking her over. Eden wondered if Fiona could tell by simply looking what she and Linc had been doing just a short time earlier. Not that it mattered, of course, since they would soon be married.

"No, I'm fine, really," Eden said. "Linc came right away. Blaine grabbed me around the neck and tried to hide behind me, just like his brother did, but I got away before he could do anything."

Marcus and Linc stared at each other for a long moment. Marcus's expression was questioning, Linc's was solemn. At last Linc said, "I'm going after him."

Marcus nodded. "The other men will want to go with you when they hear what happened. It's past time we paid that bastard a visit."

"What will you do?" Fiona asked apprehensively, her Dresden face suddenly deathly pale.

"Whatever we have to," Marcus told her grimly. "No man molests my daughter and lives to tell about it."

For a moment Eden thought Fiona would object or at least beg Marcus not to go. Instead her stepmother laid a hand on his arm. "You'll be careful, won't you? If anything happened to you . . ."

"Don't fret yourself," he assured her, his voice rough with emotion. "The only person who's got anything to worry about is Dirk Blaine." He turned to Linc. "Let's take care of the horses."

Eden watched the two men leading the horses toward the corral, knowing they would be making plans for the confrontation as soon as they were out of earshot. She put a comforting arm around her stepmother's shoulders. "They don't have any choice," she said apologetically.

Fiona nodded. "I know. I don't like it, but I also know there simply is no other way to stop a scoundrel like Dirk Blaine."

For a few minutes they watched the two men unsaddling the horses and rubbing them down before turning them loose. Then Eden recalled that for once she also had some good news to tell. "Fee? Linc asked me to marry him."

Fiona's astonishment made Eden smile. "He did! Oh, my dear, how on earth did he find the time? And how on earth did you manage to bring it about?" she added slyly.

"It took some doing," Eden admitted, although she had no intention of explaining any further. "But you were right. The instant I told him I loved him, he surrendered."

"Oh, darling, I'm so happy for you." Fiona hugged her, and Eden felt the sting of tears. These were happy tears, though, and so she let them gather.

"Come inside and tell me all about it. This calls for a celebration. What shall we have for supper?" Neither of them mentioned what would happen after supper, when the men returned and Linc told them what Dirk Blaine had done. The knowledge shadowed Fiona's eyes, but Eden resolutely went along with the charade, wishing she could put her worries from her mind as easily as she had pretended to.

"I don't like it," Linc insisted when he had heard Marcus's plan. "I ain't afraid to face him down."

"Of course you ain't," Marcus agreed. "But only a fool would ride in there just asking for somebody to shoot him in the back. If we wait until they're all asleep, we can round up the rest of his men so you don't have to worry about getting ambushed while you take care of Blaine."

Linc grunted his grudging approval as they walked back to the house. He didn't like waiting. He wanted Dirk Blaine's hide right now.

Once inside Fiona's comfortable parlor, Linc sank gratefully into one of the overstuffed chairs and massaged his aching side. He should probably be taking a nap, he thought, figuring he wouldn't be getting any sleep tonight, but he also knew he was much too angry to rest. When Marcus handed him a shot of whiskey, he downed it in one gulp, relishing the burning warmth of the liquor.

The two men sat and talked for a few minutes, then Eden emerged from the back of the house. She'd had a bath and wore a frilly, flowered dress. Linc's heart lurched at the sight of her. Remembering how she'd looked a short time ago, her exquisite body mounted on his, he felt the surge of renewed desire, and the answering heat spread inexorably through his body.

Eden smiled, a little shyly, he thought, as if she could read his thoughts. Then she came forward and perched on the arm of his chair, laying a hand on his shoulder. She smelled of soap and woman, and Linc was hard pressed not to pull her over into his lap.

Still, the intimacy of their pose gave them away. "What's this?" Marcus demanded.

"What's what?" Linc replied, clearing the hoarseness out of his throat. Eden simply smiled innocently.

"What's this with the two of you?" Marcus said, gesturing toward them.

"Didn't you tell him?" Eden asked Linc in feigned surprise.

"Tell me what?" Marcus snapped impatiently.

Linc waited for Eden to break the news, but her green eyes laughed down at him defiantly. He cleared his throat again. "Me and Eden are getting married."

"Wh . . . ? *Married?* Well, I'll be damned!" Marcus's homely face split into a grin, and he jumped up from his chair, grabbed Linc's hand, and began pumping it exuberantly.

"I see you've heard the news," Fiona remarked with a sly smile as she entered the room. "Mr. Scott, please accept my congratulations."

Linc jumped to his feet, almost toppling Eden from the arm of the chair, and took Fiona's outstretched hand. To his surprise, she used it to pull him closer, slipped her other hand around his neck, and kissed him very softly on the cheek.

"I . . . uh, thanks, Mrs. Pauling," he muttered, his face scalding with embarrassment.

"You must call me Fiona from now on," she said.

When she released him, Marcus put his arm around her and smiled expansively. "Ain't this something, Fee? It's like we're all a family."

"Pretty fancy figuring since not one of us is really related to anyone else," Eden pointed out with a delighted laugh, slipping her arm through Linc's.

Linc wanted to say something, but Marcus's reference to a family had made it impossible for him to speak. Never in his wildest dreams had he imagined such an opportunity. Not only was he getting the most beautiful girl God had put on this earth, but he would have his best friend as a father-in-law and the second most beautiful girl in the world for his mother-in-law.

Even as he smiled in acknowledgment of Marcus's exclamations of delight, Linc couldn't shake the feeling of unreality. What had he ever done to deserve such a fate?

Nothing, a nagging voice said. In fact, he'd done quite a bit to guarantee no one like Eden Campbell would ever look at him twice. And tonight he'd do it again.

A Comanche moon lit the sky as they rode toward the Blaine ranch. In years past, the Indians would have used the light of the full moon to raid. The men who rode this night were raiding, too.

They approached the darkened ranch buildings quietly, depending on the element of surprise. Marcus and Linc dismounted and stole over to the house while Melancholy led the rest of the men to surround the bunkhouse. In keeping with their plan, Marcus and Linc waited until they heard the shouts arousing the sleeping cowboys.

Yelling and swearing, Blaine's men emerged from the bunkhouse, prodded by the Paradise crew and their Winchesters.

"Come out, Blaine!" Linc called, clutching his

own rifle. Flattening himself against the wall by the front door, he braced himself for Blaine to emerge shooting.

From his position on the other side of the door, Marcus lifted his rifle expectantly, but only silence greeted Linc's command.

"He's playing 'possum," Marcus whispered.

Linc nodded and stepped away from the wall. Lifting a foot, he kicked out viciously, splintering the front door, which flew open and slammed against the inside wall.

Ducking out of the doorway, Linc whipped the rifle to his shoulder, prepared to return Blaine's gunfire, but no sound came from within.

"What the hell?" Linc muttered, then said more loudly, "Blaine, come out of there!"

"He ain't here," someone called from the ranch yard where Blaine's men had been herded. Someone had found a lantern in the bunkhouse and lit it now.

"Who said that?" Melancholy demanded, taking the lantern and holding it aloft to illuminate the scene.

"I did," Blaine's foreman said. "He come in this afternoon for a little while, but he rode out again. We ain't seen him since."

"Son of a bitch," Marcus muttered.

"Bring that lantern," Linc called. "Be careful!"

Cautiously, Melancholy approached the cabin, still holding the lantern high. Eerie shadows danced across the porch and into the doorway. Linc motioned for Melancholy to hand him the

317

light.

Holding it at arm's length in his left hand, he stuck it inside the cabin, braced once again for a volley of shots. But none came. Swearing, he stepped into the cabin, lifting the lantern high, but he saw only an empty room. The unmade bunks mocked him. He swore again.

Linc left the cabin and strode out into the yard with Marcus and Melancholy close behind.

When he came face to face with Blaine's foreman, he said, "Where is he?"

"I don't know."

"You lying son of a—"

"I don't know!" Ace insisted, refusing to be intimidated although he wore only a pair of dirty long johns and stood barefoot and unarmed. "He don't ask my permission when he goes someplace."

"You must have an idea," Marcus insisted, but Ace's expression told them he had no intention of expressing those ideas to his captors.

Linc drew a ragged breath, fighting the rage that threatened to overwhelm him.

"If you want a fight, I'll give you one!" a voice said.

Linc looked over into the face of Garth Hamilton. The boy's eyes sparkled with the same fury and frustration Linc felt. He wore only a pair of cotton drawers which revealed a body still scrawny with youth. "You're too young to be in such a hurry to die," Linc remarked, tasting the gall of his own bitterness.

"Who says I'll die?" Hamilton wanted to know.

His hands closed in fists at his sides and his downy cheeks mottled. "Give me a gun, and we'll see who lives and who dies."

"Don't be a fool, boy," Marcus cautioned, stepping up beside Linc. "This ain't even your fight."

"He killed my brother. That makes it my fight!"

"Your brother wasn't worth dying for," Linc said, feeling unutterably weary. How many times would he have to play this scene in his life? "He was a fool to keep on fighting when he was wrong and he was already licked."

"You stole his land!"

"He didn't have any land! He was a squatter and a fence cutter and a rustler."

"God damn you to hell!" the boy howled. "Somebody give me a gun!"

"Let's get out of here," Marcus said in disgust. Still keeping Blaine's men covered, the Paradise crew mounted up. Garth Hamilton continued his tirade, cursing Linc and demanding the opportunity to face him down, but no one paid him any attention.

When they were ready, Marcus looked down at Ace. "You tell Blaine he signed his death warrant this afternoon. If he's smart, he'll get the hell out of this country, and the rest of you boys, too, because if we find out you've been involved in the rustling . . ."

He let the sentence hang ominously, and Ace's face hardened with understanding.

Turning their horses, the Paradise crew rode off into the darkness. Linc maneuvered his horse until

319

he was beside Marcus. "Where do you think he's gone?"

"Hard to tell. Maybe he's run away for good. He must've known we'd come after him."

Linc couldn't let himself believe it. "We ought to check in town."

"We will, tomorrow. No use rousting a lot of honest folks out of their beds for nothing. Somebody will have seen him."

Linc grunted his assent, but his failure to find Blaine rankled. He hadn't even wanted to wait until tonight to go after him. When he remembered the sight of Blaine with his filthy hands on Eden, he wanted to choke the life out of him with his bare hands.

Patience, he told himself. Tomorrow would be plenty of time.

Chapter Ten

"Wake up, you shitbag."

Dirk Blaine groaned and swung his fist in the general direction of the voice. A woman cackled when he missed. "I mean it, Blaine. You've spent all your money, now get the hell out of here. I've got paying customers want to use this room."

Slowly, painfully, Blaine opened his eyes a slit and saw bright morning sunlight filtering through the dusty windowpane. He knew good and well she wouldn't have any customers at this hour. He opened his mouth to refute her claim, but his voice came out a hoarse croak and the effort made his head pound. Goddamn rotgut. His mouth tasted like he'd had breakfast with a buzzard.

"Go to hell, you bitch," he managed finally, but the woman only cackled again.

"If you don't get up on your own, I'll get Herman in here to throw you out," she threatened.

Herman was the huge, simple-minded bouncer. Rumor said he was married to one of the 'hogs' at the hog ranch, but no one seemed to know which one. Blaine just flat didn't care. He did wonder exactly which of the pigs he'd slept with the night before, though. Forcing his eyes wider, he turned his head slightly to where she stood just out of reach beside the rumpled bed.

He groaned again. It was the same red-haired horror he'd been with the last time. In the morning light, her sallow skin hung in unhealthy-looking pouches beneath her eyes and jaw. The red hair was plainly dyed with dark roots showing, and it stuck up in untidy tufts all over her head.

A filthy wrapper which had once been red silk was draped around her ample figure, but what had seemed luscious and inviting last night now looked merely fat and sloppy.

Her eyes weren't even green.

"Let me sleep, you fat whore. I'll pay you next time."

"I don't give credit. Get up and get your pants on, or Herman'll throw you out without 'em. You got five minutes."

With that she walked out in a huff and slammed the door. The sound reverberated like thunder through his head, and he cursed her thoroughly, if silently. Still cursing, he pushed himself upright, holding his head in both hands until the room stopped spinning. When he finally was able to look around, he decided the place looked better spinning. Aside from the rusty iron bedstead, the room contained only a rickety washstand. A rag rug of indeterminate color lay askew on the floor, which hadn't been swept for many months. Sunlight filtering through the foggy window reflected off the dust motes. The sheets on which he lay were a dull gray and reeked of countless unwashed bodies and sex.

He knew a pressing need to vomit, but fought it, not wishing to incur any more of the harridan's wrath. Gritting his teeth against the pain in his head, he slid his legs over the side of the bed and found the clothes he'd discarded sometime the previous night. As he dressed, slowly and with infinite care, he tried to remember how he had come to the hog ranch in the first place. The last time he'd awakened here, he'd sworn never again to waste himself on the slatterns who populated this squalid brothel. Oh, no, he'd had big plans then. He'd planned to have Eden Campbell to share his bed from now on.

The mere thought of that red-haired bitch filled him with rage. All this time he'd thought she was different, a lady, but she was just like all the other women he had known, his mother and the whores who had raised him, even the pig who'd just left this bed. He'd caught his precious Eden practically in the act, wallowing with that gunfighter. How many others had there been?

The thought drove him wild, and by the time he was dressed, he had almost forgotten about his hangover. All he could think of was getting his revenge on Eden Campbell. The vision of her naked body haunted him, her white, satiny skin, the full breasts with their pink tips, the thatch of auburn hair between her thighs, and beneath that . . .

Well, he might not have been the first, but he'd

sure as hell be the last. Eden Campbell would carry the memory of Dirk Blaine between her legs into perdition.

Jamming his hat on his head, he stormed out of the room into what passed as the parlor of this seedy parlor house. Herman sat at a table in one corner shoveling food into his mouth. The sight made Blaine gag, and he hurried on through, barely glancing at the woman in the faded wrapper glaring after him.

Someone had thoughtfully saddled his horse and tied it out front . . . or maybe that's where he'd left the animal all night. Blaine took no time to decide. He was mounting when he heard the woman cackling again. She stood in the doorway in what she must have thought was a provocative pose, one arm braced on the jam, her doughy breasts spilling out the opening of her robe. "Don't come back again unless you can get it up, Blaine!" she called. "And the next time you pay me in cattle, be sure it has your brand on it."

He briefly considered pulling out his pistol, but the effort was more than he could manage. Cursing her viciously, using all the words his childhood in a whorehouse had taught him, he rode away.

For a second he thought of going home to Alvin, who would sympathize and tell him what a fool he was to go to that whore. Then he remembered Alvin wasn't there, would never be there again. The old fury boiled up again, and Blaine recalled another reason for hating that gunnie, Lincoln Scott. Well, now he knew just how to pay him back, in spades.

Halfway to the ranch, Blaine stopped beside a small seep and downed a hatful of water before scrubbing the sleep and the smell of the woman from his hands and face. When he got home, he'd strip down and burn these clothes, he decided. Then he'd figure out exactly what he would do to Eden Campbell.

That morning Linc, Marcus, and Melancholy rode to town, leaving the rest of the men to guard the women at the ranch.

As they rode, Linc noticed Melancholy watching him speculatively.

"Something on your mind?" Linc asked him at last.

His mustache twitched. "I was just thinking it seems like you must've made things up with Miss Eden."

Linc smiled in spite of himself. "You could say that. She's promised to marry me."

"The hell you say!" Melancholy replied in feigned outrage. "Next thing I know, you'll be wanting me to congratulate you."

"Not hardly," Linc replied, still grinning. "Although I reckon I'll probably have to ask you to stand up with me since Marcus'll have to give the bride away."

"You got more guts than a slaughterhouse, Scott! First you steal my girl and then you want me to help get her married off to you."

325

Linc shrugged. " 'Course if you don't want to . . ."

"Oh, I'll do it," Melancholy said sourly. "It's the least I can do for a poor helpless critter like you."

"Much obliged," Linc said, glancing at Marcus, who was coughing suspiciously.

Then the town came into view, and they sobered immediately, remembering their mission. They had to find Dirk Blaine.

The storekeeper, Ben Deal, hadn't seen Blaine for several days. They had better luck in the saloon.

"No, I ain't seen him," Sam Ferguson said, "but I can guess where he is. You been out to Hazel's?"

Marcus grimaced in distaste, and Melancholy grunted.

"Is that a whorehouse?" Linc asked.

" 'Whorehouse' is a pretty fancy name," Sam said. "It's more like a hog ranch."

Linc had no trouble imagining what kind of a place it must be. "Does Blaine go there?"

"Yes, only God knows why. The women there are sluts, and probably carry every disease there is. One of them died last month. She had the pox so bad —"

"Where is this place?" Linc asked.

"Everybody knows where it is," Sam said.

"Even Marcus," Melancholy informed Linc solemnly.

"Come on," Marcus said, frowning with distaste. He pointed to a bottle of whiskey on the back bar. "Put it on my tab. We may need it to scrub down with later."

326

Sam grinned and handed the bottle over. "Good hunting."

As they rode out of town, Linc asked, "Is this Hazel's as bad as he said?"

"Worse," Melancholy said.

"It's enough to put you off women for good," Marcus added.

"You've been there?" Linc asked, unable to hide his amusement.

"Only long enough to see what it was like," Marcus replied, ignoring Linc's grin, "and Sam is right. I can't picture Blaine there, either."

Linc considered what he knew about Blaine and the things he and his brother both had said to threaten Eden. However nattily Dirk Blaine might dress, his ideas about sex ran to the cruel and bizarre. Perhaps he could only meet his perverted needs in a place like this hog ranch.

Or with a helpless captive, he thought furiously, recalling how helpless Eden had looked, half-naked, in Blaine's grasp. Unconsciously, he touched the smooth handle of the Colt riding low on his hip. If he found Blaine today, it would be the last day the man would pose a threat to anyone.

The hog ranch was about what Linc had expected. The tumbledown buildings spoke of neglect and decay. The house itself was a sprawling collection of rooms added helter-skelter with no consideration for appearances. A few cows stood in the corral, eying the newcomers sleepily.

"Hazel takes payment in cattle," Marcus said as they rode up to the house. "She ain't particular about the brand, either."

A red-haired woman came out to greet them. "Well, now, ain't this a surprise," she said with obvious pleasure. She wore a soiled calico Mother Hubbard and little else, judging by the way her generous figure shifted beneath the cloth. Her welcoming smile revealed yellowed teeth. "All my girls are asleep, but I'll be glad to wake up a few if you'll tell me your preferences. . . . Or maybe you'd like to share?" she added suggestively.

"We just want some information, Hazel," Marcus said as Linc studied the house for signs that Dirk Blaine might be lurking inside and Melancholy rode off to have a look at the back. "Have you seen Dirk Blaine recently?"

Hazel frowned, but her eyes narrowed with animal cunning. "Dirk Blaine?" she said, as if she had never heard the name before.

"We know he comes here regular," Marcus insisted.

"I don't rightly recollect . . . ," she mused thoughtfully.

Impatient now, Linc reached into his vest pocket, pulled out a gold coin, and tossed it to her. She caught it deftly and studied it for a moment before looking back at Marcus. "Now that you mention it, I think Dirk Blaine was here."

"When?" Linc demanded.

"Well, now, let me think." She eyed the coin suggestively.

"Don't get greedy," Marcus warned. "We could pull this place down around your ears."

328

"Herman!" the woman called sharply, and like an obedient dog, a huge man appeared in the doorway. He glanced at the visitors uncertainly. "Get your rifle, Herman."

"Don't move, Herman," Linc said, pointing his Colt at the man's chest.

Herman muttered an amazed curse at the speed of Linc's draw. "Did you see that, Hazel? Slick as slobbers."

"Shut up!" Hazel snapped, thoroughly irritated. She glared at Melancholy, who reappeared from around the corner of the house, his pistol drawn. "I don't have to tell you nothing about my customers," she reminded Linc.

"No, you don't, but like Marcus said, seems like the community would be a better place to live without this old eyesore cluttering up the countryside."

Hazel's glare was murderous, but she said, "He was here last night. Came in before supper and left this morning. If you want to know what he did, it'll cost you extra."

"Where did he go when he left?" Linc asked.

"How the hell should I know? I ain't his mother," Hazel reminded them in annoyance. "Now, if you ain't planning on doing business, get out."

"Thank you for your help, Miss Hazel," Marcus said with mock civility.

As they rode away, Linc headed straight for Blaine's ranch.

"Hey, hold on, partner," Marcus said when he

realized the direction they were going. "We can't corner Blaine now."

"*I* can, and I intend to!" Linc said, not slowing down. "You two can do what you want."

"Then why don't you just let us shoot you right here and save yourself the ride!" Melancholy suggested.

Startled, Linc reined up, and the others stopped on either side of him. Their horses blew while the riders glared at each other. "You can't mean to let him go," Linc said at last.

"Hell, no," Marcus said. "We want him just as bad as you do, but it'd be suicide to ride in there now. His men are still pretty mad about last night. They'd as soon shoot you as look at you, and God knows Blaine'd pay a bonus to the man who does."

"And don't forget about young Hamilton who'd shoot you for the hell of it," Melancholy added.

"All right!" Linc snapped. "So what do we do? Hope we can catch Blaine alone sometime? What about what he did to Eden?"

"Don't be a jackass. We're going to get Blaine and get him good, but we'll need some help. We'll go by the ranch and get the rest of our men. Maybe we ought to ask some of the other ranchers, too."

"Are you talking about vigilantes?" Linc asked.

"I'm talking about the community uniting to get rid of something rotten."

"You'll have to tell them what he did to Eden," Linc warned. "Some of them'll say she got what she deserved for riding around the countryside in pants. It won't be good for her reputation."

"Linc's right," Melancholy said, his mustache drooping even lower than usual. "It won't be very pleasant for her."

"I hadn't thought about that," Marcus mused. "I reckon we'd better ask Eden first. If she wants to keep it a secret, we'll try to handle it ourselves."

When they arrived back at the ranch, Eden ran out to meet them, throwing herself into Linc's arms the instant he dismounted. She felt so wonderful pressed up against him that he simply held her, oblivious to the dust and dirt he was grinding into her dress. She looked like an angel in her pale green gown, with her auburn hair pinned up to expose her long, elegant neck. He inhaled her scent greedily, wishing he had the right to carry her off somewhere so they could be alone. Instead he pushed her resolutely away.

"Did you find him?" she asked, her emerald eyes clouded with concern.

"We know where he was last night, but he's not there now," Linc told her. "We figure he's gone back to his ranch."

The other men had gathered around them, and Fiona, who had come across the yard more slowly than her stepdaughter, arrived in time to hear his last remark. "You won't go after him without the other men, will you?" she asked.

"We know we need some help," Marcus explained. "But we've got to talk to Eden first. Let's go in the house."

Turning the horses over to the other men, Marcus instructed Melancholy to tell them what had happened that morning. Then he led Fiona, Linc, and Eden up to the house.

Holding onto Linc's arm, Eden sensed his tension and felt renewed apprehension. "What is it? You're frightening me," she said when they were inside.

"Sit down," Marcus said, and Linc led her over to the sofa and sat down beside her, still holding her hand. When he wouldn't meet her eye, her stomach clenched.

Fiona perched nervously on a chair while Marcus paced around in a circle and Eden's apprehension grew.

"Linc? What is it?" she asked at last.

"Marcus thinks we ought to ask the other ranchers for help."

"Of course you should!" she agreed, instantly relieved. The more men who went after Blaine, the safer Linc would be.

"But if we ask them, they'll want to know why we're going after him. We still don't have any evidence Blaine was personally involved in the rustling. We'd have to tell them he attacked you."

"Then do it!"

"Oh, Eden," Fiona objected, but Marcus cut her off.

"Think about it, first, honey. You know what people will say. They'll say you asked for it, riding around like a man and showing your legs and — "

"Oh, for heaven's sake!" Eden exclaimed in exasperation. "You don't think I care what people say, do you?"

Linc's eyes were like blue flames. "*I* care, Eden, and I don't want people talking about you."

"We all care," Fiona added. "People can be quite unkind, particularly when a young woman has behaved in an unseemly manner."

Eden felt the heat rising in her face. At least Fiona didn't know exactly how unseemly her and Linc's behavior had been. Linc's hand tightened on hers, but she didn't dare look at him. Even still, she could guess what he was thinking: Dirk Blaine knew she and Linc had been making love, and he certainly wouldn't hesitate to blacken her name, especially if he was accused of attacking her.

"I know I ain't your real pa," Marcus was saying, "but if was, I reckon I'd try to keep this thing as quiet as possible. It was my idea to get some help, but maybe it ain't such a good one, not if it'll cause you more harm than good."

"And I'm not your mother," Fiona said, leaning forward earnestly, "but you know I love you dearly, and I simply can't allow you to hold yourself up to public ridicule."

"They're right," Linc said before Eden could object. "You're going to be my wife, and I do have some say-so in what you do. I've been thinking this thing over, and hearing what Marcus and Fiona said convinced me. If we ask other folks for help, it might hurt you, too, and even if we just use our own men, some innocent people could get killed. This really ain't nobody's fight but mine, so I'm going to handle it myself."

"No, Linc!" Eden cried.

"Don't worry, I'm not going to ride up to his front door and get myself shot down," he said, implacable. "I'll wait until we're on neutral ground and it's a fair fight."

"Linc won't be alone, either," Marcus assured her as she gaped at Linc in horror. "The rest of us'll be backing him to make sure none of Blaine's gunnies try to horn in."

"Please, don't, Linc," she begged, holding his arm with both hands as if she could physically restrain him from doing this thing. "I'd rather Blaine got away scot-free than you got hurt!"

"It's not your choice to make," Linc insisted.

She'd seen a glimpse of this stubborn streak, but she'd never imagined he could be completely immovable. For a wild moment she considered going to the other ranchers herself and telling them what had happened; then she realized that would only make things worse. They would wonder why her men weren't standing up for her. They'd think her behavior unseemly, as Fiona had said, and even worse, they would probably believe Dirk Blaine and side with him.

Overwhelmed with frustration, Eden wanted to scream and stamp her foot and forbid Linc to ever go near Dirk Blaine again. But of course she did none of those things because she knew nothing would change his mind. Instead, she asked, "When?"

"When what?"

She swallowed the lump in her throat. "When

will you meet him?"

Linc glanced at Marcus, who said, "We'll send somebody to watch his ranch and let us know when he leaves and where he goes."

At least it won't be today, she told herself.

"Well, if that's settled, I'll go tell the other men," Marcus said, heading for the door.

Fiona rose from her chair. "I'm sure you two would like to be alone." Giving them a reassuring smile, she walked purposefully away toward the kitchen.

Eden looked up at Linc. His expression was still grim and determined. No amount of charm or wheedling would stop him. Terror coiled inside her. "Oh, Linc, I'm so scared I'll lose you!"

His arms closed around her like a vise, pulling her to his chest, and she could hear his heart thundering against her ear. "Don't be," he whispered. "Now that I've found you, I'm not going to let anyone or anything keep me from having you. If you ever want to get rid of me, you'll have to shoot me yourself."

She tried to laugh at his feeble joke, but the sound came out as a sob. Clinging to him, she wept out her fear and anger and frustration. For the first time in her life she wanted to be a man so she could ride at Linc's side and protect him.

But she wasn't a man, and there was nothing she could do for Linc except pray. As he held her to his heart, she did.

"What are we going to do, boss?"

Dirk Blaine gave his foreman an ugly look, but Ace refused to back down. They were sitting on the steps of Blaine's cabin, and Dirk was still nursing a bad headache.

"They know about the rustling," Ace said. "Pauling warned me they'd be back, and that Scott is one mean hombre. I wouldn't want to mess with him."

"Then it's lucky for you you won't have to, isn't it?" Blaine told him in disgust. "Dammit, I never took you for a coward, Ace."

"You know I ain't a coward," Ace insisted. "And I ain't a fool, neither. A smart man would cut his losses and get out while he still had his hide."

Blaine's hackles rose at the implication. "Do you think my brother would've run?" he demanded.

"Alvin always avoided trouble if he could," Ace reminded him.

"But we weren't supposed to have any trouble here," Blaine complained. "Alvin promised me this would be the place we'd settle. We wasn't going to take much cattle, just enough to give us a good start, then we'd quit. They can't prove nothing, anyway."

"Then why'd they come here looking for you last night?" Ace asked skeptically.

Dirk waved away the notion. "That's something personal between me and Scott. It don't have nothing to do with the rustling."

"Then what does it have to do with?"

"That whore, Eden Campbell."

Ace stiffened in outrage. "That kind of talk'll get you hanged."

"Not when I tell folks what I saw. Her and Scott was buck naked wallowing on the ground when I come across them. Scott got mad when I wanted a little piece for myself."

Ace considered his employer's claim. "Nobody'll believe you."

"It's the God's truth!" Dirk insisted. "Two of our men saw them together, and her wearing britches like she was selling her legs by the inch."

"Don't forget they knew her pappy for years. They ain't likely to take your word against hers," Ace said, relentless. "I still say we'd be smart to get out while the getting is good. Alvin would've known it was time to go."

Dirk swore at the reminder of his brother's cunning. Dirk knew only too well he needed Alvin's advice right now. It was so hard to know what to do. They'd made a pile of money here, but Dirk didn't want to give up the dream of a home, the home he and Alvin had never known. Still, without Alvin, the dream seemed empty, and the ranch wasn't much when you came right down to it. Certainly not enough to die for.

Maybe Ace was right. Maybe they should cut their losses. He could start over anyplace. "Tell the boys to get their gear together. But," he added when Ace would have gotten up, "tell them we've got a little business to take care of first . . . over at the Paradise."

* * *

Eden slept poorly that night, worried about Linc's coming confrontation with Dirk Blaine. When she did doze off, her dreams were haunted by a leering Blaine tearing her clothes off or shooting Linc or both. She was wide awake when the rider came charging into the ranch yard shouting a warning.

She grabbed her robe, shrugging into it as she ran. Nearly colliding with Marcus and Fiona in the parlor, she followed them out to the porch. Melancholy, still astride his dancing horse, was shouting fit to wake the dead. The other men poured out of the bunkhouse in various stages of undress. Marcus, shirtless, buttoned his hastily donned pants as he listened.

"Blaine and his men are coming. I'm only a minute or two ahead of them. They're carrying torches."

This was all anyone needed to hear.

"Get your clothes on, men, but don't light any lights. Let 'em think they caught us napping. Melancholy, come in and help me with the rifles."

Eden and Fiona pitched in, and between the four of them they carried all the Winchesters out to the bunkhouse, where the men were stomping into their boots, cursing the darkness and Dirk Blaine.

Linc materialized out of the shadows and took a Winchester from Eden's hands. "What will we do about the women?" he asked Marcus

"I'd like to send them off somewheres, but I wouldn't want Blaine to catch them out."

"Give me a shotgun, and I'll fight right along with you," Eden said, but Linc shook his head.

"They'll be firing at every powder flash. I don't want to take a chance of you getting hit. Besides," he said when she started to argue, "somebody's got to guard Fiona."

"We'll put them in the root cellar, and Eden you can have your shotgun," Marcus said, thrusting it into her hands. "Come on, before they get here. Melancholy, you and Linc and I'll take the house. The rest of you split up between the bunkhouse and the barn. We'll have them in a cross fire."

"Linc!" Eden called when Marcus would have dragged her away.

"I'm coming," he said, taking her arm and hurrying her along toward the house. By the time they reached the porch, Eden was cursing herself for not having thought to wear shoes, but there was no time for such niceties. Already they could see a distant glow. Since it was much too early for dawn, it had to be Blaine and his men coming to keep his promise to burn the Paradise to the ground.

"Linc, be careful!" she cried.

His only answer was a desperate kiss which ended much too quickly. "I love you," she called as Fiona took her hand and pulled her into the house.

"I love you, too!" His words echoed through the darkness.

Stumbling along, feeling their way, the two women hurried to the kitchen, where they picked up a lantern and some matches, then raced out the back door. Eden heaved open the cellar door and held it while Fiona backed down into the black hole. After handing down her shotgun, Eden followed, holding the door open above her head. The instant her feet hit the dirt floor, she let the door drop into place, sealing them away from the danger.

Fiona struck a match and lit the lamp, keeping the flame low. Their shadows loomed large against the rows of canned goods and piles of potatoes and onions. Eden shivered.

"Are you cold, dear?" Fiona asked.

"No, scared spitless," Eden replied with the ghost of a smile.

"So am I, I'm afraid."

The two women looked up, as if they might miraculously be granted the ability to see through solid matter and witness what was happening outside. Then they heard the first shot, a muffled pop, followed by a smattering of others.

Fiona drew her breath in on a gasp, and instinctively Eden slipped an arm around her. "Oh, God, don't let anything happen to them," Eden whispered.

"Amen," Fiona replied.

The two women clung together as the shots went on and on.

Linc had just taken up his position by the window in Eden's bedroom when the raiders rode into the yard, torches held high. Linc had no trouble at all picking out Dirk Blaine, who rode in the lead.

Aiming carefully, he fired, but Blaine's horse moved and the bullet sped harmlessly by. By then, every one of the Paradise men had started firing, and the would-be raiders were thrown into a panic.

"Don't run!" Blaine yelled, too late. But caught in the killing cross fire there was no place for them to run.

Chaos reigned as men shouted and horses screamed in pain and panic. One animal went down, throwing his rider, who lay motionless, stunned or dead. The raiders dropped their torches to pull their guns, further terrifying their horses, which reared and danced wildly. In spite of the confusion, a few of the raiders managed to get their pistols out and began to return fire, shooting frantically into the darkness where their unseen attackers kept up a relentless fusillade.

Linc fired methodically, unable to chose a particular target in the milling mass, but doing his best to aim for Blaine whenever he caught a glimpse of him. Unlike the rest of the raiders, Blaine still held his torch aloft. In desperation, he finally broke from the others and charged the barn, heedless of the withering gunfire coming from the doorway. Swinging the torch, he let it fly toward the open loft door, and by some miracle, it reached its target. The hay inside instantly exploded in a ball of flame, illuminating the entire yard with a horrible orange glow.

Linc dove through the window and raced to the edge of the porch, jacking shells furiously and firing as he ran, but Blaine sped by unscathed, heading for the safety of the outer darkness. When it had swallowed him up, Linc whirled, ready to take aim on another raider, but the yard stood empty save for the fallen rider and his mount, which thrashed and screamed in agony. The rest of Blaine's men had charged off into the night.

The Paradise crew emerged from their hiding places. Marcus had already run to meet them in the yard. Linc and Melancholy followed at a trot.

One of the other men was bent over the fallen rider. "He's a goner," he pronounced after turning the man over so they could all see his vacant, staring eyes by the light of the burning barn.

Satisfied the fallen man presented no danger, Linc turned to the injured horse and saw it was bleeding copiously from a wound in its neck. Without hesitation, he lifted the rifle to his shoulder, took careful aim, and fired. The horse shuddered and went still.

"Thanks," Melancholy muttered beside him.

"Are we going after them?" one of the other men asked.

Marcus hesitated, torn between his desire for revenge and immediate necessity. "We'd better see to that fire, first," he said after a few seconds of consideration. "We know where to find them, and this time we won't have any trouble getting the other ranchers to help us go after them."

By sunup the neighbors had started to arrive, drawn by the flames and smoke easily visible in the lightening sky. All of them were appalled to discover the barn had been deliberately set afire by Dirk Blaine, and they all were more than willing to accompany Marcus on a mission of revenge.

They hadn't been able to save the barn, but by working through the night, they had managed to keep the fire from spreading to the other buildings.

When the cook rang the bell for breakfast, Eden found Linc slumped on the front porch, his back against the wall, sound asleep. Loath to wake him, she also knew she couldn't leave him there. Kneeling beside him, she gently kissed his soot-blackened cheek.

He awoke with a start and was already reaching for his pistol when he recognized her. The gesture tore at her heart, but she forced herself to smile.

"What's wrong?" he asked, looking around as if to get his bearings.

"You were sound asleep. You really ought to lie down somewhere. You must be exhausted."

He rubbed his side unconsciously. "I guess I could use a nap, but we'll be going after Blaine as soon as everybody eats."

"Can't it wait until you've had some rest?"

"It can't wait for anything, Eden."

She wanted to shake that implacable expression from his face, but she knew he was right. Even now Blaine might already be miles away. "Then at least go lay down until it's time to leave. You can use the room off the kitchen. I'll bring you some food."

His meek compliance with her suggestion was

343

some measure of his fatigue. She sent him off into the house while she hurried down to the cookhouse for his breakfast. When she got back with the plate of flapjacks he was asleep again. After putting his meal in the warming oven over the kitchen stove, she went back into the tiny room and slumped down onto the floor beside the bed where he lay.

Her own body was fairly numb with fatigue from having helped carry buckets of water all night to soak the roofs of the other buildings, but she felt no urge to sleep. Instead she used this rare opportunity to study him.

In repose, his face looked younger, closer to his true age of twenty-three. The crinkles around his eyes had smoothed into tiny white lines, and the furrows in his forehead had disappeared. His raven hair hung across his brow, and a vicious set of whiskers had sprouted on his jaw, but in spite of his disheveled appearance and the soot from the fire which still coated him, she wanted nothing more than to climb up on the bed beside him and take him in her arms. If he hadn't needed sleep so badly, she would have.

Instead, she contented herself with watching the steady rise and fall of his broad chest and admiring the length and breadth of his body sprawled so negligently on the cot. She could easily recall how he looked without his clothes, the bold virility that even now, as weary as she was, could stir her blood and make her yearn for his touch.

The strength of her desire once again triggered her abiding fear that she might lose him before she ever really possessed him. Why did men have to be so stubborn? When faced with the choice of punishing Dirk Blaine or losing Linc, Eden would have gladly let Blaine go. Unfortunately, the choice was not hers. With a sigh, she laid her head on the bed beside him and savored the few, precious moments of peace left to her.

She didn't know how much time had passed when she heard Marcus calling for him. She only knew it had been far too little. Reluctantly, she shook Linc awake. Once again he jumped and reached for his gun, and Eden silently vowed that once they were married, his life would become so ordinary he would lose that instinct to defend himself.

"Linc?" Marcus called again. He was outside on the back porch.

"He's in here," Eden called back, rising stiffly from her post by the bed.

"Why did you let me sleep?" Linc asked, his voice endearingly hoarse.

"Because you needed it, and I'm not going to let you go until you've eaten, either. I'll tell Marcus you'll be right along. Your breakfast is in the warming oven."

When Eden returned to the kitchen, she found Linc sitting at the table wolfing down the flapjacks she had brought. He'd washed off most of the soot at the kitchen sink, and he'd found some ancient coffee still warming on the back of the stove and poured himself a cup. It must have been strong enough to float a horseshoe, but that was probably just what he needed.

She pulled out a chair and sat down beside him, needing to be close. As if reading her thoughts, he reached out his left arm and slid it around her, pulling her against his side while he continued to eat.

"If you hadn't let me sleep so long," he told her between bites, "we would have had time for a little spooning."

His grin made her want to weep. "Oh, Linc, promise me you won't get yourself killed."

His grin vanished. "I told you before not to worry about me. I'm coming back, and you can count on it."

She laid her head on his shoulder for a few seconds while he gulped down the last of his coffee. Finally, he said, "I've got to go."

Reluctantly, she got up with him, but she didn't let him go. Holding him close, she lifted her face for his kiss.

"I haven't shaved," he warned her.

"I don't care," she replied. She would've walked barefoot over cactus to feel his mouth on hers.

His kiss was gentle at first, as if he were afraid of hurting her, but she slid her arms around his neck and pressed herself against him, wanting to feel every inch of her touching every inch of him. His control snapped and his arms tightened around her. She opened to him, offering the sweetness of her mouth, greedy for the rough invasion of his tongue.

His hands traced her curves possessively, molding

her to him until she felt the hard evidence of his desire. Cupping her buttocks, he pulled her into the cradle of his thighs, silently telling her what he wanted.

Then they heard Marcus calling again, and slowly, reluctantly, Linc released her. "Just wait until I get back," he whispered, his eyes glittering with the same need thrumming through her own body.

"If I can," she replied saucily.

"You'd better." He grabbed her bottom and squeezed, startling a cry from her lips, before snatching up his hat and heading for the door.

She ran after him, but stopped on the porch when she saw Marcus had brought his horse around. She didn't want to see him riding away with the others to God-knew-what.

Almost three dozen men rode with Linc and Marcus as they made their way to Blaine's ranch, but they were too late, as they'd suspected they would be.

"The place looks deserted," Gus Olsen remarked from where they had stopped the instant the ranch buildings came into view.

"Could be a trap," Melancholy suggested without much conviction.

"If I was Blaine, I would've hightailed it after last night," Marcus said. "He ain't too bright, but I don't think he's completely stupid, either. At least his men would've gone. If he's there, he's alone."

347

"Then let's see if he's there," Linc said, fighting the frustration of possibly once again having missed Blaine. "Fan out and ride in slow in case it's an ambush." He pulled out his pistol, and the others followed suit.

Linc scanned the ranch buildings for any sign of motion, but saw none. Even the corrals stood empty, the gate hanging open as if someone had turned the horses loose in a hurry. He especially watched the house in case Blaine was hiding inside, but the door there hung open, too, mocking him. The only sounds they heard were the clip-clop of their horses' hoofs, the creak of saddle leather, and their own breathing.

When they were in the ranch yard and no shots had been fired, the men visibly relaxed. "Keep your guns handy until we've checked the buildings," Linc cautioned, even though he was already certain they would find no one. He had known too many men who'd died because they'd been certain of something that wasn't true, to take a chance.

The men climbed down from their horses and spread out. Linc and Marcus took the cabin where the Blaine brothers had lived. Turning up his nose at the squalor, Linc nevertheless began to root around among the abandoned junk.

"What are you looking for?" Marcus asked.

"I won't know until I find it. Maybe some clue that Blaine was involved in the rustling or something to indicate where he might've gone."

Marcus joined the search, and when Melancholy came in to see what they were about, he went to

348

tell the others to search the remaining buildings. No sooner had Linc and Marcus determined there was nothing of importance left in the house, someone shouted from the bunkhouse.

"Hey, look here!"

Marcus and Linc went running, joining the crowd already gathered inside.

"Let Marcus through," Gus Olsen commanded, and a path opened for Marcus and Linc to pass.

At first Linc didn't see what was so interesting. The wall, like the walls in most bunkhouses, had been plastered with pictures of ladies in various stages of undress which had been torn from magazines, most notably the *Police Gazette*. Then he saw it, tacked up amid the girlie pictures.

"I'll be damned," Marcus muttered, pulling the yellowed paper from the wall and holding it so Linc could see it, too.

It was a series of sketches of the brands of every rancher represented in this posse and more. Beside each brand was another drawing showing how to position Blaine's Daisy brand over it to cover it completely.

"Do you need any more proof that Blaine was behind all the rustling?" Marcus asked.

"No," Olsen said, and the rest echoed his sentiments.

"Then let's go after them."

"Wait a minute, Marcus," Olsen objected. "You and your men ain't in no condition to go after anybody. You've been up all night fighting that fire. We don't know where Blaine went or how far he's got by now. If he left last night, we'll be days catching up, and none of us brought supplies or blankets with us."

"But if we don't set out now, the trail will be cold," Linc objected.

"Then how about if we send a couple men to track them," Olsen suggested. "Bob here is the best tracker in these parts. He can blaze a trail for the rest of us to follow. We'll meet back here tomorrow at first light. Each man can bring an extra horse and switch off. That way we can catch up with them quicker."

Linc had to admit it was a good plan. If he hadn't been so exhausted, he might have thought of it himself. Even though his gut reaction was to strike out immediately, his side felt like it was on fire, and his ears were ringing from fatigue. And if they didn't start out until tomorrow, he'd have tonight with Eden.

"Linc, what do you think?" Marcus asked.

Linc nodded. "Don't try to catch up to them," he warned the tracker, Bob. "No use tipping them off that we're on the trail. When you get close to them, just stop and wait for the rest of us to catch up."

The ride back to the ranch seemed longer than usual, which made Linc acutely aware of just how hard he had pushed himself. Back at the ranch, Eden once again greeted him with a joyous cry, raining kisses all over his face. Too weary to protest, he let her fuss over him, fixing him a much-needed bath and fetching him clean clothes from the bunkhouse.

She would even have stayed to scrub his back if Fiona hadn't sternly reminded her of the proprieties. She did manage a minute alone with him before he went back to the bunkhouse with the rest of the men to catch up on some sleep.

"Hmmm, I wish I didn't have to leave you tonight," he whispered after he had kissed her thoroughly.

"You don't," she replied with an impish grin.

"What do you mean?"

"I mean maybe you should move back up to the house. If you're sleeping out by the kitchen, you might get a visitor tonight." Her green eyes glittered with promise, and Linc's body throbbed in response.

"I suppose there *should* be another man up here to guard the house," he murmured before pulling her into his arms again.

Thinking about their scheduled rendezvous didn't prevent Linc from sleeping, but it did provide him with some fascinating dreams. By the time he joined the family for supper that night, the ache in his side had faded into insignificance in comparison to the ache Eden had started.

Fortunately, Marcus and Fiona seemed as anxious for bedtime to arrive as Linc was. Citing the early hour at which they must leave in the morning, Marcus excused himself long before the regular time. Eden demurely suggested Linc should get along to bed, too. Somehow managing to keep a straight face, he did so.

Once in the small room, he noticed the narrowness of the cot. Well, he thought with amusement, he and Eden had made love under more adverse conditions than this. At least they'd have a mattress under them this time. The prospect brought with it a surge of urgency. In response, Linc quickly stripped off his clothes and climbed, naked, into the bed, pulling the crisp white sheet up to his waist. Not feeling the least inclination to sleep, he lay back to wait.

Eden needed much more preparation. The instant she shut her bedroom door, she too began to strip out of her clothes. When she was naked, she found the bottle of rosewater she had been saving and poured a generous dollop into the warm water she had brought in earlier. Dipping a soft cloth into the mixture, she wiped it over her entire body until her flesh tingled. Her skin felt as if it were charged, as if lightning were just about to strike, and her stomach quivered with anticipation.

Was this the way new brides felt? she wondered, thinking she and Linc had things a little out of order. At least she wouldn't have to be nervous on her wedding night, because she'd know exactly what to expect.

She reached into her drawer and pulled out her summer gown, a sheer scrap of lawn that left her arms and throat bare. It felt like gossamer as she slipped it over her head and settled it around her hips. With trembling hands she tied the satin ribbon at the neckline and imagined Linc pulling it loose in just a few more moments.

"Oh, Linc," she whispered, laying a hand over her pounding heart. How would she ever bear to say good-bye to him yet again in the morning, knowing he might be hurt or killed? The worst part was knowing he hated to go just as much as she hated seeing him leave. If only there were some way . . .

The idea came to her so suddenly, she couldn't imagine why she hadn't thought of it before. Linc *did* hate the killing, and he wanted to change. He simply didn't know how to make the break. But Eden did. He would be so happy when she told him how to do it! Of course, he might feel honor bound to go with Marcus anyway, but she had the answer for that, too: if he *really* loved her, he'd do as she asked.

Swiftly, she pulled the pins out of her hair and shook it loose. Dragging a brush through it with one hand, she plucked her robe from the cabinet with the other and began pulling it on. Almost as an afterthought, she found her slippers under the bed and stepped into them, recalling the perils of running through the darkened house in bare feet. She certainly didn't want to cry out in pain and awaken Marcus or Fiona.

She took one last look in the mirror and was startled to see how happy she looked. Her eyes shone and her cheeks glowed in the lamplight. She really did look like a bride, except her white gown was a nightdress and she was going to her honeymoon long before the ceremony.

But of course the illicit nature of their meeting

353

only added to the excitement. Eden had to cover her mouth to keep from giggling aloud as she stole from her room, past Fiona and Marcus's door, and out to the kitchen. When she opened the door to Linc's room, she saw he'd put the light out.

"Linc?"

"Who else did you think would be here?" he challenged wryly.

She could just barely make him out in the shadows. Slipping off her robe, she let it fall to the floor and kicked off her slippers on the way to the bed.

She put out her hand, and he took it, pulling her down on top of him. His mouth found hers with unerring accuracy. For long moments she simply savored the kiss, bracing herself against his satiny shoulders.

His hands caressed her through the thin material of her nightdress, tracing the plain of her back and down to clutch her buttocks. Shivers raced up her thighs as his fingers kneaded her pliant flesh.

When forced to breathe, she lifted her mouth from his, and he trailed kisses down her throat until he reached the pounding pulse. One hand came up to find her breast, and her nipples hardened obediently at his touch.

"What is this thing?" he murmured, tugging at her gown.

"It's called a nightdress," she informed him in amusement.

He tugged again. "Does it come off?"

She laughed in delight. "Of course it does."

When she offered no assistance, however, he lightly nipped the swell of flesh above the lacy neckline, startling a cry from her.

"Are you going to show me how or do I have to tear it off of you?" he growled.

The shivers were racing all over her now. "Just like unwrapping a present," she said breathlessly, guiding his hand. "Untie the bow."

He jerked it free impatiently and the garment fell open. In the next second he had it over her shoulders and halfway down her arms. Her breasts spilled free, and she pressed them to his naked chest.

Echoing his gasp of surprise, she pulled her arms loose and began to stroke his shoulders again while he pushed the gown past her hips. Then there was nothing between them. Chest to breast, belly to belly, thigh to thigh, they lay in an ecstasy of sensation. Eden wondered vaguely if she would ever get used to the feel of his body against hers or the wonderful differences between them.

"Oh, Eden, you feel so good," he murmured against her breast.

His hands were everywhere, worshiping her with tenderness. Her skin ignited in response, as if every nerve were sparking at his touch. Want became need and need became compulsion. She moved against him, coaxing and tantalizing, until his breath came in ragged gasps that echoed her own.

"I love you," she told him between kisses.

"I love you," he replied, rolling them over until she lay beneath him.

She took his weight gladly, greedily, lifting her knees and offering herself. With a groan, he took her, plunging into her welcoming depths. She moaned in pleasure, wrapping her legs around him to hold him even closer. Whispering her name, he pressed his mouth to her eyes and cheeks and nose and lips, adoring her with kisses.

He moved in her, rocking gently as if to tease. The rough hair of his chest tormented her aching nipples, chafing them to tingling awareness, and her loins clenched in response. Desire pulsed through her, and her caressing fingers clutched, digging into the solid muscles of his back.

She called his name, and his control snapped. His mouth closed over hers, demanding and devouring, and his hips began to churn with frantic urgency. She met him thrust for thrust until the heat she had felt before coalesced into one central place, the place where their bodies joined.

The flame burned hot and hotter still, slickening their skin. They panted, desperate now in their quest, clasping, pounding, until Eden thought she couldn't stand it a moment longer. The end came in a wrenching spasm of white-hot ecstasy that melded them into one.

They clung together as the spasms continued, shuddering and gasping in delighted surprise, savoring the aftershocks that seemed to go on forever. Just when Eden thought it was over, another one trembled through her, startling a chuckle from Linc, whose cheek was pressed to hers.

"God, Eden, I never dreamed . . . ," he gasped.

"How do you do it?"

"I thought you were doing it," she replied, dangerously close to giggling herself. Joy was like a bubble ready to burst inside of her.

He sighed blissfully, and nibbled at her ear, sending chills sweeping over her.

"I never knew I could love anyone as much as I love you," he said finally, and the bubble burst.

Eden wrapped her arms around his neck and laughed aloud. "Oh, Linc, just think, when we're married, it'll be this way all the time."

Linc groaned in mock horror. "I doubt I'll last a week."

She kissed him long and hard as he rolled them over so she lay on top again. Eden couldn't ever remember being so happy. "And the best part is," she informed him when the kiss finally ended, "you don't even have to go after Dirk Blaine."

Chapter Eleven

Linc smiled tolerantly. He was still a little dazed from the lovemaking, and surely he'd misunderstood her. "Did you say I didn't have to go after Dirk Blaine?"

"No, I mean, yes, I said it and no, you don't have to go after him." He could hear the excitement in her voice, but she wasn't making any sense at all. She didn't give him an opportunity to point that out, though. "I've been thinking about it all day, and I realized it doesn't matter any more."

"What do you mean, it doesn't matter? He burned down your barn," Linc reminded her, thoroughly confused.

"I know, and Marcus can go after him for that, but *you* don't have to go. I know you're mad about what he did to me the other day, but he really didn't hurt me, and I'm certainly willing to forget it happened if it means you'll be safe."

Safe? What was she talking about? Convinced he must be confused because the feel of her naked body against his was such a distraction, he eased her off of him and pushed up on one elbow.

"Eden, nobody's going to forget anything. Dirk Blaine crossed the line, and it's up to us to make sure he doesn't get away with it."

She touched his face, her fingers soft and gentle. "It's not up to *you*. How many times have you pointed out that you don't have any claim to this place? This isn't really your battle, and remember when I told you you'd have to find another way to fight? Well, this is it! Tomorrow you let Marcus and the others go out after Blaine, and you stay here with me."

"Eden," he began, then realized the futility of discussing this when he couldn't even see her face. For all he knew, she could be teasing him. "I'm going to light the lamp."

Groping in the dark, he found his pants and slipped them on before locating the lamp and the matches. By the time he had the lamp lit, Eden had shrugged back into her nightdress and was sitting up on the cot. When he turned to face her, his breath caught. She was even more beautiful than usual, with the lamplight turning her disheveled hair into a flaming halo around her. One look at her green eyes convinced him she wasn't teasing, though. She was deadly serious, and he felt a cold knot of dread forming in his stomach.

"Eden, why don't you want me to go after Blaine?"

"Because I don't want people shooting at you," she said, jumping up from the bed and flinging her arms around his neck. "Do you know how frightened I've been for the past few days? Every time you leave, I wonder if I'll ever see you again."

Instinct told him to pull her close and kiss her, but he resisted the impulse, knowing he had to settle this once and for all. He placed his hands on her waist and pushed her slightly away. "Are you afraid I'm going to get shot or are you afraid I'm going to shoot somebody else?"

Her confusion looked genuine. "Why would I be afraid you'd shoot somebody else?"

"Because the killing really does bother you, doesn't it? You don't want me to get any more blood on my hands."

"Of course I don't! But that's not nearly as important as keeping you alive. It's awfully hard to have a wedding without a groom. Oh, Linc . . ." Her eyes went soft, and his heart began to pound. She stepped closer until her breasts brushed his chest through the thin fabric of her nightdress. "You know you don't have to go. If you really loved me, you wouldn't leave me."

Fury melted his sensual fog. *"If I really loved you?"* he echoed, pushing her away again. "You *know* I love you, and that's exactly why I have to go after Dirk Blaine. That bastard put his hands on you, and God only knows what he would've done if I hadn't been there."

"But it's not important anymore!" she insisted, clinging when he tried to pull away. "Don't you understand?"

"Oh, I understand, all right," he told her, pulling free of her embrace at last. "I understand *perfectly*. I reckon I finally convinced you that you didn't want to get hooked up with a killer and now you're trying to change me, but you're too late, Eden. I told you before, I can't change what I am."

"Yes, you can!" she cried as he snatched up his shirt and began to pull it on. "You were the one who said you hated being a gunfighter."

"I do, but I can't be anything else."

"Not even for me?" she demanded.

Linc paused in the process of buttoning his shirt and looked into her eyes. No longer soft, they held a silent challenge, and for one heart-wrenching moment he wished he held the power to meet it. "Especially not for you, Eden. As long as Blaine is alive, you'll be in danger, and I love you too much to let that happen.

"So you'll go off and get yourself killed instead!" she fumed.

He stuck his feet into his boots and stomped them on as he stuffed his shirt into his pants. "I told you before, you don't have to worry about me."

"What are you doing?" she asked, as if she'd just noticed he was dressing.

"I'm going back to the bunkhouse where I belong."

"Linc!"

She tried to hold him, but he shook her off and reached for his gun belt. The pain of leaving her was like a knife in his heart, but he couldn't stay. If he did, she might yet be able to weaken his resolve, and he couldn't let her make him a coward, not even if it meant losing her. "I tried to tell you this wouldn't work," he said, his throat thick. "You said the killing didn't matter, but I guess we both know it matters a lot."

"Don't be a fool, Linc!"

"Too late," he said grimly. "I was already a fool to think you'd want a man like me. I'm too wild to housebreak, Eden. If you want a trained puppy, you'll have to find somebody else."

She grabbed his arm as he turned toward the door. "I don't want anybody else! I want *you!*"

"Do you, Eden? Do you want *me* or do you want the man you think you can make me into?"

Shock widened her emerald eyes, and he saw she had no answer. Her hand dropped from his arm.

"When you make up your mind, let me know," he said, snatching his hat from a peg on the wall. He left the door open behind him, but she didn't follow.

For a long time after he was gone, Eden stared blindly into the darkened doorway, horrified at what she had done. Dear heaven, was he right? Did she really want to change him? Was that the real reason she'd tried to talk him out of going after Blaine?

Hugging herself against a sudden chill, she sank down on the cot. She tried to imagine a different Linc, a man who minded his business, a man who didn't reach for his gun when he was startled, a man who could be talked out of going after someone who had molested his woman, the man she'd tried to convince him to become. Was that the kind of man she wanted, a 'trained puppy'?

Of course not! She wanted him safe and alive, but not at the price of changing who he was. She jumped up and ran after him, heedless of the hazards of the darkened house, darting around the shadows of furniture, straight to the front door.

But she was too late. He was already inside the bunkhouse. For a moment she considered going after him but quickly discarded the idea. Not only would she scandalize all the other men by chasing after Linc in her nightdress, but he'd almost certainly interpret her pursuit as another attempt to henpeck him. No, she'd have to wait until morning to tell him he was wrong and that she loved him just as he was.

And to beg him not to get himself killed before she had a chance to prove it.

The men worked swiftly in the predawn darkness, saddling the horses and packing the food they would take. Linc kept glancing up at the house, expecting Eden to appear at any moment. Her bedroom window faced the ranch yard, so surely she must have heard their preparations.

But she didn't come, and by the time the men were ready to leave, Linc had to conclude she simply did not want to see him off. For the hundredth time he cursed his own stupidity. Why had he stomped out last night? Why hadn't he stayed and talked to her some more? She must think he was a pigheaded clod. No wonder she didn't want to speak to him now. Maybe she didn't even want to marry him anymore.

The thought filled him with despair even though he couldn't blame her one bit. But it wasn't going to keep him from going after Dirk Blaine. The bastard wasn't going to get away with attacking Eden, and if nothing else, Linc owed Marcus the help in getting revenge for his lost barn.

"Looks like everybody's ready," Melancholy said, startling Linc back to the present. "Sure wish I was going with you."

Linc smiled sympathetically. They had decided to take only half the men with them. "We've got to leave somebody here we can trust in case they come back, and next to me, you're the best man Marcus has got."

Melancholy gave Linc his most ferocious scowl. "What do you mean, 'next to you'? *I'm* the best man Marcus has got, and everybody knows it. In fact, if you're not careful, I may just beat you out with Miss Eden while you're off chasing bad men."

Somehow Linc managed to maintain his smile. "Just try it," he challenged, fearing Melancholy might have more chance of success than he dreamed.

"Do you want me to go up to the house to fetch Marcus?"

"No, I'll go," Linc said, knowing he was probably asking for trouble. If Eden didn't want to see him, he was a fool to force a confrontation, but he couldn't resist the opportunity for one last look at her face one more time before he left.

He strode quietly across the porch. The door stood ajar, and he pushed it open, his heart in his throat at the prospect of meeting Eden, but the parlor was empty. Before he could decide whether to call for his friend or not, Marcus's bedroom door opened and he came out.

His expression was grim, even more grim than

Linc would have expected under the circumstances. "Is something wrong?"

Marcus closed the door softly behind him and came close to where Linc stood before replying. "Fiona's sick. She says it's nothing, but she can't hold anything on her stomach."

"Maybe you should stay behind then," Linc suggested.

"She won't hear of it. Says she'll be fine, and I'm not to worry about her while I'm off giving that 'scoundrel Blaine his comeuppance.' "

Linc had no trouble at all imagining Fiona issuing such an order. "She wouldn't tell you to go if she was really bad sick."

"That's just it, I don't know if she would or not," Marcus said with a worried frown. "Damn that Dirk Blaine to hell." He shook his head, then glanced around. "Where's Eden?"

"I . . ." Linc shrugged, at a loss. "Still asleep I guess."

"I'll go wake her up then. You'll want to say good-bye."

"Oh, no," Linc said, stopping him when he started for her door. "We, uh . . . we said our good-byes last night."

"Are you sure? She'll be mad as a wet hen if she finds out I didn't call her."

Certain Eden was already wide awake, Linc considered the prospect of her refusing Marcus's summons and firmly shook his head. "Let her sleep. Besides, we'd better get going if we want to meet Olsen and the others by first light."

"Well, all right," Marcus agreed reluctantly. His

frown said he didn't quite understand Linc's attitude, but Linc had no intention of explaining the situation. "I just hope that tracker of Olsen's didn't lose the trail."

Eden awoke with a start and a sense of impending disaster. *Linc!* she thought, throwing off the covers and bounding out of bed. But when she pulled back the curtains she saw the sun peering boldly over the horizon and the ranch yard strangely deserted.

They couldn't have left! her mind screamed. Surely she would have heard them. But perhaps not. She had lain awake most of the night worrying about Linc, so once she fell asleep she might have been sleeping too soundly. But why hadn't Fiona awakened her? And why hadn't *Linc* awakened her? He wouldn't leave without saying goodbye, would he? But when she remembered how they had parted the night before, she knew he very well might.

Muttering a curse, she flung on her robe and went in search of her stepmother to demand an explanation. One quick sweep through the house convinced her Fiona was not about, however. Puzzled, Eden started back to her bedroom to dress so she could go outside in search of her when she noticed Fiona's bedroom door was shut. Was it possible? Could Fiona still be abed at this late hour?

Eden tapped lightly on the door. Receiving no answer, she opened it a crack and peeked in to find her stepmother sleeping soundly.

"Fee?" she said aloud before she could stop herself.

Fiona stirred and opened her eyes. Seeing Eden, she jerked upright in alarm, then groaned, clamping one hand to her stomach and the other to her mouth.

Instinctively, Eden grabbed the washbowl from the stand and shoved it under Fiona's face just as her stepmother wretched.

"Good heavens, I didn't know you were sick," Eden said as soon as Fiona had finished and slumped wearily back against the pillows. "What's wrong?"

To Eden's amazement, her stepmother smiled. "I believe I am *enceinte*."

"Oh, no! Is it fatal?" Eden exclaimed in horror, setting the bowl on the floor and climbing on the bed beside her.

"Good heavens, I hope not," Fiona laughed. "Eden, I am with child."

"With child?" It took a moment for the sense of it to sink in. "Fiona! Oh, how wonderful!" She would have embraced her, but remembered Fiona's delicate condition and caught herself just in time. "But you're so sick," she protested. "Is that normal?"

"Completely, I'm afraid, at least for the first few months."

"But you were fine yesterday," Eden pointed out.

"I've been a little nauseated for several days, but I'd been afraid to hope. Then when Marcus left this morning, I was upset and . . ." She shrugged, her perfect mouth still smiling beatifically.

"Which reminds me," Eden said, recalling her grievance. "Why didn't you wake me up this morning when the men left."

Fiona's smile vanished. "Oh, dear, didn't Marcus call you? I was too ill to get up, but I felt certain the noise would have awakened you. I can't imagine why Marcus didn't . . ." She frowned suspiciously. "Or why Linc didn't call you. Didn't he want to bid you farewell?"

Eden looked guiltily away. "We . . . we had another fight last night after you went to bed."

"Honestly, Eden, I can't imagine why poor Mr. Scott doesn't lose patience with you completely!" Fiona scolded, pushing herself up gingerly.

"Be careful. Will you be all right?" Eden asked in concern.

Fiona nodded. "So long as I move slowly. It usually passes in an hour or two and then I'll be fine for the remainder of the day. Now about you and Mr. Scott, are you saying he was so angry he wouldn't even see you this morning?"

"Well, maybe," she allowed, "or else he thought I was still mad at him."

"But you aren't," Fiona surmised, "which means your quarrel was over something inconsequential again."

"Not exactly. In fact, it was over something pretty important, but he misunderstood me. He thinks I want to change him."

Fiona smiled wisely. "Women always want to change the men they love."

Eden sighed. "Then I guess I'm normal. For a

few minutes there it actually seemed like a good idea for Linc to just lay down his guns and stay home with me. I mean, I was so afraid something would happen to him if he went after Dirk Blaine," she hastily explained, seeing Fiona's disapproval.

"Don't you think I'm terrified at the thought of Marcus out there, too?" she asked. "He doesn't even know he's going to be a father."

"You mean you haven't told him? Why on earth not?"

"Because I was afraid he might be distracted if he were concerned about me," Fiona informed her pointedly. "I certainly don't want him to be distracted if he's going to be involved in a gun battle."

"Oh, Fee," Eden cried in despair. "Linc still thinks I don't love him the way he is. What am I going to do?"

Fiona opened her arms, and Eden embraced her gratefully. "You will do what women everywhere have always done," Fiona told her. "You will pray."

As she clung to her stepmother, Eden did pray. She prayed with much more fervency than she had ever prayed before because for the first time she considered the possibility that she, too, might be carrying a child who might never know his father.

Staring up at the stars, Dirk Blaine sipped the bitter brew that passed for coffee in this outlaw camp and considered his next move. They'd been on the run for three days, and he was thoroughly sick of it, sick of the bad food and sleeping on the ground and riding until his balls were numb. But mostly he was furious that he hadn't gotten Linc Scott before he left.

And that he hadn't screwed Eden Campbell.

Oblivious to his boss's mood, Ace hunkered down beside him. "The boys want to know what we're going to do."

"Oh, they do, do they?" Blaine asked sarcastically.

Ace was immune to such subtleties. "Yeah, a lot of 'em think we oughta split up, make it harder to follow us."

"What do you think *Alvin* would've done?" Blaine inquired bitterly.

Ace frowned, finally recognizing Blaine's mood for what it was. "I think any man with sense would decide on a place for us all to meet and split up."

"Well, I'm thinking of doing something different," Blaine informed him. "We're going back."

"Back? Are you crazy? They'll hang us."

Fury boiled up in him. "No, I'm not crazy!" Blaine shouted, flinging his coffee away and lunging to his feet. He trembled with rage, and his fingers itched to grab his pistol. Only the fact that he couldn't trust the rest of his men stopped him.

Recognizing his danger, Ace rose slowly, lifting his hands placatingly. "Listen, boss, I didn't mean nothing. It's just pretty dangerous for us to go back. They saw us trying to burn down the Paradise. I know the rest of the boys won't go."

"They won't? How about it, kid, wouldn't you like to go back?" he demanded of Garth Hamilton, who hunkered nearby and had overheard the entire conversation.

370

"I wouldn't mind another chance at Linc Scott," he said sourly. Three days without a shave had left his cheeks downy with golden fuzz, but the hate in his eyes belied his boyish appearance.

Dirk strolled over to him. "Think you could kill him if you got the chance?"

"I know I could."

Dirk squatted down next to him. "You'll go back with me, won't you?"

"Hell, yes. I never run from trouble yet, and I don't aim to start now."

Rubbing his chin thoughtfully, Dirk considered the boy for a long moment. "You ever had a woman?"

"Well, sure," Hamilton said, blushing to the roots of his hair.

"You ever had one who wasn't willing? When she was fighting and scratching? When you had to beat her to hold her still and hold her down to get it in?"

Hamilton's eyes widened. "What're you talking about?"

"I'm talking about Eden Campbell. You remember that red-haired girl who's supposed to marry Linc Scott?"

"What's she got to do with anything?"

"She's part of it, boy. Don't you see? It's her cattle we was stealing."

"I never stole anybody's cattle," the boy protested. "I was hired for my gun."

"You rode with us when we burned the Paradise."

"Because I wanted to get Scott. I got nothing

371

against Miss Campbell."

"But she's got something against you now. Her pappy'll kill us all if he gets the chance, but he won't get the chance because we're too smart for him. While he's chasing us to hell and gone, we'll circle back to his very own ranch where Little Miss Eden and that limey wife of his are waiting all alone. Did you see his wife? She's a pretty little thing, looks like a china doll and talks like a stage actress. I tell you what, boy, if you go back with me to get Scott, you can have her."

"What do you mean, have her?"

"I mean whatever you want. She'll be yours. If you can't think of nothing, you can watch what I do to the girl." He grinned. "I'll give you all the ideas you can use. What do you say, boy?"

"You're the best tracker I've ever seen," Linc told Bob as they watched the outlaw camp from a safe distance. It was well hidden and carefully dark. If Bob hadn't told them where to find it, they would have ridden right by without noticing.

"Blaine didn't make much effort to hide their tracks," Bob demurred. "What I can't figure is why they're still together. They've got to know we'd follow them. All they had to do was split up in ten different directions, and we wouldn't've stood a chance of finding them."

"I guess Dirk Blaine is dumber than we thought," Marcus remarked. "I always did think Alvin ran things. They must be feeling the loss."

"Do you think we oughta attack tonight?" Gus

Olsen asked. "Or wait till dawn?"

"They've got a guard posted, but only one," Bob reported.

"Let's wait a while," Linc suggested. "They won't be going anyplace until morning anyway. We'll give our men a chance to rest up a bit, and give Blaine and his bunch a chance to get good and asleep. Maybe their guard'll nod off, too."

"I'll tell the rest of the men to get some shut-eye," Olsen said. "Call us when you're ready."

When he was gone, Marcus and Linc rose from where they had crouched to observe the camp and walked away a bit, out of earshot of the tracker.

"What are you going to do with Blaine's men once we catch them?" Linc asked.

Marcus drew a ragged breath. "I'm gonna pray they all get shot when we overrun the camp, because we'll have to hang whoever's left."

"I figured," Linc said grimly. He dreaded the prospect, but they really had no choice. Without laws and courts and jails, the honest citizens were forced to take such matters into their own hands, and criminals were summarily dealt with. It wasn't a pleasant task, but if this country was ever to be safe for women such as Eden and Fiona, their men would have to do what was necessary.

Marcus went to join the others, leaving Linc alone with his thoughts. As usual, they turned immediately to Eden. In retrospect, his decision not to see her before he left seemed idiotic. Even if she'd still been angry, he at least would have known where he stood, and maybe they would've been able to come to some kind of understanding.

Instead he could only wonder if he'd somehow ruined the only chance of happiness he was ever likely to get.

Pushing aside such speculation, he forced himself to observe the camp and study it for signs of life or watchfulness. After a while, he saw the guard strike a match and light a cigarette. The tiny red glow from its end showed Linc his movements as he paced the perimeter of the camp. Slowly, Linc began to formulate a plan.

Several hours later they were ready to ride. In the last hour of the night, Linc and the others mounted their horses and moved into position so they could attack the camp from three sides. When everyone was in place, Linc let loose a rebel yell, the signal for the four men who had been sent in ahead on foot to light the torches that would guide them.

One by one the makeshift lights flamed up, the men holding them crouched low so as not to present too great a target. When the last one illuminated, all the riders echoed Linc's yell and charged in, guns blazing.

Roused by Linc's first call and the shouts of warning from their guard, the outlaws bolted up from their blankets, scrambling for guns, searching in vain for cover.

The first wave of riders overran the camp from the west, driving the outlaws back into the second assault as the attackers closed in around them. Herded together in the darkness and the gunsmoke, the outlaws began to fall one by one, screaming and shouting, firing until their guns clicked empty and they threw up their hands in surrender.

When not one of them was left fighting, Linc called a halt and shouted for the torches to be brought into the camp. By then the smoke had started to clear, and in the lessening haze, Linc could see the havoc they had wrought.

"Keep 'em covered," he commanded, sliding down from his horse for a closer look. Several more of his men dismounted and began to collect the discarded guns, tossing them into a pile. Another lit the campfire and tossed on enough wood for a blaze to illuminate the whole camp, making the torches unnecessary.

Linc scanned the cowering outlaws, once and then again. "Where's Blaine?" he demanded, feeling the old frustration once again.

When no one answered him, he asked again, turning his gun on the most frightened-looking of the men.

"Gone," the man said hastily, clutching his wounded chest. "He rode out last night."

"Where'd he go?"

But this time the man shook his head abjectly. He didn't know, and if any of the others did, they weren't talking. Or they simply couldn't talk. By the time Linc and the others got the outlaws sorted out, only four of them were still alive, although not one of their own men had sustained a wound.

By then dawn was breaking, and Marcus had sent the tracker Bob out to find a likely tree for disposing of the surviving outlaws.

One of the wounded men was Garth Hamilton, Linc noticed. He had come out of the fight with little more than a flesh wound on his upper arm. In the cold light of day, the boy looked more like a frightened kid than a fierce gunfighter, and Linc couldn't help the wave of pity he felt for him. Seven years ago he'd been much the same, full of piss and vinegar and ready to take on the world. If Linc hadn't met up with Marcus Pauling, he, too, might have taken the wrong road and ended up with a noose around his neck. The thought of hanging Garth Hamilton brought Linc little satisfaction.

When Hamilton saw Linc looking at him, he affected a defiant scowl. "Ain't you gonna see to our hurts? Ace here is bleeding something awful."

Linc glanced at the foreman whose thigh had been torn open by a large-caliber bullet. His pants were soaked in blood.

Ace laughed mirthlessly, his eyes hard and knowing. "Ain't no point in doctoring us, kid, not when they plan to hang us."

"Hang?" Hamilton repeated in horror. His boyish face went white, and when he looked around for confirmation, no one would meet his eye.

"They hang rustlers in these parts," Ace explained, his lips pulled back in what was either a grin or a grimace of pain. "Blaine should've warned you."

"But I ain't no rustler!" Hamilton insisted, jumping to his feet. He held one hand over his wound and blood seeped out between his fingers.

"You rode with them the night they burned my barn," Marcus reminded him.

"I only came 'cause I wanted a chance at Scott!

I thought you was just having a feud. I never knew about no rustling!"

"Is that true?" Linc asked Ace.

The older man shrugged. "Blaine hired him to kill Pauling, or rather Alvin did after Dirk botched the job the first time."

"Oh, yeah," Linc recalled. "He shot some stranger by mistake, didn't he?"

Ace grimaced again. "How'd you know?"

"Because I was the one he shot."

"I'll be damned," Ace said in amazement. "That son of a bitch is so stupid, he couldn't find his ass if he was tied in a tow sack."

"Then why don't you tell us where he went so we can put him out of his misery?" Linc suggested.

"If I do, will you let me go?"

But Linc couldn't lie, not even to find Dirk Blaine. He shook his head.

"Then you can go to hell," Ace informed him solemnly.

Bob rode back into camp, drawing everyone's attention. He glanced at the wounded men and then quickly away. "I found one about half a mile east of here."

Linc looked at the outlaws. One of them had a sucking chest wound. It would be inhuman to put him on a horse, especially when he'd be dead within the hour anyway. "Let's wait awhile," he suggested, gesturing toward the fellow, and Marcus and Olsen nodded their consent.

"Wait?" Garth Hamilton shouted shrilly, jumping to his feet again. "If you're gonna hang us, get it over with, for God's sake. Are you trying to torture us?"

"No," Ace said coolly, "they're hoping some of us'll die natural. They don't have much stomach for hanging, do you, boys?"

No one bothered to reply, and Linc saw Hamilton looking the other outlaws over, judging their chances. Plainly, one would die soon, and Ace might well bleed to death, too. His wound had already formed a puddle beneath his leg. The third man had been hit in the back and kept coughing painfully.

But Garth knew *he* wouldn't die, not if they waited all day. Linc could see the knowledge on his face and felt sick at the waste. Without even thinking about it, he walked over to where the boy stood.

"Come over here," he said, motioning the boy away from the rest of the prisoners.

Hamilton blanched. "You're going to take me now?"

"No," Linc hastily assured him. "I just want to talk to you a minute."

With an uncertain glance at Ace, who nodded his approval, the boy followed Linc until they were out of earshot. Linc pulled out his tobacco and began to roll a smoke. Hamilton watched him hungrily, and when it was done, he handed it to the boy and made another for himself. When they were lit, Hamilton inhaled gratefully, his hand unsteady as he removed the cigarette from his lips. "What'd you want to talk about?" he asked at last.

"Is it true you didn't do any rustling?"

"Hell, yes! I'm a hired gun. You heard what Ace

said. They sent for me to kill Mr. Pauling."

Linc studied the boy for a moment, trying to judge his sincerity. "You ever killed a man before?"

"Sure! I killed Jack Winters," he said, naming a man who had once been a legend.

"*You* were the one?" Linc asked, unable to hide his contempt.

"It was a fair fight," Hamilton defended himself, easily reading Linc's expression. "I don't know what you heard, but he was the one started it. He picked a fight and called me out."

"Had you ever killed anybody before that?" Linc demanded.

"Uh . . . no," he admitted reluctantly, unable to meet Linc's eye.

"Then it don't make sense. He never would've picked on a green kid."

Hamilton looked away again. "He . . . he might've thought I had a reputation."

This Linc could understand. "You'd been bragging some, I guess."

The boy nodded and took a long drag on his cigarette.

"So he thought you was somebody, and he called you out so you'd kill him," Linc said.

"What're you talking about?" Hamilton asked nervously.

"Jack was going blind."

"The hell you say!" Hamilton said in outrage.

"It's the truth. Not many knew it, but he'd got so bad he couldn't make out much more than colors and shapes. He swore he wasn't going to live like that. I reckon he figured he'd make your reputation for you on his way out."

"No!" the boy cried, but Linc could see he recognized the ring of truth in the story. Linc had destroyed his vaulting self-confidence in his ability as a gunfighter.

"So you came here thinking you were a big-time gunfighter who was going to knock off Lincoln Scott," Linc continued.

"I . . . I didn't know you was here," Hamilton protested weakly. "Blaine just sent word to a friend in Dodge City that he needed somebody handy with a gun. They asked me to come, so I did. I didn't know nothing about the rustling or anything, I swear to God."

Linc wasn't sure why, but he believed him. Maybe there was hope for the boy yet. "I don't want to hang you, Hamilton, but I can't speak for the others. Marcus Pauling had his barn burned, and you was with the ones who—"

From the corner of his eye, Linc saw Marcus squatting down to offer Ace a drink from one of the canteens. Something about the gesture bothered him, but before he could think what it was, Hamilton said, "I know where Blaine went! He tried to talk me into going along."

"Where?"

"He went back to the Paradise. He figured the place wouldn't be guarded because all the men would've come after us. He . . ."

"He what?" Linc urged, fear coiling in his stomach.

"He went after Miss Campbell."

Linc swore just as a gun exploded. Instinctively,

he grabbed the boy, and they both hit the dirt as half a dozen shots went off in response, sending up a cloud of gunsmoke that obscured Linc's view of the camp.

Linc pointed his gun, not even remembering having drawn it. Ready to fire, he waited in vain for a target. The shooting had stopped as abruptly as it began.

"What's going on?" he shouted.

"It's that fellow Ace," someone shouted back. "He's done for, now, though."

Linc scrambled to his feet, dragging a stunned Garth Hamilton with him. Still clutching his pistol, Linc marched the boy back to the camp where he found three dead outlaws.

"What the hell happened?"

Marcus looked up sheepishly. "I bent down to give him a drink," he explained, gesturing to the staring corpse of the man known only as Ace. "He snatched my gun right out of my holster and started shooting."

"Of course we all started shooting back," Olsen explained hastily. "He only got off two or three shots before we got him."

"And before we realized who he was shooting at," Marcus added, pointing at the other two outlaws who had each been plugged neatly in the forehead.

"That's a lie!" Hamilton shrilled. "He'd never shoot his own men!"

"He would if he wanted to save them from hanging," Linc said quietly. "He knew if he started shooting, our men would kill him while he got the others. It was a pretty gutsy thing to do."

This time all the color drained from Hamilton's face, and Linc sat him down quickly, calling for some water. The boy drank gratefully, and when he was done, Linc made him lie down until the weakness passed.

"My God," Hamilton moaned a few minutes later. "He would've shot me, too, if I hadn't've been off talking to you."

"Maybe he waited until you were out of range," Linc suggested. "Remember he told us you weren't involved in the rustling."

Aware of the other men watching in disapproval, Linc wet his bandana from the canteen and began to scrub the dirt out of Hamilton's wound.

"What're you doing?" Hamilton asked, his voice cracking from pain and astonishment.

"Can't have you bleeding all over the place," Linc said off-handedly, pulling off Hamilton's bandana to use as a bandage.

"He's one of them," Olsen protested, speaking for the others.

Linc lifted his gaze to them defiantly. "He told me where Blaine went, just before Ace started shooting. He said Blaine doubled back to go after Eden."

Marcus swore viciously, and the others stared back in stunned silence.

"That ain't all," Hamilton said, struggling upright. "He wanted me to go with him. He said if I did, he'd . . ."

"He'd what?" Linc prompted when the boy hesitated.

Hamilton glanced at Linc as if for courage. "He said I could have Mrs. Pauling if I'd go with him."

Marcus howled his outrage above the murmurs of the other men, and he had already started for his horse when Linc called him back. "Remember we left Melancholy to guard them. Blaine won't ride up to the ranch when he sees they aren't alone."

"He's right," Olsen said. "We've got some business to take care of here, first."

Everyone looked at Hamilton, whose fear shone plainly on his youthful face.

"I say we let him go," Linc said, rising inexorably to his feet.

"Let him go?" the cry rose from the other men.

"You heard Ace say he didn't do any rustling. He was hired to kill me, but I think he's changed his mind about that, haven't you?"

Hamilton nodded vigorously. "Yes, sir, I sure have. If you let me go, I swear you'll never see hide nor hair of me again."

"You don't believe him, do you?" Olsen scoffed.

"Yes, I do, and since I'm the one he's after, I don't see as how the rest of you have any say in this at all."

"Well, I've got some say," Marcus protested. "He rode with the bunch who burned my barn."

Linc looked at his old friend for a long moment. "Sometimes all a boy needs is a chance to do right. I want to give him that chance."

He didn't have to explain. He saw Marcus's weathered face soften with the memories of another boy he had helped once, long ago.

"All right," Marcus said at last. "We'll turn him loose, but on my terms. All he gets is a horse and a saddle. No gun, no food, and no water."

When Hamilton would've protested, Linc silenced him with a look. "Take what you can get, boy," he whispered as he helped him to his feet. "They could've set you off afoot."

Hamilton swallowed loudly and, cradling his injured arm, hurried to his horse.

"He's took you for a fool," Olsen grumbled. "Someday he'll shoot you in the back."

Linc only grunted in reply, but he thought that if Hamilton didn't, someone else probably would. At least when the time came, the boy would be one less burden on his soul.

"Olsen, you'll understand if we don't wait around to help you bury these fellows," Marcus said.

"Go on," Olsen urged. "We'll take care of things here. Send us word if you need any help."

Linc, Marcus, and the rest of their men rode swiftly away. They hardly spoke during the long trip back, but each of them was thinking the same thing: if Dirk Blaine had a twelve-hour head start, they didn't stand a chance of getting to the ranch in time to help.

The sun had long since set and the ranch looked deserted as the riders approached, but the moment they were close enough to call out their identity, lights flickered on and the other men emerged from their hiding places, waving lanterns and shouting greetings.

Linc felt his heart slide back down from his throat into its proper place. Of its own accord, his gaze turned toward the ranch house porch, where he saw two women standing silhouetted in front of the lighted window.

At least he'd gotten here before Dirk Blaine.

The riders stopped their horses in the yard, and Marcus was out of the saddle in an instant.

"I'll take care of your horse, boss," Melancholy offered. Marcus waved his thanks as he hurried into Fiona's embrace.

Linc forced himself not to watch the tender reunion or even to glance in Eden's direction.

Melancholy looked at him quizzically as he dismounted. "Should I take yours, too?"

"No need," Linc said gruffly, leading his horse over to the corral. Ignoring Melancholy's curious stare, he began to unsaddle the animal. "We caught up with them late last night," he explained as he worked. "We attacked the camp just before dawn." Briefly he told the story up to the place where Hamilton had informed them Blaine was headed back here and why he was coming.

Melancholy swore eloquently. "We ain't seen no more 'n a tumbleweed until you fellows rode up just now. If he'd so much as showed his face, I'd've shot it off for him."

"I figure he probably knew that." When Linc picked up a rag to start rubbing his horse down, one of the other men took it from him and began to do the job. Suddenly the weariness of four days of hard riding caught up with him.

"Come on, partner," Melancholy said, clapping a

hand on his shoulder and starting him in the direction of the bunkhouse. He asked a few questions to which Linc mumbled the answers, then they heard Eden's voice calling across the yard.

"Linc?"

Linc stopped dead, and his heart began to slam against his ribs. New vitality flowed through his body, banishing his exhaustion.

"She's probably put out 'cause you haven't gone over to say howdy," Melancholy suggested, a questioning note in his voice. He obviously couldn't understand Linc's failure to greet her.

Of course, Linc had been uncertain of his welcome, but now . . . "I'll see you later," he mumbled as he started toward the ranch house at a trot.

In the shadow of the porch, he couldn't see her face so he couldn't guess her mood. Silhouetted by the lamp that still burned in the front window, she stood with her arms crossed. Protectively or belligerently? He couldn't be sure. She wore a loose-fitting dress, probably one she'd thrown on quickly upon hearing the approaching riders. She might not have anything on under it. His body stirred at the thought and at the prospect of holding her willing flesh next to his, but as he mounted the steps, he recalled he'd been wearing the same clothes since he'd left the ranch four days ago. She certainly wouldn't want him close now, regardless of her mood.

He stopped a few feet away from her, and when she didn't speak, he said, "You wanted to see me?"

"Yes, I . . ."

Eden stared up at him, cursing the darkness that

hid his face from her. What was he thinking? Was he still angry with her? He hadn't come to her willingly, but perhaps he was just uncertain of his reception. She drew a deep breath, inhaling the scent of leather and horses and male sweat. Her blood quickened in response, and her heart ached with longing. "Marcus told us what happened. Are you all right?"

"You can see for yourself."

But what she really wanted to know wouldn't be visible. "That boy . . . the one you let go . . ."

"What about him?"

He sounded irritated, but she had to know. "Why wouldn't you let them hang him?"

"Because he wasn't a rustler."

"Is that the only reason?" she insisted.

"What does it matter?" he snapped.

"It matters because you told me you could never change. It would have been real easy to kill that boy, but you didn't, and you wouldn't let the others do it, either. Why, Linc? Was it because of what we talked about before?"

"Do you think you've reformed me, Eden?" No doubt about it, he was angry now. She swallowed the lump in her throat.

"I wasn't the one who thought you needed reforming," she reminded him. "You're the one who said I shouldn't marry a gunfighter."

"And you shouldn't."

"Not even if . . ." She caught herself just in time. She had no intention of holding him with threats of pregnancy, particularly when she had no reason to think she carried his child. "Not even if I love you?"

She could actually feel his reluctance to accept the idea. "Do you really love *me*, Eden?"

"Of course I do! If I didn't, I wouldn't have . . ." She bit back the words, conscious they were outside, where anyone might overhear. "I wouldn't have made love with you," she said more softly. "Linc, you told me to let you know when I decided what I wanted, and I've had a lot of time to think while you were gone. I was wrong to ask you not to go after Dirk Blaine, but you were wrong when you said it was because I didn't want you killing anyone else. I know what kind of man you are, and I know you'd never take another person's life unless you had no choice. You proved that today when you let Hamilton go."

"I'm not a hero, Eden. Don't try to make me out to be one."

"But you *are* a hero, Linc, at least to me. You're brave, and you're strong, and you don't let people like Dirk Blaine get away with the evil things they do, not even when some silly woman tries to make you. I love you, Linc. I love you just the way you are."

He made a groaning sound, and Eden flung herself into his arms. He clasped her to him fiercely. "I'll get you all dirty," he whispered into her hair.

"Do you think I care? Please kiss me before I die of desperation."

With a strangled laugh, he found her mouth and captured it. His beard tore at her face, but she reveled in the sensation, opening to his possession and rising up on her bare toes to press herself more closely to him. They clung together for a long time, kissing and whispering love words and recklessly promising never to quarrel again.

"So," she said finally, still breathless, "are you going to make an honest woman out of me, or do I have to tell Marcus to load up his shotgun?"

"If you're trying to make me feel guilty, you're wasting your time," Linc informed her as he nibbled on her neck. "You know good and well I already proposed to you. I might've even done it more than once."

"But this time we'll set a date and invite the neighbors so you can't back out again."

"I never backed out before," he protested, pulling her more snugly into the cradle of his thighs. The hard evidence of his desire sent a thrill through her, and she wished she dared lead him into the privacy of her bedroom.

"Oh, Linc, I want you so much."

He groaned and pressed his lips to hers again for a long, lingering kiss. "I want you, too," he said hoarsely when they broke for air, "but this ain't exactly a good time. I've hardly been out of the saddle for four days, and I haven't slept for two."

"You seem lively enough to me," she replied, rocking her hips against the proof of his vitality.

With another groan, he kissed her again, but this time when the kiss ended he pushed her reluctantly away. "Although I'd like nothing better than to prove just how 'lively' I could be, we aren't exactly alone." He gestured toward the front window, through which they could see Fiona moving about in the parlor. "And besides, the next time we're together, I want you to be my wife, Eden. No more sneaking around and worrying about getting caught."

"I never noticed you worrying too much before," she teased, touched by his determination. "But maybe you're right. Actually, I should have thought of it myself. I can't imagine a better way to get you to set the date. How long do you think you can wait?" Once again she pressed herself against him provocatively.

"Mmmm, how about tomorrow?" he murmured against her mouth.

"Tomorrow it is," she gasped when she could speak again.

He stiffened in her arms.

"Linc?" she asked in sudden alarm. She touched his face, and he kissed her fingers.

"You know it can't really be tomorrow," he said, his voice heavy with regret. "Dirk Blaine is still on the loose."

"Oh . . . yes . . ." She'd almost forgotten. "Oh, Linc, promise me nothing will happen to you. When I think about losing you—"

"Hush." He pressed his fingers to her lips. "I've told you before, nothing's going to happen to me, not when I've got the most beautiful girl in the world waiting to marry me."

"Eden!" Fiona called from the doorway. "It's getting quite late."

"I'm coming," she said, then turned back to Linc. "Don't go off without saying good-bye tomorrow."

"I won't," he promised.

They said their tender good-nights and parted reluctantly. When Eden entered the house, she found Fiona waiting expectantly. "Well?"

"Well what?" Eden replied coyly.

"Judging from the way you and Mr. Scott were embracing outside, I suppose I should begin making wedding plans."

"Quite right," Eden said in her best imitation British accent. "And quite soon, too."

"Oh, Eden, I'm so happy for you."

Eden accepted Fiona's hug with a delighted laugh, but sobered when Fiona asked her how soon the wedding was to be.

"As soon as they catch Dirk Blaine," she replied grimly.

Blaine stared into the small fire, watching the flames dance around the wood. Damn Eden Campbell and Lincoln Scott and Marcus Pauling and all the rest of them. If only Alvin was here . . .

Memories of his brother stirred his anger to life. Alvin never would've let them get caught. Alvin would've known just what to do. But Alvin had been a fool to get himself killed by a two-bit gunnie like Lincoln Scott. Dirk's fury boiled up, dark and ugly, raging against Scott and Alvin alike.

Even his own men had deserted him. Not one of those bastards had been willing to come back with him. Not one of them had any loyalty to the man who'd paid their wages for the last year. What was this world coming to when a man couldn't depend on one living soul?

Now Dirk was alone, but that was fine, because with Alvin gone, there wasn't anybody he really trusted anymore. Besides, he didn't need anybody's help to get Linc Scott. The hell with Hamilton and the rest of those hired guns. This time he'd get Scott for sure. He'd show Alvin and all the rest of them.

Dirk shivered and cursed the dampness of the cave. As he reached for his pack to pull out a blanket, he thought about how lucky he'd been to find it. When he'd discovered that Pauling hadn't left the Paradise unprotected like he'd thought, he'd been desperate for a place to hide. Then he'd remembered finding Eden that day. That little whore had been off screwing Linc Scott, but he knew she'd never do it out in the open where anybody could see them. No, she was too clever for that. Dirk knew they had a hidey hole someplace nearby, and he'd found it without any trouble at all once he set his mind to it.

Now, of course, he'd have to wait. He'd never liked waiting before, but he'd never had something this good to wait for either. After thinking all day, he'd come up with the plan. Sooner or later he'd catch them alone, Scott and Eden. This time he'd be the one in charge, and this time he'd have the advantage.

Linc Scott would die but not before he watched Dirk tame and mount that little red-haired vixen. And Eden . . . Well, she'd just *wish* she was dead.

Chapter Twelve

As tired as he was, Marcus couldn't fall asleep until Fiona was beside him. After helping him get cleaned up, she had gone to see about Eden. He'd left the lamp burning low on the bedside table so when she came back in, moving quietly so as not to disturb him, he could clearly see the shining gold of her hair and the peachy glow of her face.

She slipped off the dress she had thrown over her nightdress when Melancholy had announced their arrival earlier and hung it in the wardrobe. Still moving quietly, she came to the bed and was about to blow out the lamp when he spoke her name.

"I thought you'd be sleeping," she said with a smile. Her eyes were like sapphires in the lamplight.

"How's Eden doing?"

"Quite well. She and Lincoln have made up their latest quarrel and might well be able to get themselves married before their next one. At least they are making plans."

She blew out the lamp and slipped into bed beside him. He took her in his arms, overwhelmed with gratitude to have her close again. For a moment he simply held her, inhaling her sweet scent and savoring the precious softness of her body.

"I've been awful worried about you," he whispered.

"About me? Whatever for?"

"Because you were sick. I'm real glad to see you're better."

"Well, actually, my recovery is only temporary. I'm afraid I shall be ill again tomorrow morning."

Fear formed a fist in his stomach. "What do you mean?"

"The illness from which I suffer only occurs in the morning, which is why it is called 'morning sickness.' "

"I never heard of it," he said, feeling the fist tighten. "Is it . . . serious?"

"Terribly serious."

"Oh, God, Fee, don't be afraid. I'll take you to the best doctors. I'll—"

"Marcus, my darling," she protested with a laugh. "I'm terribly sorry to have frightened you, but you're so deliciously easy to tease, I simply couldn't resist."

At the sound of her laughter, his fear began to dissolve. "You mean you're not really sick?"

"Not exactly. You see, I'm with child."

"With . . . child?" The words didn't register for a moment and when they did, he still wasn't quite certain he'd understood. "You're going to have a baby?" he asked, hardly daring to believe.

"Yes, my darling, or rather I should say *we* are

394

going to have a baby, since you are entirely responsible for my condition. Your attentions to me of late have been so—"

"But you're sick," he said, still not quite able to comprehend.

"Many women suffer from morning sickness during the early months. It will pass, and then I shall get terribly fat, and I shall crave all sorts of unusual foods and grow irritable and quite probably make your life totally miserable."

She paused, and he knew she wanted him to say something, but his throat was too thick with emotions he'd never expected to feel.

"Marcus?" she asked uncertainly. "Aren't you pleased?"

"God, yes," he said hoarsely, pulling her against his pounding heart. For one terrible moment he was afraid he might actually cry, but he swallowed down hard on the lump in his throat, and the urge passed. "I thought the day you married me was the happiest day of my life, but now . . ."

"I shall remind you of this one day when the baby has kept us awake all night crying and you are fervently wishing you had never set eyes on either one of us."

Marcus smiled in the darkness, knowing such a thing would never happen. "I love you, Fee."

"Then you must promise me you will not go out looking for Dirk Blaine," she said, her voice solemn once again.

At the mention of Blaine's name, a brand new rage welled up in Marcus. That bastard had offered his precious Fiona as a prize. When he got his hands on him . . .

"Marcus, listen to me," Fiona insisted. "I've buried two husbands and two children in my life. I can't bear the thought of losing you, too."

"You didn't seem worried when you sent me off after him a few days ago," he reminded her.

"That was necessary. He and his men had stolen our cattle and burned our barn, and he had assaulted Eden. You dealt with the rest of his men, and no one will fault you if you leave Dirk Blaine to Lincoln Scott. It's really Lincoln's fight now anyway."

"But Eden is my stepdaughter, and Blaine was the one set fire to the barn. I've got to—"

"Marcus, my dear, of course you must protect your honor, but you must protect your wife, too. If Dirk Blaine is planning to attack Eden, you must have someone here to guard us. Why can't you do it yourself?"

She had a good argument, and Marcus knew he'd be a fool to resist it. The argument sounded awfully familiar though. He smiled at a memory. "And if I refuse, are you going to stand on the porch and cry in front of the other men and shame me into it?"

"Most assuredly."

"Then I don't reckon I have much choice. Although I'm warning you, I get mighty restless just sitting around the ranch. How are you going to keep me entertained?"

"Oh, I don't know," she murmured, running her hand down his bare hip. "Perhaps we can think of something."

Linc lifted his face to the pewter-colored sky and let the rainwater pour off his hatbrim and down his back. The storm, one of those that boils up without warning and dumps torrents of water over the ground, had caught them in the open prairie. Now their horses were muddied up to their bellies and every man in the posse was wet through to the skin beneath his rubber slicker.

Linc glanced at Bob and shouted over the roar of the storm: "I don't reckon even you can track Blaine in this."

" 'Fraid not," Bob replied, adjusting the collar of his slicker against the downpour. Olsen had lent them the tracker for the duration of their hunt. "But if we haven't found him in three days of looking, the rain won't make no difference. I figure he's long gone."

"It's the only thing that makes sense," Melancholy offered. He looked even more morose than usual with his mustache drooping wetly over his mouth. "Maybe he did think he'd come after Miss Eden, but he ain't a complete fool. When he saw we had her guarded, he must've thought better of it and lit out."

A jagged bolt of lightning streaked across the sky, and almost instantly the thunderclap split the air.

"We might as well head on back," Linc said in disgust. "Even if he is somewhere around, he'll be holed up in this weather."

They turned their horses in the direction of the

ranch. With Bob, they numbered a half dozen. Linc felt guilty keeping so many of Marcus's men away from their work for so long, but he couldn't just sit around and wait for Dirk Blaine to show his hand.

The tension at the ranch was thick enough to cut. The women hadn't so much as been to town since the trouble started, and unless he could find Blaine, Linc didn't think they ought to go. But they were both dropping hints about needing fabric for a wedding gown, and now that Fiona was pregnant, Linc felt an added pressure to eliminate the threat Blaine presented.

To complicate matters further, Fiona's pregnancy had suggested yet another reason for Linc to hurry his marriage to Eden: Eden might already be carrying his child. He hadn't dared broach the subject with her, but he didn't need much imagination to interpret her eagerness as necessity. Damn that Dirk Blaine.

When Linc and the other men arrived at the ranch, Linc took care of his horse, then went to the bunkhouse to get cleaned up before going to see Eden. She awaited him anxiously, greeting him with a kiss in what had become her accustomed manner. He didn't need to tell her they hadn't found anything. She took him straight into the kitchen for a cup of hot coffee.

Marcus and Fiona were already there, sitting around the table as a fragrant stew bubbled on the stove.

"This rain's a heck of a thing," Marcus remarked sourly.

"Bob and Melancholy don't think it makes much difference," Linc said, taking his seat at the table. "They figure Blaine lit out when he found out he couldn't get near Eden."

"Surely he would've showed his hand by now if he was still around," Eden argued, handing him his coffee and taking a seat beside him.

"And you haven't found any sign of him," Fiona reminded Linc, equally eager for the search to end and life to return to normal.

"I think they're right," Marcus said thoughtfully. "Blaine never was much of a planner. His brother did the thinking, and his whole outfit's been going off half-cocked ever since Alvin died. Blaine ain't a patient man, neither. I can't see him biding his time like this. He must be gone for good."

"Are you saying we should stop looking for him?" Linc asked.

"I'm saying we can't let the ranch work go much longer. The men can keep their eyes peeled while they work. If he's around anyplace, somebody'll spot him sooner or later."

As eager as he was to call a halt to the search, Linc couldn't quite feel comfortable. Some sixth sense told him Blaine wouldn't give up so easily, but he also knew he couldn't keep the men riding indefinitely. Marcus was right: if Blaine was around, their riders would spot him or his sign while they were out doing their regular work. "All right," he agreed at last.

"Does this mean we can set a wedding date?" Eden asked eagerly, slipping her arm through his.

Her touch electrified him, reminding him of his

foolish promise not to make love to her again until they were married. "I reckon it does," he said unsteadily.

"How about Saturday?" she suggested, looking to Fiona for approval.

To their surprise, Fiona frowned. "We don't even have a gown. Surely you can wait another week. Besides, have you considered where you will live?"

Eden hadn't given the matter a moment's thought. "I just assumed we'd live here with you. Since we're all partners . . ."

But Fiona was shaking her head. "You won't have much privacy living here. Remember, you'll be newlyweds."

Her blue eyes sent Eden a message that brought the heat to her face. She well knew how little privacy the thin walls in this house provided. But on the other hand . . . "You don't expect us to wait until we can build our own house, do you?"

Fiona glanced at Marcus, who took up the argument. "I been meaning to talk to both of you about this. If you recollect, we each own a fourth of the ranch, which means the two of you together will own a half once you're hitched. It seems kind of silly to keep running the place as one big ranch when it was meant to be two ranches in the first place. What do you say we split it down the middle. Me and Fee'll keep the Paradise and you two can take over my old spread."

"Which means we can live in your old house," Eden added, delighted.

But when she looked at Linc, he seemed less than pleased. "You can't just turn over a quarter of your ranch to me," he protested.

"The hell I can't," Marcus replied cheerfully. "If you won't take it no other way, I'll give it to Eden as a wedding present."

"Then I'll own half, and when you marry me, it'll become yours," Eden added. "And don't try to convince us you haven't earned it either. I believe if we'd pull down your britches, we'd find the saddle sores to prove exactly how much you've done to earn it."

"Eden." Fiona scolded, but she couldn't quite hide her amusement. Marcus coughed discreetly, and Linc glared at her. She glared back, unrepentant.

At last Linc said, "What's Marcus's house like?"

Laughing in triumph, she kissed him on the cheek. "It's absolutely terrible, fit only for a bachelor to live in. It's just one big room, but we could divide it into a bedroom and a kitchen, I think."

"And add more rooms as you need them," Fiona said. "Perhaps a parlor first and then room for children."

Linc shot Eden a funny look which made her think he also must have considered the possibility that they might need a child's bedroom quite soon. Hoping they would, Eden squeezed his arm.

" 'Course, the place might be falling down for all we know," Marcus said. "Nobody's lived in it for months. You'll have to make some repairs before you can move in."

"And you might as well divide the rooms, too," Fiona added. "You won't want to do that work after you're living there."

Eden's initial excitement faded somewhat as she realized they were adding days and possibly even weeks to the time she and Linc must wait to be married. Of course, there was no reason to rush, or at least none she knew of, and certainly no reason to let Marcus and Fiona think there was. "How long do you think that will take?"

"Three weeks oughta do 'er," Marcus estimated. "We can all ride out to there tomorrow to see what has to be done."

"And afterwards we can go into town," Fiona said. "You'll probably need to order some furniture, and we must make Eden a gown."

"And they'll need supplies for the house," Marcus added.

"And I reckon I'll be needing a suit," Linc confessed.

By the time Fiona served supper, all the plans had been made, and Eden, at last, had a wedding date.

Eden stared blindly out the window, as if simply willing Linc's presence could make him appear on the road.

"Is someone coming?" Fiona asked as she entered the parlor.

"No," Eden grumbled. "And I'm starting to wonder how anxious Linc really is to marry me. He's hardly had a minute for me in over two weeks, and he hasn't so much as shown his face around here in two days."

"He has a lot of work to do," Fiona reminded

her. "The wedding is a week from tomorrow."

"Well, if he's too busy to come here to see me, he could at least invite me over there. Surely there's some work I could do. The place must need cleaning if nothing else."

"I'm certain it does. Perhaps you should take it upon yourself to see."

Eden looked up in surprise. "You mean just go over there?"

"Perhaps it isn't strictly proper, but you are engaged, and you are surely entitled to inspect the progress on your future home. Linc would most certainly appreciate it if you take him his dinner when you go, too. He must be tired of eating his own cooking by now."

"What a wonderful idea! What should I take him?"

"Let's see what our larder holds," Fiona said with a smile, leading the way to the kitchen.

Linc looked up from hitching the wagon to see Marcus and Melancholy riding into the yard. He waved a greeting and walked out to meet them.

"How's it going?" Marcus asked.

"The house is about done. I figured I'd go into town and pick up the furniture we ordered today, then bring Eden out tomorrow to look things over and make sure it's to her liking."

"You know," Melancholy confided solemnly, "I'm starting to think maybe I was the lucky one. All this settling down looks like a lot of work to me. I don't reckon nothing short of a broke leg could keep me in a house for two solid weeks."

"It's been a trial all right," Linc admitted with a grin. "I just keep thinking about what I'm working for, though, and it don't matter quite so much."

" 'Course you'd say that," Melancholy allowed dourly. "Me, I think I'll just enjoy being single for a while yet."

"I don't reckon you fellows saw any sign of Dirk Blaine," Linc said after Marcus had brought him up to date on the ranch business.

"Not so much as a hoofprint," Marcus said. "I can't imagine he's gone to ground for all this time. He must be a hundred miles from here by now."

"In another state, if he's smart," Melancholy added.

"He's probably gone to Indian Territory," Linc guessed. "A man like that'd get along fine where there ain't no laws."

" 'Course, he'd have to hold his own with some really bad men, and I don't think he's got the starch for it," Marcus said. "Could be we'll never hear another thing from Mr. Blaine."

"I just wonder if I'll ever be able to stop looking for him," Linc mused. "When I think about him going after Eden . . ."

"She knows better than to be caught out alone someplace," Marcus assured him. "I've got a feeling she's getting a little restless, though, and there's no telling what she'll do when she's restless. Maybe you oughta come over and stay at the ranch tonight."

Linc grinned. "Don't worry, I was planning to do just that. I'm getting a little restless myself."

Marcus scowled down at him in mock disapproval. "Don't go getting any funny ideas now. There's still another whole week before the wedding."

"How could I forget when my future father-in-law is looking over my shoulder every minute?"

"And a bunch of heartbroke waddies is looking over your other shoulder," Melancholy reminded him.

"You just better not go planning no chivaree," Linc warned, only half in jest. "If somebody tries to steal Eden on our wedding night, there'll be hell to pay."

"Reckon I'd better start saving up for it then," Melancholy replied, deadpan. "I always did say a man who can't hold onto his own bride don't deserve to have her."

"Now, boys, don't fight," Marcus cautioned with amusement. "Melancholy, you oughta feel sorry for poor Linc here getting his wings clipped, instead of acting jealous. Don't forget, he'll have Eden telling him what to do for the rest of his natural life."

Melancholy shook his head sadly. "When you put it that way, it does sound sorta pathetic."

"Get out of here, the both of you, before I come after you with a pitchfork," Linc said cheerfully. "It don't matter what you say, you won't change my mind."

"Let's go then, boss," Melancholy suggested. "The poor fellow's past helping."

Marcus turned his horse and raised a hand in farewell. "I'll tell Eden you're coming over this evening."

"See you later," Linc replied before returning to his wagon.

A little while later, Marcus and Melancholy stopped to water their horses in the creek that separated his ranch from Linc's. The two men climbed down to get themselves a drink, and when Marcus looked up, he noticed a gouge in the cutbank where a horse had recently climbed up.

"What do you make of this?" he asked Melancholy. On closer examination, he saw that perhaps more than one horse had crossed.

"Looks like a horse went by," Melancholy replied, scanning the horizon for signs of a rider. "Not long ago, either."

"Who'd be riding around here?"

"None of our men."

"Funny we didn't see whoever it was."

"Maybe they went another way. We didn't exactly come straight here," Melancholy said, reminding him they had followed a circuitous route checking the cattle. "Or maybe they didn't want us to see them."

Neither of them mentioned the suspicion they shared. "Looks like they might've been headed out to Linc's place," Marcus observed.

Melancholy climbed back up the bank and tried to pick out the intruder's prints. "Ground's too hard to tell which way they was headed."

Marcus felt the first frisson of fear. "Who'd you leave to guard the ranch today?"

"Shorty."

Marcus nodded thoughtfully. "I think I'll go by there just to make sure everything's all right. Why don't you—"

"—go see if anybody's paid Linc a visit since we left," Melancholy finished for him. "I'm on my way."

The two men parted swiftly, not bothering to exchange another word. Marcus rode hard, harder than he needed to, he realized when he arrived at the ranch and discovered nothing amiss.

Or almost nothing.

"Where's Eden?" he asked after Fiona had greeted him in surprised delight.

Fiona gave him a conspiratorial smile. "She's gone to visit Lincoln. The poor thing was simply dying of boredom and—"

"You let her go alone?" Marcus exclaimed, horrified.

She blinked in surprise, then lifted her chin in outraged innocence. "Certainly not. I sent Shorty with her."

"Dammit, Fee, don't you remember Dirk Blaine's still on the loose? Me and Melancholy saw sign some riders had crossed the creek over by Linc's where no riders should've been and—"

"Honestly, Marcus, use some sense," Fiona scolded. "The riders were Eden and Shorty, on their way to Linc's. You yourself told me just the other evening that Blaine must be miles away from here by now."

Marcus opened his mouth to protest, then realized he was only growling because he'd been so worried. Fiona was probably right. He pulled off his hat and ran a hand through his thinning hair. "Even still, you shouldn't've let her go off like that.

Besides, Linc ain't even home. Me and Melancholy stopped by there, and he was on his way to town."

"Oh, dear, she'll be so disappointed. She hasn't seen him for two days, and she has become unbearably curious about how the house is progressing."

"Linc was planning to come see her tonight and take her over there tomorrow anyways." Marcus shook his head. "I warned Linc he'd have his hands full with that one. Can't stay put for more than a minute."

"Just like her stepfather," Fiona said affectionately. "Although I can't say I mind your showing up here so unexpectedly. Now we can dine together."

"That is kind of a treat since you can't never eat breakfast with me anymore," he replied, somewhat mollified. "I reckon when they find out Linc ain't home, Shorty'll bring Eden straight back, and they'll meet Melancholy on the way. Don't think I ain't gonna give her what-for for going off like that, though. When she's Linc's wife, she can do what she wants, but as long as she's living under my roof—"

"Hush, now," Fiona chided. "I don't want to hear another word about it, and if I do, I promise to become quite ill. I may even faint."

"You're teasing, ain't you?" Marcus asked as he followed her into the kitchen.

"Perhaps," was all she would say.

When Melancholy saw the lone rider heading toward him, he instinctively reached for his pistol; then the man waved, and he recognized Shorty. Melancholy spurred his horse to a run, slowing as he approached the other rider.

"What in the hell are you doing out here?" he demanded furiously. "I left you to watch the ranch."

"Miz Pauling sent me to keep Miss Eden company," Shorty protested.

"Keep her company? Then where the hell is she?"

"She's at Linc's place. She took him his dinner," he added slyly. "I figure they plan to spend some time together."

"You jackass! Linc's gone to town for the day. Didn't you notice he wasn't around?"

"Well, sure," Shorty admitted sheepishly, "but we figured he'd be back in a little while. Miss Eden said she didn't mind waiting 'cause she had to cook his meal anyways."

"So you just rode off and left her alone," Melancholy fumed.

"What harm can come to her? Nobody even knows she's there."

Melancholy considered this for a long moment. "She'll be right irritated when she's got to sit there all day kicking her heels, but I reckon you're right: no real harm can come to her."

Dirk Blaine watched the man who had accompanied Eden to the ranch ride away, and he chuckled silently to himself. It had taken a long time, much longer than he would've suspected, but Alvin had been right: he had finally caught Eden alone.

If Alvin hadn't come back, Dirk might've given up long ago. At first he'd been surprised to see his brother hovering in the darkness of the cave, surprised and more than a little frightened. After all, everybody knew you were supposed to be afraid of ghosts. But Alvin didn't mean him any harm. He'd only come to help Dirk wait and keep him from making any more stupid mistakes.

Dirk couldn't help resenting his brother's interference a little. Did Alvin think he couldn't do one single damn thing without his help? Did he think Dirk was so helpless he had to come back from the dead just to pull him out of trouble? But now he saw how much help Alvin had been, and his resentment drowned in the flood of excitement as Dirk contemplated what he was going to do to Eden Campbell while they waited together for Scott to return.

He'd seen Scott leave a little while ago and had followed him long enough to figure out he was heading for town. Dirk supposed he needed some more supplies for whatever he was doing to the house. That meant he'd be gone most of the day, certainly more than long enough for Dirk to have his fill of that little redheaded bitch.

He had Alvin to thank for that, too. Ordinarily, he would've returned to his cave when Scott left, but Alvin had told him to go back to the ranch and wait. Dirk was getting so good at waiting. He could sit for hours at a time now, never moving, hardly even breathing, just waiting and waiting, knowing his time would come.

He'd hardly gotten settled in his hiding place above Pauling's old ranch again when Eden and the cowboy had come riding up. For a while he'd been afraid Eden would leave when she saw Scott wasn't home, but he should've known better. She was a stubborn little bitch. She'd wait until hell froze over if necessary. He could hardly believe his luck when she turned her horse loose in the corral and sent the cowboy away. It was just like Alvin had said it would be.

Of course, she might just have sent the cowboy to look for Scott. Alvin would say he should wait awhile just to be sure, and Alvin was right. Dirk would wait. It was second nature to him now, and when he was sure she was alone, he'd get her.

Eden couldn't believe what Linc had done to the house. Just as she had thought, the place had divided nicely into two good-sized rooms. The one would serve as their kitchen and parlor while the other would be their bedroom. After admiring the kitchen, she succumbed to temptation and went into the other room.

To her disappointment, the room was empty except for a neat pile of bedding stacked in one corner, but then she recalled they had ordered a brass bedstead and some other furniture. It should be arriving in a day or so, certainly in plenty of time before the wedding. Eden closed her eyes and pictured the room as it would look on her wedding night with the light burning low. Tiny shivers danced over her as she imagined Linc lifting her in his strong arms and carrying her to the bed.

With a sigh, she pushed the vision aside. There was no use tormenting herself with daydreams. Besides, Linc himself would be back soon and she wouldn't have to imagine anything at all. The thought lightened her steps as she walked back into the other room. When Linc showed up, she wanted to have a hot meal waiting for him.

Fiona had been giving her instructions in all the housekeeping skills she had successfully ignored up until Lincoln Scott came into her life, and she had finally learned how to prepare a decent stew.

At least Linc wouldn't starve to death once they were married, she thought with a smile as she began to unpack the foodstuffs. She noted with some surprise how clean Linc had left the place. The floors were spotless, and he had scrubbed the pine table within an inch of its life. The room would be quite cozy once the sofa they had ordered arrived. Fiona had promised to give her some pictures to hang on the walls, and Eden was already piecing a quilt for their bed. She only hoped it would be done before winter.

She found a knife and a cooking pot without any trouble at all, and set to work building up a fire in the stove. Linc had banked it before he left, and the heat of the coals told her he hadn't been gone too long. The coals flamed quickly when she sprinkled on some tinder.

After removing her jacket—she was wearing the same riding outfit she had worn the first time she had ever seen him; would he notice?—she put the meat on to brown. Then she began to peel the vegetables. She had just completed the stew and put it on to boil when she heard the rider approaching.

Her heart leaped in anticipation, but she turned slowly, wiping her hands on her apron. She wouldn't run out to greet him, she thought, hastily removing the apron and reaching up to check her hair. No, she'd wait until he came inside and surprise him.

If she could stand the wait! Although she knew it was only a matter of minutes from the time she heard the horse approaching until it stopped right outside the cabin, she was already fairly trembling with excitement. He hadn't gone to the corral as she had expected, and she supposed he'd seen the smoke from the fire and wondered who was inside.

Biting her tongue to keep from calling out, she nervously smoothed her shirtwaist, then twisted her hands anxiously in her skirt. Above the pounding of her heart she heard the creak of saddle leather as he dismounted. Then his shadow darkened the threshold, and he was there, filling the doorway.

Only something was wrong. Something was *very* wrong.

"Hello, Eden," Dirk Blaine said.

Terror clutched at her throat, stopping speech and even breath. She stared in mute horror at the man she'd never thought to see again, and he stared back, his eyes glittering with maniacal glee.

Panicked, she glanced around frantically for some means of escape, but the cabin had only one door and the two windows were too high and too small. She wanted to scream, to run, to hide, but

413

she knew her only hope was to remain calm.

Placing a hand over her churning stomach, she managed the semblance of a smile. "Dirk, what a surprise."

"I'll bet," he replied, stepping into the room.

He looked like a wild man. His clothes were filthy, his skin gray from lack of washing. He hadn't shaved in quite a while, and his blond beard had grown in scraggly. The man she had known before had taken great pride in his appearance, so she knew something terrible had happened to change him.

"We've been wondering where you got to," she tried while her mind raced. A weapon. She needed something with which to defend herself. Then she remembered the knife she had used. It still lay on the table.

Don't look at it, she told herself. Don't let him know it's there.

"I found a place to hide," he told her, coming closer. The sour smell of his unwashed body gagged her. She backed up instinctively, but the wall was behind her, and she could go no farther.

"It must have been a good one," she said with false brightness. "Nobody's seen hide nor hair of you."

"Oh, you know exactly where it is. You and Scott spent some time there. Tell me, did he wallow you right there on the bare ground?"

Eden's breath caught. Of course! He'd been hiding in her secret cave. Why hadn't she thought of it before? He must have guessed Linc was in some sort of cave when Dirk found her by the creek that

414

day, and he'd remembered it when he needed a hideout.

"You're awfully clever, Dirk," she said, speaking slowly and trying to gauge his mood. He didn't seem angry, but she suspected he was no longer rational and could become violent at any moment. "Do you know how many people have been trying to find you?"

His grin was feral. "Doesn't seem like anybody's looking for me at all anymore. I figure you must've thought I was long gone."

"I . . . yes, we . . . Well, I guess you heard what happened to your men," she said, fighting to stay calm as she inched her way toward the table where the knife lay.

"No, I didn't hear nothing. What happened?" he asked with some concern.

Eden cursed herself for mentioning the subject. "Marcus and our men found them. They . . . they're all dead." She decided not to mention Garth Hamilton, or Linc's role in all this either.

He laughed, an eerie, cackling sound that sent a chill over her. "Stupid bastards! Alvin was right about them, just like he was right about everything else. I'm glad now that none of them came with me. I don't need any of them. I don't need anybody but Alvin."

Eden stared at him in disbelief. Didn't he remember that his brother was dead? But she couldn't let herself get distracted, not if she wanted to survive. She had to get to the knife. When she took another step toward the table, he shifted, too, apparently thinking she was trying to get around

415

him so she could run toward the door.

"You won't get away from me, Eden," he warned. "Not this time."

She took another step. But what would she do when she got the knife? He'd most certainly draw his pistol the instant she picked it up, and a knife was no match for a gun.

"This time you're all mine," he continued. "I wanted Scott to be here so he could watch, but this is even better. When he gets back . . ."

"Dirk, Linc *is* coming back," she tried, grasping at this straw. "I'm expecting him any minute. That's why I'm cooking his dinner. He'll never let you get away this time, Dirk. If you're smart, you'll leave now—"

"I'm smart!" he shouted, making her jump. His face contorted in fury for a moment before he almost visibly got hold of himself. Then he smiled, a slow, knowing grin that made her flesh crawl. "But Scott *isn't* coming back. He went to town this morning. So you see, we've got *hours* yet to wait."

"No, you're lying!" she cried, terror swelling within her.

"He took the wagon, and I followed him a ways to make sure," Blaine informed her, taking demented pleasure in her fear.

She knew he was telling the truth. She hadn't even thought to check to see if Linc's wagon was gone. How could she have been so stupid? Linc wasn't coming, and she'd sent Shorty away. There was no one to protect her, no one at all.

Panic paralyzed her for a heartbeat, then surged over her in a mighty wave, propelling her to action.

She flung herself at the table and grasped the knife, then whirled, clutching it in both hands.

His eyes widened in surprise, but before he could react, she lunged at him. Instinctively, he dodged, and her lunge carried her forward, past him. Then nothing stood between her and the door. Still hanging onto the knife, she picked up her skirt with her free hand and ran toward freedom.

His roar of outrage thundered from the cabin, but she hardly heard it. All she saw was his horse standing ground-hitched in the yard. She raced toward it.

The animal danced away in fright, but she dropped the knife and caught the trailing reins. With a strength born of desperation, she held the horse still, lifted her foot, and plunged it into the stirrup.

Blaine was close, so close she could almost feel his breath on her neck, but freedom was closer. Grasping the pommel, she hauled herself up, up . . .

"Oh, God!" she cried as she went not up but down. Her weight brought the saddle sliding over the horse's back. Blaine must have loosed the cinch! The animal whinnied and bucked in terror, and Eden hit the ground with a bone-jarring thud.

As if she'd bounced, she scrambled up again almost instantly, but Blaine caught her around the waist and turned her toward him. "Thought you'd get away, did you?" he said, his stinking breath hot on her face.

The gorge rose in her throat, and she flailed frantically, kicking and clawing in a struggle she had already learned was futile.

He laughed, holding her easily, and in one last, desperate effort, she spit in his face. As she had hoped, he loosened his hold, but before she could break away, the hand that had released her came whooshing back to smack her face.

The impact sent pain roaring through her head, and specks of light danced before her eyes. Her ears rang, and her body passed out of her control for a moment. She could not resist when he began to drag her back toward the house.

Linc! her mind cried, but she knew he wouldn't come. Blaine had her now, and he could do whatever he wanted. She couldn't stop him, but she could make him pay dearly for what he took. Ignoring the pounding in her head, she fought her way back to full consciousness and dug in her heels.

He muttered a curse, and they struggled for a minute before he simply threw her over his shoulder and carried her into the house. She pounded with her fists and tried to kick, but he held her feet fast. Then she saw his gun and grabbed for it, but it hung in the holster.

Feeling the tug, he cursed viciously and flung her away from him. She landed with a thump on the cabin floor. Once again, she scrambled to her feet, dodging his kick, and seeking refuge behind the table. But he caught her easily, grabbing her by the hair. Pain seared her scalp, jarring a cry from her throat, and she fell backwards against him again.

Holding her hair with one hand, he pulled her up against him again and ran his other hand over her, squeezing her breasts and belly, then clutching between her legs. She screamed her protest, thrashing wildly, fighting his hand until she thought he would tear the hair from her head and the agony brought tears to her eyes.

Suddenly, he released her and shoved her into the corner. She slumped against the wall, her breath coming in sobbing gasps. He grinned down at her, panting like a beast, his arms spread to catch her if she tried to run.

"Strip."

At first the word held no meaning for her, and when she did not respond, his face contorted in fury.

"Take off your clothes!" he shrieked. "Just like you did for Scott!"

"No!" she screamed back. When he lifted his hand to strike her, she ducked beneath it in a desperate lunge for freedom.

His fist came down on her back, knocking the wind from her body and sending her sprawling onto the floor. As she frantically tried to suck air into her empty lungs, Blaine threw her over on her back. Straddling her helpless body, he grasped the neck of her shirtwaist with both hands and tore it open, sending buttons flying.

He was pawing at her camisole when her breath came back in a rush. The delicate fabric gave just as she grabbed his hands to pull them away. He wrenched loose of her grasp and smacked her. Once again stars danced before her eyes and pain echoed through her head, but she fought the debilitating weakness.

His fingers dug into her naked breasts. "No!" she cried, or thought she did as she tried to pull his hands away. Then from some distant part of her brain, she remembered the gun which still hung on his hip.

Once more she grabbed for it, and this time it slid free, but his right hand clamped over hers, and before she could overpower him, his left fist plummeted into her temple.

Darkness enveloped her for a few seconds, and her whole body went numb. As if from a great distance, she heard him cursing and felt him take the pistol from her nerveless fingers. Where was he putting it? High, up high, on the table which was almost above her head now. How would she ever get it?

Desperately she fought the wave of blackness that threatened to drown her in unconsciousness. Blinking furiously, she tried to focus, and saw to her horror that he was unbuckling his gunbelt and tossing it aside.

When he began to unbutton his pants, terror sent a surge of energy through her. Pushing up on her elbows, she began to scramble backward to free herself from his imprisoning legs. She didn't get far before he caught her, clutching at her skirt and hauling her back with a maniacal laugh.

"You can't get away," he told her. "But keep on fighting. I like it that way."

He fell forward, pinning her to the floor, crushing her with his weight. When she tried to scratch, he caught her hands and held them above her head.

His stench enveloped her, and she gagged, making him laugh again. "Do you know what I'm going to do?" he taunted. "Of course you do because you've done it with Scott. I'm going to strip you naked and breed you like a sow in a shoot. And when I'm done, you're going to beg me to do it again."

"Never, you bastard!" she gasped, nearly breathless with horror.

"Oh, maybe not at first," he allowed. "I might have to take my belt to you, but sooner or later you'll get down on your knees and you'll . . ."

He went on, but Eden didn't listen, didn't let herself listen to the filth pouring from his mouth. Instead she tried frantically to think of a way of escape.

Then he shifted until he held both her hands in one of his. She struggled in his grip, but to no avail. With his free hand, he reached down and pulled up her riding skirt, but he had to slide off her body to get the skirt up over her hips, and as he half-knelt beside her, she suddenly remembered something her father had taught her years ago.

The instant he had her skirts above her knees, she struck, driving her knee into his crotch. His howl of agony told her of success, and she tore her hands free as he clutched himself.

Rolling, scrambling, she lurched to her feet, but she had only taken one step when Blaine's arms closed around her legs, driving her to the floor again. She screamed in renewed terror, kicking against his grasp, pummeling him with her fists, but when he lifted his face to hers, she saw he was beyond pain. Pure madness burned in his eyes.

"You whore!" he raged. "You're just like *she* was! You're just like all the others! But this time you won't leave me! This time you won't get away!"

He released her legs, but before she could move an inch, he threw himself on her once again. His weight held her fast, and oblivious to her clawing hands, he wrapped his fingers around her throat.

"Dirk!" she croaked in the last instant before he cut off her air. She dug in her nails, raking his flesh, drawing blood, but he felt nothing. His terrible eyes stared down at her, blank and distant, as if she weren't even there at all, and finally she knew she wasn't. Everything began to fade, blurring around the edges, then growing darker until she saw nothing except Blaine's crazed eyes.

"Blaine!"

Linc fired, aiming high so he wouldn't accidently hit Eden, then bounded into the room.

Blaine looked up, but he didn't let go of Eden's throat, so Linc kicked, planting a booted foot alongside of Blaine's head. The force of the blow sent him sprawling, wrenching his hands free of Eden's neck.

To his relief, Linc heard Eden's desperate gasp for air, but he couldn't see to her just yet, not until he'd taken care of Blaine.

The rustler bounded up with a roar, as if Linc's savage kick had merely grazed him, but instead of lunging for Linc, he went for the table. Too late Linc saw the gun lying there, and as Blaine swung it on him, they fired together.

From years of training, Linc darted to the right and dropped to his knee to make a smaller target. Blaine's gun exploded again, the flash bright in the smoke-filled room, but the bullet struck where Linc had been. This time Linc took careful aim at the figure dimly visible in the haze and fired.

Blaine grunted as if he had been hit, and Linc moved again, scrambling as far away from Eden as he could get in order to keep Blaine's shots at him from striking her accidently.

"Damn you, Scott!" Blaine said, his voice garbled and strangely liquid. The smoke was so thick, Blaine was no more than a shadow.

Linc heard a thud, like a pistol hitting the floor, then another as Blaine keeled over on his side.

"Blaine?" he called, but the only response was the sound of Eden's gasping breaths.

Crouching, moving carefully through the haze, Linc made his way to where Blaine lay. The rustler didn't move, but Linc kicked his pistol out of reach before kneeling down to check.

Blaine clutched his throat in a vain attempt to stop the blood from pouring out. His eyes glittered with the remnants of life, and when he saw Linc leaning over him, he gurgled, "Damn you to hell." Then he released his breath on a long sigh and went still.

"Eden?" Linc called, hurrying to her side.

She stared up at him blankly, each breath a shuddering gasp.

"Eden, honey, can you hear me? He's dead, Eden. He'll never hurt you again."

He stared down at her, willing her to respond.

Dear God, when Melancholy had intercepted him on the road to town, he'd done so simply to save Linc from Eden's wrath at being kept waiting alone all day. Thank heaven Linc hadn't shrugged off the warning, and thank heaven he'd talked Melancholy into lending him his horse so he could make the trip back more quickly. If he'd been even one minute later . . .

But Eden did not respond, did not even blink. For the second time in minutes, Linc knew real terror. Had he still come too late?

"Eden?" he tried again, and she began to tremble. Instinctively, he knew she was cold. With one last glance at Blaine, Linc holstered his gun. Carefully, he picked Eden up and carried her into the bedroom, where she could no longer see Dirk Blaine's body . . . if indeed she could see anything at all.

He laid her tenderly on the pile of bedding and pulled out a blanket to spread over her. Rage welled in him as he noticed her torn bodice and the marks of violence on her milk-white flesh. If he could have killed Dirk Blaine again, he would have done so in that moment. With unsteady hands, he pulled her torn shirtwaist closed before covering her.

Still she stared unseeing up at the ceiling, and her breath rattled in her throat. He would have to get her home. Fiona would know what to do, but he couldn't take her until Melancholy got here with the wagon. Then Linc thought of taking Eden back through the other room, past Blaine, and he knew he couldn't let her see him, not ever again.

Rising slowly, leaving Eden reluctantly, he returned to the other room and dragged the rustler outside and around to the side of the cabin, out of sight. After checking on Eden again and finding her still unresponsive, Linc found a scrub brush and some lye soap and removed Blaine's blood from his floor.

He also found the stew Eden had prepared for him, and when he thought of how he had almost lost her, tears stung his eyes. Returning to her side, he knelt beside her and took her cold hands in his.

"Eden? Honey, can you hear me? It's Linc, and I'll never let anybody hurt you again. Do you hear? Not ever again."

Her trembling seemed to increase, and responding to instinct once again, Linc lay down beside her and took her in his arms.

"I'll always take care of you, sweet girl. I love you so much."

He held her for a long time, cradling her head to his shoulder and cushioning her quaking with his own body. At last her trembling ceased, and she gave a shuddering sigh. "Eden?" he asked in alarm, pushing her away so he could see her face.

She blinked, and her eyes cleared. "Linc?" she said, her voice hoarse. "What happened . . . ?" She lifted a hand to her throat, which Linc supposed must have been sore from Blaine's attack. Then he saw her memory return, and terror widened her eyes. "Blaine!" she croaked.

"He's dead," Linc assured her, tightening his embrace protectively. "He'll never hurt you again, I swear it."

"He was choking me," she said as if she hadn't quite understood. She shuddered, and Linc pressed a kiss to her forehead, his heart aching.

"I know," he murmured, brushing the tangled hair away from her face. She looked so shattered, not like his Eden at all, and once again he wanted to do murder.

"You . . . you shot him?" she asked tremulously.

"Yes, he's dead. You never have to worry about him again."

"Oh, Linc . . ." Her voice broke, and tears flooded her eyes. As much as he hated to see her cry, her weeping was far better than her earlier lack of response.

"It's all right," he whispered, but his assurance made her cry out in anguish, and once again he drew her close.

For long minutes she sobbed against his chest. The sounds she made were wrenched from her soul. They tore at Linc's heart until he wondered if either of them would ever be whole again.

At last, exhausted, she fell silent, still quivering slightly, like a frightened bird. Accustomed to fighting with his hands or with his gun, Linc felt helpless battling Eden's unknown terrors. When he thought of Blaine putting his hands on Eden, he knew the swift death the man had suffered was too merciful an end. For the first time in his life, Linc sincerely hoped the hellfire the preachers talked about really existed. Only such a punishment would repay a man like Dirk Blaine. The only thing Linc didn't know was whether Blaine had raped Eden before he tried to kill her. The thought was too horrible to contemplate, and Linc wasn't even sure he wanted to know. If he had . . .

"Linc?" Her voice was still hoarse.

"Yes, love?"

"He didn't . . . He tried to, but he didn't rape me," she said as if she had read his thoughts.

"Thank God," Linc whispered, knowing he could never have lived with the guilt of having arrived too late to save her from that humiliation.

They heard the wagon rattling into the yard and Melancholy's surprised shout. Linc guessed he had seen the body in the yard. Gently he pried himself loose from Eden's clinging arms. "I've got to go tell Melancholy what happened, then we'll take you home."

It took every ounce of strength he possessed to leave her lying there.

Chapter Thirteen

Slowly, painfully, Eden made her way across her bedroom to the mirror which hung above her dressing table. Every bone and muscle in her body ached, and the night's sleep she had just finished — with a little help from the laudanum Fiona kept for emergencies — had only made her discomforts worse.

When she finally reached the mirror, she suddenly felt reluctant to look. Blaine had struck her several times in the face, and she could feel the swelling on her cheek and temple. Did it look as bad as it felt? Taking a deep breath, she stepped in front of the mirror and let out her breath in a horrified gasp.

One eye was purple all the way back to her hairline. Her other cheek was not discolored, but it looked as if she were carrying a wad of tobacco. Her neck was equally bad. She could clearly see the imprints of Blaine's ten fingers, and it still hurt to swallow. Wanting to know the worst, she reluctantly untied the bodice of her nightdress and spread it slowly to reveal the lacerated flesh of her breasts. Black bruises blotched her pale skin and red streaks marked where Blaine had scratched her.

She moaned aloud.

"Eden?"

Eden swiftly covered herself before turning to face her stepmother. Fiona stood in the doorway of her bedroom, her lovely face pinched with worry. "The bruises will fade, darling," she said, closing the door behind her.

"But not in time for the wedding," Eden replied. "I can't be married with my face looking like this." She didn't add that she couldn't let Linc see the other marks on her body either. She didn't want Linc to know the extent of Blaine's violation.

"Do you want to postpone the wedding?" Fiona asked solicitously. "I'm sure everyone would understand, considering the circumstances."

"I . . . I think so, yes," Eden replied, making her careful way back to the comfort of her bed. At least when she lay perfectly still on the feather mattress, most of the pain ceased.

Fiona hurried there before her to turn back the covers and plump the pillows. "Oh, my, what's this?" she asked in alarm, lifting a handful of auburn hair from the pillow.

Automatically, Eden reached up to touch the back of her hair and another handful came away in her fingers. "Blaine . . . he pulled my hair . . ." she admitted, feeling nauseated at the thought of his assault. Resolutely she pushed the memory away. She simply couldn't think about it now, not yet.

Fiona muttered something incomprehensible as

she helped Eden back into bed. "Perhaps you would like a hot soak a little later, after you've eaten," she suggested. "I can have Linc bring the tub in here and . . ."

"No." Eden said too loudly, making her head throb. Seeing Fiona's startled expression, she said, "I mean, yes, I'd like to soak, but could you ask Marcus to bring in the tub? I don't want . . ." She couldn't quite make herself say the words.

"You don't want Lincoln to see you like this," Fiona guessed. "Eden, you can't think it would make any difference to him. The poor man spent the entire night sleeping on the floor outside your room in case you called out in your sleep."

"You didn't let him see me, did you?" she cried in alarm.

"Certainly not. It would be most improper for him to see you in your nightclothes. But surely you want him to visit you. He's about to drive me to distraction asking after you."

"No, please, Fiona. Keep him away until . . . until I look normal again."

"You won't look normal for at least a week, perhaps much longer," Fiona warned.

"Then for a few days, anyway. Please, I can't . . ." Tears clogged her throat, and before she knew it, she was sobbing.

Crooning words of comfort, Fiona sat down on the bed beside her and took Eden's hand in hers. Eden let the tears run onto her pillow, helpless to stop them, until her spate of weeping was over.

"I know you must be feeling ashamed because of what happened," Fiona said gently, "but no one blames you, least of all Lincoln."

"But I *feel* so filthy. Last time Blaine attacked me was bad enough, but at least when it was over, I didn't have any marks to remind me or . . . or anyone else of what happened. But this time . . . Linc must . . ."

"He most certainly does not." Fiona insisted. "The only thing that concerns him is your well-being."

But Eden remembered his reaction when she'd told him Blaine hadn't raped her. His fervent "Thank God" told her how important it was to him to know she hadn't been defiled. If he saw how badly Blaine had hurt her and how fragile her emotions were, he might even think she'd lied about the rape. Would he still want her then?

"Just a few days, please," she begged, and reluctantly Fiona agreed.

"You can't blame her," Marcus told Linc later that day. "No girl wants her man seeing her like that."

Linc nodded, but he couldn't quite bring himself to believe Eden would care about such a thing. Hadn't he held her and cared for her right after the attack? He knew all about her injuries.

No, she wasn't afraid for him to see her. Linc very much feared she was afraid of *him*.

And she had every right to be. Anybody who'd been beaten and almost killed would naturally be terrified. And of course he had been right there when it happened, and she had seen him kill

Blaine, just as she had seen him kill Blaine's brother. If she was afraid of Linc, no one could blame her.

"Just give her a day or two," Marcus said. "She'll come around."

"Sure," Linc muttered. Marcus was probably right. How many times had Eden insisted she didn't care about the killing he had done? But she also thought he could change. Hadn't she tried to talk him out of going after Blaine in the first place? She probably still thought he could put away his gun and become an honest, peaceful citizen, but after his confrontation with Blaine, Linc knew that could never happen. He'd always feel compelled to fight against injustice. Would she still want him when she found that out?

The hot baths helped, although Eden thought her skin might shrivel right off her bones if she soaked any more. By the next day she could move without too much pain and had begun to experiment with rice powder to see how thoroughly she could cover her bruises.

Her hair finally stopped falling out in clumps, and Fiona managed to get it brushed and braided without causing her too much agony. Eden was still horrified when she looked in the mirror, but she was beginning to think she would survive.

When Fiona brought her noon meal that day, Eden asked the question uppermost on her mind. "How's Linc doing?"

To her surprise, Fiona refused to meet her eye.

"Fine, I'm sure," she said, setting the tray down on Eden's lap and making quite a fuss about rearranging the silverware.

"Fee, is something wrong?"

"Why, no, not a thing," Fiona replied with false brightness. "How are you feeling, darling? Would you like me to rub you with some linament?"

"Fee, is something wrong with Linc? Tell me." Eden insisted, catching her stepmother's hand and holding her fast.

Fiona maintained her fixed smile. "I can't imagine why you think something is wrong with him. He's so fine, in fact, he's gone on a little trip."

"A trip? What kind of trip?" Eden asked, fighting a sickening sense of foreboding.

"I believe Melancholy said he had some business to attend to in . . . in Dallas, I think."

" 'Melancholy said'? Didn't he talk to you or to Marcus?"

"Uh, no, he left quite early this morning, before any of us were awake."

"He left without saying good-bye?" Eden asked in despair.

"He did say he would only be gone a few days," Fiona hastened to assure her, although Eden could see her stepmother was as worried about the situation as Eden herself. "And don't forget you have postponed the wedding and refused to see him until your face looks better. He probably thought he would use the time productively."

Doing what? Eden wanted to demand, but she didn't because she was afraid Fiona wouldn't be able to answer. Linc couldn't possibly have any business that would take him away so suddenly, and if he did, why hadn't he told Marcus about it?

"He *will* return," Fiona said confidently, although Eden thought she might have been trying to convince herself as well. "He left that stallion of his, so he *must* intend to return. You can't possibly doubt it."

"What if I can?" she challenged.

"Whyever would he leave?" Fiona scoffed.

"Because he doesn't want me after Dirk Blaine had me."

"Eden." Fiona cried. "You told me he didn't—"

"He didn't, but what if Linc doesn't believe me! What if he thinks I'm damaged goods now and—"

"Nonsense! Dirk Blaine must have struck you much harder than I thought to have knocked all the sense completely out of your head!"

"But Linc left! How else can you explain it?"

"I have no idea, but he most certainly did not leave because he thinks you are 'damaged goods.'"

Eden looked at her stepmother in despair. "What am I going to do?"

Fiona frowned down at her. "First of all, you will concentrate on recovering from your ordeal. Secondly, when Lincoln returns, you will forget this nonsense about hiding your face, and you will speak to him about your fears."

"I couldn't do that!" Eden cried.

"Of course you can, and you will. Believe me, Eden, I have far more experience in these matters than you, and I know how quickly a love can sour if you keep your fears a secret."

"But what if he doesn't come back at all?" she

asked, voicing her greatest fear.

"Then you must decide if it's 'good riddance' or if you want to go after him."

"You mean chase him?" Eden gasped.

Fiona shrugged delicately. "Certainly not, but a man like Lincoln Scott wouldn't be too difficult to find. A chance meeting perhaps . . ." She shrugged again.

Would she let Linc go? The very idea was unthinkable, especially when she remembered how much he had loved her once. If he had forgotten that, she would remind him so he would never forget it again. Eden smiled up at her stepmother. For the first time since she had seen Dirk Blaine standing in the doorway, she began to think everything might work out after all.

Linc walked into the store and looked around in amazement. It was the biggest mercantile he had ever seen, and he supposed he could find whatever he wanted here. He only hoped he could find what he *needed*. His wandering gaze drifted to the front of the store where a young girl stood behind the counter.

Sunlight streamed in from the skylight above, touching her auburn hair, and Linc felt the shock of recognition. The girl looked up and smiled a greeting, and Linc's shoulders sagged with relief. She wasn't Eden. She didn't even look like Eden.

He laid a hand over his pounding heart and took a deep breath. He was going to have to stop acting like such a jackass. Did he intend to spend the rest

435

of his life looking for Eden around every corner? The prospect was appalling, but that was exactly what would happen if he let her send him away now.

He couldn't blame her if she no longer wanted to marry him, but he also couldn't forget how much she had loved him once. With a sad smile he recalled how often she had told him so in no uncertain terms. Was he going to let her go now?

The girl's smile had grown quizzical. "May I help you?" she asked prettily.

Linc made his decision. "Yeah, I, uh . . ." He approached the glass counter and glanced down at the baubles displayed inside. The very number of them overwhelmed him. "I need to buy a present."

"For a young lady?" the girl asked with a knowing smile.

He managed to smile back. "Yeah, a girl with red hair like yours."

The girl considered him for a moment. "What is the occasion?"

"A wedding . . . I hope."

She nodded sagely. "You've quarreled."

"Not exactly."

She leaned forward conspiratorially. "Then what, exactly?"

"Well, we . . . we were supposed to get married, but something happened, and now I don't know if she still wants to or not."

"Why haven't you asked her?"

"I'm going to," Linc replied impatiently. "But I thought . . ." He gestured toward the baubles in the counter.

Understanding lighted her eyes. "You thought if you brought a gift, you might ease your way."

"Something like that," Linc admitted.

"Then we must find exactly the right gift, so you must tell me about your lady so I'll know how to advise you."

"What do you mean?"

"Well, I need to know if you want something fancy or something funny. Does she have a sense of humor?"

"She used to," he replied, thinking of the many times she had teased him.

"Then we'll think of something to make her laugh," the girl decided with a smile. "It's hard to say no when you're laughing."

When Linc arrived, he found the ranch nearly deserted. It was Saturday afternoon, and everybody had gone to town. Under ordinary circumstances, Eden would be gone, too, but Linc suspected he would find her inside. He didn't think she would show her bruised face in town.

Uncertain of his welcome, he left his horse tied in the shade and approached the house cautiously, not calling the traditional greeting. The front door stood open, and Linc walked quietly across the porch and stepped inside.

"Oh!"

A figure jumped up from the sofa, and although his eyes weren't adjusted to the interior light, Linc recognized Eden at once. As she came gradually into focus, the sight of her discolored eye tore at his heart. With great difficulty, he resisted the urge to charge across the room and take her in his arms.

"Didn't mean to scare you," he said, nervously shifting the package he held from one hand to the other.

"Linc," was all she said. She sounded more than surprised.

"How are you doing?"

Her hand fluttered up to her eye. "I . . . I'm fine. Much better than I look."

"You look good to me," he said, love and desire thickening his voice as he let his gaze drift over her slender figure.

"Do I?"

He nodded, wishing he knew how to ease the awkwardness between them. When he'd imagined this scene, he'd imagined Eden happy or angry, but either way, she'd been talking a mile a minute. This silent Eden worried him.

"Where is everybody?" he asked lamely.

"They went to town, Marcus and Fiona, too. It's Saturday."

"Yeah, I know." The day they should have been married. The knowledge lay between them, no less real for being unspoken.

"You were gone a long time," she said at last.

"Longer than I expected. My horse went lame out in the middle of nowhere, or I would've been back a couple days ago."

"Oh," she said. The information seemed to cheer her. "You didn't say good-bye before you left."

"You didn't want to see me, remember?"

"But I didn't want you to leave me, either!"

Linc blinked in surprise, but his tension eased somewhat at her outrage. "I didn't *leave* you. I had some business to attend to."

"What kind of business?" she demanded, crossing her arms belligerently.

Linc struggled to hold back a smile. This was more like it. With growing confidence, he glanced down at the package. "I wanted to get you a little something, sort of a wedding present."

"You had to go all the way to Dallas to buy me a present?"

He was hard pressed not to laugh out loud at her skepticism, but he managed a regretful grimace. "Well, I had a little thinking to do, too."

"What did you have to think about?"

Her cheeks were pink with fury, and Linc almost regretted baiting her. "I had to think about us."

"You had to decide if you still wanted to marry me after what Dirk Blaine did to me!" she accused, and once again Linc stared at her in surprise.

"No! I never—"

"Don't lie to me! I know how much you hated him and how you probably can't stand the thought that he put his hands on me, but—"

"Eden!" he shouted, startling her to silence even as he quickly closed the distance between them. Tossing the package onto the sofa, he took her by the arms. "Listen to me! I did hate Blaine, and I do hate the thought that he ever touched you, and if I could, I'd kill him all over again, and *that's* what I had to think about! When you wouldn't see me, I knew it was because you were scared of me, and I can't blame you—"

"Wait a minute! What makes you think I was scared of you?"

"Because you'd seen me kill a man, *two men* in fact. I'm a violent man, Eden, and I know you think I can change, but I don't think I can."

"You killed those men to save my life!" she protested. "Surely you must know you aren't like them. You *hate* violence."

"But I'll always use my gun when I have to."

"I certainly hope so! I wouldn't want to live in a world where good men weren't willing to fight for what's right. Linc, I love you! How many times do I have to tell you that before you believe it's the only thing that matters?"

He looked down into her emerald eyes, glittering now with the tears of frustration. Even marred by Blaine's fists, she was still the most beautiful woman he had ever seen. "I'm pretty thick headed," he admitted hoarsely. "I reckon even if you tell me every day for the rest of my life, it might not sink in."

"Well," she mused, her slender body straightening resolutely in his grasp, "I'm certainly willing to take on the project."

"You mean you'll marry me?"

"If you still want me."

"If I still . . . ?" He caught himself just in time. There was no use in going over all this old ground again, so he took advantage of the fact that she wasn't saying anything at the moment and kissed her.

She felt so good and tasted so sweet and melted

so willingly into his arms that he kept on kissing her until his knees wouldn't support him anymore. They collapsed together on the sofa.

Right on top of Linc's package.

"What in the world?" Eden wondered, breaking from Linc's kiss long enough to rescue the parcel. "Oh, yes, my gift," she said, squeezing the brown wrapping paper in an attempt to guess what might be inside.

Linc tried to take it from her so he could kiss her again, but she held him off playfully, intrigued by the mystery of what he might have brought her all the way from Dallas. "Now wait, I think I'd better look at this first. I might change my mind about marrying you if I don't like what you've brought me," she teased.

His grin was wicked. "You might at that. The girl who helped me pick it out—"

"Girl!" she echoed in feigned outrage. "What girl was this?"

"The girl who worked at the store." His sky blue eyes twinkled with mischief, and Eden knew a quiver of excitement. "She warned me it was scandalously improper for me to give you this unless we were married."

"She did, did she?" Eden murmured as she eagerly tore away the paper and string to reveal white silk and lace. At first she thought he must have brought her something for her wedding dress, but the garment was awfully small. Taking two corners, she lifted it out of its wrapping, shaking out the folds. "Linc!" she squealed when the legs of the pantalettes fell free.

Her own cheeks felt hot, so she was delighted to see Linc's had reddened also. "To replace the ones you tore up to bandage me," he explained sheepishly.

Somehow controlling the laughter that threatened to bubble out, she asked, "But how did you know what size?"

"Oh," he replied with a semblance of his old cockiness, "I just said about this big."

Before she guessed his intent, he'd cupped her bottom in both hands and pulled her into his lap. She wrapped her arms around his neck, still clinging to the pantalettes, and allowed him to nibble hungrily on her throat. "Shouldn't I try them on just to be sure they fit?" she whispered into his ear.

He shivered in response. "Only if you let me help," he replied provocatively.

"Mmmm," she said, throwing back her head to grant him better access. "All right."

He went completely still. "All right?"

She nodded eagerly.

"But . . . I thought we were going to wait until we were married," he reminded her.

"You were the one who made that silly rule. Of course, if you insist," she said, bringing the pantalettes back to her lap and spreading them out as if to see how they might look, "I could try them on all by myself."

Before she even finished the sentence, Linc was on his feet with Eden in his arms and heading for her bedroom.

* * *

"Whose horse is that?" Fiona asked as she and Marcus drove into the ranch yard later.

"Never saw it before." He squinted as they passed by the animal. "Wait a minute, that's Linc's saddle."

"Thank the good Lord," Fiona breathed in relief. "I know poor Eden had almost given up hope."

Marcus chuckled. "I wonder if they've kissed and made up."

"And if they've managed to have yet another argument," Fiona added with a smile.

"Well, it's understandable," Marcus allowed. "A man gets mighty testy when his basic urges ain't being met. I recollect a time when I was pretty near howling at the moon—"

"Marcus!" Fiona scolded, pinkening.

Pedro met them at the barn and confirmed that the horse did indeed belong to *Señor* Linc, who had gone into the house quite some time ago and hadn't been seen since.

"Maybe you'd better unsaddle the poor animal then," Marcus suggested. "Looks like Linc'll be staying for a while at least."

"*Sí,* I will take care of the wagon, too. I know you are in a hurry to see *Señor* Linc."

"Thanks, son," Marcus said as he helped Fiona down. "I'll be back for the supplies in a few minutes."

Marcus and Fiona hurried across the yard and into the house, expecting to find Eden and Linc cuddling on the parlor sofa.

"Where could they be?" Fiona asked when they found the room empty.

443

"Maybe she fixed Linc a bite to eat," Marcus guessed. A few minutes later they had ascertained the two lovers weren't in the kitchen either.

"Where could they have gotten to?" Fiona mused. "Pedro said they hadn't left the house and—"

Marcus muttered something incomprehensible and turned to the closed door of Eden's bedroom.

"Oh, Marcus, you don't think . . ."

His only reply was a low, growling noise as he strode over to Eden's door and threw it open.

"What the hell do you think you're doing?" he bellowed just as Fiona ducked her head beneath his outstretched arm to view the scene within. Eden and Linc were sound asleep upon her bed, entwined in each other's arms. They appeared to be wearing nothing beneath the sheet that had been negligently pulled up around their waists.

They both awoke with a start at Marcus's shout, and Eden instinctively grabbed for the sheet to cover her naked breasts. Then she saw Marcus and Fiona staring down at them in wide-eyed horror and knew a horror of her own.

"Oh, Fee!" she cried in dismay.

"It's all my fault," Linc was saying, holding the sheet up to cover his own nakedness. "I forced her into it—"

"You most certainly did not force me!" Eden informed him in outrage. "In fact, it was all my idea, if I remember correctly. You didn't even—"

"Eden," he growled in irritation, "shut up, and let me do the talking."

"*Shut up?*" she echoed furiously. "How dare you

444

speak to me like that, Lincoln Scott?"

"I'm trying to protect your good name," he snapped. "Any other woman would—"

Fiona made a strangled sound, and they both looked up to find her weeping against Marcus's shoulder.

"Oh, Fee, I'm so sorry," Eden wailed, feeling close to tears herself when she realized how hurt her stepmother must be by her shocking behavior. "But we really are going to be married this time, I promise!"

"Damn well better be," Marcus muttered, his face red.

Fiona lifted her head from Marcus's shirtfront and swiped at the tears that were streaming down her face only because she was laughing too hard to contain them. Eden gaped at her in astonishment.

"I can only wonder how Mr. Scott ever managed to keep you quiet long enough to seduce you," Fiona gasped. "And Marcus is right, you shall be married immediately, tomorrow if we can arrange it, but," she added, taking a calming breath, "I do believe we shall see to it that the two of you are not allowed to even see one another between now and then for fear you might quarrel once again and ruin everything!"

"Fiona!" Eden protested. She might have jumped up to argue with her stepmother's ridiculous prediction had she not been naked.

"And you've got two minutes to get out of that bed and get your clothes back on," Marcus grumbled, pointing at them accusingly. "Two minutes and not a second longer!"

Fiona was still laughing when Marcus pulled her from the room and slammed the door behind them.

For a few seconds Eden and Linc didn't move; then she hazarded a guilty glance in his direction. She couldn't quite gauge his expression.

"Well," he mused, "I reckon I'm lucky Marcus didn't shoot me on the spot."

Eden grinned. "Maybe he thinks marrying you off to me is a worse punishment."

He pretended to consider. "Maybe he's right."

Eden tried to punch him, but he caught her hand and pulled her into his arms. The delicious sensation of his flesh against hers wiped all thoughts of revenge out of her mind. "No one's forcing you to marry me," she murmured against his lips.

"I think Marcus is," he replied, "and I also think Fiona may be right about us staying apart until the wedding. You're awful hotheaded and—ouch!"

"And I'll pinch you again if you aren't careful!"

Pounding on the door startled them apart. "A minute and a half, and then I'm coming in!" Marcus warned from the parlor.

Linc drew her close for one last, quick kiss.

"Wonder if we could get ourselves married tonight," he said when their lips parted.

"I'll speak to Marcus about it," she promised.

Author's Note

I hope you enjoyed reading about Eden and Linc, Marcus and Fiona, and all the rest of the characters in *Wild Texas Promise*. I love to hear from my readers. Please write me at the address below and include a SASE for a reply.

Victoria Thompson
c/o Zebra Books
475 Park Ave. South
New York, NY 10016

447

THE BEST IN HISTORICAL ROMANCES

TIME-KEPT PROMISES (2422, $3.95)
by Constance O'Day Flannery

Sean O'Mara froze when he saw his wife Christina standing before him. She had vanished and the news had been written about in all of the papers—he had even been charged with her murder! But now he had living proof of his innocence, and Sean was not about to let her get away. No matter that the woman was claiming to be someone named Kristine; she still caused his blood to boil.

PASSION'S PRISONER (2573, $3.95)
by Casey Stewart

When Cassandra Lansing put on men's clothing and entered the Rawlings saloon she didn't expect to lose anything—in fact she was sure that she would win back her prized horse Rapscallion that her grandfather lost in a card game. She almost got a smug satisfaction at the thought of fooling the gamblers into believing that she was a man. But once she caught a glimpse of the virile Josh Rawlings, Cassandra wanted to be the woman in his embrace!

ANGEL HEART (2426, $3.95)
by Victoria Thompson

Ever since Angelica's father died, Harlan Snyder had been angling to get his hands on her ranch, the Diamond R. And now, just when she had an important government contract to fulfill, she couldn't find a single cowhand to hire—all because of Snyder's threats. It was only a matter of time before the legendary gunfighter Kid Collins turned up on her doorstep, badly wounded. Angelica assessed his firmly muscled physique and stared into his startling blue eyes. Beneath all that blood and dirt he was the handsomest man she had ever seen, and the one person who could help beat Snyder at his own game.

Available wherever paperbacks are sold, or order direct from the Publisher. Send cover price plus 50¢ per copy for mailing and handling to Zebra Books, Dept. 3090, 475 Park Avenue South, New York, N.Y. 10016. Residents of New York, New Jersey and Pennsylvania must include sales tax. DO NOT SEND CASH.